KILL ZONE

KILL ZONE

KEVIN J. ANDERSON
and DOUG BEASON

FORGE®

A TOM DOHERTY ASSOCIATES BOOK
New York

KILL ZONE

Copyright © 2019 by WordFire, Inc., and Doug Beason

A Forge Book
Published by Tom Doherty Associates
120 Broadway
New York, NY 10271

www.tor-forge.com

Forge® is a registered trademark of Macmillan Publishing Group, LLC.

The Library of Congress Cataloging-in-Publication Data is available upon request.

ISBN 978-1-250-18344-6 (hardcover)
ISBN 978-1-250-18343-9 (ebook)

Our books may be purchased in bulk for promotional, educational, or business use. Please contact your local bookseller or the Macmillan Corporate and Premium Sales Department at 1-800-221-7945, extension 5442, or by email at MacmillanSpecialMarkets@macmillan.com.

First Edition: August 2019

Printed in the United States of America

0 9 8 7 6 5 4 3 2 1

To Tom Doherty,
for supporting our writing for twenty-five years

Some technical and operational details in this novel have been purposely altered for National Security reasons.

Kill Zone: the area centered on the point of a nuclear explosion, which guarantees total destruction of human life

DOE's proposed repository as designed will be capable of safely isolating used nuclear fuel and high-level radioactive waste for the one-million-year period. . . .

—*[Independent] Safety Evaluation Report Related to Disposal of High-Level Radioactive Wastes in a Geologic Repository at Yucca Mountain, Nevada. Office of Nuclear Material Safety and Safeguards, U.S. Nuclear Regulatory Commission, January 2015*

A SAP [Special Access Program] is a program established for a specific class of classified information that imposes safeguarding and access requirements exceeding those normally required for information at the same classification level.

—*U.S. Department of Energy website (unclassified)*

KILL ZONE

1

Though the airport wasn't the nearest one to the target, it was close to New York City. And more importantly, it had a privately owned Daher TBM 930 aircraft available, no questions asked.

He'd paid two thousand dollars cash to rent the fast plane dry—unfueled—which allowed him to load the minimum amount of gas. That way he could take off with three-quarters of a ton of payload. He wouldn't have to fly far, only thirty miles, and he'd chosen the single-engine Daher for its speed, up to 380 miles an hour.

By his calculations, he should be able to achieve more than 500 mph when he came straight in at a dive. At that speed, carrying 7,400 pounds max weight, he'd easily punch through the containment building's roof.

And that was *before* his payload of ANFO exploded.

The entire Sanergy activist group would be proud that he'd made such a clear, indisputable statement. They would wish they had listened to his urgings, because now the nuclear power industry would grind to a halt thanks to his bold statement this morning. His only regret was that he wouldn't live to see it and bask in the praise of like-minded people. But he saw no more effective way to stop the madness, put a halt to the never-ending, poisonous buildup that continued to grow out of control.

Though dawn's glow lit the eastern horizon, the sun hadn't risen yet. The TBM 930 was parked behind the general aviation terminal, and he drove his windowless van up to the large passenger door, where he could transfer the plastic bags of ammonium nitrate fuel oil explosive without being seen. He took his time, careful not to rip the sides of the packaging. He couldn't afford to be caught, not after all the planning, the endless flight lessons, and even assembling the ANFO.

It had been easy buying fertilizer at a dozen different landscaping stores, rather than making the ammonium nitrate himself, and he'd discovered that #2 simple-distillate home heating oil worked better than diesel for the fuel oil part of the explosive mixture. He'd tested a small batch of his concoction in a remote field, a hundred miles from where he lived, and the one-pound explosion worked like a charm.

Working swiftly and efficiently, trying not to think beyond the task at hand, he finished loading the Daher without raising suspicions. After driving the van to a nearby parking area, he jogged back to the plane in the dawn silence and started the preflight checklist. He only bothered with the takeoff part of the flight. No need to worry about the return or the landing.

He dispensed with everything except the correct protocols to take off and fly thirty miles, gaining altitude all the way so his dive would attain the max velocity possible before impact.

As the new day brightened, he saw hints of an early morning storm coming in, a nor'easter with strong winds. A silver lining, he thought. The storm would help disperse the radioactive cloud over New York City in the aftermath of the crash.

The time for endless talking was over. Time to kick the tires and light the fires. He had a date with destiny.

2

Adonia Rojas surveyed her domain of Granite Bay, frowning—not from what she saw, but from what she *couldn't* see.

As the site manager, she held absolute power over all operations and people at the nuclear power plant. When she spoke, people scrambled to do her bidding, although she didn't abuse her power. Adonia was tall and attractive, young for her position of authority. She was the only female site manager of a nuclear power plant in the U.S., and at thirty-five she was also the Nuclear Regulatory Commission's youngest executive. She'd only had this job for six months, but any doubters needed less than five minutes of conversation to be convinced that Adonia's rapid rise in her career was due to her brains rather than her looks.

Like all site managers, she hadn't had a grace period to deal with the backlog and bureaucratic crises, a chance to get her feet under her so she could face the larger challenges. Some of her colleagues had been hit with disasters on their first day on the job. At a bustling, high-tech nuclear power plant, site managers couldn't afford to have a learning curve.

Colonel Shawn Whalen, her former boyfriend, had once told her that her authority at Granite Bay was equivalent to that of a commander in a war zone.

Instead of being confident, though, this morning Adonia had arrived at the plant after two sleepless nights in a row, not sure how she would deal with the buildup of spent fuel rods. The storage problem was completely out of her control, and it wasn't going away.

Overlooking the placid shores of the Hudson River sixty miles north of New York City, the morning view looked serene. Columns of white steam roiled out of two massive natural-draft cooling towers, each four hundred feet high.

Directly below, next to the wet-storage facility one building away, Adonia could see sparks flying at a worksite as a welding crew repaired a vacuum tank. In the middle of the one-point-seven-square-mile complex, a fuel tanker truck toiled around temporary storage buildings as it approached the admin center.

Adonia's headquarters building, a glass-faced administrative tower, was strategically located at the southwest corner of the site. From the tenth floor, she had an unobstructed view of the fenced Granite Bay facility. And except for the constant buildup of spent rods, all was running smoothly.

No aircraft, not even small drones, were allowed to fly within five miles of Granite Bay's restricted airspace. Only satellite infrared sensors could detect which building on the large site housed the two-unit pressurized water reactor, filled with over 7,500 highly radioactive uranium rods. A quarter of the rods were retired to cooling pools and exchanged for new ones every year.

Granite Bay provided nearly two gigawatts of electricity to New England. The power plant itself didn't cause Adonia's headaches, but all those spent uranium rods still emitted large amounts of radiation *after* they left the reactor's core. Though not sufficient to keep powering the reactor, the 13.1-foot-high rods were more than active enough to emit a lethal radiation dose within minutes.

Granite Bay's spent rods were stored upright in cradles, immersed in forty feet of water, safely covered with constantly circulating liquid that absorbed the radiation and carried away the heat so the pool didn't come to a boil.

After five years of cooling down, the still-radioactive rods were removed from the deep pools and encased in massive steel and concrete containers, which were filled with inert gas. These containers were then stored inside newer "temporary" buildings.

And just sat there. The dry, high-level nuclear material kept accumulating in storage.

That was where the process ground to a halt. Granite Bay—as with every other nuclear power plant in the nation—had no place to store the deadly material. The containers of high-level waste were ready to be shipped to permanent storage, far from Granite Bay, where they would be safe from any mishaps. But with decades of politics and inaction, there was no facility to receive them. Anywhere.

That was what kept Adonia up at night. It was a disaster waiting to happen. Granite Bay was a power-generating plant, not a permanent storage facility, but all those cooled rods just sat here temporarily— in other words, "forever"—in a place not designed for long-term storage. And she couldn't do a damn thing about it.

Adonia's only consolation was that at least she wasn't alone. Her fellow site managers in thirty states were in the same boat. Granite Bay, like every one of the sixty-one commercially operating nuclear power plants in the U.S., was simply running out of room.

As the early-morning storm blew in, wind whipped dust and leaves around the site and swift clouds closed in to smother the brightening dawn. When the outside temperature plummeted twenty-one degrees in ten minutes, moisture condensed on her office window.

Adonia watched the back of the fuel tanker truck come around the corner near where the workers were welding the vacuum tank, rushing to finish before the storm. Flashers on, the fuel truck backed up slowly toward the bright welder's arc. A shower of sparks swirled in a macabre dance, swept up by the errant breezes, fed by the welder's arc, rising high.

Adonia looked up into the darkening clouds high above the site, saw one spark much brighter and higher than the others. For a moment she didn't realize this wasn't just a spark from the welder. It moved in a straight line, heading down, growing larger. Like an incoming missile.

She sucked in a quick breath. It wasn't a spark at all, but rather light reflecting off a single-engine plane. The plane accelerated in a nearly vertical dive toward the wet-storage facility one building away. The cooling pools inside that facility housed thousands of uranium rods.

What the hell! That plane *couldn't* be overhead—Granite Bay's restricted airspace stretched five miles in all directions!

She heard the whine of the engines now as the aircraft continued its dive, hurtling toward the storage building as if on a bombing run. Adonia realized that the pilot wasn't going to pull up. Intentionally.

She spun from the window, raced to her desk, knowing she had only seconds. She had to do something, contact emergency ops, stop that pilot—

Before she could grab the phone, the plane smashed into the building's roof, and a bright, double-pulsed light erupted and overwhelmed her view, like a giant flashbulb.

Adonia's vision was saturated by flash-blindness. She collided with her desk and fumbled for the phone, trying to find the intercom button. The handset skittered across the desktop.

A second later a *boom* slammed the windows, and the entire admin building seemed to sway from the explosion.

Stunned, she tried to clear the dazzling blotches from her vision. Outside on the ground below, she saw the welders scramble to their cutoff valves, but before they could kill the power, a sheet of yellow and red flames gushed over the ground, transported by thick, viscous fluid that spewed from the tanker truck.

A piercing siren warbled throughout the admin building. Identical alarms would be sounding throughout the site.

Adonia slapped the red intercom button that tied directly to Granite Bay's emergency operations desk, but nothing happened.

As the waves of flame and smoke expanded from the crash site, she jabbed at the button again, but heard no response. She worked her way around the desk, still trying to see through her flash-blindness. She found the phone handset dangling from its cord over the side of her desk. Again, nothing. The explosion must have cut the landline.

She found her purse and grabbed her cell phone instead. She speed-dialed the ops center, hoping that cell coverage hadn't failed as well. As the phone clicked and tried to connect, she grabbed an old emergency handheld radio from the back credenza. She needed to get to the crash site, do something to help.

She ran out of her office holding the bulky radio with one hand and her cell phone to her ear with the other. She bypassed the elevator and veered to the emergency stairwell. How many times had it been drummed into her: never use the elevator in an emergency.

The ops number rang, but no one answered as she jogged down the empty stairwell. It was still early morning, just at shift transition, but the emergency desk had to be manned! Granite Bay was a twenty-four/seven operation.

She made it down five of the ten flights when a voice finally answered her cell. "Ops desk!" Half a dozen people were shouting over each other in the background.

Still running down the steps, she yelled into the phone. "This is Adonia Rojas. Give me an update."

The man's voice stiffened when he realized who she was. "Radar picked up a small plane at thirty-one thousand feet two minutes ago, heading for our restricted airspace at high speed. We couldn't raise the pilot, so we notified the Air National Guard and started broadcasting warnings to the plane. But it kept coming. And . . . and it hit Wet-Storage Building 22A."

"Status?"

"The impact breached the roof and a Class B fire is spreading outside the facility. Extent of damage is unknown, but we're preparing to go to General Emergency. Fire crews are on their way, should arrive within minutes."

"Copy." Adonia's stomach twisted. The plane had crashed into the overflow wet-storage facility—intentionally. That building was hardened, but not against that type of attack. The structure was never meant to be more than a stopgap measure to house the additional cooling pools.

When the government refused to let her ship the deadly waste to a proper storage complex, she had begged for facility upgrades on the "temporary" holding structures, including measures to strengthen the buildings to meet nuclear standards against even a terrorist attack. Her pleas had fallen on deaf ears and tight wallets back in

Washington, so Adonia had taken the initiative and scraped together enough funds to fortify what she could. She now hoped it had been enough to avert a complete disaster.

As the new set of alarms kicked in, she knew this was the first time since Three Mile Island that a nuclear plant had gone to General Emergency—and on her watch. "Response?"

"Emergency response and cleanup teams deployed. We're in voice contact, but no detail has been forwarded." The speaker consulted with someone in the background, then said, "We don't have an optical link set up yet. We'll notify you ASAP when we're receiving visuals from inside."

She approached the second-floor stairwell. "Copy. I'm heading to the wet-storage facility to assist the on-scene commander." She didn't want to think about how hazardous the area would be. "Did the containment hold? Have you implemented the emergency planning zone?" One more flight of stairs, and she was out of breath.

"Yes, ma'am, and we're preparing potassium iodide tablets for distribution to the general public if any radiation is detected, all part of General Emergency."

"Good." She stopped herself from calling out further orders as she reached the last set of stairs. She wasn't going to jump in and confuse an already chaotic situation. The best thing she could do was to let her people do what they had been trained to do, but she had to make sure they were following procedure. "Have you notified DOE?"

"We're on the line now. The Department of Energy emergency operations center is trying to set up a call with Dr. van Dyckman, but he's not in the headquarters building. They said they'd patch him through to you as soon as they find him."

Good thing Stanley's out of the loop, Adonia thought. Knowing van Dyckman, he might try to micromanage from Washington.

Stanley van Dyckman was the poster child for the Peter principle, promoted well beyond his level of competence, always taking credit for other people's work. And now as a Deputy Assistant Secretary of Energy, he wielded just enough clout to really screw things up.

But as long as the bureaucrat was out of contact, he couldn't do any damage.

Having taken care of her legal obligation to notify the Department of Energy, Adonia could focus on helping her team succeed.

The man from the ops desk kept talking as she reached the bottom of the stairs and the emergency exit door. "Ma'am, your phone ID has you calling from one of our Granite Bay cells. Can Dr. van Dyckman reach you on this number?"

"Yes, but if we drop coverage, try this." She flipped over the emergency radio in her other hand and read out the serial number and contact frequency.

She slammed through the exit door and burst outside, then came to an abrupt halt. She stared at the soot and smoke, smelled burning fuel. Black columns roiled into the air not far from where she stood, but another building blocked her view of the actual burning wet-storage facility. Site alarms competed with loud sirens from emergency vehicles, making it difficult to hear. She felt drops of rain spitting down from the storm.

She pressed the cell closer to her ear as she jogged toward the smoke rising over the next building. "Any better idea what happened? I saw the plane come down—it wasn't an accident."

Rustling papers came over the speaker. "He must have been carrying an explosive payload to cause this much damage. Emergency response has detected above-ambient radiation levels, which are steadily rising. There's still no fiber optic inside the burning facility to visually assess the damage, but it's possible the cooling pools were breached, exposing the uranium rods to air. If so, there's enough radiation bouncing around in there to fry anybody in seconds. And if the fire gets to the unshielded rods—"

Adonia knew full well that radioactive contaminants would be swept aloft by the smoke and fire. This was already an unprecedented disaster, and unless the incoming nor'easter dumped a downpour fast, a radioactive cloud of deadly debris could expand to the southwest—straight toward New York City.

More raindrops splattered the ground. She reached the corner of the building as two additional fire trucks rolled around the corner at top speed. But these weren't her on-site ladders—these trucks were outside civilian firefighters.

And that meant they were untrained for this kind of disaster. They didn't have the proper shielding or equipment! Local county units were on call in case of emergencies at Granite Bay, but this was not a typical fire. With the amount of radiation present, the first responders would be putting themselves in danger that they couldn't even see.

Adonia shouted into her cell. "Ops! Who the hell authorized county ladders onto the site? They don't belong here!"

A new voice came over her speaker. "Dr. van Dyckman ordered them, ma'am. We're speaking to his staff now. He personally called all local fire districts and asked them to provide additional support to our Granite Bay engines—"

"Pull them back!" Adonia stopped running so she could shout directly into her phone as the rain increased. "Our people can commandeer their equipment, but those responders need to stay away from the crash site if they don't have the proper decontamination gear. Do it, *now*!"

"Yes, ma'am. Stand by one." The phone went silent for a moment. "Calls are going out canceling all off-site units, but van Dyckman's Chief of Staff says the Deputy Assistant Secretary is now setting up a conference call with the news media, and he'd like you to participate. He wants you to tell the news media exactly what happened—"

Nobody knows what happened yet! She wanted to scream, but calmed herself, just barely. "Tell him I'm not able to participate in any media circus right now." She hadn't even seen the crash site. Furious at the meddling bureaucrat, Adonia thought quickly. "Has DOE notified the other sites across the country? This might be a coordinated attack on *all* nuclear plants. Think of nine-eleven."

"Yes, ma'am, they've all been alerted."

Adonia watched as her on-site emergency response crews garbed in yellow decontamination suits covered the gas fires with foam, while moving inside the breached wet-storage facility to contain any radiation release. The impermeable whole-body garments each had a self-contained breathing apparatus, protecting the workers from any hazardous materials.

The wind died down as the rain increased, gradually becoming a morning downpour. Hopefully, the heavy rain would wash the smoke out of the air and inhibit the dispersal of any radioactive cloud.

"Has radar detected any other planes approaching our airspace? Is this an outright attack?"

"No, ma'am, and the national command authorities haven't detected anything abnormal over any of the other nuclear power plants, but they are all on high alert. The New Jersey Air National Guard established a combat air patrol to overfly our restricted airspace with two F-16s, just to be safe."

She sighed. With the military involved, no other aircraft would get near Granite Bay, or any other power plant. "If anyone from the media wants to know what happened, tell them to contact DOE Headquarters. We'll let them release details as they come out."

She shifted the phone to her shoulder. "And tell Dr. van Dyckman's office that I'll be able to speak with him once my emergency response has the situation under control. But it may take a while. Got it?"

"Yes, ma'am. Loud and clear."

She knew the cleanup crews had their job cut out for them, mopping up any contaminants and repairing the cooling pools, but at least a near catastrophe had been contained—for now, helped by the rain.

The media catastrophe was about to begin.

The White House

The Oval Office was exactly what Stanley van Dyckman expected. He had seen it countless times on TV and the movies, but it was different to be here in person and on official business.

Throughout his career as a senator's Chief of Staff and at DOE, van Dyckman had attended many high-level meetings, had rubbed shoulders with four-star generals and Nobel Prize–winning scientists—that was par for the course—but now he had the opportunity to meet with the President himself. And not merely for a photo op either; he would not be an anonymous person in a large crowd of officials and representatives. This was a real meeting, and the President genuinely wanted to hear what van Dyckman had to say.

The country was in crisis after the near disaster at Granite Bay, and van Dyckman held the solution the nation had desperately needed for more than half a century. Thank goodness the DOE Secretary was out of the country; otherwise, van Dyckman would have been relegated to holding the young Secretary's briefcase while the neophyte political appointee was the center of attention and would probably take credit for the whole idea.

Van Dyckman wore his best pinstriped suit, and he had shaved an hour before the meeting so there wouldn't be even a hint of a shadow on his face. The President's calendar allotted only half an hour for the meeting, but if everything went well, maybe he'd be in the Oval Office for a lot longer than that. The President was famous for throwing the schedule out the window and spending whatever time he felt a subject required.

He mentally ran over his talking points. The answer he proposed seemed so obvious, the decision clear, even though the nation had avoided action for decades. This President, at least, had a "damn the torpedoes!" mindset, and he could make a real decision to solve a difficult problem.

Van Dyckman was so eager he barely noticed the surroundings of the outer anteroom, and when he finally entered the Oval Office, he was ready. He had been waiting for the right opportunity, and this was it.

Smiling, he shook the President's hand, trying to convince himself this was just like any other high-level meeting. The man was smaller in stature than he had expected after seeing numerous raised-voice speeches and rallies on TV, but van Dyckman could sense his larger-than-life presence. It reminded him a little of a buried land mine. "Thank you for seeing me, Mr. President. I'll try to be direct, so as not to waste your time."

"Sounds like this nation's been wasting a lot of time," the President said. Blunt, aggressive—and that was good, as far as van Dyckman was concerned. "Wait a minute before we get started." The President stepped back to his desk and picked up the phone. "Stephanie, is Colonel Whalen on his way?"

"Just arrived, sir," said the intercom.

The door opened again and a military officer stood there in Air Force blues, a full colonel but obviously young for his rank. He was sandy haired and handsome with blue-green eyes, and van Dyckman couldn't help but make an unkind comparison to a Ken doll.

The President said, "Dr. van Dyckman, meet my military aide, Colonel Shawn Whalen. He's an expert on nuclear matters, and I trust his advice."

The officer shook the President's hand, then turned to van Dyckman. "We've met before at several DOE functions."

"Of course." Van Dyckman squeezed Whalen's hand as if competing with his grip. He had no memory of meeting the man previously—Whalen was only a colonel, after all, and he met so many more important people in his duties.

A White House steward brought in a coffee service tray. Van Dyckman had imagined holding a cut-crystal rocks glass and sipping fine Scotch with the President as they discussed matters of national importance. But it was only mid-morning, which was a little early to drink even by Washington standards.

It didn't matter. He expected to be coming to the Oval Office many more times. This proposal was the only real near-term solution for the nuclear storage crisis.

The three men sat on the sofas, leaning forward as van Dyckman removed his portfolio from his briefcase. He unbuttoned his suit jacket, brushed away imaginary lint. "Let me start off by saying, sir, that the attack on Granite Bay could have been worse—much worse. Fortunately, through fast thinking and decisive action, we managed to avert a widespread dispersal of radiation from the spent rods. Good thing I was managing the situation from Washington so I could employ the correct emergency procedures without red tape or delays."

Colonel Whalen raised an eyebrow. "We've studied the transcripts of the phone conversations, and I believe Adonia Rojas was the person instrumental in saving the facility—as well as having the foresight to fortify her own buildings ahead of time, without help from DOE. If she hadn't done so, the plane crash would have caused a far greater disaster."

Van Dyckman opened the binder as a distraction to cover his frown. He didn't need to hit a conversational speed bump just when he was about to present his main points. "Ms. Rojas and I work very closely, Colonel, and I admit, funds are scarce. But we dodged only one bullet at Granite Bay. Over the years, other incidents occurred that were nearly as bad, but they were quietly covered up. Right now, our entire nuclear industry is under heavy fire, and Granite Bay only exacerbated the problem. More nuclear disasters are just waiting to happen, and we can only put on so many layers of Band-Aids to solve a problem that needs a tourniquet."

The President frowned, already growing impatient. He looked down at the presentation folder, waiting to see the report. "Enough with the metaphors, Dr. van Dyckman. Tell me how to fix this. I want a real solution, something we can implement right away."

Van Dyckman tried not to show his relief. "And I have a solution, sir, but first let me give a quick overview. We currently have ninety-nine commercial nuclear reactors spread over thirty states. They're all vital to our economy and our power grid, but short-sighted protesters would have us shut down all the nuclear plants—which would be a disaster, since the U.S. derives about twenty percent of our total energy output from nuclear power."

Colonel Whalen thumbed through the charts. "Yes, the people at Sanergy are having a field day after Granite Bay." He looked up. "In a way I don't blame them for their concern, but do they really believe our nuclear power plants are that fragile?"

Annoyed, van Dyckman twisted his mouth, but he kept his voice steady. "You would rather we tell everyone the truth? That the majority of our temporary storage facilities aren't hardened against wackos flying kamikaze planes? We're lucky this was a lone-wolf event. A Sanergy extremist, not a larger-scale assault."

"It's not clear that Sanergy was really involved, or if it was just a single fanatic," Whalen said. "In any case, Sanergy wants to use the incident as a lever to force their own goals, to move away from nuclear power and embrace green energy, but that's simply not realistic in the near term. No matter how optimistic Sanergy might be, we can't just shut down a fifth of our nation's electrical capacity overnight because of wishful thinking."

"Right," van Dyckman said, glad that the young colonel wasn't arguing with him. Maybe they were on the same page after all.

Whalen continued, "And the plane that hit Granite Bay shows that our current stopgap practice of storing so much high-level radioactive waste in local holding areas is not only a safety issue, but a *security* concern as well. A big one. Now, no one could make nuclear weapons out of even high-level waste, but a terrorist could easily create a dirty bomb with the material. And that, fueled by public hysteria, would dwarf any threat we've seen."

Van Dyckman felt a warm glow. The colonel was making his case for him! He turned the page in his binder to show another chart and continued, "The problem is that our nuclear power plants generate two thousand tons of high-level radioactive waste each year in the form of spent fuel rods and other hazardous materials. We need a safe *and* secure place to store it, preferably out of public view, and right now we've got nothing." He paused to let the words sink in.

The President's brow furrowed as he concentrated. "So it's just sitting around? How much waste are we talking about, total?"

"Over one hundred thousand metric tons across the nation. Currently, as we just saw at Granite Bay, most of those spent fuel rods are in temporary storage areas at each site, either in cooling ponds or dry-storage casks. They're safe, but Sanergy argues they have the potential to leak into groundwater, streams, or even the air."

Van Dyckman leaned forward. "We've had commercial power plants since 1958, when President Eisenhower launched the Shippingport Atomic Power Station in Pennsylvania. And they've been generating nuclear waste ever since. One hundred thousand *tons* of it."

"Someone must have foreseen this," the President said. "What about that underground storage facility in Nevada, Yucca Mountain?"

"As you know, sir, it never opened," van Dyckman said. "After thirty years of construction, some estimates put the total price including setbacks, legal and environmental reviews at over one hundred billion." He hesitated. "A previous administration completely shut it down."

"Political pressure," Whalen said.

Van Dyckman felt the need to hurry, and his voice rose as he rattled on. "Yucca Mountain is the most studied piece of geology on Earth. Even though it's the most godforsaken wasteland in the entire country, people insisted 'not in my backyard.'"

The President pressed his lips together. "Well, whose backyard do they want it in? It's got to go somewhere."

"But it's not going anywhere," van Dyckman said. "Right now, the waste is in everybody's backyard, stored in casks spread over sixty-one nuclear sites, waiting to be transferred, someday, to a single, consolidated permanent storage area . . . which doesn't exist."

"The casks are extremely safe, sir," Whalen said, "made of concrete, steel, and other material. But I agree with Dr. van Dyckman's assessment. This much waste is both a safety and a security risk."

Van Dyckman sat back on the sofa and sipped his coffee, enjoying the fine bone china, the rich roast. Across from him, the President straightened. "We need to do something." He looked around the room.

"One option is for you to reopen Yucca Mountain," van Dyckman said. "An Executive Order. As simple as that."

"We've already looked at that, and it's not that simple," Whalen said. "The legal reviews alone would take years, and the public may not allow it despite the reassurances and current uproar over Granite Bay."

The President looked back and forth between the two men and drew his mouth tight. "We need a place to store it that doesn't need public approval. If Granite Bay was a wake-up call, we can't afford to keep the status quo."

Van Dyckman nodded. "Correct, sir. The whole high-level nuclear waste problem is one of the most maddening examples of bureaucracy and foot-dragging I've seen in my entire career. We need to implement a solution now and without interference, even if it's just a temporary answer while we work through the red tape and get a permanent facility online once and for all."

"What do other countries do with all their radioactive waste?" the President asked. "We're not the only ones with nuclear power plants."

"Some nations are starting to bury their waste underground, sir," Whalen said.

"Other countries don't have our political environment," van Dyckman said. "In order to take care of this emergency while we pursue a longer-term solution, it'll require some discretion." He added something he knew would resonate with the President. "And bold action." He hesitated for effect. "But I have a way to do it."

"Then I'll sign an Executive Order."

Van Dyckman felt giddy. He already had the President convinced, and he hadn't even offered his proposal yet.

"Where exactly do you propose to put the material?" Colonel Whalen said slowly. "What other facility do we have that's adequate to hold that much high-level nuclear waste? You'd still need to get all the assessments and environmental approvals for storing it permanently."

Van Dyckman flipped the page, showed a map of the New Mexico desert along with photos of the rugged terrain south of Albuquerque, around Kirtland Air Force Base. "We already have a perfectly acceptable facility that was designed for long-term storage and protection of our nuclear weapons stockpile. Hydra Mountain. It's honeycombed with tunnels and shafts, vaults carved out of the granite, but with the stockpile reduction, all the nukes were removed, and the Hydra Mountain facility is just sitting there empty, mothballed. *And,* best of all, it's deep inside a secure military base."

He started speaking faster. "If you call it a temporary site, rather than a permanent one, then by classified Executive Order, sir, you could reopen the doors and start transporting casks of high-level waste almost immediately. You'd start solving the problem before the next accident happens. And you wouldn't even have to tell anyone about it publicly, much less obtain any legal reviews or hold any hearings, while at the same time you go through the process of openly constructing a permanent site somewhere else."

The President lifted his head. "Hydra Mountain. Why does that sound familiar? Someone was talking about that just the other day. . . ." He shook his head. "But I like it." He glanced over at his military aide. "Shawn?"

Wearing a thoughtful expression, Colonel Whalen pulled the binder toward him, flipping through the printouts van Dyckman had brought. "It is a possibility, sir, but I'd have to study it further. It may be on an Air Force base, but I don't know enough about Hydra Mountain off the top of my head."

"Look into it," the President said, "and get back to me quickly. I want to move on this if it's an acceptable solution. Granite Bay was a real wake-up call."

Whalen said, "The need is great, sir, but after all this time we shouldn't take precipitous and ill-considered actions either. There could be unintended consequences, cascading effects. After all, Yucca Mountain was studied for over thirty years, and it still didn't open."

"Granite Bay," the President repeated, as if that answered everything. "I don't ever want to have another Granite Bay, or anything like it—not under my administration. Make it happen."

His heart racing, van Dyckman closed his binder and saw that their half hour was up. He hadn't even needed the extra time he'd hoped for.

Smiling, he picked up his materials and casually swept up a pen from the coffee table, one with the Seal of the President of the United States, and pocketed it.

4

Kirtland Air Force Base
Southeast of Albuquerque, New Mexico

Armed military police. Razor wire. Fences. Locked gates.

Adonia was surprised to encounter so many defenses, even though she was already well inside the security perimeter of Kirtland Air Force Base. *A nice welcoming way to start the day*.

She wished she knew why she'd been called here.

One of the MPs came forward from the security gate and opened the back door of the escort car. The uniformed man peered inside, squinting. His face looked very sunburned, which was not surprising, considering the New Mexico heat. "This way, Ms. Rojas. You'll be processed into the Mountain through the intake office over there. Lieutenant Peters will meet you momentarily."

Mystified, Adonia swung out of the backseat, taking her briefcase and purse. Her heels crunched against gravel as she stepped out into the brilliant sunlight; a gust of hot wind blew dust into her eyes. Judging from the scenery around here, she had overdressed for the occasion. Her black pumps and red business suit were more appropriate for her usual meetings in Washington, D.C., than the desert Southwest.

Out of habit before rushing to catch the red-eye out of LaGuardia, she had dressed for a formal meeting, but it was now apparent that Hydra Mountain was no typical government office building—and quite different from Granite Bay back in New York.

Only eight hours ago she'd received a phone call requesting her immediate presence in New Mexico for a vital, high-level review. *Nothing like planning ahead,* she thought. Her old boss, Assistant Secretary van Dyckman, had made it clear the invitation was mandatory, and as a contractor, Adonia didn't want to burn any bridges.

She raised a hand to her forehead against the glare and desert wind as she surveyed the area. She'd left her sunglasses at home, expecting to be confined in a typical conference room under banks of fluorescent lights, not deep inside a huge Air Force base.

Standing beside the blue government escort car, she faced the tall security gate and four sequential barricades of chain-link fence, each topped with razor wire. Behind the fences loomed the imposing mountain—a scrub-covered mound rising five hundred feet from the desert and spreading three miles wide. *Hydra Mountain.* Not many people got a chance to see this rugged and ominous place up close. *Who would want to?*

Official blue-and-white government signs identified electrical fences and warned that trespassers would be met with deadly force. Granite Bay had similar warnings, as did the entire nuclear industry, and she was perfectly familiar with them. But this security exceeded anything she normally saw. Adonia felt a chill, despite the heat. The terrain around her was unwelcoming enough, but the mountain was downright *ominous.*

According to publicly available sources, Hydra Mountain had been a secure nuclear weapons storage depot back in Cold War days, decommissioned at least two decades ago. In its heyday, this place must have bustled with activity, military personnel working in and around the complex as nuclear warheads were stealthily transferred into the storage tunnels from Safe Secure Transports. Now, the rocky buttress seemed quiet and empty, a ghost town. Hydra Mountain should be shut down.

So why had she been called here, of all places? And on such short notice?

She turned to the MP who walked her toward the fence. "I was expecting to be taken to DOE's Albuquerque Field Office. This is an odd place for an official meeting." She tucked her long brunette hair behind her ear, already suspecting the man wouldn't give her any useful answer.

The sunburned guard nodded. "They're expecting you inside the facility, ma'am. Mr. van Dyckman's orders were very clear."

As clear as welder's goggles, she thought, but it was on par with the rest of the obtuse information that van Dyckman had provided, other than his demand that she travel to Albuquerque for the high-priority Sunday review. "High priority" and "Sunday" didn't usually mesh in the government, especially since she normally reserved the weekend for catching up on her own work at the power plant, but her old boss often had a flair for the dramatic.

She'd forgotten about van Dyckman's priorities, which were more often based on his own sense of importance than actual emergencies. She secretly called them "Stanley-isms." For Adonia, the best defense was to agree only as much as necessary and get the work done, either *with* him, or *around* him. That was one reason she'd left government service and gone to Granite Bay, but now damage control after the plane crash disaster had occupied her for more than a year.

At least she'd managed to finish some unclassified paperwork on the plane, four blessedly uninterrupted hours in the air, wedged in a middle seat two rows up from the rear lavatory, while two heavyset brothers snored away on either side of her. She had a lot of important work to do managing Granite Bay, which still hadn't entirely recovered from the incident but was still producing significant power for the Northeast. More eyes than ever were watching over everything she did, though.

Forced to rely on stopgap safety upgrades, even after the attack, Adonia constantly worried about compliance, operations, logistics, finance, security, personnel, and a hundred other concerns. She didn't have time to waste taking a tour of some long-mothballed nuclear weapons storage facility, but she tried to convince herself that Stanley's last-minute request might result in future contracts. Still, she hoped this meeting would wrap up in time for her to catch a red-eye flight back home so she could go to work on Monday morning. She hadn't brought an overnight bag, made no hotel reservation in Albuquerque.

Adonia followed the MP up to the first fence gate, while the driver pulled the blue staff car around, leaving her behind. *Stranded in the desert . . . a wonderful way to spend a Sunday.* Just inside the innermost fence, she could see a squat brown corrugated structure abutting the stony slope, a small administrative outbuilding that gave no hint as to what might be inside the Mountain.

The first main security gate led into a large sally port, but she could see a smaller pedestrian sally port that led through the sequential fences to the ugly admin building.

The inner gate opened, and a dark-skinned woman in U.S. Air Force battle fatigues strode toward her. Adonia shaded her eyes, able to make out that an ID dangled around the young woman's neck.

The Air Force officer gave an uncertain salute as she exited the second gate and came forward. "General Rojas? I'm sorry to keep you waiting. I'm Lieutenant Peters."

Adonia realized that by shading her eyes she must have given the impression she was saluting. With an embarrassed laugh, she dropped her hand. "Terribly sorry, Lieutenant. I'm just a civilian. It's so bright out here, I couldn't see with the glare."

The officer's shoulders relaxed as they exchanged handshakes. "My mistake, ma'am. The paperwork was rushed through, and the local DOE protocol office relayed that you're a general officer. Sometimes our high-ranking visitors don't wear their uniforms for operational security reasons."

Adonia was amused by the mix-up, but Shawn Whalen would have been floored that anyone could mistake her for military! The two of them would have had a good laugh about it. She paused. Now where had *that* stray thought come from? Even though they had parted as close friends, she hadn't thought of Shawn in almost two years, since he'd been assigned as the President's military aide. Maybe just being on an Air Force base had started the wheels turning in her mind. . . .

Thinking of him was a lot more enjoyable than worrying about her overcrowded fuel rod storage at Granite Bay. At least *he* wasn't a problem that needed to be solved.

She followed Peters through the first fenced gate. "Rest easy around me, Lieutenant. The DOE used to consider me a general officer equivalent when I was still in civil service, but it's only a protocol rank. That's far different from being a real general, trust me, and I'm not a hard-ass in disguise. Just treat me as a civilian."

Lieutenant Peters nodded formally and closed the first gate behind them. "No worries, ma'am. We're still getting used to transitioning Hydra Mountain to the Department of Energy, away from military control. Some of the protocols are a little contradictory."

Adonia couldn't hide her surprise. "Transitioning to the DOE? That's news to me. When did that happen?" Maybe that was why she had been brought here in such a rush. As site manager of Granite Bay, she was much more involved with the Department of Energy than with the military.

Peters stiffened. "I . . . shouldn't have said that. You'll be briefed at the proper time and place." She lowered her voice. "Please don't mention it once you get inside. Regulation Rob wouldn't take it very well. He's a real stickler."

Regulation Rob? That was strange. "Don't worry, I'll be sure to act surprised. My ex-boss already has plenty of questions to answer. Has Assistant Secretary van Dyckman shown up?"

"Yes, ma'am. I believe all the others have arrived as well."

"Good, I look forward to catching up with him." Her comment sounded breezy, but she wanted to strangle Stanley for keeping her in the dark. Oh, how different it was being a contractor!

While she was here, Adonia hoped for some quality time alone with him for a no-nonsense debriefing. As Assistant Secretary, van Dyckman knew full well the pressure she was under at Granite Bay. Overseeing the nation's nuclear waste was his primary responsibility, and the inadequate temporary spent fuel storage area at her site was a problem that wouldn't solve itself. She was swamped, far behind schedule, and she needed to oversee the additional holding pools being built after the plane crash. In the meantime, she had to monitor the crowded reconfiguration of the immersed fuel rods.

She had no interest in joining in some blue-ribbon review committee. Stanley must be in showoff mode, especially after his promotion to Assistant Secretary. Why couldn't he just hold a videoconference like everyone else?

As she followed the officer to the pedestrian gate, Adonia saw two flatbed eighteen-wheelers, side by side near an enormous metal vault door set into the mountainside. Gray canvas covered both flatbeds, disguising the huge load, which was twice as high as each tractor unit.

Adonia frowned. After being decommissioned back in the post-Reagan era, Hydra Mountain should be empty, so why were the big trucks delivering a substantial cargo load? Something was definitely going on here. . . .

Adonia presented her ID to the guard stationed at the next sally port gate. It was a bad photo, par for the course in government-issued identification, showing her long dark hair, large brown eyes, naturally thick lashes, generous lips, and a startled-looking goofy expression. Years ago Shawn had teased her about the picture, not that his Air Force photo ID was any better.

The sergeant at the gate inserted the common access card into a reader that verified her identity. "Are you carrying any cell phones or other electronic devices, Ms. Rojas?"

"Just my NRC cell. I need it to keep in touch with my facility back in New York—"

The guard didn't flinch. "You're not allowed to bring it inside, government cell phone or not."

Adonia couldn't afford to be cut off from her Granite Bay team, not even on a Sunday. "It's an operational necessity, Sergeant. Nuclear power plants don't take care of themselves. I have the necessary clearances, and I have to be available on a moment's notice."

With the Nuclear Regulatory Commission's urgent orders to reconfigure Granite Bay's overcrowded storage array of fuel rods, she needed to oversee the high-risk activity. They were pointedly aware that her spent fuel rods were packed to capacity—beyond capacity, for her own comfort level—and even repacking the array would buy only a little time. Nuclear waste couldn't just sit there, swept under a rug, yet Granite Bay wasn't legally allowed to move the rods anywhere else. Even after the near disaster at her site, no one seemed in a hurry to pick up the political hot potato.

Adonia started to insist on keeping her phone when Lieutenant Peters intervened. "Sorry, Ms. Rojas. It really is a classification issue. In addition, strict protocols prohibit electromagnetic transmissions inside the Mountain, as it may affect the sensors. No exceptions. Brand-new safety and security systems are being installed throughout the facility and the integration has been . . . problematic at times. If you accidentally trigger a lockdown, you'll have to cool your heels for six hours while the systems recycle." Peters gave her an understanding look. "Better safe than sorry, ma'am."

The guard pointed to a metal cabinet set in concrete at the side of the sally port, which held two dozen lockboxes. Keys dangled from the locks of the few available ones. "Pick an empty box, lock your phone inside, and take the key. You can pick it up when you leave, ma'am. Nobody will touch it."

Adonia sighed. Knowing that further argument would solve nothing, she powered down her cell, stowed it in an empty lockbox, and placed the key in her purse. "I'll look on the bright side. I can't tell you how many times I've wished I could be away from the phone."

The sergeant waved them through the port, and the gate behind them rolled shut, closing them in an arched tunnel of barbed wire under the hot sun.

When the opposite gate swung open and granted them access to the squat admin building, Adonia felt a welcome blast of air-conditioning. The building held only a few small offices, a closed conference room, and, at the end of the hall, a large vault door that led into the Mountain. Just outside the conference room, an older Hispanic man sat behind a table covered with neatly stacked government forms. He gave Adonia a smile that seemed full of anticipation.

A different kind of gauntlet, she thought. *Red tape instead of barbed wire.*

Lieutenant Peters bowed out. "That's all I can do for you, ma'am. Out of my jurisdiction. Once you enter Hydra Mountain, you aren't officially on a military base anymore, so I'll hand you over to Mr. Morales."

The man at the table picked up a stack of forms and gestured her to the seat in front of him. "Good morning, and welcome to the Mountain. Prior to receiving any programmatic information in the conference room, you need to sign these required security documents and waivers."

She looked at the size of the stack. "Looks like I'm refinancing a house."

Adonia knew that the military and DOE each had convoluted and mutually exclusive administrative protocols, which doubled the red tape. Morales asked for her ID—again—and Adonia dug out her white government common access card. She was accustomed to having her ID verified at every turn, although back at Granite Bay or in NRC meetings, her colleagues recognized her on sight. But she had never been inside Hydra Mountain, and she didn't even know the names of the other review committee members who were already inside the conference room.

What a fine Sunday outing. She picked up the top form and scanned it. Stanley van Dyckman certainly had some explaining to do.

While the clerk accessed a security database with his laptop, Adonia could hear voices in muted conversation from behind the closed door. After Morales verified her clearances, he pushed another set of forms across the desk. "Please acknowledge and sign these security statements before you enter the conference room."

Reading the documents in detail would have taken her hours, but Adonia already knew the standard DOE security forms; she'd left the government only two years ago to run Granite Bay. She flipped through the form, spotting the clear and explicit warnings, then noticed that the terms were more draconian than usual: divulging *any* information about *any* Hydra Mountain program constituted a felony offense, punishable by what looked to be an infinite number of years in Federal prison. Somewhere in the fine print she was probably also offering up her firstborn if she ever had children, or her left kidney if she didn't.

Adonia grimaced. "This makes me accountable for something I don't even know about yet. Why am I signing these?"

Morales smiled at her again. "I can't tell you, ma'am, because I really don't know." He nodded toward the large vault door at the end of the corridor. "I'm not allowed inside the Mountain. Although this perimeter facility qualifies as a SCIF, a Special Compartmented Information Facility, you'll have to wait until you actually go inside before you can discuss any program-specific material. At that point, someone will explain everything." He nudged the pen closer to her and lowered his voice. "At least according to Regulation Rob."

That again. Adonia grunted and picked up the pen. "I wouldn't want to miss out on all the fun. After all, this is my day off."

In the past, some national security programs had been so hush-hush that their very existence was highly classified. Even Vice President Harry Truman had never heard of the Manhattan Project until he was sworn in after the death of Franklin Roosevelt. That had been a crash program to develop an atomic bomb at the height of World War II, though, and this place was just an old, mothballed nuclear weapon storage site. Maybe in Stanley's mind the two programs were equivalent. It was the sort of melodramatic maneuver her former boss loved, since it made him seem important. Another Stanley-ism.

She signed the papers. "I guess it's the government way."

"Especially the DOE way." Morales handed her a red badge clipped to a radiation dosimeter on a plastic lanyard. "Now that you've signed in, I'll notify Mr. Harris that everyone's here. He'll be taking you all inside the Mountain."

Adonia placed the lanyard around her neck as the name rang a bell. "Wait, you mean Rob Harris? *He's* Regulation Rob? I used to work with him at Oakridge, but I haven't seen him in years. A really good guy."

"But he is a stickler for the rules," Morales said as he picked up the phone. "Everything by the book, chapter and verse."

Adonia smiled as she remembered. "Yes, that's him."

Rob Harris had had a long career in DOE, and she knew him to be competent, detail-oriented to a fault, and generally well liked. Harris hadn't been the most charismatic manager, but he was thorough, and he was a straight shooter. Morales was certainly correct—Regulation Rob had never seen a procedure he didn't like.

"I thought he'd retired, though." She remembered talking to Harris at a DOE mixer in Oakridge five years ago, when he told her he intended to take advantage of a government golden parachute that year. He yearned to leave work behind in favor of a nice beach and a stack of novels.

"The retirement didn't last long." Morales pressed the phone closer to his ear and spoke into it. "Yes, sir. Everyone is present. I'll send in Ms. Rojas."

Even before he hung up, the conference room door opened, and Stanley van Dyckman emerged to meet her, all smiles. "Adonia! Glad you could make it." As always, his brown hair was slicked back. He was nattily dressed even out in the New Mexico desert: blue pinstriped suit, white shirt, a maroon tie, brown wingtips.

She adjusted her new badge and dosimeter, keeping her expression neutral. "Always glad to help." He chuckled at her sarcasm, and she pressed harder: "Why exactly *do* you need me here, Stanley? And why in such a hurry to get me here on a Sunday morning? A little bit of warning would have been nice."

Van Dyckman often insincerely tried to play down his position as a DOE Assistant Secretary, but ever since he'd received his political advancement after the Granite Bay incident, Adonia had noticed something standoffish about him. "This inspection team had to be put together quickly, a pro forma review committee, and we've got a ticking clock here. The Senator has a big meeting in Washington on Wednesday, and he needs our blessing for the Hydra Mountain project." Before she could ask any more questions, he cut her off, anxious to take her into the briefing room. "You'll find out once we're inside the facility. We can't talk out here in the hall." After glancing at the completed paperwork, van Dyckman ushered her into the room, eager to make introductions. "I think you'll be impressed with what we're doing here, Adonia. I really do. It solves a lot of crucial problems for the nation. You've been complaining about it yourself."

She had no intention of letting him sweep her along before she had a chance to speak candidly. She grabbed his arm, forcing him to stop just inside the door. "Just a minute, Stanley. First, you and I have to discuss my backlog of spent fuel rods. For some reason the NRC keeps deferring to you."

He brushed her off as his smile became more brittle. "We can talk at a break. The others have been waiting for you to arrive."

Translation: he intended to avoid her at every opportunity.

Adonia insisted, "Stanley, you know we've exceeded capacity for wet storage, but the fuel rods keep piling up. My cooling pools are crammed, and I don't have any additional space. No room at the inn! I simply can't store any more spent rods unless we build larger *per-*

manent pools on site, not temporary ones. Immediately. And that takes money, as well as government approval. The NRC keeps booting the problem over to you, but your staff is sitting on my request. I don't know why they're stalling. This is not the sort of thing you can avoid—unless you want to shut down Granite Bay entirely."

"Permanent pools are a different line item in the budget, with additional regulations," van Dyckman said. "I don't have as much leeway as I do with temporary construction." He obviously didn't want to talk about it, leading her into the conference room. "Trust me, Adonia, I'm taking care of the problem. Just be patient and make the stopgap measure work for a little longer, as I suggested a few months ago—"

She shook her head. "I won't do that. The NRC is still looking for any reason to shut me down after the crash, and I won't ask them for another waiver. I *need* funding for permanent pools, and I need it yesterday!" It seemed absurd to construct "permanent" temporary pools, as opposed to even worse "temporary" temporary pools, but she wouldn't compromise safety. Granite Bay had enough of a black eye as it was, thanks to the attack by the antinuke fanatic.

Stanley was clearly impatient with her interruption. "Just erect the temporary pools and let me worry about the NRC. That'll give you breathing room and ease the crisis."

"It shouldn't always be a crisis," Adonia said.

His expression looked strange. "I *said* I'd take care of it. I fixed the last problem after the attack, didn't I? We stopped a radiation release that could have dwarfed Three Mile Island."

"*Dodged* is a better way of describing it." Adonia's eyes flashed. And "we" prevented it? He'd been busy preening before the press while she directed the emergency response, and the morning rainstorm had done as much to mitigate the radiation release as anything else. Talk about revisionist history!

It wasn't the first time he'd tried to take credit for other people's actions. Three years ago when Adonia was still in the government and assigned to DOE Headquarters, right before his appointment as Deputy Assistant Secretary and while he was still Chief of Staff for a powerful senator, van Dyckman had refused to release funding unless the DOE packed additional fuel rods in their reactor's cooling pools, crammed closer together than what the NRC had approved. He'd offered his own plans for yet another "temporary emergency solution," but he had made a minor—and crucial—error in his calculations that would have resulted in a major criticality. It was only *Adonia's* quick action countermanding his commands that had saved the day. Although van Dyckman happily took credit for preventing the "mishap," they both knew who had stopped a possible catastrophe, and they both knew who was responsible for it in the first place.

What mattered most to Adonia was that a disaster had been averted, but it made Stanley insufferable. She had felt great relief when she left government service to become the manager of Granite Bay.

Later, his response to the plane crash, as well as the powerful senator's backing, had somehow led to van Dyckman being appointed as Assistant Secretary of Energy, which placed him in charge of the nation's nuclear waste. Yet he hadn't done anything to solve the growing storage problem.

At least he was so busy that he couldn't micromanage her, and Adonia was able to do her work without being harassed. He knew that she could hold the truth over him if she wanted, revealing to the public how his botched calculations would have resulted in a disaster, but she had never threatened to do so. It was an uneasy truce between the two of them.

Now, he tugged her toward the conference room. "Please just wait until we've finished this meeting. You'll see what I'm doing, and believe me, you'll thank me for it." He seemed more intense than she had ever seen him.

She lowered her voice. "One week, Stanley. I'll take a tour of this place if it makes some senator happy, but you've got *one week* to hold off the NRC and come up with the funding for Granite Bay's permanent wet storage. It can't wait."

"After you enter the Mountain, I guarantee you'll change your mind." His smile brightened. "Now, ready to meet the rest of the committee?"

Adonia held his gaze, but didn't return the smile. "One week."

He took her elbow and finally steered her into the conference room.

6

Despite all the fences, gates, and guards on the outside, the bland conference room could have been in any government or military facility: outdated motivational posters and a picture of the President adorned the walls; workhorse plastic chairs with metal legs surrounded a faux-wood table with a laminate finish. A metal cylinder coffee dispenser sat on a blocky credenza in the corner.

Two men and an older woman chatted as they clustered around picked-over pastries next to the coffee urn. The larger of the two men wore a light gray suit; he held himself erect and kept his chin raised, as though to elevate himself. The other man had wild gray hair and wore a black corduroy jacket, tan button-down shirt, and blue jeans. The woman was short and petite, and her brown pants suit with matching flats were in contrast to Adonia's red power suit and heels. Again, she felt overdressed.

The woman finished her cherry Danish and wiped her fingers on a napkin, and Adonia recognized her as the Undersecretary of Energy. Victoria Doyle was a powerful, no-nonsense woman in a very influential position in the DOE . . . but Doyle was responsible for nuclear *weapons,* not nuclear energy, which made her a square peg here. In the Department of Energy bureaucracy, Weapons and Energy were not only physically and administratively separated, but each area had its own culture, not to mention significant rivalry.

Adonia whispered to Stanley, "What's Undersecretary Doyle doing here? She isn't even in your chain of command." As soon as she asked, she remembered the rumors that Stanley had once had an affair with Victoria Doyle. Maybe she shouldn't have mentioned anything. . . .

His voice held a touch of annoyance. "Good question. You'll have to ask Rob Harris—he's the one who assigned her to the committee, though this was supposed to be my show."

"Then how did her name get on the list? Why was she invited?"

He tightened his jaw. "I asked Harris to pull together the best senior experts for this team, but I should have vetted it first. I thought I could trust my own site manager to make the call."

Your site manager? "I don't understand what Rob is doing here. I know he retired—"

Ignoring her, van Dyckman raised his voice to get the others' attention. "Everyone! Ms. Rojas has arrived, and Mr. Harris is on his way in from the operations center, so let me introduce you all." He rubbed his hands briskly together, more comfortable now that he had taken charge. "This is Adonia Rojas, site manager of the Granite Bay nuclear power plant in New York. I like to think of her as my protégée, especially after the unfortunate events of a year and a half ago. Her position at Granite Bay gives her a real hands-on, boots-on-the-ground perspective for our review. That's why I wanted her here."

Though she bristled, Adonia forced herself to smile and nod at the other committee members as Stanley continued his introductions. "I'm sure you recognize my old boss, Senator Pulaski. He's here in his official capacity as Chairman of the Senate Energy and Natural Resources Committee. Senator Pulaski is the reason we called all of you together so quickly. On Wednesday back in Washington he has a vital meeting about the future of Hydra Mountain, and he needs us to conduct an objective and broad-based review."

The big man in the light gray suit vigorously shook Adonia's hand. "Glad to meet you, young lady." He held her hand for an uncomfortably long moment until she pulled away.

Van Dyckman said in a stage whisper, "Be nice to him, Adonia—he still controls the purse strings to the entire nuclear complex." He brightened and made his tone artificially upbeat as he turned to the man with the unruly hair. "If you watch the news or any of the talk shows, you've seen Dr. Simon Garibaldi, the 'loyal opposition' from Sanergy."

No one laughed, and Adonia felt her stomach sour. *What the hell is he doing here?* She knew the nutcase who had crashed the small plane into her site had been a fringe member—vehemently disavowed—of the Sanergy protest group.

"More like devil's advocate," Senator Pulaski muttered, not afraid to show his dislike for the man.

The tall, casually dressed Garibaldi responded with a distant smile. "Objective and open-minded. And willing to consider alternatives." He sounded professorial.

Because of his technical background and his quick wit, Simon Garibaldi was a favorite of talk-show hosts, an outspoken, erudite critic of nuclear power despite having previously worked for DOE. As a gadfly in the media, Garibaldi felt it was his mission to make nuclear power obsolete by transitioning to cleaner, sustainable options . . . none of which were sufficient in the near future, though. Nevertheless, Garibaldi wanted to stall plant operations, claiming that his actions were a catalyst to force a change.

Coolly, she reached out to shake Garibaldi's hand, in part to cover her uncomfortable reaction. "I've heard a lot about you, Doctor. You're still President of Sanergy?"

"Sane energy for the masses," he said with a brief nod. "It's not a radical group, as some try to paint us, especially after that obviously misguided man crashed his plane into your facility. He was clearly disturbed." He glanced at the Senator. "Sanergy is a watchdog organization, that's all. My chief role is to serve as spokesman for alternatives."

He looked from Victoria Doyle to Stanley van Dyckman, who stiffly exchanged glances. Garibaldi's tone was biting as he added, "Who would have thought I'd finally meet DOE's head of nuclear energy *and* the head of nuclear weapons together in the same room, along with the moneybags who funds them? And here we are, alone without any referees." He chuckled with an icy humor. "This was worth all the cloak-and-dagger routine getting me here."

Pulaski growled, "We're well aware of your antinuclear bias,

Dr. Garibaldi. But I hope we can convince you differently. Your blessing on this project will go a long way with the Congressional Oversight Committee. We're doing the right thing here for the nation, you'll see."

Garibaldi seemed intrigued. "There's a difference between wanting to do the right thing, and having a self-serving agenda, Senator."

Annoyed, Pulaski stiffened. Garibaldi was tall, over six feet, and his unruly hair stuck out in all directions. The Senator was even taller, and outweighed him by fifty or sixty pounds, but he seemed outmatched nevertheless.

Van Dyckman glided between them. "Now, Senator, Mr. Harris specifically asked for Dr. Garibaldi because of his broad knowledge and unique perspective. I suppose he'll keep us on our toes, and one can't question his credentials." He looked around the group. "I ask you all to keep an open mind. We're doing great things here in Hydra Mountain, solving a national crisis. We've needed something like this for a very long time, and it's finally operational."

"I can be objective, but not a patsy," Garibaldi said. "If you can't convince me about whatever it is you're doing here, you'll never convince the public at large."

Pulaski looked as if he had found a sour pickle inside his cheese Danish. "We aren't ready to reveal this project to the public. That's why you signed all those security forms."

Interrupting the conversation, the conference room door opened, and two men entered, one in a dark blue sport jacket and a white shirt open at the collar, the other dressed in Air Force battle fatigues with silver eagles on either lapel. Red access cards hung around their necks.

Adonia caught her breath as she recognized them both. Rob Harris was a thin, mid-sixtyish African American with smoky gray hair and a bland expression. Early in her career she had worked with him for two years at Oakridge National Laboratory in Tennessee.

But her attention was immediately drawn to the handsome, smiling colonel, with his close-cropped sandy-brown hair and green-blue eyes. Ever since their bittersweet parting, she had spoken to Shawn Whalen only on the phone, and she certainly hadn't expected to see him here. Their high-powered jobs had separated them, which made a long-distance relationship unsatisfying and impractical. Shawn had gone to Washington to work as the President's military aide and special adviser. If he was here for this meeting, then Hydra Mountain was indeed an important project.

Spotting her, Shawn broke into a broad smile, but he turned his formal attention to the group, all business. Clasping his hands behind his back, he said, "Senator, Madam Undersecretary, Mr. Assistant Secretary, Ms. Rojas, and Dr. Garibaldi—on behalf of the President of the United States, let me welcome you to Hydra Mountain. Thank you for coming on such short notice. I'm Colonel Shawn Whalen, the President's military aide. This is Rob Harris, site manager for the Mountain."

Garibaldi looked intrigued and suspicious. "I read up on Hydra Mountain before coming here. Why does a decommissioned Cold War military facility need a site manager?"

Van Dyckman interjected, "Because we've found a viable new use for this complex."

When Rob Harris spoke, his voice was monotone, even plodding. "*That's* why you're all here for this vital review. Sorry for the inconvenience, but Senator Pulaski is on a time crunch to conduct his classified oversight hearing later this week."

"The Senator should look at his calendar ahead of time and plan better," Garibaldi muttered. "A government meeting on a Sunday is a little unusual."

Harris seemed to know Garibaldi. "There's a purpose to it, Simon. I arranged for us to meet on a Sunday morning so as not to interfere with normal weekday operations. Except for one delivery this morning, we have the facility to ourselves. I've canceled today's shift, and we only have a skeleton crew in the operations center."

Harris obviously knew Victoria Doyle as well. He had worked in the nuclear industry for so long, Adonia realized, he'd probably interacted with all the currently influential people at some point in his career. "Madam Undersecretary, it's been a few years since you've been here in person, and things have changed . . . quite radically. I specifically requested your presence because I think you have a unique perspective on our operations."

"I was wondering why I was asked to participate," Doyle said. "Stanley certainly didn't request my presence."

"We're at the one-year point for operations," Senator Pulaski explained with a hint of a drawl. "These types of programs are required to be periodically reviewed to continue operations, but we can take care of this quickly, get your sign-off, and you can fly back home." He seemed to think the inspection was a perfunctory activity.

"Hydra Mountain really is an impressive operation. You'll see soon enough," van Dyckman interjected. "What we've accomplished here in a relatively short time—"

"You've been operating for twelve months without any public knowledge?" Garibaldi asked. "Sanergy keeps close tabs on nuclear ops. Don't expect me just to give you a rubber stamp. What exactly *is* going on inside this mountain?"

Shawn broke in, his voice calm and reassuring. "And we are eager to show you, as soon as we go into the next SCIF. Before we enter the Mountain, does anyone have electronics on them—cell phones, iPads, smart watches, pagers? Anything at all that transmits radio-frequency energy?" He held up a small blue zippered bag to accept any wayward devices. "Anyone? Anything? We're about to enter a very sensitive area."

Van Dyckman said, "We took care of all that before entering the admin building, Colonel."

Senator Pulaski let out an impatient sigh. "I have to stay in touch with Washington, coordinate with my staff. Senate business doesn't stop on weekends, and this isn't the only classified program I'm responsible for, you know." He looked from Shawn to Harris. "Once we're inside, you'll make phones available at regular intervals? So we can conduct our business?"

Though the Senator was too sententious for her tastes, Adonia sympathized with his concerns. "I'll need to call my Granite Bay staff before the day is out, as well. We're in the middle of major construction."

"We know you're all very busy," van Dyckman said. "We wouldn't have asked you to join us for this review if you weren't at the top of your respective fields. We'll try to make arrangements."

When no one offered up any phones or electronics, Shawn stuffed the bag in the thigh pocket of his fatigues. "Very well. Everyone follow me, please." He led the way out of the conference room to the narrow hall and the large vault door against the rock wall.

The outside wind shook the admin building's flimsy corrugated wall as the group gathered at the door. "Once we're inside the Mountain, we'll be able to get into the specifics of our operations," Shawn said.

Van Dyckman was barely able to contain his excitement. "A final reminder about those forms you signed, restricting your rights about revealing what's going on inside." He almost sounded smug. "It's a special-access area and is the most classified thing you are ever likely to see."

Garibaldi stepped toward the vault door. "This had better be good if I signed away my freedom."

Harris swiped the card hanging from his neck, keyed in a code, and pressed his palm against a screen. Once his access was approved, Adonia heard an audible click as the thick metal door swung open to reveal well-lit tunnels carved into the living rock. "Ladies and gentlemen, welcome to Hydra Mountain."

7

As Adonia followed Undersecretary Doyle through the vault door and inside the mountain facility, she glanced again at Shawn, tossing silent questions at him. He gave her a quick smile as she passed, and mouthed *Later,* but maintained a professional demeanor. He had always considered it a matter of pride never to let anyone get a hint of their relationship, though he'd certainly been warm and loving in private. She still didn't have any answers about Hydra Mountain, but she relaxed a little, reassured by Shawn's involvement.

Stepping to one side, he gestured the Senator, Garibaldi, and van Dyckman through the doorway, then brought up the rear. Once the group had entered the cool dustiness of the tunnels, he closed the pedestrian vault door behind them and twirled the combination, locking them in.

"Buried under a mountain," Adonia muttered to no one in particular.

As her eyes adjusted, she felt a growing sense of wonder, realizing the immensity of this place. The group stood at the left-hand side of an arched chamber fifty feet high and three times as deep, with an enormous tunnel feeding in from the left and right. The giant chamber carved into the granite was large enough to house a three-story building. Though its floor was level concrete, the walls were rough, raw rock, with some patches covered by metal mesh to hold back loose debris. The air smelled damp.

To the right down the wall was a massive vault door, similar to the one she had seen outside in front of the waiting eighteen-wheelers. Though she had little sense of direction after entering the Mountain, she realized that she was looking at the *other* side of the giant entry she had seen earlier.

Directly ahead of them, on the chamber's far wall, was a sealed guard portal that prevented unauthorized entry deeper into the Mountain. The tunnel leading off the main chamber stretched so far to the left and right that the passage shrank to a point in the distance. Every twenty-five feet, bright LED lights hung from a ventilation duct that ran along the ceiling. Obviously, the modern lights and bright metal air ventilation system had been recently installed. Back in the old Cold War days, she was sure garish bulbs had shone in these tunnels.

Dr. Garibaldi tilted his head back to take in the enormity of the place. "Well, well, so much for this being a decommissioned facility." His voice echoed off the rock walls.

"Recommissioned and repurposed," van Dyckman said. "Hydra Mountain is the perfect answer to our needs."

"What needs?" Garibaldi asked.

Shawn interrupted in an even voice, "Now that we're in this internal SCIF, we can brief you in greater detail."

"The suspense is killing me," Adonia said jokingly, but she was deeply curious to know how this project could be relevant to the members of this impromptu inspection team.

She knew that during the Cold War, the warren of tunnels deep inside Hydra Mountain had been filled with nuclear warheads, even though the storage facility was so close to the city of Albuquerque, just southeast of the airport. The public had no clue what was going on right under their noses. But the Mountain had been shut down for decades. What was van Dyckman using this place for now? And what did it have to do with her?

Shawn casually found a way to step close to Adonia, although he paid her no special attention as he addressed the entire group. "Ladies and gentlemen, I had exactly the same reaction the first time I visited Hydra Mountain, just after I started working at the White

House. I haven't been through all the levels here myself, but with today's review, we'll be seeing the entire facility."

"My intent is to show you the whole complex, for completeness in your review," Rob Harris said. "As required."

Undersecretary Doyle frowned, suddenly wary. "Does that include the lower level?"

"Of course, everything," van Dyckman said, brushing aside the comment. Adonia wondered how the Undersecretary knew anything about other levels. "Otherwise Dr. Garibaldi would accuse us of hiding UFOs."

"And what, exactly, will we be seeing?" Garibaldi crossed his arms over his chest. "If not Martians?"

Van Dyckman looked at each one of them, his eyes sparkling. "You have been granted access to Valiant Locksmith, an unacknowledged, waived DOE Special Access Program—a SAP—established over twelve months ago by the President himself."

Valiant Locksmith? Where do they get these names? Adonia wondered, without surprise.

Garibaldi kept looking around. "I may be out of the government now, but I still have my SCI clearances, and Sanergy monitors all DOE projects. If this is a DOE program, why haven't I heard about it?"

Senator Pulaski spoke to the older scientist as he would to a child. "Just because you have a clearance, Doctor, doesn't mean you have the right to know about every secret program in the government. Valiant Locksmith is one of the most highly classified SAPs in existence—"

Shawn interrupted smoothly, "Again, this is an unacknowledged and waived program, Dr. Garibaldi. A SAP is *unacknowledged* if its very existence is kept secret, and *waived* if it is immune to statutory reporting requirements. No one at Sanergy would have been informed." He nodded to the Senator. "As Chairman of the Senate Energy and Natural Resources Committee, Senator Pulaski is one of the few members of Congress who even knows about Valiant Locksmith. He both funds and oversees the work here, but the program undergoes a yearly review by the select Congressional

Intelligence Oversight Committee, which is coming up in a few days. That's why all of you are present today. I'm here as the President's personal representative."

Garibaldi did not look pleased. "Unless this is a matter of national defense, the public has a right to be informed and to provide input in all such programs. I was led to believe this had something to do with the nuclear energy infrastructure?"

Pulaski interrupted with an impatient sigh. "The government has conducted waived, unacknowledged SAPs for decades, Doctor. The National Reconnaissance Office running our nation's spy satellite program was a SAP for over *thirty-one years*. All that time no one knew the Air Force Assistant Secretary was really the Director of the NRO."

"Very few government programs qualify for that classification," Shawn said. "Valiant Locksmith is one of them. You'll see why very soon."

"That still doesn't explain anything," Adonia said. "Just come out and tell us why we're here, Shawn. What is Valiant Locksmith?"

He turned to van Dyckman. "I think the Assistant Secretary would like to explain."

Of course he would, Adonia thought.

Wearing a pleased smile as if he had just stepped out on a Broadway stage, van Dyckman began to lecture. "This is a rather ingenious solution to a perennial national problem, and we're very proud of—"

Before he could finish his sentence, a pulsating horn blared through the tunnels. Amber cautionary lights embedded in the rock flashed as the large vault door slowly began to rotate open, spilling sunlight into the cavernous stone-walled chamber.

Rob Harris raised his voice over the alarm as he ushered them to the opposite side of the chamber. "Good timing. This will answer some of your questions. Though it's Sunday, the Mountain is about to receive a delivery. Please stay within the painted safety lines on the floor."

As the others moved forward, Shawn maneuvered himself next to Adonia. "I told you we were going to keep crossing paths with our careers."

Frowning, she nodded to Garibaldi. "What about him? One of his Sanergy nuts nearly destroyed my site."

"I've read the classified report, and Garibaldi's telling the truth. The pilot wasn't one of theirs, just inspired by the rhetoric. Garibaldi's clearance would have been pulled if we found any hint of a connection. And for some reason the approval for his appointment to this committee came straight from the DOE Secretary's office. Somebody wanted him here, and badly. We'll need his support, and I think we'll get it."

The others stopped against the far rock wall and watched as the vault door swung all the way open. He gave her a warm smile, and she found herself missing him again. "You haven't begun to see the real surprises we've got in store for you. Just wait—I think you'll approve."

Adonia was intrigued. "I'll take your word for it." If van Dyckman had said the same things, she would have been skeptical. But Shawn wouldn't lie to her.

She looked around at the others, trying to gauge their reaction. Rob Harris was cool and businesslike, preoccupied, not that he had ever been Mr. Charisma. Garibaldi looked curious, as though trying to solve a puzzle, and Undersecretary Doyle was keenly focused, maybe a little worried. Stanley, though, was practically giddy.

When the giant metal door fully opened, Adonia heard the guttural growl of truck engines as the two flatbed eighteen-wheelers crawled inside. The sound of alarms and diesel engines filled the chamber, along with exhaust fumes. Several minutes later, after the flatbeds had completely entered the chamber, the mammoth vault door slowly swung shut behind them and seated itself into place with a reverberating bang. The truck drivers throttled off the rumbling engines, and exhaust air rushed through vents along the tunnel ceiling, pulling the diesel fumes away.

When the alarm horn stopped pulsating, a startling silence filled the tunnel. Five workers in blue facility overalls came forward to pull the tarps from the flatbeds, unveiling the cargo. Each flatbed held two large upright concrete cylinders, fifteen feet high and six feet wide, adorned with the bright yellow-and-black labels of the universal radiation symbol.

Garibaldi's eyes widened. "Those are high-level nuclear waste containers! You're transporting radioactive casks across country under a . . . tarp?"

"Nothing to worry about," van Dyckman said. "These casks weigh one hundred thirty-seven tons apiece, so nobody is going to steal them."

"Also," Shawn pointed out, "they have unmarked, armed security escorts along the entire route."

As she looked at the tunnels, the transport trucks, and the excessive security, Adonia began to put the pieces together. She muttered, "Waste casks delivered to a mothballed nuclear weapons storage depot, on a secure military base . . ."

"That's right," van Dyckman said, still grinning. "On Federal property, not public, a place with a full suite of safety and security systems already in place."

Garibaldi's expression changed. "You're storing high-level waste! Hydra Mountain was designed to secure nuclear weapons, and now you're using the facility for spent fuel rods and other radioactive waste without public oversight."

"It has to go somewhere," van Dyckman said.

Rob Harris looked relieved that he was finally able to reveal the answer. "*This* is Valiant Locksmith, and Dr. van Dyckman is my supervisor and the program's manager. His job position is an unacknowledged, waived fact."

Adonia tried to wrap her mind around the idea. Her ex-boss was a political appointee, an assistant secretary, and he was also secretly the national program manager of an unacknowledged SAP? How was that possible?

Grinning from ear to ear, van Dyckman spoke quickly. "Valiant Locksmith is a covert Special Access Program established by the President himself to solve a crucial problem facing our nation. And Hydra Mountain is the perfect place, a ready-made, turnkey facility exactly suited to the requirements of the mission. It was empty, just waiting to be used."

Adonia couldn't cover her surprise. The lack of any approved place to store the power industry's backlog of hazardous waste created an ongoing crisis that no one wanted to talk about. For years, politicians had ignored the issue, as if the problem would just go away on its own. The only permanent solution, the giant Yucca Mountain complex deep in the Nevada wasteland, had been stymied at every turn by legal challenges and politics, until even its staunchest proponents were forced to surrender. The problem of waste storage remained unsolved. For *decades*.

Now Stanley was storing deadly waste in this mothballed nuclear weapons facility? No wonder the Nuclear Regulatory Commission kept deferring to him. Even Adonia couldn't deny the appropriateness of the solution.

Victoria Doyle seemed both annoyed and confused by this revelation, and Garibaldi was clearly alarmed. He said, "You can't possibly be authorized to turn this into a permanent storage facility. We're practically within the Albuquerque city limits! Yucca Mountain took decades to build, with countless levels of oversight and review, and it was finally shut down because studies clearly showed—"

"It was shut down because of politics, not science," van Dyckman interrupted. "Even outside experts confirmed it could safely store high-level waste for over a million years."

"Plus or minus a few hundred thousand years!" Garibaldi snorted. "Have you seen the error bars?"

Shawn said, "The President is fully aware that Valiant Locksmith is only a temporary program, but he has embraced Hydra Mountain as an immediate stopgap solution to a problem that was growing more and more out of control every day. Reopening the Mountain allows us to store the nation's high-level waste in one safe and secure location until a permanent storage facility is approved, built, and opened."

"Or until Hell freezes over," Senator Pulaski muttered.

Adonia knew what he meant, doubting that a permanent nuclear waste storage facility would *ever* be opened. Despite the obvious and vital need, any public storage site would be strangled by politics before it got off the ground. Every facility ever proposed had been embroiled in decades of lawsuits, political grandstanding, and environmental protests.

But the plane crash at Granite Bay had only demonstrated how vulnerable the numerous inadequate holding areas were. This place certainly couldn't be any worse.

At Granite Bay, Adonia was forced to deal with the escalating problem every day. Such a staggering amount of nuclear waste at nearly a hundred different sites was a disaster waiting to happen, even without extremists flying small planes.

Hydra Mountain had been designed to securely store nuclear *weapons,* which were far more dangerous than spent fuel rods. Though she was inclined to make a quietly sarcastic comment, Adonia realized she was impressed that Stanley van Dyckman—of all people!—had somehow pulled the strings to make it all happen. The more she pondered the idea, the more she decided that this did make sense, at least in the interim. "You may be onto something here."

While an overhead crane swung down over the flatbeds, jump-suited workers drove two low-slung tractor-crawlers up to the containers. Wearing gloves, the workers secured the crane's hook assembly to a large concrete cask, carefully moving one giant cylinder at a time from the flatbed to the crawlers. Like ants struggling with a gigantic crumb, they prepared to haul their treasure off to a hoard somewhere in the tunnel.

Harris spoke to the group. "The President had no choice but to establish Valiant Locksmith, because Congress wouldn't act, and the environmentalists wouldn't let them. Over the years, several nuclear accidents were hushed up around the country, each one increasingly more severe." He nodded to Adonia. "Ms. Rojas knows from personal experience how we dodged a bullet and avoided a real catastrophe at Granite Bay. If just one minor detail hadn't gone right that day, we might have been looking at an incident worse than Three Mile Island or Japan's Fukushima."

Adonia shot a quick glance to van Dyckman, thinking of how he had meddled during the response, as well as his earlier botched calculations for the density of the fuel rod storage array. *A lot of other bullets,* she thought, *barely dodged.*

Stanley studiously ignored her.

Harris continued, "There were many other incidents before

Granite Bay, such as the incident at the Waste Isolation Pilot Plant in New Mexico. Fortunately, only low-level waste is stored in WIPP, but several workers were accidentally exposed to a slight amount of radiation. There was no real danger to the public, and the incident itself should have been inconsequential, but the slipup was indicative of the much larger high-level nuclear waste problem. Even because of that minor lapse, the contractor lost its $2.5 billion yearly contract to run the Los Alamos National Laboratory."

Garibaldi looked queasy. "There's no such thing as an *inconsequential* radiation incident."

Shawn stepped in. "You're right. That incident at WIPP was only the second time since the Manhattan Project that the government really shook up its nuclear infrastructure. Granite Bay pushed the President over the edge."

Senator Pulaski pulled himself up. "We take this very seriously, and that's why Hydra Mountain is so desperately needed." He lifted his chin, as though lecturing his staff. "All nuclear waste is dangerous. That's why it belongs in here instead of out there."

Adonia was surprised Pulaski would make such a broad and ill-informed comment, considering he was the one man who funded the country's nuclear infrastructure. "Actually, it's a matter of degree, Senator. WIPP stores only the lowest-level waste, such as contaminated gloves and paper, objects that may have briefly come in contact with radioactive material. It's mostly secondary material and poses no immediate danger—"

"Immediate danger is a relative term, Ms. Rojas." Garibaldi fixed his eyes on the last of the concrete cylinders as workers removed it from the second flatbed. "I'll admit that a pair of lightly contaminated gloves is a lesser concern than radioactive spent fuel rods, but what level is truly safe? Unshielded rods emit enough radiation to kill a person after only a few seconds of exposure. The WIPP incident may have been minor, but if the same mishap occurred at your Granite Bay site, we'd be having an entirely different conversation."

"At least there would *be* a conversation," van Dyckman said. "And that's the point. Nobody wants to talk about storing nuclear waste. Protest groups throw up roadblock after roadblock against any proposed solution, Congress doesn't act—it's as if everyone thinks the problem will just go away if we ignore it long enough."

The tractor-crawler drove away carrying the large concrete cask, but the members of the group were caught up in their own conversation. Garibaldi rocked back on his heels near the rough wall. "Sanergy is aware of the magnitude of the present problem, but the only permanent solution is to *stop producing more waste* in the first place. If we expand safe, clean energy alternatives, then there will be no more high-level nuclear waste."

Undersecretary Doyle was impatient with the debate. "That still doesn't explain why we're here. Why am I part of this group? Just to add another perspective before the Senator's congressional oversight meeting? Sounds like half-assed planning to me."

Garibaldi seemed troubled and curious. "And why did the President want me here as the . . . loyal opposition?" He seemed to be amused by the term. "I would think I'd be the last person he wanted to see this."

"The President didn't ask for anybody specifically," Shawn said. "We took recommendations, and Rob Harris was very persuasive. You're all here for a reason. Ms. Rojas, for example. Considering her hands-on familiarity with the problem, and as site manager of the nation's largest nuclear power plant, she was a natural choice."

Van Dyckman frowned. "Rob Harris also suggested Dr. Garibaldi, as well as Undersecretary Doyle, even though she doesn't have as much background in nuclear energy." His voice turned sour. "His approvals were rubber-stamped, and by the time I actually saw the names, it was too late to postpone."

The site manager said curtly, "I wanted a well-balanced group with fresh eyes, people who could provide an unbiased perspective—a review team outside of your part of the DOE, Dr. van Dyckman, who wouldn't have a personal stake in the program. Even though Ms. Doyle's nuclear expertise is in Weapons rather than Energy, her engineering credentials are impeccable."

Out of the corner of her eye Adonia saw Victoria Doyle give a curt nod to Harris. There was obviously something else going on between them. . . .

As the second flatbed was unloaded and the workers finished their paperwork, Harris guided them to the interior guard portal and a smaller vault door embedded in the granite wall. "Let's go inside to the storage locations."

"Then you'll see the good stuff," van Dyckman said. He gathered the group into a small semicircle next to the gate. "Keep in mind that DOE is already moving an incredible amount of high-level waste into Hydra Mountain, under the strictest security guidelines. Our intent is to rapidly reduce the amount of nuclear waste stored in inadequate holding areas at a hundred different sites across the nation. This will dramatically reduce the risk of an accident outside. Valiant Locksmith has been operational for a year since the President signed the classified Executive Order, but this is still a dangerous place—not an office building. However, Rob's team is doing a great job."

The Senator added, "And we'd like you to reach that same conclusion for your report to the Intelligence Oversight Committee."

Van Dyckman kept smiling. "By law, once a year we're required to conduct an outside and unbiased assessment of the entire program. The President is keenly interested, and as his military aide, Colonel Whalen is his eyes and ears. The rest of you constitute his blue-ribbon committee to review what we've accomplished, and, we hope, give Hydra Mountain a clean bill of health to present to the oversight committee."

"If it's warranted," Garibaldi said.

"No pressure," Adonia muttered.

"Of course it's warranted," van Dyckman said. "I've added DOE upgrades to the old military safeguards, supplementing the antiquated Cold War protective systems. With all the safety and security systems, this is the ideal place for our operations. Brand-new technology alongside tried-and-true legacy systems."

Garibaldi turned to Shawn. "Ms. Rojas manages a nuclear power plant, so I understand what she brings to the table, but what is your actual expertise in these matters, Colonel Whalen?"

Shawn smiled. "I've had hands-on experience with nuclear material as a bomber pilot—I periodically carried nukes in my B-2. Because of the short notice and importance, the President asked me to expedite the review, but this is Mr. Harris's facility, so he'll lead us through. I'm just an observer, too."

Harris said, "I'll go over everything, step by step, corridor by corridor. You'll see for yourselves, and reach your own conclusions." He stepped up to the security door and swiped his card to open the vault. "The interior storage facility is isolated from this staging area by yet another layer of security. Once inside, we'll head up to my office in the operations center, where you'll see how we keep track of Valiant Locksmith ops nationwide, as well as the status of the waste stored inside the Mountain. That'll give you some idea of how extensive the program is."

The heavy door opened. Harris turned back to them, touching his lanyard. "Make sure your badge and dosimeter are visible at all times. And please, don't touch anything." He hesitated, then gave an uncharacteristic smile. "If you hear a high-pitched warbling siren, just run like hell to this exit. It's the only way in or out of Hydra Mountain."

The cool tone in his voice made Adonia uncertain whether or not he was joking. Something told her he wasn't.

On the other side of the second vault door, the long granite tunnels looked identical to what they had just left behind. "This is a giant maze," Adonia muttered, "like in Dungeons and Dragons."

"An entirely different kind of dragon in here," Shawn said.

During her undergrad years at Texas A&M, majoring in nuclear engineering, many of her classmates had spent weekends on role-playing games, following imaginary adventures across graph-paper mazes and battling monsters with a roll of the dice. Some of her friends had harangued her to participate, not because she would have been a particularly skilled elven warrior, but because they wanted more young women in the game. Although she had joined in a few sessions, Adonia preferred to spend her scant free time swimming for recreation, getting exercise. Most of her hours, though, were consumed by her studies. Becoming a nuclear engineer wasn't easy.

As the group walked along, they heard the hum of electric carts, louder tractor-crawlers moving both ways down the wide tunnel thoroughfare. Some of the crawlers had an extended cargo flatbed to accommodate the concrete casks the big trucks had just delivered. Yellow traffic lanes were painted on the sealed concrete floor, with a pedestrian walkway on either side.

"You'll see much more activity inside the main areas, even though we have only a skeleton shift today." Harris ushered them out of the way, carefully within the painted safety lines, as he pointed out some of the larger tunnels. "A quarter mile in either direction is a main, perpendicular passage that runs deep into the Mountain. The right-hand tunnel over there leads to storage vaults on this level, while the left tunnel descends to the lower level."

Adonia frowned, unable to completely grasp the three-dimensional layout. Van Dyckman saw her expression and quickly said, "We'll show you a diagram once we get into the operations center. You'll see what he means."

Harris waited until a cart hummed past, then led them across the tunnel to a metal door marked with a wooden sign: *Hydra Mountain Ops Center*. He opened the door and paused before entering. "The crew is expecting visitors, but I'd prefer that we continue the briefing up in my Eagle's Nest office, where I can watch over the center."

He led them inside the large chamber where dozens of men and women milled around desks and computer monitors with a sense of intensity and purpose. Stadium-sized displays covered three of the walls, showing live video grabs of canvas-covered flatbeds departing from nuclear sites across the country. Another screen showed a C-17 cargo plane taking off from an airport near the Idaho Nuclear Site; a third showed a train pulling railcars covered with gray tarps.

Analysis and diagnostic screens on the workstations were set next to tunnel monitors, showing views from cameras mounted in various places throughout the Mountain. Smaller graphic windows displayed radiation levels as well as ambient gas readings from sensors scattered around Kirtland AFB. One monitor showed a scrolling list, which Adonia realized was a running status of nuclear waste shipments leaving NRC and DOE sites—shipments she had always been prevented from making at Granite Bay.

Adonia was both amazed and incredulous at the extent of the operation, unable to believe she'd been kept out of the loop. How desperately had she needed this at Granite Bay! Van Dyckman must have intentionally left her in the dark. She glanced at Senator Pulaski. "You said this is the *twelve*-month review? You've been moving shipments into Hydra Mountain for the past year already?" She swung her gaze toward van Dyckman. "And nobody bothered to inform me it was happening?"

Obviously guessing her thoughts, Stanley flashed a satisfied smile, as if expecting her to applaud him. "The speed and efficiency of this program is remarkable. In just twelve months since Valiant Locksmith went fully operational, we've moved nearly fifteen percent of the backlogged high-level waste from the holding areas designated as the most hazardous to this safe and secure facility." He looked proudly at her. "Believe me, Adonia, Granite Bay has always had one of the best-managed temporary storage areas—which is a good thing!—but that put you at the back of the line. The other, more risky sites were considered higher priority. They were in far worse shape."

"But you've still asked me to build temporary holding pools at Granite Bay." She had argued against it from the start. "If you knew this option—"

"Your new pools are only for the short term, six months at most. I knew we'd take care of the fuel rods soon enough. And even better, we're accelerating the pace of waste movement!" Brushing aside her concerns, he pointed to a flashing red entry in a Gantt project-management chart on the main wall display. She knew how to read the complex charts and immediately noted a slip in a complicated logistics schedule. Stanley seemed to think it was a gold star. "That's Granite Bay, Adonia. Your site was going to start shipping waste next week."

Looking at the screens, all the shipments of nuclear waste being secretly moved from various sites across the country, Adonia couldn't help but feel annoyed at her boss. "I'm the site manager of the largest nuclear power plant in the country. When were you planning to read me into Valiant Locksmith?"

Van Dyckman looked uneasy. "Actually, I'm not reading *any* site managers into the program; the others don't know about it either. On your side of the business, only the NRC Chairman is cognizant of what we're doing here."

"But you're shipping their high-level waste! Where do the other managers think it's going?"

He shrugged. "The cover story is that the waste is being transported under the direction of Homeland Security because of the terrorist threat. The plane crash at Granite Bay made that explanation highly plausible. That lets us keep the shipments classified from the public, just like the movement of nuclear warheads. DOE tells them their waste is being transported to another, random location for secure distribution. Once it's gone, it's not their problem. And Granite Bay's problems will be solved soon enough."

"Pending the results of this review," Harris cautioned. "The Senator has his oversight hearing on Wednesday."

Garibaldi's face darkened. "Well, pending a lot of things. The . . . *scope* of this is very disturbing. So much nuclear waste being moved around like radioactive chess pieces. I don't deny that the present storage areas are accidents waiting to happen, but so is such a large-scale movement of nuclear waste."

Van Dyckman said, "The casks are thoroughly shielded and they end up in a far more secure holding facility. It's a win-win for everybody."

"There are *always* unintended consequences," Garibaldi said. "Nothing's perfect."

As if adhering to a rigid schedule, Harris led them through the operations center and up a short flight of stairs to a glass-lined office that overlooked the busy room. Adonia thought the name "Eagle's Nest" was a good description for the upper-level office.

Harris waved them to an oval conference table in the center of the room. The Senator interrupted, "Where's a phone? I need to check in with my staff. We should take a half-hour break before going any further."

Harris's expression fell at the prospect of a delay. "We were just getting started, Senator. There's so much for us to review."

Shawn smoothly interrupted, "We just need a few more hours of your time, Senator. It's still Sunday morning, and I'm sure your staff can handle the office for the time being. We'll get you access to a secure phone when we break for lunch."

Pulaski looked disappointed, but Harris was anxious to begin his briefing. He produced a chart of the warren of tunnels and chambers inside the Mountain. "As you are aware, we have repurposed the Mountain's original nuclear weapons storage areas into vaults for high-level waste. We'll spend the rest of the morning in the storage vaults on this level. The safety and security systems may look like overkill, but bear in mind that this place was built to store nukes, not waste, so we have an entire layer of existing defenses we're exploiting, in addition to DOE's upgrades. Hydra Mountain is considered adequate until such time as a truly permanent and acceptable solution is found."

Garibaldi looked exasperated. "Best-case scenario is that will take decades! The issue isn't even under active discussion, as far as I know."

"Would you rather we waited until a genuine disaster occurs before we do anything?" van Dyckman asked, looking around the room and focusing on Undersecretary Doyle. "Right, Victoria?" She had remained quiet during the entire interchange, her arms crossed; Adonia thought she was out of her element.

Garibaldi remained calm and professorial. "Well, I would rather we devoted our efforts to emphasizing clean energy, which wouldn't generate any more hazardous waste."

The Senator was impatient. "Even if a fairy waved her magic wand and shut down every nuclear power plant today, we still have a hundred thousand tons of high-level nuclear waste piled up *right now*. Planting daisies and singing 'Kumbaya' doesn't make it disappear."

Not wanting the meeting to degenerate into a circular argument, Shawn interrupted. "Let's tour the facility so you can see what we have here. In the debriefing afterward, we can discuss the merits and any shortfalls of Hydra Mountain as an alternative storage area. Agreed? We want your opinions and expertise. That's why we brought you here."

Harris faced the group. "Undersecretary Doyle, Dr. Garibaldi, and Ms. Rojas—each one of you will have insights and a unique perspective, and I'm eager to hear your views once you've seen the complex. As Colonel Whalen said, we're pressed for time and have a lot to see." He motioned to the door. "Please leave your briefcases and purses on the table. They'll be safe in here. This way, please."

As everyone followed, Harris stopped at the door and turned to Doyle. "Madam Undersecretary, may I have a word before we go? Alone?"

Victoria opened her mouth to answer when Senator Pulaski took her arm. "You can catch up with him later, Victoria. You've really got to see what Stanley has done in here!"

Harris started to protest as the Senator ushered her out of the office before he had a chance to speak. Adonia watched as the site manager shook his head and hurried after them.

9

As van Dyckman and Garibaldi filed down the stairs from the Eagle's Nest, Adonia was the last to exit with Shawn. She had so much more to talk with him about, but she doggedly stuck to business. "I still can't believe Harris brought in Garibaldi as part of this team—you know he'll never agree to any of this, on general principles. And despite what your classified report concluded, some of those Sanergy people are still extremists." It was hard to stomach the idea that the suicidal pilot had no proven official connection.

"Garibaldi himself isn't so bad, more willing to listen than you might think," Shawn said. "Sanergy has been outspoken and skeptical, but their objections have a strong scientific basis, not just paranoia. Remember, Garibaldi does know what he's talking about. He used to work at DOE Headquarters, and before that he was with Harris at Oakridge."

"That was way before my time there."

Shawn allowed a small smile. "He'll drive van Dyckman nuts, that's for sure. He may be a devil's advocate, but he understands the industry and he's smart."

Adonia nodded. "But when he was at Oakridge, something happened that turned him against the entire nuclear complex."

"He's never said what it was," Shawn said. "The DOE Secretary wanted him on the team for objectivity; she and Garibaldi seem to have some history. Despite all his grousing, though, Garibaldi must realize we're at a tipping point with the nuclear waste piling up. If we can just get him to accept Valiant Locksmith . . ." He lowered his voice even further as they followed the group back down to the ops center floor. "At least he understands a lot more science than Senator Pulaski does. Even though the Senator controls the purse strings, he doesn't know a thing about nuclear engineering."

"Wonderful," Adonia said. "The inmates in charge of the asylum."

"Congress has a lot in common with an asylum." When he lightly took her arm and led her toward the rest of the group, Adonia appreciated his touch, and she knew it wasn't just an accidental courtesy. He left so much unsaid, and she wished they could just have an hour together to clear the air.

Another time they had been in such close quarters, she'd beaten him swimming in the Fort McNair lap pool, and then they had walked hand in hand around the Tidal Basin, enjoying the warm spring night in Washington, D.C., and ended up back at his apartment.

Even with all the opportunities she'd experienced, her relationship with Shawn had been the best part of being a DOE Fellow at the National War College. But thanks to the two of them excelling in their respective fields, their follow-on assignments had made a long-term relationship unrealistic. Adonia was posted to DOE Headquarters before leaving government work for Granite Bay in New York, while Shawn went off to command the 509th B-2 Wing in Missouri before his assignment as military aide to the President. Romance was shunted farther and farther down their list of priorities.

If she had stayed in Washington and continued working in the Forrestal Building at DOE Headquarters, their relationship might have grown instead of fading to the back burner. Who knew where they might be now? But Adonia had never lived her life by shaking a Magic 8 Ball and waiting for answers.

Outcome uncertain.

Catching up to the Senator, Rob Harris led the group out of the control room and back into the main passageway leading deeper into the Mountain. They stopped before a vault door that led into a side tunnel. In staggered intervals down either side of the smaller passageway, Adonia saw seven-foot-tall vault doors embedded in the granite wall, like prison cells.

"This side tunnel extends for a half mile and intersects another main passageway," Harris said. "In an emergency, you can get out by following this tunnel to the end and taking a left. A right turn slopes down to the lower level." He motioned to the vault doors that were built flush into the granite walls. "These storage chambers were originally designed to hold nuclear warheads."

He led them to where an older woman waited for them in front of one of the sealed vaults. The technician wore a white jumpsuit and black work boots; a plastic mask dangled from her neck. Mounted on the wall was an old-fashioned intercom box with a speaker and a black Talk button.

In his bland voice, Harris introduced her. "Mrs. Garcia is a level-three nuclear technician and will be taking us through this dry-storage chamber. It's a high-hazard area."

Garibaldi stepped back with exaggerated alarm. "We're . . . going inside one of the chambers?" His voice wavered.

"Nothing to worry about." Mrs. Garcia held up her badge. "Does everyone have a dosimeter? We'll be opening two of the chambers so you can see the safety and security features, new ones and legacy ones."

Van Dyckman said in a bright voice, "State of the art. When DOE transitioned Hydra Mountain from military jurisdiction, we enhanced the existing safety and security of the entire facility, ranging from upgrading air ventilation to adding classified security measures."

"I've worked my whole life in the nuclear industry," the technician said with a grandmotherly smile. "And this is the most sophisticated technology I've ever seen. Things certainly have changed."

Adonia looked to Shawn. "DOE health and safety regulators must have had a field day upgrading Hydra Mountain from Cold War standards to get a present-day certification."

"The old countermeasures were good enough to guard nuclear warheads, and with our new systems we can certainly protect radioactive waste," van Dyckman said.

Garibaldi broke in, "Have you tested all possible combinations of the old Department of Defense systems and your new technology? What about unforeseen interactions? Cascading nonlinear effects?"

Van Dyckman answered stiffly, "Hydra Mountain meets all DOE standards, which are far more stringent than the older military requirements. The two layers provide a high level of redundancy."

Victoria Doyle finally joined in the conversation. "The DoD and the DOE have different ways of handling nuclear material. The DoD is the end user of nuclear weapons. They don't build them; that's the DOE's job—"

Van Dyckman cut her off. "The Department of Energy designs and manufactures nuclear weapons, conducts research using nuclear reactors, and so they have to deal with the waste generated by those operations. Both departments have outstanding systems for nuclear safety and security, but they are different, and we had to account for that difference when Hydra Mountain was transferred from the military to the DOE."

"Well said." Mrs. Garcia was cheery but uninterested in the discussion, hurrying them along so she could do her part. "Let's go inside and have a look." She entered a code in the keypad next to the old-fashioned intercom outside the vault door. "This is a typical chamber where we now store dry high-level waste." As the door moved, a magenta light flashed at the ceiling and an alert buzzer sounded in the tunnel. "Step back, everyone."

As the thick metal vault slowly rotated open, Mrs. Garcia pointed at the line of similar oval doors staggered at intervals down the long tunnel. "Back in the day, when the military stored warheads here, each vault was staggered to make sure that stray radiation from one device couldn't interact with others. Fail-safe systems ensured that when one chamber door was open, all the other doors had to be sealed. That kept any radiation from getting inside—"

"But Hydra Mountain's mission has changed," van Dyckman interrupted. "So we modified these systems to hold high-level waste, which can't go critical like a nuclear weapon."

Harris added in his bland voice, "Because of the schedule imposed, we needed to open more than one chamber at a time just to accommodate the volume of material we're bringing inside. Otherwise, we could never keep up, and shipments would pile up in the main corridor staging area, causing an even greater hazard."

"We wouldn't want to slow things down, now would we?" Garibaldi said in a biting tone.

Adonia frowned at the site manager, surprised that "Regulation Rob" would bend the rules. "You modified the systems so you could open multiple chambers at the same time, in order to move in more shipments as they arrived."

"You know the sheer amount of backlog in our nuclear facilities," van Dyckman said. "The faster we ease the pressure on power plants like Granite Bay, the safer the nation will be. And we have all these empty vaults just waiting to be filled."

"We keep receiving shipments," Harris said. "It seemed the best way, and calculations showed a significant safety margin in these specific vaults."

Harris had a fine reputation at DOE, and he had even mentored her when she'd been a young intern at Oakridge National Laboratory, working on her first reactor. But now his hair was thinning and much grayer than she remembered; his face was lined with stress. He seemed to be going through the motions, following the rules without any passion for the work. She hadn't realized at first, but now she saw that he looked *old*. And worried.

Mrs. Garcia waited patiently as the vault door ground all the way open. "Wait here while I do my safety check. Don't go inside yet."

Adonia and her companions crowded up to a bright yellow line painted on the floor just outside the entrance. Inside the large chamber, alcoves had been carved into the inner granite walls, each twenty feet high, ten feet across, ten feet deep. A yellow rope hung across each cubbyhole. Like a sarcophagus, a metal cylinder marked with the universal yellow radiation symbol stood upright inside each alcove.

"Those are dry-storage containers," Adonia said. "Granite Bay is overflowing with them."

"Those alcoves were originally designed to hold nuclear warheads, each separated by two feet of granite. That's more than sufficient to absorb any line-of-sight radiation emitted by plutonium cores," Harris said. "Or in this case, more than enough to shield high-level nuclear waste."

Garibaldi seemed reluctant to move near the chamber. "What's the ambient radiation in there now?"

"Negligible," van Dyckman said reassuringly. "The containers themselves have sufficient shielding. It's overkill, believe me."

"It's naïve to say that any radiation is negligible," Garibaldi growled, looking at Harris as if they shared some kind of secret. "Right, Rob?"

The site manager balked, but refused to answer. Adonia got the impression this was an old argument—from all the way back at Oakridge?

Senator Pulaski peered inside. "Look at all that shielding rock. Opening two vault doors at the same time couldn't possibly be a safety hazard. Or am I missing something?"

"It used to be," Mrs. Garcia said, "when nuclear weapons were stored here. But now that they're gone, there's no kill zone surrounding the Mountain."

"That's overstating it," van Dyckman sighed. "She means a possible contamination area."

"No, she means a kill zone," Garibaldi said. "It's the area around a nuclear explosion where there's total destruction of human life. Hiroshima's kill zone had an average diameter of one point six miles, and that blast was 'only' fifteen kilotons. If the conditions are right, a megaton's kill zone can reach sixty-three miles across—an area of over three thousand square miles. That's why these doors were never opened at the same time."

"Let me show you the principle, Senator," Mrs. Garcia said, sounding like a schoolteacher. "Watch me."

She stepped back into the corridor and walked fifty feet to the next sealed storage chamber. "Suppose this vault door were open. Now pretend I'm radiation emitted from a nuclear warhead stored inside." She crossed the tunnel and stopped at the granite wall on the opposite side, slapping it with her hand. "Most of the radiation is absorbed, but some of it—me, in this case—will reflect off the wall and bounce down the corridor." She walked back toward the group in a zigzag pattern, "bouncing" from one side to the other.

"Now imagine billions upon billions of particles either being absorbed or reflected, following a similar path." When she reached the group of observers and the open vault door, her trajectory now headed straight toward the open chamber. "Eventually, some of the radiation could find its way in among the warheads, where it would bounce around and interact with the cores—"

"And possibly initiate a catastrophic chain reaction," Garibaldi said. "A nuclear detonation that would ruin everyone's day." He looked around. "It's a small probability, but with enormous consequences."

"Worse than that." Doyle spoke up, surprising them after her long silence. "In a warhead storage area, since the weapons are so close together, it wouldn't be just one detonation. The radiation from each device might initiate another cascading explosion . . . and another . . . and another. It's called sympathetic detonation—the absolute worst-case scenario." She glanced at Harris.

"You're right," Garibaldi said. "Multiple megaton explosions even deep inside Hydra Mountain would result in a kill zone hundreds, if not thousands of miles in diameter, perhaps extending to the East Coast."

Van Dyckman lifted his chin. "But of course that can't possibly happen now, since we're only storing waste here, not warheads." Undersecretary Doyle seemed to be raining on his parade. Adonia recalled their alleged affair; the two probably considered each other competition now. "Nukes haven't been stored in Hydra Mountain for decades. This is the safest SAP the government has ever run, and I *will* keep it that way."

Doyle seemed to roll her eyes. "This is a huge place, Stanley—"

The technician held up a hand, then glanced at her watch. "I came in on a Sunday for this. Before we enter, I need to disengage the internal sensors." She turned to controls at the side of the vault and looked up at a camera installed in the metal ducts along the ceiling. After making a cryptic motion to some unseen observer, she turned to another inset panel and ran her fingers over an LED display.

"As you saw, I had to give the authentication code before I could switch off the motion detectors. Otherwise, alarms would go off and initiate all sorts of old, nasty countermeasures specifically designed for the military—sticky foam, knockout gas, that sort of thing. During the Cold War days, they weren't messing around." She entered the Disable code and motioned for everyone to follow her inside the large storage chamber. "Don't touch anything, or you might trigger one of the other sensors. Nobody wants that."

As the visitors crowded into the vault, Garibaldi hung back outside the chamber. Mrs. Garcia urged him to join them. "Come on in. There's plenty of room." She stepped back and motioned with her arm.

Garibaldi drew in a breath. "No . . . thank you. I can hear you fine."

"But you can't see," van Dyckman said, annoyed. "How are you going to give an unbiased assessment if you can't even see what she's showing us?"

"I'm fine staying here."

"Not an option." With a huff, van Dyckman grasped Garibaldi by the elbow, steered him into the vault, and brought him to the front of the group. "Here." He turned to Mrs. Garcia. "Go ahead, please."

The technician nodded curtly, then started explaining the packing, transportation, and storage procedures for the dry containers. From her experience at Granite Bay, Adonia could have given the tutorial herself.

Garibaldi barely paid attention; he fidgeted and appeared to be trying to find something that didn't make sense, or uncover a bad procedure. He was clearly uncomfortable in the chamber.

In contrast, Senator Pulaski showed little understanding of the technical details, although he tried to look intent and even nodded once in a while. He glanced around the chamber. "I don't see any fuel rods. Where are they?"

When Harris and van Dyckman hesitated, Adonia explained,

"After they've been removed from a reactor, spent fuel rods are submerged in pools for up to five years so the water can absorb the radiation they emit. Once they've cooled sufficiently, the rods can be broken down and sealed inside these dry containers, which are much safer to handle and store."

Mrs. Garcia motioned them closer. "Here, take a look."

As the visitors crowded closer to the alcoves, a young man in tan pants, short-sleeved blue shirt, and yellow tie hurried down the corridor and stuck his head into the chamber. Adonia remembered seeing him at one of the stations in the operations center, but now he looked alarmed. "Mr. Harris, you're needed in ops." He swallowed visibly, but tried to hide it. "It'll take only a few minutes of your time."

Harris did not like to have the routine interrupted. "What is it, Mr. Drexler? Can it wait?"

"No, sir. It's . . . important. The Operations Officer requires your presence."

Harris kept his expression carefully neutral as he turned to the group. "I apologize. Hopefully, I'll be back before we go to the next vault. Ms. Rojas, since you're the only site manager present, will you accept temporary transfer of safety responsibility for this committee in my absence? I don't have a handover-of-liability form for you to sign, but we can do this verbally if you agree."

Regulation Rob. She had not forgotten that Harris was such a by-the-book person. "Of course."

"Thank you, I relinquish my responsibility." Without waiting for their reply, he hurried after Drexler down the tunnel, leaving the committee to wonder about the emergency.

10

After Harris rushed off, Mrs. Garcia continued explaining the systems in the vault, but as she droned on, her words went right through Garibaldi's head, unprocessed, though no one could tell he wasn't fully engaged.

He'd perfected the look years ago, as a simple psychological defense after being locked in that . . . *place* in Oakridge, a look he used when he needed to retreat. It didn't matter what topic was being discussed, or who else was in the room. If the dark memory clawed back, he knew how to put his mind in neutral, adopt a knowing expression, and nod once in a while.

And then he'd wall away that horrible past and find himself in a much better place. His thoughts often returned to the highlight of his time after he'd been enlightened about the hidden dangers of the entire nuclear industry. And, yes, he had achieved some enormous successes.

Shutting down Yucca Mountain was like stopping a giant oil tanker, a huge and bloated project moving under the momentum of decades of time and billions of dollars. But Simon Garibaldi had done it, he and his powerful lobbying and public awareness group. Sanergy had taken advantage of a groundswell of public opinion, people who didn't like the idea of filling Yucca Mountain with countless tons of radioactive waste, spent fuel rods from nuclear power plants, and who knew what other kind of nuclear poison.

If the nation had thought ahead rather than ignoring the problem, the waste never would have been generated in the first place. The very idea of relying on nuclear power forever was a dangerous dead end. Had no one paid attention to Chernobyl? Or Three Mile Island? Or Fukushima? It was like a five-year-old still sucking his thumb because no one made him grow up. . . .

Glory days. He and fifty Sanergy volunteers had gathered at the southern tip of Nevada just outside the well-patrolled boundary of Nellis Air Force Base. The gates were heavily guarded by MPs. The protesters would have been arrested if they forced their way inside, and Garibaldi's followers would have done that if he'd demanded it, but such a sacrifice would have served no purpose. They could make their point outside, where the TV crews could watch them wave their signs decrying nuclear power, demanding that this storage facility never be opened.

Inside the sprawling military base, distant Yucca Mountain was visible on the wrinkled landscape, a long line of rock that towered above the surrounding desert. So pristine.

Garibaldi had given many impassioned speeches and written numerous op-ed pieces in major publications. He was a perfect spokesman, not a wild-eyed radical but a former DOE employee, well educated and well spoken. He had played for the other team for so many years, he knew how to play the game . . . but after his own personal ordeal in that vault in Oakridge, he had seen the error of his ways. Now, Dr. Simon Garibaldi gave voice to the concerns of a large part of the population.

Out under the baking Nevada sun, he stood in a light tan dress shirt, khaki pants, and comfortable shoes. His fifty protesters wore all sorts of clothes, T-shirts and cutoffs, even two in Grim Reaper costumes. Their signs were imaginative, their angry chants loud even in the great emptiness.

The news cameras had captured it all, particularly the Las Vegas TV stations. "This doesn't just affect Nevada. It affects the entire nation," Garibaldi shouted as he stood on the gravel in front of the fenced entry gate to the base, and his people cheered.

From behind the base gates, the MPs stood wary and ready to act.

The base had tripled security, aware of the protest. Several jeeps as well as armored vehicles had pulled up near the fence and the entry portal in a threatening posture. Now, the MPs stood with their rifles shouldered but obvious, making sure Garibaldi's volunteers didn't try to charge the base. The intimidation didn't work.

"The state of Nevada has no nuclear power plants of its own. Why should you be forced to store someone else's dangerous waste?" Garibaldi continued. "Is your state just a dumping ground?"

"It's not fair!" shouted someone. "Nevada was screwed."

"We're all being screwed if we keep nuclear power," Garibaldi said. "It's an addiction, and it's time we go cold turkey. We will suffer from withdrawal, but in the end we'll be strong and we'll be healed."

Some of the volunteer protesters were members of the Western Shoshone tribe in full traditional costume. The Shoshone tribe had objected strenuously to Yucca Mountain being turned into a waste storage facility, claiming that the site was on sacred lands that held great cultural importance.

The Walker River Paiute tribe had also added their voices to the dispute, because their reservation lands were directly on the transport route for any nuclear waste to be delivered to Yucca Mountain. By a large margin, the people of Nevada were opposed to the facility, although the seven counties immediately surrounding the designated land were in favor of it. They just weren't seeing the big picture.

Because his scheduled protest had drawn so much publicity, he wasn't surprised that a group of counterprotesters came to cause trouble. Local ranchers and miners, construction workers and government employees. Like an opposing team, they stood in a group, angry and shouting, waving handmade signs in sharp contrast with the professionally designed placards Sanergy had produced. *Yucca Mountain now!* said one of the signs. *Save Our Jobs and Store It Here!*

"It's perfectly safe," yelled one gruff, broad-shouldered man in a plaid shirt. "I've read the reports."

"Reports can be doctored," Garibaldi said. "No one can be certain there won't be a quake or a fracture or a leak. They can't guarantee the waste won't be disturbed for a hundred thousand years."

The man shouted back, "That's bullshit. Scientists can't predict anything for a tenth that long." The two groups remained separated, but the TV cameras approached, closing the gap.

One of the other locals stood beside the first man. "Opening that facility will create hundreds of jobs. If it isn't here, they'll put the stuff somewhere else, in Texas or New Mexico."

"If the government tries that, we'll protest it there, too," Garibaldi said. "It's a fundamental problem, and we have to stop it."

A young woman on the opposing side sounded shrill and frustrated. "But it exists. The nuclear waste *exists*. You can't ignore it. We have to do something about it."

"And the nuclear power plants will keep producing more and more," Garibaldi said. "If we find a simple and easy solution to store the waste, then what's their incentive to shut down the plants? We need to get off this addiction! The only way for us to wean ourselves from nuclear power is to force the development of alternative energy."

"What are we going to do in the meantime?"

"We may have some tough years, I won't lie." Garibaldi was prepared for that. He'd used the same argument when he advocated for dramatically increasing gasoline prices, even though it would hurt consumers in the short run, because then people would demand greater fuel efficiency and get themselves off dependence on gas and oil. People would not voluntarily change when they thought the system was working. They were like a frog sitting complacently in the pot of water as the temperature increased one degree at a time until the water boiled. . . .

Someone threw a rock. Garibaldi didn't see where it had come from, but it struck the sign held by a protester next to him. Suddenly, a howl of outrage erupted from his own followers, mirrored by a chorus of mocking jeers from the locals.

"You aren't even from around here!" said the man in the plaid shirt.

Garibaldi knew that many of his volunteers did come from Las Vegas, but the difference between the city of Las Vegas and rural Nevada couldn't be more dramatic.

The MPs at the gate edged forward, sensing violence—as did the TV cameras.

"This is America," said one of the local supporters waving a *Store It Now* sign.

Garibaldi seized on that. "Yes, this is America, and Americans can achieve great things. America created the Manhattan Project. America created the Apollo program. We can solve this, not sweep it under the rug. But we all have to work together."

"Yucca Mountain does solve the problem, you idiot—but you hate nuclear power so much you just can't see it!"

One of his own volunteers picked up a rock and hurled it at the man, and that was just the start. Like a chain reaction gone critical, the two sides began shouting, hurling rocks, and then they rushed together in a brawl. The Air Force MPs hesitated just a few seconds, then they emerged from the gate, charging into the fray to break up the violence, but not before both sides of the debate suffered cracked skulls, multiple bruises, and lacerations.

The TV news had covered it all, and Garibaldi became even more of a celebrity. Thanks to the publicity from the Yucca Mountain incident, he had booked dozens more talk-show appearances, and he had also learned how to make his point. He would be calm and reasonable as he presented his case, not just fearmongering but genuinely looking at the big picture. Simon Garibaldi could be very convincing.

Even with his successful actions, he couldn't take full credit for shutting down the Yucca Mountain project, but the protests continued. The grassroots opposition persisted, and the next administration had made sure that Yucca Mountain would never open. . . .

Now, Garibaldi blinked, bringing himself back to the present, and Mrs. Garcia and the dry waste storage chamber swam into focus. He drew in a breath, remembering where he was. Yes, it had been like stopping a giant oil tanker, but he, along with countless other like-minded people, had succeeded. So he knew it could be done.

But now Hydra Mountain! An astonishing solution accomplished by fiat. No, he couldn't support this. Not at all.

11

Rob Harris tried to maintain a calm, professional demeanor as he followed his exec from the storage vaults, but the urgency was plain on Drexler's face. The young man was not one to cry wolf, and he would never have interrupted the high-level tour unless something truly unexpected had happened. Moving at a brisk pace, Harris imagined dozens of dire scenarios on the site, but both men remained silent as they hurried to the ops center.

As site manager, Harris was used to dealing with unexpected circumstances, but the timing was unfortunate with so much at stake here today. His entire plan relied on the review team members being able to see the looming problem with their own eyes, and draw the right conclusion. He knew they would put the pieces together.

Harris wished he'd had time to speak with Undersecretary Doyle alone, now that she'd finally been read into Valiant Locksmith. Because of her own Special Access Program, Doyle was the only person on the team besides Senator Pulaski with the proper access to understand the real dangers of having so much high-level waste inside Hydra Mountain—especially down in the lower cavern.

The Undersecretary needed to see for herself what van Dyckman had done, but until just a few minutes ago she hadn't even known that his covert program existed. Once Doyle got to the lower level, though, she would fully understand.

Then all hell would break loose.

Thanks to draconian SAP security constraints, Harris was restricted from telling anyone else not cognizant of both programs about the problem. Period. Each person had to see their own part, and Harris had to hope they would put the clues together. It was like the parable of blind men trying to describe an elephant, each touching only one part of the animal and not grasping the whole thing. If they could only use their eyes!

No one but himself knew about *all* the Special Access Programs in Hydra Mountain; Doyle's and van Dyckman's were only two of several. Due to the very nature of a SAP, rigid classification firewalls prevented each program manager from knowing anything but their own work. With their various SAPs, the agencies using the Mountain—Department of Energy, Department of Defense, Department of State—were like foreign countries with walled borders. As site manager, Rob Harris had a legal right to see the whole picture, but he was the only one.

And that was the problem.

Even though he knew the very real hazards of continuing present operations, Federal law forbade him from pointing anything out to the people who needed to know. Harris would go to jail for the rest of his life if he told the left hand what the right hand was doing. He knew the regulations well.

Going by the book, Rob had reported to the DOE's Inspector General that he had a classified concern, but even the IG didn't have access to Victoria Doyle's unacknowledged State Department SAP, and thus the IG couldn't grasp the reason for Rob's urgency. And when he had brought it up through the State Department's Inspector General, they likewise didn't have access to the DOE Valiant Locksmith SAP . . . and so the State Department had the same lackluster reaction. Neither was *allowed* to see the problem, prohibited by Federal law.

But when Senator Pulaski suddenly needed a perfunctory, rubber-stamp review committee, and Stanley van Dyckman had simply asked for a list of names, Harris seized the opportunity. He couldn't break the law, but he could move the chess pieces.

Victoria Doyle had the access now. She had the knowledge, she had the eyes, and most importantly she had the smarts to see the big picture. If he couldn't get her alone to discuss the urgent matter, then she could see for herself what he had been forbidden from explicitly telling her.

She would understand the danger. She had to! And if Dr. Garibaldi also pieced together what was going on, then Adonia Rojas could back him up; Rob knew her to be a clear thinker, not motivated by politics.

Then Harris could finally sleep easy again at night.

But right now he had some other emergency that threatened Hydra Mountain. Drexler was clearly sweating, his face drawn.

As soon as they passed out of earshot down the main corridor, the younger man started briefing Harris in a quiet but urgent voice. "Sir, there's been an incident inside the facility perimeter. We've contacted HQ, and they're setting up an immediate call with the Secretary of Energy. The threat level is still being assessed, since both safety and security sensors have been triggered."

"Security *and* safety detectors?"

"Yes, sir. That's why we pulled you out. Protective Services are rushing to the crash site right now."

Harris stopped. "Crash? What type of vehicle? How bad?"

"It's . . . it's a Class A."

Harris's heart skipped a beat. "A *plane* crash?" His mind immediately raced to the suicide bomber who had tried to take out Granite Bay nearly eighteen months before. *Oh crap, not again.* Was this an attempt to do the same to Valiant Locksmith's high-level waste by yet another misguided Sanergy protester? Had Garibaldi set it up? Impossible! He couldn't have known beforehand. And with the heavy security cloaking Hydra Mountain, how would Sanergy even know the program existed . . . unless there'd been a leak? What if someone had discovered why Dr. Garibaldi and the SAP review team were really here?

Doubling his pace, he rushed toward the ops center. "How big of a crash? Was the Mountain breached, and was anyone hurt?" He pictured a fireball from a fully loaded plane diving into the rugged mountainside. What would they hope to accomplish?

"It appears to be minor, sir, and no one was injured. On first glance, it seems to be a genuine mishap, a piloting accident. There are a lot of thermals in the area because of the unusually hot weather, and the winds are high today. A small six-passenger plane strayed into Hydra Mountain airspace after taking off from Albuquerque International. The pilot radioed that he was having engine trouble. The aircraft lost altitude and made a hard landing just inside the perimeter fence on the slope."

After Granite Bay, Harris wasn't convinced anything was an innocent crash. And it was too much of a coincidence, especially on the day of the VIP tour, and especially with Simon Garibaldi's presence. "That sounds exactly like one of our preparedness scenarios. I don't care what it looks like, we can't let our guard down."

Drexler struggled to keep pace, breathing hard. "Unclear at this moment, sir, but it doesn't appear to be a terrorist strike. The plane knocked down a few power lines as it came in for a landing, and some scrub brush caught on fire. The pilot may have been trying to reach the perimeter road, not the interior, but with all the wind . . ." He shrugged.

"It *might* have been a textbook precautionary landing. Maybe." Harris relaxed a little, but wasn't that exactly what a secret strike might look like? Hydra Mountain had originally been designed to withstand the impact of a fully fueled 707, the largest jet of the day, so a small plane shouldn't cause too much damage, even if it was filled with fuel or explosives. Since Kirtland AFB shared the runway with the civilian airport, the military would help DOE with the investigation. But still, could it really be that innocent? "No facility breach?"

Drexler shook his head. "No, sir. That's why the operations center commander didn't initiate an immediate facility lockdown, but we sent for you instead. Security personnel have joined the emergency response team, and we're awaiting confirmation that it was just an accident and not an attack. Kirtland's military police and fire crews are on their way to provide backup."

They reached the main floor of the operations center, and he headed for the Eagle's Nest, ready for the call from HQ. At the door, he paused and turned to the young exec. He spoke in a firm voice, deciding to be cautious rather than naïve. "It may be nothing, Ken, but the timing is just too suspicious. Our operations are quiet on a Sunday, and we have a group of VIPs inside the Mountain. We follow the rules here, and DOE procedures dictate that *any* violation of restricted Hydra airspace must be considered a threat until proven otherwise. Besides, we don't know what type of cargo that small plane was carrying." Everyone knew what had happened at Granite Bay, and this reminded him too much of that second plane hitting the World Trade Center, which had immediately proved the first impact wasn't an accident. . . .

He made his decision and nodded to himself, knowing he was right. "Have the ops commander order an immediate security lockdown as a precaution. Better to be safe. I'll take the call from the Secretary of Energy and assess the situation from my office."

Drexler looked back toward the dry-storage tunnels outside the ops center. "What about the review committee, sir? Once you initiate a lockdown, the alarms will go off and those people will be rattled."

Harris knew they wouldn't like it at all, especially not Senator Pulaski, and van Dyckman would be furious. But Harris would not cut corners. "They'll be safe enough if they just sit tight. It's happened before. I'll lift the lockdown as soon as I'm certain what happened outside. I left Ms. Rojas in charge, and I know she's perfectly competent." He jogged up the stairs to his office. "That's my decision. Execute a security lockdown, Mr. Drexler. Now."

12

Without warning, an ear-splitting siren wailed through the tunnels and echoed in the granite-walled chamber. Adonia spun to van Dyckman. "That's a safety alarm, Stanley. We need to leave."

He looked more confused than worried. "I'm sure it's a drill," he said, trying to sound reassuring. "Probably for our own protection."

"You don't know for sure, Mr. National Program Manager?" Garibaldi said with clear sarcasm.

Victoria Doyle added a biting comment: "Stanley's often more enamored with the job *title* than with the job *knowledge*."

Van Dyckman stiffened. "We've had dozens of drills and test exercises here in the Mountain, not to mention false alarms. Makes it hard to get work done, let me tell you." His chuckle was strained. "Just wait here for the drill to be over."

Amidst the alarms, Adonia saw the heavy storage chamber door was automatically closing, which would shut them inside the chamber. She called, "Everybody out, unless you want to be sealed inside!" Leading the way, she herded the nearest person—Victoria Doyle—through the opening with her. Van Dyckman was right on their heels.

Instead of bolting out into the corridor, though, Mrs. Garcia ran to an embedded console on the far interior wall, where she furiously keyed codes into the LED display. "All of you, get out to the corridor! This isn't supposed to be happening. These vault doors should remain open to let people escape. I have to disable these sensors."

Even as Adonia and Doyle rushed out, Senator Pulaski hesitated, like a deer caught in the headlights, blocking the chamber opening. Shawn shouldered him hard. "Senator—out, now!" He knocked the man unceremoniously out into the tunnel, charging out after him.

With a constant hum, the heavy door continued to close, leaving Garibaldi and the technician inside. Mrs. Garcia called to him. "Stay here. We'll just wait it out."

Though the gap seemed too narrow, the tall scientist raced through it, desperate. He twisted, squirmed, and Adonia was sure he would be crushed. But with a gasp he squeezed through the vanishing inches just in time. The vault door snagged the back of his tweed jacket and crunched shut against the stone wall.

Caught in his jacket, Garibaldi struggled. He tugged so hard he ripped the fabric. Shawn helped him shrug out of the coat as Adonia hurried to assist them. "You could have been killed!"

Garibaldi was gray and sweating, clearly shocked. "I wasn't going to be locked inside." He swallowed hard.

"It's just a drill," van Dyckman said, sounding more embarrassed than terrified. "Harris will reset it soon enough. You were overreacting."

Out in the tunnel, Senator Pulaski sat on the concrete floor, indignant, nursing his elbow. Undersecretary Doyle stood looking incredulous.

Garibaldi brushed his shirt, looking back at the torn jacket caught in the heavy door. "And that technician is trapped in there! We've got to get her out."

Van Dyckman dismissed the problem. "Believe me, the radiation levels are so low in there it's no worse than getting a dental X-ray. Mrs. Garcia will be fine."

"But what happened?" Adonia asked, then narrowed her eyes. "What triggered it?"

"Harris went to investigate something, so he probably did what the manual told him to do," van Dyckman said. "He's too cautious. Whatever happened, I'm sure the systems functioned exactly as designed."

Adonia looked back at the sealed vault doorway, realizing how much it reminded her of a crypt. "But Mrs. Garcia said it shouldn't have closed. And she's right—that was a safety alarm, and chamber doors are supposed to remain open, so people can escape, not be trapped inside. Something's wrong, Stanley."

Shawn said, "She's in no immediate danger. The chamber has power and plenty of air, and she knows that. Mrs. Garcia will just have to cool her heels." He glanced down at Adonia's feet. "Speaking of which, you lost one of your pumps."

Adonia looked down, realizing that in her scramble, she must have knocked off one of her shoes and left it inside the chamber. Since she couldn't walk in only one shoe, she removed the other one, dropped it on the tunnel floor. "They weren't very practical inside a mountain anyway. I knew I overdressed for this meeting."

The sirens continued to wail, reverberating off the granite walls.

Queasy, Garibaldi stepped close to the sealed chamber door, tugged uselessly at his dangling jacket, and then placed his palms against the metal. "That woman is in danger . . . sealed in the storage chamber."

Van Dyckman spoke over the alarms. "Like all the staff here in Hydra Mountain, Mrs. Garcia believed in Valiant Locksmith, so she did her job, stayed behind to disable the chamber's sensors. I think she's a hero." He nodded, reaffirming what he had said. "Yes, a hero. She'll be fine."

A flare of anger ignited in Garibaldi's gray eyes. "If the radiation levels are so low, you sure seemed in a hurry to get out of there, Dr. van Dyckman. Have you ever been locked inside a nuclear vault?"

"Stanley normally stays locked behind a desk in his Washington office," Doyle said, drawing her mouth thin. Van Dyckman shot her a glare.

Senator Pulaski sat against the wall with his knees pulled up, more upset than frightened, despite the ratcheting alarms. "Why would Harris pick today to stage a drill? That's an idiotic thing to do. We were supposed to have a straightforward, thorough review to show that everything works perfectly."

Why indeed? Adonia thought. Unless a genuine crisis had initiated the alarm.

Shawn tried to help the Senator to his feet, but the man brushed him aside. "Can someone stop this infernal noise? Van Dyckman?"

Garibaldi was agitated. "Does it indicate a radiation leak? Some kind of spill?"

Van Dyckman shook his head, yelled so he could be heard above the noise. "No, it'll cycle off shortly. Whatever it is, I'm sure we aren't in any danger. Someone probably just opened a door without getting the proper approval."

Garibaldi pounced. "So there's been a *security* breach? Terrorists taking over Hydra Mountain?"

Adonia knew that was unlikely, but she still had a sick feeling as she remembered the suicidal plane streaking down toward the wet-storage pools at Granite Bay. "Stanley misspoke. That safety alarm is identical to what we use at my site. It's standardized across the nuclear industry."

Suddenly, the siren stopped, leaving their ears to ring in the silence. "Thank God," the Senator muttered. Adonia could hear only the low thrum of air exchangers in the metal ventilation duct overhead.

Shawn looked toward the main corridor where they had entered from the operations center. The massive entry door had also sealed off this side tunnel from the main corridor. He frowned. "How are we supposed to get out?"

Though she felt a growing chill, Adonia kept her voice calm. "Like it should be open. Safety systems are designed to allow people *out* of areas, not keep them inside."

Shawn considered. "You're right. If anything, that main tunnel door should let us exit the secure facility, and allow the guards access."

Adonia drew in a breath. *Maybe we are all trapped just like Mrs. Garcia, but in a much bigger cage.* She remembered that she was technically in charge, even if she didn't know what Rob Harris had in mind for them. "Just stay calm. Mr. Harris is in the operations center, trying to figure out the problem. We need to stay here, wait until this exercise ends."

"And then what?" Pulaski demanded, climbing to his feet and looking up and down at the sealed chamber doors. "We all get infected by radiation? I can feel it in the air right now."

Doyle and van Dyckman both rolled their eyes. Garibaldi looked surprised by the comment. "You don't get *infected* by radiation, Senator. You should at least have a basic understanding of the science if you're in charge of funding all these programs."

Pulaski angrily cut off the lecture. "I don't care what word you use. It doesn't seem safe, trapped in here and surrounded by so much nuclear material. We were supposed to move quickly through the facility."

"Mountain personnel spend entire work shifts here, day after day," Shawn said. "We're well shielded from any radiation. You'll be fine."

Garibaldi still looked shaken. "How rigorous was your review of this old facility before you recommissioned it last year? If you think a small amount of ambient radiation in a sealed tunnel is dangerous now, just wait until all these vaults are full. Are you certain you understand every aspect of the situation?"

Pulaski lifted his chin. "Dr. van Dyckman performed the review, and I accepted his recommendation."

Garibaldi was exasperated. "And that poor woman is trapped in the chamber. None of you can even imagine what she's enduring in there."

Adonia looked at the controls of the vault that trapped Mrs. Garcia, but they had reset themselves and steadily blinked with spurious characters. Instead of doing nothing, she punched in a few options and tried to activate them. Nothing happened.

Van Dyckman spoke as if he knew what was going on. "Is there any way we can communicate with Harris in the meantime? At least he can tell us what's going on."

Walking on bare feet, Adonia headed down the tunnel to the sealed main door. "Maybe there's some other way to open that vault door in an emergency. Shouldn't there be a crash bar? A fallback egress?"

Van Dyckman followed her. "The analog systems were present on the old vaults, not on my upgrades. I made sure Hydra Mountain was up to modern specs before we received our first shipment for storage."

"Just get me the hell out of here." Pulaski brushed off his knee, which had suffered a bruise when he'd fallen.

Standing at the sealed exit door that closed off the entire tunnel, Adonia scanned the controls, a mishmash of old 1950s-style switches and a modern LED panel. She saw neither a safety bar nor any other mechanical means of opening the thick metal door, not even an old-fashioned combination dial. Nor a phone.

Adonia recognized a leftover relic that wasn't one of the new digital upgrades. "Look, an intercom—Cold War vintage. I wonder if it still works." When she pushed the Talk button, feedback screeched out of the speaker. After releasing the button, she twisted a black ribbed knob, which she guessed was a volume control. She leaned close and pushed the button again. "Hello?"

"Operations center. State your identity." The voice sounded scratchy. The intercom probably still had its original speakers.

Adonia was losing patience. *Who do you think it is? We're the only ones inside a top-secret facility on a Sunday morning.* Then she remembered how much of a stickler Harris was. By the book, all the way. She drew in a breath, calming herself. "Adonia Rojas, with the review committee. Is Mr. Harris there? We're trapped in one of the tunnels, and our escort, Mrs. Garcia, is locked in a dry-storage vault. Can you open this door?"

"The lockdown will be lifted shortly, ma'am. We've had a Class A incident, and Mr. Harris is managing the situation."

Adonia frowned. *A plane crash?* The sick feeling returned to her stomach. "Can I talk with him? He put me in charge of these people."

The scratchy voice sounded terse. "You are safe. Please remain where you are while I get Mr. Harris. Stand by one." The speaker clicked and fell silent.

As the others gathered round, Adonia tried to offer some encouragement. "They're working on the problem. At least they know where we are, thanks to the intercom. I imagine it won't be too much longer."

"I hope not," Senator Pulaski said. "This Valiant Locksmith review is one thing, but I have other classified programs being discussed at this week's oversight hearing." He turned to van Dyckman. "Is there any way I can contact my staff, Stanley? With all that upgrade funding I approved, you must have included some modern means of communication down here."

Van Dyckman opened his mouth to speak just as the intercom speaker clicked. "This is Rob Harris. Ms. Rojas, is everyone all right?"

"We're fine, but Mrs. Garcia is trapped—"

Senator Pulaski pushed forward and demanded, "Harris, lift the damned lockdown and open this door."

Undersecretary Doyle spoke from the back of the group. "Calm down, Senator."

Harris's voice came from the speaker. "I apologize. A small plane made a hard landing inside Hydra Mountain's restricted perimeter, and DOE policy required that I initiate a security lockdown. Response teams are on their way to assess the downed aircraft, but preliminary indications are that it is merely an accident. As soon as that's confirmed, the lockdown will be lifted."

Adonia pushed the Talk button. "You *are* aware that we heard a safety alarm, and not a security one, much less a facility-lockdown alarm."

Harris took a moment to answer. "Yes . . . we're aware."

"Are you in contact with Mrs. Garcia? Is she safe inside the chamber?"

"And can we do anything to help her?" Shawn added.

"She's waiting it out, just like everyone else," Harris said. "I've spoken to her on a separate line. The storage chamber has an independent suite of detectors from the tunnels, so she had to disable the sensors. In the meantime, we're working to open the main tunnel door and get you out of there as soon as the lockdown's lifted. We're still trying to understand why the different systems are bleeding over."

Garibaldi stepped close to the speaker. "We were brought here to review your storage operations, Mr. Harris. This is a unique and serendipitous opportunity to hear about the safety and security features, and how they interact. Have all your different systems been fully tested in an integrated fashion? These are ancient, analog DoD artifacts interacting with your new digital DOE systems. Old-school and new technology don't always play well together."

"We've tested the sensors and alarms, but not in every conceivable combination." Harris's voice hesitated on the intercom, as if he was embarrassed. "And I'm well aware that you heard the safety alarm and not the one for a facility lockdown, but we're working on that problem as well. Just stay put and don't tamper with any sensors you see."

Shawn looked concerned as he pressed the Talk button. "What about the plane crash? How serious is it? Any casualties? Damage?"

"None that we know of. The pilot made a rough landing in high winds after taking off from Albuquerque International. He's inside our fence, which set off both our legacy and newer sensors. When the lockdown was executed, my staff thinks the old safety and networked security systems bled over. That led to, uh, unexpected interactions in the lockdown. Not what was anticipated."

"You're saying it's a goat rope," Senator Pulaski fumed.

"What a surprise." Garibaldi lifted his brows at Stanley. "Crossover between decoupled systems can never happen, right, Dr. van Dyckman?"

Van Dyckman opened his mouth, but Pulaski nudged the others out of the way so he could reach the intercom himself. "Harris, can you patch me through to my staff back in Washington? It's important."

"Sorry, Senator. Since you're inside the tunnels, communications have to go through Valiant Locksmith channels, and most of your staffers aren't read into the program. You'll be able to contact your office on a secure line as soon as we get you out. Just be patient, please."

Before Pulaski could complain further, Adonia asked, "Do you have an estimate when things will get back to normal?"

"Could be a few minutes, could be an hour. Please stay close to the main tunnel door. I don't want anybody to trigger any countermeasures."

Frustrated, the Senator stalked partway down the tunnel, turned his back to the committee, and pulled something out of his jacket pocket. He fumbled, then pressed it against his ear. It took Adonia a moment to realize what he was doing.

She reacted with alarm. A phone! He had smuggled in a cell phone, an RF transmitter in these tunnels and chambers filled with delicate sensors—

Shawn spotted it, too. "Senator, drop that!"

Adonia yelled, "Stop!"

Pulaski found the speed dial and pushed Send.

13

Tense and overwhelmed, still waiting for clear instructions over the phone, Rob Harris used his shoulder to press the red handset against his ear as he riffled through his old personal security paperwork. He'd signed the original documents over twelve months ago before he stepped into the site manager job, before even *knowing* what he had agreed to.

The secure telephone on his desk was doubly encrypted, which was deemed adequate for discussing normal SAP material, but the Undersecretary's program was a *State Department* SAP, not DOE. The bureaucratic convolutions, restrictions, and interagency legalities were maddening, but the law was clear, and rules were rules. Harris hadn't been dragged out of retirement to start cutting corners and breaking Federal law now.

After a long moment, a digitally reconstructed voice broke the silence on the secure line. "The Secretary will be with you momentarily, Mr. Harris. Sorry for the delay."

As he waited, Harris continued to scan the documents, which legally granted him access to the most important secrets in the DOE and the Department of State. Those papers acknowledged his trustworthiness, while threatening horrific consequences if he broke the law.

He understood and accepted the dire constraints; that was part of the package when he agreed to become site manager. By supervising the Special Access Programs inside the Mountain—*all* of them—Harris held the keys to the kingdom. Only the President himself and Senator Pulaski, as chair of the oversight committee, could say the same. The Secretary of Energy and Secretary of State were not even cognizant of each other's SAP. Here inside the giant mountain facility, the DOE, DoD, and State Department were like the three hear no evil, see no evil, and speak no evil monkeys.

And that caused problems.

Van Dyckman's Valiant Locksmith was a vital program, yes, but Victoria Doyle's Velvet Hammer was *incredibly* important, one of the last options the U.S. possessed if faced with an existential, nation-ending threat.

Ah, there it was. He scanned the paragraph. He'd been right: Velvet Hammer operated under State Department rules, not Energy. As such, Harris couldn't even hint about its existence, or its potentially dangerous interactions with other SAPs in the Mountain, not even with the Energy Secretary herself.

So here he was—in a crisis, with a gag tied over his mouth.

The red headset clicked. "Rob, this is Caroline Nitta. How's the review committee going? Is Dr. Garibaldi behaving himself?" Her youthful voice sounded pleasant, cheery. She had to know this was no social call!

He dropped the documents on his desk, devoting his full attention to the call. Perhaps she didn't know why he'd called the emergency lockdown; after all, her high-profile experience as a public defender had secured her political appointment, and not her knowledge of DOE's inner workings. "Yes, Madam Secretary. He keeps us all on our toes." He paused, cleared his throat. "But right now our facility is under a precautionary lockdown due to a Class A mishap. I thought you needed to know."

Secretary Nitta rustled papers over the encrypted phone, which sounded like a staccato pattern of raindrops hitting the line. "You mean the small aircraft in restricted space? I have the first-look assessment in front of me. Seems like it's just an accident." She paused, and he assumed she was scanning the material. "The intel folks don't hear any chatter related to Hydra Mountain or the nuclear waste shipments. No one should have known about the review committee ahead of time, so this couldn't have been planned in advance as an outright attack, like at Granite Bay. The downed aircraft seems more a case of inept flying in high winds, rather than a nefarious plot. Could be innocuous."

Harris wasn't ready to relax so quickly. "You may be correct, ma'am, but agency regulations call for a lockdown during any Class A incident. I'll lift it as soon as I have confirmation that the crash was indeed accidental. Our teams are converging on the downed plane now. We have to be certain." She shouldn't be challenging her own rules.

"And you did exactly what you were supposed to, Rob." She sounded a little patronizing. "Even if this was truly an accident, I've asked my Chief of Staff to set up a face-to-face with the Air Force Secretary to tighten the security envelope around Kirtland airspace in the future. Hydra Mountain's too damned close to the Albuquerque airport. I want to make sure this never happens again."

"Yes, ma'am, I agree. And, uh, thank you for letting Undersecretary Doyle participate on the review committee at the last minute," he said. "I'm sure her knowledge will provide valuable insights as we complete the review—once the lockdown is lifted."

"Yes," Nitta said in a dry tone. "And she'll also give Stanley some adult supervision."

Harris started to respond, but kept his thoughts to himself; he'd always suspected that the young DOE Secretary and van Dyckman didn't get along. Stanley's direct line to the President must be unsettling to the meticulous Caroline Nitta.

Thank goodness for Victoria Doyle's presence. Even if he couldn't meet with her alone, he knew that the Undersecretary would recognize the danger as soon as she saw what van Dyckman had done in the lower level. She would understand the whole picture, just as he did, the possible cascade of unintended consequences. And as a DOE Undersecretary, Doyle had enough clout to call a halt to all this madness. "When she reviews Valiant Locksmith and the activities inside the Mountain, the Undersecretary can help us accurately assess the project."

While Senator Pulaski did have access to the State Department SAP, the man didn't have the technical background to understand the implications. Adonia Rojas and Simon Garibaldi did, and possibly Colonel Whalen; van Dyckman might, if he paid attention, but none of them knew anything about Velvet Hammer.

He knew, though, that Victoria would figure it out. He had brought them all together for that very purpose.

Rob continued on the secure line, "The good news is that when I placed the Mountain in lockdown, the facility was completely isolated from the outside."

"And what's the bad news?"

"Well, ma'am, although we recently upgraded Hydra Mountain to DOE standards, were still depending on legacy military systems to help cut costs, and those old systems weren't meant to function with newer standards. The interface between the old and new systems is not as clean as we'd thought."

Secretary Nitta sounded concerned. "Meaning?"

He knew he was going into too much detail, but she had to know. "When our current lockdown was initiated, a sensor that should have initiated a feature to herd intruders to the nearest security portal actually triggered *another* security feature designed to protect personnel against an attack. The review committee has been accidentally—and temporarily—confined to the first storage tunnel. One of my techs is sealed in a dry-storage vault as well. They're all stranded."

"Was anyone hurt?"

"No, ma'am, but Senator Pulaski is a little, uh, agitated, as is Mr. van Dyckman. He's upset that the tour wasn't a flawless demonstration of the Valiant Locksmith program. I'm sorry about that, Madam Secretary."

"No one anticipated an unfortunate plane crash, Rob. Are they safe for the time being?"

"Of course. We should have them out the moment the lockdown is lifted. They just have to wait patiently in the meantime."

"Patiently?" Harris heard a suppressed chuckle across the line. "Keep me in the loop, and give my regards to the Senator. It's good for him to have some genuine in-the-field experience, and for Assistant Secretary van Dyckman as well. They both think the real world ends outside the Beltway." She hesitated. "That was a good call on your part getting Undersecretary Doyle and Ms. Rojas on your committee. And a personal thanks for asking Dr. Garibaldi. We go back a long way."

"Yes, ma'am. I remember."

Still unsettled, Rob hung up the red phone and went to the window of his Eagle's Nest, hoping to hear confirmation from his own people that the crash was as innocent as it seemed, that the pilot and his handful of passengers posed no national security threat. After that was confirmed, he could rejoin the review team and keep them moving along. He would insist that they inspect the rest of the Mountain, and he'd make sure the committee saw what he needed them to see.

Through the large window overlooking the operations center floor, he spotted a light blinking on an enlarged schematic of the Hydra Mountain tunnels. Another sudden flurry of activity on the floor sent a chill down his spine. What now?

He hurried back to his desk and scanned the monitor, unable to believe what he was seeing: a disruptive electronic signal had been detected in the first storage tunnel, a radiofrequency transmission! He caught his breath. Who was sending a signal? A transmission like that would trigger a series of countermeasures cascading through the sensitive safety and security systems!

He hit the intercom and his voice boomed out onto the ops center floor. "Who's sending a signal? Who's transmitting in there? That'll cause—"

Before anyone had time to react, higher-level countermeasures automatically engaged to address the threat.

Simultaneously, the Mountain's entire system crashed, freezing the lockdown.

14

Right after the Senator activated his cell phone, another ratcheting alarm blasted through the tunnel. The deafening interruption startled him, but he seemed oblivious to what he had done. Pulaski scowled and pressed the phone against his ear, ready to shout as soon as anyone on his staff answered.

Shawn reached him first, grabbing his arm. "What the hell are you doing!" He tried to seize the cell phone.

Simultaneously, Adonia yelled, "Any signal will trigger RF sensors—"

The Senator yanked his arm away from Shawn, dropping the phone to the ground. As it clattered on the sealed concrete, Adonia dove for it, hit End Call, then powered it off, but it was too late. She held the phone and looked up at Shawn, her eyes wide as the emergency alarm continued to clang.

Pulaski looked at both of them, indignant. "What the—"

Adonia shook the phone in front of his face. "Your call just triggered another set of security countermeasures on top of the lockdown!" She wanted to strangle him, whether or not he was a senior senator. As she considered how he had just thrown the equivalent of a live hand grenade into all the interconnected sensors inside Hydra Mountain, the safety and security systems, the automated responses, she couldn't articulate how furious she was.

Shawn barely restrained himself from shouting. "How many times were you told no electronics inside the Mountain? We couldn't have been more clear!"

Pulaski looked at the two of them as if they were nothing more than insects. "You can't talk to me like that. Hydra Mountain is under my oversight. This is an encrypted phone, approved by the NSA—"

Adonia made a disgusted noise. "Missing the point! With all the defensive systems in this facility, who knows what your signal just triggered?"

Garibaldi pursed his lips, rocked back on his heels. "Well, I think the technical term for the situation is 'The shit has hit the fan.' Good job, Senator."

Booming alarms continued all around them.

Glaring, Pulaski turned to van Dyckman, but the other man looked just as distressed. His expression began to waver. "But what does it matter? I couldn't even get a connection—all this rock must be blocking the signal."

"You're deep inside a mountain—of course you won't get a signal," Victoria Doyle said in a withering voice. "But your transmission triggered a lot of detectors and automatic countermeasures."

Battling anger with every diplomatic skill he possessed, Shawn opened the thigh pocket in his battle fatigues and yanked out the blue electronics-storage bag. He took the cell from Adonia and zipped it inside the bag, which he held in front of the flummoxed Senator's face. "I'm confiscating this phone. This packet is a miniature Faraday cage, so signals can't get in or out."

Pulaski raised his voice into the continuing alarms. "Colonel, I will have that phone back. It contains my calendar and all my contacts."

With forced calm, Shawn secured the packet in his thigh pocket; Adonia knew him well enough to read even his well-concealed expressions, and she had never seen him so upset.

Shawn spoke in a measured tone. "Senator, you knowingly carried unapproved electronics into a classified, special-access area and put us all at risk. That could cost you your clearance and your committee position—if not time in jail. But if it makes you feel any better, the packet is padded and waterproof." He patted his thigh. "You'll get it back when we're safely out of here."

Pulaski seemed about to lash out, but faltered as he realized that everyone else in the group looked at him with equal consternation.

Adonia raised her voice over the continuing siren. "Listen up! Mr. Harris told us to stay close to the vault door—and not set off any sensors. Thanks to the Senator's phone, we've already failed there, so let's move back near the intercom. Maybe Rob can turn off this new alarm and get us out of here."

Shawn's voice was clipped. "First, does *anyone* else have electronics on them? Anything that might emit electromagnetic radiation— including smart watches? I thought we were perfectly clear, but I don't want this to happen again. Last chance for amnesty." He looked around the sheepish group, but no one produced undisclosed electronics.

As they headed back to the vault door that blocked off the main tunnel and the ops center, Garibaldi's face scrunched up in a quizzical look. He sniffed deeply. "What's that odor? I've smelled that before." Then he coughed and staggered backward. "I remember that from one of the Sanergy protests that got out of hand. Tear gas!"

Adonia blinked, then shook her head and blinked again. Suddenly, she felt as though her skin erupted in a hot, painful rash. Her eyes watered and burned, and she started to gag, unable to breathe.

Pushing her way to the intercom, Doyle bent over and started to cough. "It's . . . coming from up ahead, by the vault door. But that's where we're supposed to go!"

"That's our exit when the lockdown ends," van Dyckman said.

Garibaldi pointed down the storage tunnel to the metal door. "Look, the vents!" Small plumes of gas curled into the tunnel, crawling out of openings in the granite wall. The plumes quickly diffused into the air, but the vapor was apparent once they knew where to look.

Pressing hands over his ears against the continuing alarms, Senator Pulaski hunched over and turned in the other direction. He lurched down the tunnel, away from the vault door. "If it's tear gas, then we have to get away."

Blinking back tears, Adonia coughed as she yelled after him, "But . . . Harris told us to stay here!"

He retched out an answer. "Harris . . . isn't . . . being gassed!" He staggered down the corridor away from the blocked exit. "I'm sure as hell not staying here."

With increasing distress, Garibaldi bent over and also lurched away from the tear gas, reluctantly following Pulaski. "He's . . . right. For once, the Senator seems to be doing the smart thing. Score another point for your wonderful system, van Dyckman." He ran blindly, reaching out to feel the granite walls. "Harris told us this tunnel intersects with the one that leads down to the lower level. We can get out that way, and we'll be away from the gas."

Although Adonia could barely breathe herself, she clung to Harris's instructions. She was in charge of these people, but the tear gas defense didn't make sense. Security countermeasures were supposed to drive people *toward* an exit, to get them out of the facility in a dangerous situation, not push them deeper inside.

As the thickening gas burned her eyes, nose, and lungs, Adonia knew it would not be possible to remain in place, as Harris had instructed them. The Senator's panicked retreat seemed more and more reasonable as the irritating gas thickened.

Coughing uncontrollably, van Dyckman hobbled after the two. "Get to the intersection with the incline," he called ahead in a hoarse voice. "It's another way to reach the main corridor, as well as the lower level. The system *is* working. It's just a temporary glitch, but we have to wait it out . . . where we can breathe."

Undersecretary Doyle followed them, while Adonia smeared her hands over the tears that flowed from her eyes, stubbornly hoping that Harris would cut off the gas and open the vault door as he had promised. They couldn't wait any longer.

Shawn grabbed her elbow. "They're right . . . and you're responsible for their safety. Let's go."

The plumes of gas were like a toxic fog, still hissing into the confined tunnel and swirling around the vault door. No exit there. Unable to stand it any longer, Adonia and Shawn staggered away, following the others deeper into the facility.

They passed Mrs. Garcia's closed storage chamber, and Adonia hoped the technician was safe from the noxious fumes. "We might have been better off sealed in there with her." She coughed.

"No thanks," Shawn said. "At least this way we can keep moving, get somewhere safe."

Behind her, in addition to the clanging alarm, a new ear-splitting siren went off, making her whole body shake. She didn't recognize the distinctive tone as any standard alarm employed by the DOE. Maybe it was one of the old military countermeasures still functioning in the facility. But this was far worse than any alarm signal; it seemed to pierce her entire being. She pressed her hands against her ears as she careened forward. It wasn't an alert; maybe some kind of sonic weapon?

The siren was only one component of the devilish cacophony. A deep, low reverberation rolled down the tunnel, an invisible force driving them from the vault door. Her entire body thrummed with the subsonic frequency, down to the marrow of her bones. The sound came in slow, crashing pulses, growing worse.

On the other end of the frequency spectrum, she barely detected a sharp, needle-like noise that pushed her eardrums to the edge of bursting. The ultrasonic dissonance seemed to slice through her head. This was a full-spectrum, multifrequency sonic attack!

She had no chance to think, could not choose where to go. She could only react. The sonic barrage drove her away, and she instinctively fled, anything to escape the overwhelming noise. She gasped for breath as the low subsonics seemed to squeeze the air out of her lungs, while the mid-range and higher frequencies shook her body, pierced her skull.

She could barely think through the pounding, shrieking pain. With her eyes burning from the tear gas, Adonia saw the others in front of her careening from one side of the tunnel to the other, like drunken partygoers.

Forcing some small amount of control, Shawn urged them faster, pushing them along, but no one paid attention. Senator Pulaski screamed wordlessly as he staggered along, his eyes closed, shaking his head back and forth.

Still pressing her hands to her ears, Adonia crowded in among the rest of the group as they kept trying to escape the noise. Shawn yelled something, but Adonia couldn't make out what he said over the cacophony.

When she tore her hands from her ears, she realized that trying to muffle the noise had not worked at all. The harsh dissonance hammered through her palms as if they were tissue paper. Maybe her eardrums had already burst, but with the incredible sonic pain, it didn't seem to matter anymore.

She collided with van Dyckman and Garibaldi, pushing them to hurry. Her ex-boss tripped and stumbled to the concrete floor, but the older scientist grabbed him, helped him forward.

As they moved farther from the main vault door, Adonia thought the insane noise decreased, at least marginally. Positive reinforcement? Slowly, step after step as they careened down the tunnel away from the main corridor, the hammering pulses abated. For some reason they were being herded away from the vault door, by countermeasures that must have been designed to drive intruders to a holding area or interception point. Maybe that was where they were headed. She didn't care. She just needed to get away from the barrage, to find some shelter, some respite from the attack. She and her fellow team members weren't aggressors or intruders, but the system couldn't differentiate among its targets.

Ahead, Senator Pulaski crumpled to the floor, and Shawn bent to help him up, even though the big man outweighed him by fifty pounds. Pulaski resisted, kicking out with his feet, as if he just wanted to curl up and die.

Barely able to see, Adonia shoved van Dyckman and Garibaldi forward to join Victoria. Helping Shawn with the Senator, she yelled in his ear. "Keep moving! The noise will grow louder unless we keep going forward." The countermeasures would ratchet up until they went in the desired direction. The intent of the system was clear.

Together, they grabbed the squirming Senator. Shawn worked his hands under Pulaski's shoulders, and he and Adonia strained to lift the big man up. They staggered forward.

As the merciless sonic barrage continued, they worked their way down the tunnel. Van Dyckman, Doyle, and Garibaldi all stumbled forward, not knowing where they were going, just heading *away* from the gas and the infernal noise.

Shawn and Adonia plodded along with the Senator in tow. She suspected the man would have died there if they'd left him. Old military countermeasures didn't have much of a humanitarian bent.

Even with the sheer reactive need to escape the hammering pain, Adonia felt increasing panic. This couldn't possibly be a test, or even a routine lockdown. She feared that Pulaski's cell phone signal had caused a catastrophic overload while the Mountain was in lockdown.

But what if there was some real outside emergency, like the extremist attack on Granite Bay? A significant threat to Hydra Mountain, and they just happened to be caught in the middle? What was Rob Harris responding to?

In their frantic escape, they passed numerous oval vault doors of sealed dry-storage chambers on alternating sides of the tunnel. Adonia didn't know how far they had run from the noise or where they were supposed to go.

Almost imperceptibly, the alarms decreased in intensity. When the haggard group slowed to a stop, pausing and panting, the sound naggingly increased again, spiraling up in volume, driving them onward again. "Must be motion sensors embedded in the walls," Adonia shouted. "We have to keep going."

The main tunnel door—supposedly their way out of the Mountain—was now far behind them. She tried to recall the diagram they had briefly seen in the Eagle's Nest. She thought this storage chamber tunnel ran parallel to the main corridor, separated by at least a hundred feet of granite. And Harris had said this tunnel intersected with another one they could use in case of an emergency. She hoped the security systems were at least driving them toward safety, that this wasn't just another glitch in the facility systems.

After they had gone another hundred yards and the mind-shattering racket diminished again, she spotted a vault door directly ahead, sealed tight. If she was right, this would be a second interior tunnel, the incline to the lower level. Harris had said it would also lead back to the main corridor.

As they approached, the thick metal door slowly opened, as if beckoning them inside.

15

With the screeching, painful noise driving them, everyone rushed to the obvious escape offered by the opening vault door.

"That way!" Doyle yelled. "Straight ahead!"

Van Dyckman was right behind her. "We'll be protected in there."

The group stampeded forward, and as they approached the door, the maddening sound dopplered down in intensity, as if to reward them for their cooperation.

From the other side of the metal door, Adonia could see another tunnel perpendicular to the one they were in. This really was like some dungeon role-playing game. The cross passage looked identical to the previous interior tunnel, which was now nearly a half mile behind them.

Shawn pulled the disoriented Senator along. He didn't seem to realize the noise was abating. They slowed, and suddenly Pulaski straightened and brushed the help aside, embarrassed at having to be carried.

The group stumbled to a halt at the open vault door; Adonia was reluctant to enter what might be a trap. By now the din had decreased to the level of a loud rock concert, and she could start collecting her thoughts.

Peering past the vault door, she spotted construction supplies, tools, and debris piled along the new passage. Apparently this area was still being reconfigured for Hydra Mountain's new mission. In the wide tunnel, massive sheets of one-inch-thick plastic panels, bags of cement, and disassembled metal scaffolding were stacked among caterpillar-like swaths of foil-backed pink fiberglass insulation that had been removed from the Cold War–era facility construction. Adonia recognized the thick black polymer panels as fiber-reinforced plastic, which were usually associated with . . . lining water tanks? She frowned. Surely not in these tunnels. The debris and construction material were stacked against the sloping granite walls, leaving a path along the center just wide enough for carts and forklifts.

Holding up a hand to stop anyone else from following him, Shawn stuck his head into the connecting tunnel. Garibaldi frowned. "Checking to make sure there's no trapdoor into an alligator pit, Colonel?"

Shawn didn't laugh at the joke. "I don't want to trigger any more countermeasures. Maybe I should go ahead alone, cautiously."

"The vault door's open—that's obviously where we're supposed to go," van Dyckman interrupted. "With the motion sensors, it's more likely we'll trigger countermeasures if we stop moving." He pointed to the left. "Look, this way leads back to the main corridor. We can get out of here."

Adonia supported Shawn's decision. "Harris charged me with ensuring our safety, Stanley. It's my call, and I agree with Colonel Whalen."

Van Dyckman scowled at her, taken aback. "And I'm the program manager. I don't need anyone's approval to head for safety. I've been inside the Mountain hundreds of times."

Shawn blocked the way and refused to move. Adonia knew he always had her back; she'd never doubted that. Shawn was fast on his feet, and he kept himself in great shape, while Stanley was the epitome of an Ivy Leaguer from Brown; his main "athletic" effort was arguing before Senate budget committees.

After seeing the expression on Shawn's face, van Dyckman backed down. He mumbled, "I wouldn't want to countermand your authority, Ms. Rojas."

Garibaldi said, "I don't suggest we agonize over the decision."

Senator Pulaski called out, "Somebody better lead the way before those sonic countermeasures start blaring again. Let's get out of this place!"

Doyle shuddered. "I don't want to experience anything like that noise again in my life. Lesser of two evils—let's go forward before the Mountain forces us to move."

Adonia made up her mind, knowing they couldn't wait much longer even if they set off more sensors. "All right then, let's head through. We've got to find an intercom so we can let Rob know where we are. I want to find out what triggered those countermeasures."

Doyle cast a sour glance at Pulaski. "We all know exactly what got us into this mess. His damned phone crashed the systems—which are clearly unstable for such an important facility."

"Unstable?" van Dyckman piped up. "These are sensitive and thorough security measures, and the systems are working exactly as designed in response to a severe anomaly." He pointed to the left, through the newly opened vault door. "The main corridor is less than a hundred feet over there. I'm sure of it. If we go the other direction, we'll walk down a decline to the lower level and the high bay. We were supposed to tour there this afternoon, according to Harris's schedule."

In a sharp voice, Pulaski said, "We can finish the review later, after we're safe."

Garibaldi muttered, "I don't think this is what they really wanted us to see. Not getting good marks so far."

Adonia stepped next to Shawn so she could study the control panel set into the granite just outside the open vault door. The panel looked identical to the other one outside the dry-storage chambers, with the same LED screen and old-fashioned intercom. She pushed the Talk button and leaned closer to the speaker. "Ops center? Are you there?"

Nothing happened. The intercom didn't function.

While the others watched in consternation, Garibaldi raised his voice to be heard above the continuing racket. "Van Dyckman may be correct in his assessment. If his new and improved defensive systems are working as advertised, we've been herded this way for a reason."

Adonia again visualized the set of tunnels in her head from the diagram, but something about the electronic systems didn't feel right. Perhaps their safety and security measures, new and old, were working at cross-purposes, thanks to the sequence of errors. The Class A event, the small plane crash, might have stressed the complicated system to its limits, and then Pulaski's cell phone signal had been the tipping point that caused the logic chain to break down. Back at Granite Bay, her experts would have called it a non-reproducible bifurcation, a manager's worst fear: different results for identical situations.

Harris had said that Hydra Mountain's safety and security interfaces had not been tested in all possible permutations before the facility was rushed into operation. Yet Yucca Mountain had endured more than three decades of excruciating design assessments and reviews, and it had still been mothballed. In addition, the Nevada desert facility had been *designed* to store high-level nuclear waste in the first place. By contrast, reopening Hydra Mountain was a rushed, classified stopgap solution, using antiquated systems appropriate for nuclear *weapons* in combination with state-of-the-art, digital devices jury-rigged for storing nuclear *waste*.

What could possibly go wrong?

Adonia would have felt much better right now if at least the old-fashioned push-button intercom worked. *Something* had to be stable in this topsy-turvy underground site.

She turned away from the wire mesh speaker. "We're on our own. Everybody, through the door and to the left—as fast as we can. Watch out for all that construction material. Shawn, take the rear and make sure no one falls behind."

"Copy that."

She looked at Pulaski. "Need any help, Senator?"

"I'm fine, as long as I can get out of here." Senator Pulaski took a few uncertain steps and then pushed forward, walking by himself now. The others followed.

Adonia called, "Stay together. Once the sensors detect that we've entered this connecting tunnel, we don't know how long the vault door will stay open."

"Be prepared to cover your ears," Shawn added. "We may set off additional sonic countermeasures."

"I can't wait," Garibaldi said.

The Senator stepped ahead, and Adonia heaved a sigh of relief when his footsteps triggered no further alarms. "See? Home free." She motioned for the rest of them. "All right, let's go!"

Ahead down the long tunnel, a bright light shone at them like an oncoming freight train. She guessed that from there another vault door should lead back to the main corridor, offering them a way out, but the powerful beam didn't look like a welcoming light. The beacon grew brighter and brighter as they hurried toward it, like a wall of intense glare.

A dark silhouette in front of her, Pulaski shielded his eyes against the brightness. Behind him, Doyle paused, placing her hands on her narrow hips as she squinted ahead, wary. The light began to pulse, each time growing brighter . . . and brighter, burning their eyes as if the glare itself intended to push them backward.

Garibaldi said, "Well, what surprise do you have for us now, van Dyckman?"

"These aren't my security systems." He sounded rattled. "I've never seen this before."

Shawn came up behind Adonia, peering down the tunnel with its intense throbbing lights. "That looks like a warning to me. I don't think that's the way to go."

"Of course it is!" van Dyckman insisted. "That's the way out. The exit door can't be more than twenty or thirty more yards straight ahead. I've used that entrance dozens of times. Valiant Locksmith transports high-level waste down to the lower level through this very passageway."

Adonia's ears were still ringing from the sonic alarms, and she shook her head. "Common sense tells us to go that direction, but it's also clear the countermeasures are trying to push us *away*. It's another deterrent." She turned around, dreading what she had to do. "We have to go the opposite direction, or it'll just get worse."

16

The wall of blinding light down the tunnel was not only intense, but it had grown more ominous. The others grew uneasy, too, even van Dyckman. The throbbing accelerated from a slow, rhythmic pulse to a jerky, random staccato, as if it was designed to disorient and confuse.

Adonia covered her eyes, flinching. Shawn said, "I've heard of this, I think. It's an optical deterrent, just like the sonic one. The system is trying to herd us in the opposite direction, down the tunnel incline."

"But that's not the way out!" van Dyckman insisted. "We can't go backward. We need to get out of here."

Garibaldi sounded pensive rather than frantic. "Hydra Mountain must have multiple layers of independent, active defensive systems. They're targeting our senses, first assaulting us by smell with that noxious tear gas, then by sound, and now with white light." He paused for a beat. "I bet this isn't the only countermeasure. Other parts of the electromagnetic spectrum could be far worse."

Shawn nodded. "It would stop an intruder cold. Anything to protect the nuclear warheads that used to be stored here."

"But we're not intruders!" Pulaski snapped. "This is my own damned program!"

Garibaldi looked down his nose. "Apparently, the automated countermeasures are not convinced of your wholesome intentions."

"Maybe the Senator should make another phone call and file a complaint," Doyle said with clear sarcasm.

"Let's not wait around to find out," Adonia said.

"But we know we don't want to go in the direction the active measures are pushing us! *This* is the way out. The system works!" Steeling himself, van Dyckman put his head down and stubbornly marched toward the bank of pulsing, intense lights. "Just close your eyes! It'll be fine."

He pushed past the Senator in his haste to prove his assertion, knocking the disoriented man out of the way. In the cycling, random lights, Pulaski stumbled against the pipes of a disassembled scaffold, lost his footing. He cried out in pain and held on to the granite wall for balance. "Damn it!"

Shawn ducked his head and refused to let the changing lights confuse him. He made his way to the Senator and stabilized Pulaski, taking some of the big man's weight as he brought him back toward Adonia.

"It hurts!" Pulaski said. "I twisted my ankle."

Garibaldi looked at him with a withering expression. "Don't expect me to carry you."

"That's enough. He'll make it, and we'll all pitch in when necessary." Adonia could feel growing antagonism among the others, as if they considered Pulaski too high maintenance for the crisis, and Garibaldi's sarcastic edge didn't help. She turned to the Senator. "Try not to put much weight on it, sir."

Still pushing toward the bright pulsing light like a man trudging against a driving storm, van Dyckman approached the end of the tunnel. The glare shimmered and throbbed like a fusillade of bright flashes. He seemed determined to defy the countermeasure and bulldoze his way to the exit. But as he grew closer, he must have triggered another sensor, as a succession of bright circles of light shot down the tunnel wall from rings of high-power strobes embedded in the walls.

Dazzling waves hurtled toward him as if converging on his head. The glowing circles dissipated once they flew past, but they shot out faster and faster, brighter than sunlight. Van Dyckman ducked his head and covered his face in the crook of his arm. Off balance, he veered away from the center of the passageway, lurching toward the left wall, but he kept going, fighting against an imaginary headwind.

As the Senator leaned against the wall, keeping one foot off the floor, Adonia watched the strange bombardment surrounding her boss.

"Now what are they throwing at us?" Doyle asked. "Some sort of . . . optical special effect?"

Doggedly plodding toward the exit door, van Dyckman reeled. The throbbing rings of light in the walls changed color, melting from white to violet, circle after circle, cycling down the spectrum from blue to green to yellow to orange, and even deeper, until it became a dark red so intense that it was almost impossible to see.

Garibaldi straightened, his eyes wide. He shouted, "Van Dyckman—turn around, now! Or you'll be fried."

Pulaski looked down the tunnel. "The bright light is fading. Does that mean it's safe?"

"It hasn't faded, just shifted down in frequency," Garibaldi said. "And if it's dropping to the infrared, our eyes won't be able to see it anymore. But he's about to experience it as heat—big time."

It was the next phase of the active defense, Adonia realized. "Like being in the middle of a giant convection oven." She bolted after her former boss, calling back to Shawn, "Stay with the Senator. I'll bring him back." She ran barefoot toward van Dyckman, and the pulsing rings of white light swept past her as well, wave after wave, increasing in intensity. "Stanley! Come back."

Rings of light shot all around her, changing colors as they swooped past. She bent her head and tried to ignore the overbearing glare. "Stanley, damn it! Turn around!"

The throbbing rings filled the tunnel, spiraling from white to intense purplish-blue down the spectrum to bloodred—and then she could no longer see it . . . but a sudden intense heat bathed her skin from the front, as if she were walking toward a supercharged heat lamp.

The temperature quickly became unbearable, and she crashed into van Dyckman, where he stood in the center of the tunnel, his head down against the overwhelming infrared radiation. He stretched his arm toward the elusive vault door, now only tens of feet away, as if trying to pull himself forward.

Adonia's face stung and burned, but she managed to grab his shirt and pull him back. He struggled. "It's . . . it's right there, just a little further—"

"You'll die before you make it." She yanked and he stumbled back into her, but she caught him, kept him upright, and dragged him toward the others. Once she turned around, even just a few steps away from the pulsing infrared, she felt her front cooling off, although the heat now slammed against her back like a physical force.

Van Dyckman stopped resisting, then he lurched along with her, retreating toward the others. As if the systems were rewarding them for making the right decision, the heat dissipated swiftly as they retreated. After only a few seconds, Adonia felt as if she had spent a day in an intense tanning bed.

Soon, the concentric rings of brighter lights flashed around them, visible again, as if they really needed motivation to keep going. Adonia felt van Dyckman sag against her. His shirt was soaked with sweat. "That wasn't smart, Stanley."

"It's not supposed to work like that."

As they reached the rest of the group, the light behind them spiraled back up to a steady white, casting long shadows on the concrete floor and all the scattered construction equipment and debris. The ceiling LED lights brightened, taunting, beckoning them in the direction the systems wanted them to head.

Into the descending tunnel.

Adonia said, "Who am I to argue against stubborn countermeasures?"

Shawn joined her, concerned. "Your face is red, like a bad sunburn."

"I could use a dip in a nice cool swimming pool. Did I mention this isn't the way I wanted to spend my Sunday?"

"And I'd rather be rock climbing," he said. "Maybe later. Once we get out of here."

"You got it." Adonia wiped the sweat from her forehead. She

looked down the tunnel that led to the lower level. "We better get going before the next defensive measures kick in."

Undersecretary Doyle joined them, ignoring van Dyckman. "In a few hundred feet the tunnel starts sloping down. There's a guard station before you reach the lower level—it should be manned. We can hole up there until this madness is over."

Adonia looked at the Undersecretary. "How do you know that?"

"Some of my own programs were located in Hydra Mountain. Remember, DOE used to deliver nuclear weapons to the military here. The lower level was used for storing plutonium pits, back in the good old days."

Adonia didn't need to hear any more. "If we get to the guard portal, we can shelter there. I bet we'll find some kind of telecommunications to contact Rob Harris."

Shawn frowned. "Why would the old countermeasures herd us down to the former pit-storage level? That makes no sense."

When Adonia ran a hand through her dark hair, her fingers came away wet with perspiration, and her red dress was rumpled. "No idea, but we're not getting to the main exit through that infrared wall."

Dazed, van Dyckman gazed back toward the glaring barrier of white light, knowing their exit was only a few hundred feet away. "So close."

Senator Pulaski struggled to his feet again, gingerly putting weight on his sore ankle. He started walking in short stutter steps. "Just get me the hell out of here."

They moved as a group, working their way down the tunnel, away from the pulsating lights. Garibaldi nodded, as if this scenario were merely an experiment. "The system is responding as if we're intruders, but the wires are crossed. Literally."

Van Dyckman threw him a disgusted look as they passed more construction material and debris against the tunnel wall. "Impossible. I told you we installed new systems. State of the art."

"Then the countermeasures should be driving us out of the Mountain, not deeper into it." Garibaldi raised his eyebrows. "Think about it, 1950s analog hardware interacting with artificial intelligence?

Back in the Cold War era, they used copper wires, not fiber optics, and mechanical, analog switches rather than digital logic. Instead of being able to computationally simulate a million test cases a day guided by self-learning algorithms, Hydra's old interface might be able to run only a few tests a day—if they're lucky."

Van Dyckman said, "We're under intense pressure from the President, and each test would have brought down the facility for hours. If we did all that, we'd never move anything in."

"Shouldn't have been a problem," Garibaldi said sarcastically, "so long as you're willing to put up with a few minor glitches, like this disaster."

17

Rob Harris's stomach roiled, and he wiped his forehead with his sleeve. Being out of contact with the team members trapped inside the Mountain was making him frantic. His ops center screens showed an increasing cascade of alarms inside, but he didn't know what they were doing in there. Hydra Mountain's safety and security systems were working at cross-purposes, triggered by that unauthorized cell phone transmission immediately following the Class A incident.

He'd been forced to reboot the facility's entire system—the only way to unfreeze the lockdown now—but that entailed a *six-hour* process that involved bringing up thousands of obsolete analog devices as well as newer digital equipment, all interconnected. They ranged from truly antique water-cooled processors and decades-old PDP and VAX computers hardwired by the military to van Dyckman's newest DOE networked clusters.

As site manager, he had pored through all of his manuals, searching for something he had missed, some workaround or shortcut. None of the procedures covered circumstances like this. He desperately needed outside input. He had to know what else he could do, how far he could push the facility.

Sitting in his Eagle's Nest office and looking through the wide windows at the urgent activity below, he once again waited for the DOE Secretary's call. A software failure in the security lockdown had blown most of the old analog intercoms in the deep tunnels, and he couldn't make contact with the stranded team. The inspection group had inadvertently triggered several unexpected crossovers in the installed countermeasures—and that wasn't even the problem that Harris had wanted them to discover! No, not what he had intended at all.

Here, above the busy ops center floor, Harris should have felt like a king in a high tower. Below, his exec Drexler and fifteen staff members urgently worked on internal operations, paying little attention to the separate video feeds from outside the Mountain, which were splashed as overlapping windows on the giant wall screens. As his team worked with obsessive focus to override the automated defensive systems, Harris longed to be down there with them, getting his hands dirty and hoping to offer some helpful insight, but those people were good at their jobs—and much better versed in the complexities than he was. He would only get in the way if he went down among them. His job was here.

But why hadn't the Secretary called back? The classified fiberoptic line to Washington was one of the only systems besides the countermeasures and monitors that were independent of the reboot, working on an isolated power supply.

Harris glanced at a digital clock, one of three in the office set to various time zones: Eastern Daylight Time for DOE Headquarters, Mountain Daylight Time for Albuquerque, and Greenwich Mean Time. Another minute ticked down. There was nothing he could do to accelerate the restart. Five hours and thirty-nine minutes remaining, and the team was stranded inside.

The functioning monitors showed the storage chamber tunnels deserted, as expected during a lockdown. Since he had sent the normal weekend crew and construction teams home during the committee's review, Hydra Mountain was mostly empty anyway. Holding its breath.

The new digital fiber-optic link in the sealed storage chamber had let him talk to Mrs. Garcia, who was not happy, but at least she was safely tucked inside. Her only wish was that she had a book to read while she killed another five and a half hours, but her boredom wasn't a crisis.

Rather than staying put, as he had instructed, Adonia Rojas and the rest of the review team had moved from the side tunnel, driven off by the active countermeasures. Obviously, that wasn't supposed to happen. Now Harris could barely track where they had gone. Only a few sensors in the tunnels were active, and the conflicting logic instructions in the integrated new and legacy systems had made a mess of the automated defenses inside.

Judging from the last active countermeasures they had triggered, the multifrequency light and infrared bombardment, he knew the team was being driven down the inclined tunnel to the large interior cavern where warhead assembly had once taken place. That would have been part of the tour anyway, and he would have led them from breadcrumb to breadcrumb. Right now in their scramble for safety, though, he doubted if any of the team members were paying close attention to the details of the review.

Harris felt guilty for dumping that responsibility on Adonia's shoulders; he had only meant to be gone for a few minutes when Drexler dragged him away. Now she had to try to keep her companions safe, even though she knew very little about Hydra Mountain.

He wished he could help and explain what was happening, but the intercoms had shut down. He had to rely on her intelligence and judgment. At least Colonel Whalen was at her side. Together, they would make the right decisions.

Right now they were in among the piled construction materials, rolls of fiberglass insulation that had been stripped out of the reconditioned chambers, sacks of concrete mix, metal bars from scaffolding, wooden boards, panels of thick plastic. As long as they kept moving and continued downhill for another few hundred feet, they would encounter no additional defenses. Once they reached the guard station that blocked access to the lower level, they could take refuge and just wait out the last few hours. The phone there might even work.

It was only a matter of time. Nail-biting, but straightforward.

Unless they triggered another detector and released more countermeasures.

Harris felt frustrated and helpless. Why didn't Secretary Nitta call?

He could do nothing to help those trapped people, couldn't even re-assure them. At least Drexler had been able to reboot some of the infrared sensors in the tunnels, connected by the new fiber-optic lines. From the readouts, Harris was reassured that the team members were still together, and hopefully unharmed.

Every tech in the operations center knew this was no drill, that they had to do everything possible to get the team members out of there. Hydra Mountain had already suffered a severe black eye, thanks to the screwups today and the bumbling small plane intrusion. Valiant Locksmith would not get the glowing report and clean bill of health that Senator Pulaski needed for his oversight meeting. It might even be a fatal blow to the program.

And he was the site manager. After this, Rob Harris might find himself back in retirement—not a bad thing, after all—and Valiant Locksmith might be shut down until these problems were fixed. Although that would solve his immediate concern about the interaction with Victoria Doyle's SAP, he did not want this to become another Yucca Mountain fiasco, which would leave the nuclear waste problem unaddressed—again.

But if the solution was almost as bad as the problem at hand . . .

Even though the system reboot would prevent them from entering the interior for six hours, his staff searched for any kind of work-around. On the floor below, technicians shouted on secure phones with various contractors, subcontractors, and consultants, anxious to thwart a system that had been designed not to be tampered with. Hydra Mountain had been built to protect nuclear weapons from both outside and inside threats; the systems would not allow for a simple bypass just because a review team was inconvenienced.

The best solution would be to wait out the remaining time and do his best to unruffle feathers afterward. Harris just hoped he could convince them to continue the review, though after being held hostage for six hours and subjected to some of Hydra Mountain's countermeasures, Adonia and her companions would not be in the best, objective mood. Now that Undersecretary Doyle had been read into Valiant Locksmith, however—a huge victory for Harris—he could privately discuss his concerns with her. One way or another, *that* problem would be addressed.

At last, the red STE phone on his desk rang; the digital ID on the fiber-optic link read SECDOE. He snatched it up. "Harris here."

"Mr. Harris, we're going to program level. Stand by." He waited a moment until the phone hissed the unique sound of double encryption, and the male voice came back on, sounding tinny. "I have you at . . . Valiant Locksmith."

Harris read from the desktop's digital display. "I concur."

"Here's the Secretary of Energy."

The phone line was silent for a moment, then, "Rob, Caroline Nitta again. I've just been briefed that your countermeasures are herding the committee to the Mountain's lower level rather than to the exit. Is that by design? It seems counterintuitive, according to the specs I have been shown."

"It took a while to figure out, ma'am, but apparently the safety and security systems interacted in a nonlinear fashion when they were simultaneously triggered. There are unforeseen incompatibilities between the legacy DoD systems and the newly upgraded DOE hardware."

"English, Rob. You're speaking to a public defender, not an engineer."

"Sorry." Harris stood at his desk, pulling the STE phone cord tight so he could keep watching the ops center through the windows. "That small plane intrusion simultaneously triggered both security and safety sensors. Though the crash itself was a minor mishap and the passengers suffered only superficial injuries, all hell broke loose with both the old legacy systems and the new systems responding at the same time, at cross-purposes. Remember, Hydra Mountain was made to protect nuclear warheads, and the defenses were not meant to be . . . subtle." He drew a breath.

"The real tipping point, though, was when one of the team members attempted to make an unauthorized cell phone call in the middle of a volatile situation. That transmission triggered a cascade of increasingly severe responses."

The Secretary made a disgusted sound. "How the hell did anyone get a cell phone inside the Mountain? I was read the riot act about wearing even my digital watch when I was out there." The encryption distorted her long sigh. "I swear, I'm going to have you conduct full body cavity searches from now on."

Harris continued his report in as objective a voice as he could manage. "No voice or data were transmitted, but whenever a phone is powered up, it automatically emits a radiofrequency ping. Our detectors are so sensitive that they're triggered by *any* electromagnetic emission—intentionally so, in order to detect intruders and prevent espionage."

"What idiot would do such a thing?" the Secretary demanded. "Was it Stanley? I wouldn't put it past the man."

"We shot DOE intelligence a copy of the waveform picked up by our sensors, and at the classified level, NSA was able to confirm the cell phone owner." He swallowed awkwardly. "It was Senator Pulaski, ma'am. Though he was asked to relinquish all electronics at the entry gate and again inside the tunnels, he apparently failed to do so."

There was a long pause, and he imagined her strangling the Senator in effigy. She heaved a deep breath and asked, "And the inspection team—where are they now?"

"They're being herded by a succession of countermeasures, but they should be approaching a guard station. They can shelter in place there. Right now we have our hands tied until the full system recycles." He looked at the clocks. "Five hours and twenty-seven minutes more. There's simply nothing I can do. It's like being locked in a bank vault with a timer."

"But are they safe?"

"They are if they shelter in place, and don't trigger any more sensors." Harris glanced out of the office at the operations center monitor. "I won't deny that some of the countermeasures they faced are aggressive and unpleasant, but they're all nonlethal."

"Such as?" she asked.

"Initially, tear gas up in the storage tunnels. Next, they encountered sonic, optical, and infrared defenses, designed to disorient them. But now that they're near the empty guard station above the lower level, they can just hunker down." He hesitated. "They'll be fine if they just stay there, but if they turn back at all, motion sensors will detect it, and the systems will respond. They'll trigger other countermeasures."

"Can't you just shut down power and cut off the countermeasures? We know they're not intruders."

"My team is trying every possible option, ma'am. The emergency backup is buried in the Mountain's interior from Cold War days, and it immediately kicks in when the system reboots—exactly as it was designed to do. The interior infrastructure is totally independent from outside influence.

"Plus, there are hundreds of old systems hardwired into the controls. We just didn't have the budget to remove them. We even have antiquated 16-bit, PDP-11 computers programmed in assembly language that still control critical functions, and that all adds to the time it takes to recycle." He realized he was probably talking over her head, and he didn't want to explain how much it would cost to bring Hydra Mountain into the twenty-first century. Stanley van Dyckman had insisted on getting the facility up and running with all due speed, using every resource available while still controlling costs. Harris couldn't blame headquarters for not wanting to spend exorbitant money on what was just a "temporary" storage facility.

Secretary Nitta remained silent for a long moment. "Once they reach the guard portal, is someone there to intercept them? Is it manned?"

"Normally, yes, but we have only a skeleton crew today. Hazardous operations were curtailed in order to make the lower level available for the inspection team, and I was expecting to guide them myself. No one else is down there." He steeled himself, tried to sound confident. "But the guard station is meant to be a safe holding area. Adonia Rojas is in charge, provisionally. I'm sure she will keep them there. She knows what she's doing."

"That's a relief. Have you been in direct contact with her?"

"Not recently. Our . . . intercoms are shut down."

The young Energy Secretary let out an exaggerated groan. "What a cluster!"

The red phone sounded muffled as Secretary Nitta covered her end and spoke to someone. In the interim, Harris heard a knock at the office door. He saw his exec and buzzed him in. Drexler slid a sheet of paper across his desk before ducking out.

What else could go wrong? Harris scanned the note and caught his breath.

When the Secretary came back, she sounded as though she was trying to make the best of the situation. "At the very least, I suppose we'll have to read Senator Pulaski out of all our DOE SAPs, whether or not he's the oversight committee head. This breach is too serious to ignore. I'll be putting out fires behind the scenes for the next month." Then she sighed. "Thanks, Rob. I know your people are doing everything they can. At least it can't get any worse. Let me know as soon as you have them back out, safe and sound."

Harris's throat seemed more dry than usual. "Actually, ma'am . . . it does get worse." He glanced at the new sheet of paper on his desk. "If the team doesn't shelter in place, they may face more severe countermeasures than the safety and security systems established for Valiant Locksmith."

He had to choose his words carefully, because he wasn't cleared to speak with the DOE Secretary about Doyle's State Department SAP. "A final defensive system is still active in the guard portal from the Cold War era, a last-ditch protection mechanism against intrusion into the lower level. If the shelter in place experiences an unauthorized breach, the last level of countermeasures will activate in order to protect the other . . . activities in the lower level."

The Secretary asked slowly, "Other *activities* . . . ?"

He swallowed hard. "Things that were well under way before the DoD decommissioned Hydra Mountain and DOE took possession, ma'am." He tried to shift her focus. "Lethal force will automatically be employed if both doors of the guard portal are simultaneously opened during a lockdown. If more than one door is open, the system's logic will assume that intruders have defeated all our nonlethal defenses, and will therefore employ more severe countermeasures."

"Oh . . . my God. Lethal force? And we won't be able to reach the team members for more than five hours? You *cannot* allow them past that last security portal. Period!"

"I'm sure it'll be fine, ma'am," Rob said, but his tone of voice said the exact opposite. "Once they get to the guard station, all they have to do is wait it out."

He imagined how impatient, angry, and frustrated the committee members were. Cut off from communication, they might not be willing to sit still.

18

Adonia moved to catch up with van Dyckman and Doyle, but the two hurried down the tunnel as if it were a race. Silent, successive circles of white light continued to pulse past them to disappear down the tunnel walls like aircraft landing lights directing them deeper into the Mountain.

"All it needs is a whooshing sound," Adonia muttered, feeling less threatened now that the group was moving in the correct direction. The scene reminded her of an old space ride in a theme park.

She realized that the effect was caused by strands of intense LED lights embedded in the tunnel walls, strobing and pulsing past in a closely timed sequence. An effective and unambiguous way to force intruders—or hapless inspection team members—out of the huge underground complex.

But they were being driven deeper instead, downhill to the lower levels. She hoped the guard portal up ahead would serve as a safe haven, maybe even with a landline phone she could use to call the ops center.

Garibaldi followed close, and she could hear Senator Pulaski grumbling to Shawn from the rear. She turned to see that the Senator had stopped in his tracks, bent at the waist and retching. Though by now she was frustrated and annoyed with the Senator, Adonia tried to retain her professional demeanor. Once they got out of here, though, she intended to document and report Pulaski's reckless behavior and disregard for security. He had no business being involved in such vital matters. He was an absolute liability.

Behind them, the light circles continued to hurtle down the tunnel, strobing faster in a sickening illusion of acceleration. Pulaski was not just being a drama queen; he was obviously sick and disoriented. Shawn gripped his shoulders, tried to steady the man. He called to Adonia. "These lights are giving him severe vertigo, and his twisted ankle isn't helping."

She waited for them to catch up, while the incoming light circles flared past, brighter and faster, as if angry that the two had slowed. Shawn supported the Senator, who convulsed with dry heaves, and then, as another disorienting flare of light streaked past, he vomited onto the granite wall.

Cowed into silence, Garibaldi, Doyle, and van Dyckman waited among the construction materials, plastic panels, rolls of fiberglass insulation, and wooden boards. Just ahead, the tunnel angled steeply down, toward the lower level.

"Sit tight," Adonia called as she turned back to help Shawn and Pulaski. "We'll be safe once we make it to the guard station."

As she turned around and headed the other direction, Garibaldi motioned urgently down the incline. "Better not reverse course, Ms. Rojas. Sensors are tracking us, and they might react. We don't want the optical and IR deterrents to conclude we're trying to retreat."

Finished retching, the Senator panted for breath. Shawn supported him as he stood shaking. "He needs a few minutes."

"I don't think we have a few minutes," Garibaldi warned. Beside him, van Dyckman looked pale and nervous. He didn't contradict the older scientist.

As before, the light rings began changing color from white, cycling down through deep violet, to light blue, through green and yellow. The rings seemed to be growing angrier as the colors shifted to deep red, then beyond visibility. "We've got to move!" Adonia shouted.

Pulaski favored his ankle and took stutter steps as he stumbled down the tunnel as if zapped by lightning. Shawn hissed in unexpected pain as the pulses descended into infrared. The temperature spiraled and he manhandled the Senator, hurrying him along back toward the rest of the group.

Adonia met up with them as a sudden flare of overwhelming heat washed over the front of her body. Her back still felt cool, but her face, neck, and exposed arms felt as if they were in a hot oven. This was far more intense than the flash of infrared heat she'd felt earlier. Barely able to think, she only wanted to turn and run in the direction the countermeasures wanted them to go. She couldn't control herself.

Shawn hauled Pulaski along, both of them running, paying no heed to the Senator's injured ankle. Unable to stand the intense heat, Adonia reached the others, who remained huddled among the construction materials. She yelled at the unresponsive walls, as if the systems could hear her, "All right! We're moving the direction you want us to go!"

But the searing heat did not abate even as they retreated. The punitive waves slapped at them, driving them away relentlessly. "But we're going downhill! What more are we supposed to do?" They could not outrun the penetrating, fiery sensation.

"This isn't heat!" Shawn yelled. "It's millimeter waves. Got to cover ourselves or we'll be cooked!"

"Cover ourselves with what?" Barely able to think, Adonia looked around.

"The insulation!" Garibaldi grabbed at the scattered debris. "The fiberglass insulation! It has foil backing, and that'll deflect the millimeter waves. Wrap yourself in it. Hurry!"

The others also experienced the overwhelming pulses. Following Garibaldi's shout, they grabbed the dusty blankets of pink insulation, yanking and unrolling them so they could wrap the fiberglass close to their bodies, with the foil backing facing outward.

Adonia didn't have time to think through the physics. The pain was too intense, like hot coals on her back. She scrabbled for an armful of the pink wooly mats that had been extracted from the old tunnels. The fiberglass prickled like sharp hairs all around her, against her stinging skin, but she needed to protect herself *now* from the intensifying millimeter bombardment.

Shawn let the Senator slide off his hip against the granite wall, and he and Adonia piled the fiberglass mats on him before snatching more of the material for themselves. They moved frantically, wincing from the pain. Somehow, she and Shawn managed to help cover each other. "Hunker down . . . until the pulses stop!" he said.

She hoped the countermeasures *would* stop, but she feared the intensity would increase until it reached lethal levels. "This place is trying to kill us!" Victoria Doyle shouted from beneath her makeshift protection.

Adonia lay buried under the thick mats, feeling blessed relief as the sensation dissipated. She could hear Pulaski moaning on the concrete floor, and Shawn yelled at the Senator, "Stay covered up, sir. It's for your own protection."

Nearby, van Dyckman groaned, not knowing what to do, but they had all followed Garibaldi's urgent instructions. "If we're wrapped in this tinfoil, won't we be cooked alive?"

Garibaldi responded, "Not heat! It's millimeter waves."

"It's called active denial," Shawn said, his voice muffled. "Our embassies use it as a nonlethal defense against rioters."

In her makeshift cocoon, Adonia felt protected from the searing heat, though she imagined she must look like a fast-food burrito wrapped in foil. The pink fibers reminded her incongruously of cotton candy.

Pulaski's faint voice came from nearby. "I . . . I'm not burning up anymore!"

"I'll explain the technical details later, Senator." Garibaldi somehow managed to sound superior even through the layers of insulation.

Shawn's voice cut through the background. "Everyone, remain as motionless as you can. The millimeter waves should stop as soon as the sensors can't pick up any movement. They'll think they've defeated the intruders."

Before long, a tense silence filled the tunnel, and Adonia began to hope the countermeasures had really stopped. She heard the sound of foil rustling next to her as Shawn moved, calling out, "Everyone keep still. I'll make sure it's safe." After a moment of silence, he spoke with greater urgency. "Okay, let's get moving. This is our chance. The sensors will detect us, and I expect they'll cycle through the defenses again, starting out with visible light rather than a blast of millimeter waves, but if we hurry we may have enough time to get to the guard portal."

Adonia clawed her way out of the fiberglass wrapping. She felt sticky and itchy. "No time to lose. Cover as much ground as we can." She shouted at the walls. "We're going! All right, we're going."

The others peeled themselves out of the fiberglass, plucking at their clothes. Garibaldi's hair was even wilder than before; Undersecretary Doyle tore herself free. Shawn helped Pulaski up while Adonia freed van Dyckman, who shucked his ruined jacket and dumped it on the floor, leaving it with the pile of insulation. "Come on, let's go! Down the incline before the countermeasures cycle up again."

Garibaldi showed an unexpected respect for Adonia. "I'll help where I can, Ms. Rojas. I may not have much in common with all of you politically, but there's plenty of blame to spread around. For now, we all need to work together to get out of here."

Together, the group hurried along. Adonia hoped the sensors would determine they were good little intruders, following directions. The next time the millimeter waves hit, they might not have piles of construction material nearby to protect them.

Nonplussed but determined, Doyle pushed ahead, while van Dyckman was pale and shaken. "I still can't understand why the systems are reacting this way. We should have been able to exit up above! Rob Harris should have been able to let us out of here."

"Get over it, Stanley," Doyle said with an edge to her voice. "The priority now is to keep from doing any additional harm until the lockdown is lifted. There can't be much time left."

"It's been hours already!" the Senator groaned.

"Harris said he'd lift the lockdown as soon as he confirmed the plane crash wasn't an attack," Adonia pointed out. "We don't have any idea what's going on outside, but we'll have plenty of time to talk about it when we get to the guard portal."

"Maybe we should go all the way through to the lower level. The main cavern is the most secure zone in the facility," van Dyckman said. "We'll be safe there."

Doyle gave him a withering look as they hurried down the incline. "You don't know what you're talking about, Stanley. You think Valiant Locksmith is the big dog in the Mountain, but other programs have been here for forty years or more. A lot of it isn't under your jurisdiction."

He blinked at her. "What do you mean? Hydra Mountain is mine—by Presidential order. Your old DOE weapons programs only had a small presence here, storing spare parts for the national labs. The U.S. isn't even building nukes anymore, so whatever leftover weapons work may still be in this facility is irrelevant at best."

Doyle rounded on him, but Adonia cut them off in a low but forceful tone. "Quibbling will get us killed. Do you really think the safety and security systems are going to get any simpler as we head deeper into the Mountain?"

Van Dyckman seemed surprised at her insubordinate tone, considering he was so much higher up the political chain, but Doyle cut him off before he could speak. "Put a lid on it, Stanley. She's right. We need to get to the guard portal." With a quick glance toward Adonia, the older woman hurried ahead, confident the others would follow.

Adonia looked at van Dyckman to gauge his reaction and saw him scrunching his forehead, as though he strained to control his anger. She imagined that so many parts of his career had begun to unravel on a day that should have been his triumph; in his high-level DOE position, van Dyckman had rarely been put in his place. Reporting directly to the young Secretary of Energy herself, he'd probably thought he was the fair-haired boy, a seasoned politician compared to her, who knew how to play cutthroat games. After all, he was responsible for running a neat and politically feasible solution to the nation's nuclear waste crisis.

Adonia guessed that she and the others were supposed to see the true worth of Valiant Locksmith and shower him with accolades for solving a desperate crisis . . . but now his solution was falling apart in front of his sponsor, his old lover, and his greatest critic.

He strode off after Doyle, ready to go on the attack, but Adonia caught him. "No more discussion, Stanley. Save it for when we get to the guard portal."

She needed to give him something to do, to reaffirm his sense of importance, to distract him. Behind them, Shawn and Garibaldi helped Senator Pulaski along. Adonia turned to van Dyckman. "Stanley, please help with the Senator. It's going to take all of us to get him through this, and you're still going to need his support after all this is over."

It took a moment, but van Dyckman forced a nod. "I know he's . . . challenging, but he's always been that way. He's an extremely important man. This program's future may depend on him, but Victoria keeps finding fault with everything we're trying to do." He shook his head. "I still don't understand why Harris even made her part of this review team."

"Rob must have had his reasons," Adonia said. As Shawn and Pulaski caught up, she, too, wondered why in the world such a disparate team had been pulled together in the first place. There had to be a deeper reason than just a simple inspection. What did Harris really have in mind?

19

As they approached the guard portal, the passageway was cluttered with even more piled materials, which they had to dodge. Adonia was surprised to see how much construction was still taking place inside the Mountain.

The facility had been mothballed for years, and when the DOE took over the site and reconfigured the storage chambers for Valiant Locksmith, she knew that substantial modifications would have been necessary. But according to Stanley, the Mountain had been reopened for over a year. If a steady flow of nuclear waste had been arriving for secure storage, the facility should have been finished and approved for operations. Even if Valiant Locksmith was deeply classified, no program was too important for DOE lawyers to waive safety regulations.

So what was van Dyckman still building down here?

She imagined that even as he helped the agitated Senator along, van Dyckman was brainstorming how they could salvage the review.

Victoria Doyle shot a dissatisfied scowl back at them, and Adonia didn't know how to read the increasing tension. She could tell the Undersecretary had some deep animus toward Stanley, which was more than scientific or political rivalry. This was personal.

As she caught up to Doyle, she remembered hearing the rumors during her own short stint at DOE Headquarters, of the poorly concealed affair between the two energetic rising stars. Supposedly, their relationship had begun back when van Dyckman was still Pulaski's congressional Chief of Staff and before Doyle received her appointment as Undersecretary to administer the DOE's National Nuclear Security Administration. Both of them were ambitious and could use each other's connections. Victoria gained influence and incomparable access to a powerful senator, while Stanley received unique insider information about one of the executive branch's most important agencies, responsible for nuclear weapon development. It wasn't a starry-eyed romance, but more of a high-level, mutual partnership with benefits.

Much younger at the time, idealistic, and determined to make a difference, Adonia had kept her head down and focused on her job. For her own part, she had been enamored with then–Lieutenant Colonel Shawn Whalen during their days at the National War College.

But when the President had commended Stanley for his role in "saving" Granite Bay after the extremist attack, his affair with Victoria Doyle had flared out and fizzled. He was rumored to have tested his connections with the President, and had overreached in an attempt to get himself appointed as the next Secretary of Energy. Instead, that position had been given to a high-profile young public defender. And, adept at the high-stakes game of political maneuvering herself, Victoria had blocked Stanley's other ambitions, landing him a mere assistant secretary job as a consolation prize.

Now, another piece fell into place for Adonia. Unbeknownst to anyone due to SAP security, he must have been offered that role because it included the covert and vital responsibilities of being the Valiant Locksmith national program manager. Not a consolation prize at all.

In effect, it appeared that Stanley had won that battle. If Valiant Locksmith succeeded in mitigating the nuclear storage crisis, then his coveted position of Energy Secretary was well within his grasp. But in order to achieve his triumph, he still had to move a hundred thousand tons of high-level waste into the decommissioned weapons facility—safely, securely, and under the public's radar.

No wonder van Dyckman was on edge as this celebratory inspection tour turned into a debacle at every turn. His entire career hinged on the success of this review.

Now it all made sense to Adonia. Judging from the Undersecretary's body language, she realized that Victoria Doyle hadn't had any idea what Stanley was up to here in the Mountain. After their affair, she must have thought she had trounced van Dyckman, relegating him to political Siberia. Now she would have realized that the importance of Valiant Locksmith placed him in day-to-day contact with the President and the White House.

And if he did indeed become the next DOE Secretary, then he would be Victoria Doyle's boss. Adonia supposed a political Siberia would be very chilly this time of year. . . . No wonder Victoria gave him such a cold shoulder.

Stanley van Dyckman was arrogant, and Adonia was thankful she no longer had to work with him on a daily basis. Ever since he'd been appointed Assistant Secretary, she couldn't understand how he had survived politically. Valiant Locksmith explained everything.

And the crowd goes wild! Adonia thought.

After today, Undersecretary Doyle wouldn't be singing the praises of the program for the Senator's classified congressional review, nor would Simon Garibaldi. While Adonia herself recognized that Hydra Mountain was a better answer than sweeping the nuclear waste under the rug, how could she give this facility a thumbs-up, after what they'd been through?

On the other hand, if the program *did* shut down in a debacle, it might take decades before another solution was even proposed. . . . How could she allow that either? There was too much at stake! She didn't dare let it fail. Despite the overlapping safety and security systems, the operational concept here was a reasonable one. Adonia knew damned well that *something* needed to be done about the high-level waste and spent fuel rods piling up at Granite Bay and the sixty-one other nuclear power plants across the country. How she *wanted* it to work! If Hydra Mountain failed without any other alternative on the table, then the crisis would only be exacerbated.

Adonia kept pace with Doyle, seeing lights ahead down the corridor, reflections from metal walls and glass windows. "It's the guard portal," Victoria said, and the relief was clear in her shaky voice. "Just like I said."

Ahead, a giant vault door large enough to admit machinery, such as cargo crawlers carrying warheads or nuclear waste transportation casks, blocked most of the tunnel. To the left of the vault door was a smaller, person-sized metal door with a mesh-embedded safety window. On a normal workday, a guard sitting behind the safety window could see anyone approaching, even if cameras and motion sensors had been disabled, such as now.

Pulling up the rear of the group, Senator Pulaski let out a sigh of relief as he slumped against the wall. "We can get inside and just wait there. Maybe there'll be a phone. I've got to contact my staff."

"There weren't any phones originally installed inside the Mountain, Senator, except for Mr. Harris's operations center," Shawn said. "Blame it on Cold War security about calling out."

"I think we'll keep you away from any phones we find, just to make sure," Doyle said.

Taking charge, Adonia stepped up to the smaller doorway, beside an LED control panel identical to what they had seen in the storage chambers above. She pressed her face against the mesh-reinforced observation window, but the guard station was empty.

"Looks like nobody's home," Garibaldi said.

With Hydra Mountain's skeleton crew, the portal was unattended, the door closed. If Rob Harris were present, as planned, he would have had access to the controls, but now they were on their own.

Victoria placed her hands on her narrow hips. "This is a shelter in place, but we need a combination to gain access." She looked at van Dyckman. "All right, Stanley, you said this was your facility. You must have the code, so make yourself useful."

He looked uncomfortable. "Site Manager Harris has the facility-wide codes."

"Thank goodness there's still *some* security left down here. But this doesn't help us much if we can't get inside." Victoria turned her back to him, as if he had proved himself worthless.

Adonia spotted the bulky intercom box near the door controls.

She pressed the black Call button and spoke into the mesh speaker. "Hello?" *Please work,* she thought. "Anybody there?"

"Operations center—ah, Ms. Rojas?" said a female voice.

The team members crowded around her and let out a round of cheers. Adonia smiled. "Yes, we're all here. Please connect me with Mr. Harris."

"And shut down those damned countermeasures! We're not intruders," Pulaski shouted in a hoarse voice. "Get us out of here!"

"Rest assured we're working on it, sir. Please hang tight—there's less than five hours remaining on the facility reboot."

The Senator looked incredulous. "Five hours!"

"I'll have the site manager for you momentarily. Stand by, one."

Soon, Harris's familiar voice came from the speaker, sounding ragged. "Adonia! What a relief to be back in touch. Is anybody hurt? Our cameras shut down, but our IR sensors saw that someone triggered the active-denial countermeasures."

"We're all right, except for a few scrapes and bruises," she said. "Senator Pulaski turned his ankle, but I think it's just a minor sprain."

As if the site manager's voice gave him confidence again, van Dyckman stepped up. "Harris, what the hell is going on? The safety and security systems are pushing us deeper into the Mountain rather than to the nearest exit. And what's this about five more hours on the lockdown? Override it! Shut down the damned system and send a party to retrieve us." Anger was clear on his face, especially now that he had a target to blame.

"Our hands are tied while we're still recycling, sir," Harris said. "We're experiencing nonlinear interactions between the old DoD systems and the new DOE ones. We had to reboot the entire system to resolve some fundamental conflicts."

"Well, that's a complicated way of saying the shit has hit the fan," Garibaldi said with wry amusement.

Harris sounded patient and professional. "The countermeasures are working, but the systems logics are competing for control. They'll continue to do so until the full system is back up. I'm just glad to hear that you weren't harmed. Frankly, I'm . . . *surprised*—pleasantly surprised, that you don't have any serious injuries. The millimeter waves are one of our newest countermeasures, and they've proven quite effective in human protocol testing, but, uh, it appears they also disrupt our legacy electronics."

Adonia said, "We shielded ourselves with sheets of foil-backed fiberglass insulation. That protected us from the worst of the bombardment."

Harris sounded surprised. "That was clever. Glad it was available."

Victoria interrupted with an edge in her voice, "What construction is still under way down here? I thought Hydra Mountain was a fully operational facility." She raised her voice. "What are you building in the lower level?"

"You'll have to ask Mr. van Dyckman," Harris said with a clear chill in his voice. "He can explain the rationale much better than I."

Van Dyckman squirmed away from Doyle. "We intended to show you during the inspection tour, but I'm afraid our schedule has gone out the window."

Adonia got down to business. "Rob, we're at the guard portal, but it's unoccupied and sealed. Can you let us in? We need a place to wait out the system reboot before the countermeasures activate again."

Harris was glad to change the subject. "Mr. van Dyckman, you have the emergency override code. It's only good for onetime use, but you could have easily gained access—"

Van Dyckman reddened. "I'd remember it if I tried long enough, but just open the door from your end."

"Yes, sir," Harris said. "But as a reminder, the mnemonic for the override code is—"

"Open the damned door, Harris!"

"Yes, sir. Please step back from the portal door."

Adonia noticed that Victoria Doyle crossed her arms and frowned at her ex-lover. Now what was that all about? Why couldn't van Dyckman remember something as important as an override code, and why should Victoria be reacting with such obvious disapproval?

Painted on the concrete floor, a yellow arc marked the path of the heavy metal door. Adonia and the others stepped out of the way as a sharp alert buzz rang out, echoing in the tunnel. The door rotated open.

The interior of the portal contained controls to open the much larger vault door, two desks with high-backed chairs on wheels, a small table, a sink, coffeemaker, a file cabinet, and even a one-person bathroom. An identical mesh-embedded door on the far side of the enclosed guardroom led to the opposite side of the tunnel, and the lower level of Hydra Mountain. Although not spacious, the portal was sufficient for them to shelter in place for several hours. Adonia relaxed slightly.

Harris's voice now came from an intercom inside the portal. "Is everyone inside? I can't shut the door until everyone has entered."

As Adonia began to usher them into the cramped room, Garibaldi paused. His brow furrowed as he looked up at the obvious cameras in the ceiling. "Why do you need to ask? Aren't you watching us?"

"The cameras stopped functioning. All we have are IR and other nontraditional sensors. You're lucky the intercom runs through the backup system with the lights."

"I'll bet your toilets leak, too," Garibaldi grumbled.

"We can discuss it later, when we're out of here." Adonia crowded the team members into the shielded portal. "Come on, everybody inside."

"Just don't let anyone retreat up the tunnel," Harris warned. "If motion sensors see you going the wrong direction, the defensive systems will reengage—and now that you're deeper in the facility, more serious legacy countermeasures will take priority."

Garibaldi lifted an eyebrow as he crowded up against the file cabinet. "More serious than getting fried by microwaves?"

"Exponentially more serious," Harris answered. "The millimeter active denial is our newest nonlethal system. Kinder and gentler. The old DoD weapons countermeasures expressly allow the use of deadly force."

20

Deadly force.

Adonia felt a chill, although the revelation made sense. Back in the day, lethal countermeasures would be justified against anyone trying to steal nuclear warheads, but no one could run off with a giant concrete cask of hazardous waste. And why would they want to? She couldn't imagine how some bad actor would even attempt it. Deadly force was no longer warranted, by any means.

But lethal legacy countermeasures were apparently still in place in Hydra Mountain. What was van Dyckman thinking? Even worse, the defensive systems couldn't tell the difference between a genuine threat and a few people who happened to be trapped through no fault of their own.

After the insanity that had already occurred, Adonia had little confidence in anything working as it should. "Everybody, crowd together and let's get this door closed. Quick." She urged the last of them into the small room designed to accommodate two people. "Now sit tight. We can tell stories around the campfire until the reboot is over." Seeing them all safe, she let out an unconscious sigh of relief.

Shawn spoke to her quietly enough that the others didn't hear, but he sounded deeply disturbed. She had seen that contemplative look on his face many times. He said, "There should never be an *automated* system that uses deadly force."

148

"The defenses were put in place to protect live nukes," she pointed out. "Harsh language wouldn't be a sufficient deterrent."

"Oh, I wouldn't have a problem with a professionally trained armed guard who is authorized to shoot to kill under extreme circumstances. DoD countermeasures *always* have a human in the loop, a person on the trigger. Is Valiant Locksmith so important that it justifies lethal automated systems with no oversight? The military doesn't kill without human oversight. It's a fail-safe: *someone* has to make the call. Deadly force shouldn't be on autopilot, especially not for spent fuel rods."

He frowned back down the tunnel. "As we've noticed, automated systems aren't always reliable."

Adonia knew he was right. From the National War College she remembered that the military was authorized to use deadly force under Title 10 of the U.S. Code. Even drones weren't completely autonomous, especially those carrying Hellfire missiles; someone had to operate them. "Land mines are the closest I can think of to automated killing machines."

"And land mines are now forbidden by international law," Shawn said. "But Hydra Mountain has even more deadly systems in place to protect *nuclear waste?*"

Victoria interrupted, showing clear impatience as she pulled on the handle, trying to draw the heavy guard chamber door closed, but it wouldn't budge. "We need to seal the portal and hunker down. Right now we could all use a safe spot."

Pulaski took a few careful steps on his twisted ankle, then slumped into one of the two swivel chairs. "I'm much better now, thank you."

Harris's voice came over the tinny intercom speaker. "IR has all six of you in the portal. Stand back, we're closing the door from here." Seconds later the metal door slowly rotated shut, humming on its pistons until it seated into the jamb. "You'll be safe there until the systems have recycled and the lockdown is lifted. Four hours and twenty-four minutes while we bring up the various components one at a time."

"Anybody have a deck of cards?" Garibaldi asked.

"I have a solitaire game on my cell phone," the Senator said, grinning slyly.

Adonia depressed the black intercom button. "Rob, what other kinds of defensive measures might be activated out there?"

"None, so long as you don't leave the safety of the portal." The intercom remained silent for a long moment. "Hydra Mountain is set up to employ escalating degrees of force, from nonlethal to near-lethal to lethal."

"*Near*-lethal?" Garibaldi asked. "Well, that sounds just as delightful as lethal!"

"Near-lethal defenses are designed to thoroughly incapacitate, but they may be lethal under certain circumstances. Take knockout gas, for example. The same dose that renders a linebacker unconscious may kill a petite cheerleader. In high enough doses, the same gas may be deadly to everyone."

Van Dyckman interrupted, "There's nothing to worry about, as long as we just stay here."

Harris's voice continued through the speaker. "When activating Valiant Locksmith, we added the nonlethal systems because high-level waste is obviously not as dangerous as active warheads."

Garibaldi frowned at the speaker. "If Hydra Mountain was decommissioned as a nuclear weapons storage facility and is only storing waste, then why haven't you deactivated and removed the deadly countermeasures? That should have been your first order of business."

Harris avoided the answer. "Once you're out of there, we can discuss everything in the briefing room, under normal circumstances. For now, the simplest answer is for you just to shelter in place. I'm trying to take care of the emergency on this end, still hoping we can find a way to accelerate the reboot. The small plane crash was apparently no security threat, so we can get back to normal."

Adonia's main priority was to keep the group together and stay in the shelter, as instructed, but Harris's convoluted explanation for the spectrum of lethality in Hydra Mountain just didn't add up. She glanced at Shawn, and he seemed to be thinking the same thing. Something was going on here beyond storing nuclear waste. . . .

"We all understand, Rob." Adonia looked around her group. "But your systems haven't exactly functioned the way they should, and you're talking about automatically triggered lethal weapons. What if there's another crossover, another glitch?"

Harris's voice was surprisingly crisp. "Ask Mr. van Dyckman if the system is working as intended. He's right beside you. And ask him about any other cascading problems that might occur with his fuel rods."

Garibaldi swung a glare at van Dyckman. "He means the disassembled rods in dry storage, right? Not any still-hot fuel rods."

Unsettled, Victoria Doyle also stared at van Dyckman, but he huffed. "Once the lockdown is lifted, you'll see the whole facility soon enough. We intend to show you everything as part of the review. We'll pick up where we left off."

"We're just going to continue the tour?" Garibaldi said in disbelief. "Mrs. Garcia was in mid-sentence when the first alarms went off. You want us to go back up there, open the vault door, and let her keep speaking?"

Pulaski moved to the opposite door and looked through the wire-embedded safety glass, peering down the tunnel that led to the lower level. Van Dyckman joined him, speaking in a low voice. "He's right, Senator. These are unusual circumstances, and our review group couldn't see everything we needed them to see. Maybe you can postpone the Intelligence Oversight Committee hearing, sir? Valiant Locksmith is still a viable program."

"Unfortunately, my hands are tied." Pulaski sounded discouraged. "This is not what you promised me, Stanley. I have everything on the line here."

"So do I," van Dyckman mumbled.

Garibaldi pushed the second chair out of his way and leaned against the wall. He scrubbed his hands through his already unruly hair, which didn't improve his appearance. "Better yet, stop generating more and more nuclear waste, which only exacerbates the problem. Shut down the power plants until you figure out what to do. Nuclear energy will always be dangerous, and it will always generate deadly by-products." He looked at the others confined in the small room. "You know nuclear power is a dead end, like burning coal. Better to focus on the longer term. There are dozens of promising options for clean power already. They just need to be scaled up and supported."

"That's a pipe dream, and you know it! No alternative can be deployed on a scale that would be remotely useful to U.S. energy needs," van Dyckman said. "Wind, solar, geothermal, algae—they're all for show. Not to mention their drawbacks: how many birds on the endangered species list are killed by rotating wind vanes? Right now, nuclear power provides a fifth of our nation's electricity, and it should be more. Plus, it's clean and it's safe."

"Not safe enough, or clean enough," Garibaldi said. "I don't see the need for any top-secret repositories for the waste generated by wind turbines!"

Even Adonia had heard the idealistic arguments, which were fine in conception, but unrealistic for the immediate future. "We need a combination of technologies, including nuclear, Dr. Garibaldi. You can't just turn off all those power-generating plants."

"I can dream, my dear Ms. Rojas, and dreams are how progress is made. We will never win the race if we don't leave the starting gate. Somebody has to keep pushing for it—and that's why I founded Sanergy."

"Which riles up crazy people and makes them fly planes into Granite Bay," Pulaski said bitterly, looking to Adonia for support.

Garibaldi responded with clear indignation. "Sanergy was not responsible for that! He was a lone wolf and mentally unstable. I can't be blamed if some extremist distorts my message. I want to safely shut down our nuclear plants, not blow them up!"

Victoria Doyle responded with a sour expression. "For once Stanley got it right, Garibaldi. Your solution is unrealistic. Even if you phase out nuclear energy over the next twenty years, your green technologies *can't* deliver twenty percent of our national power needs, on demand, at the drop of a hat when there's no sunlight and no wind. Do you *really* think that battery and energy-storage technology can advance that quickly? A combination of technologies is needed, and nuclear is one of them."

The older scientist stroked his chin and slumped back with a sigh.

"I know, I know—but we should still be *trying*. I am not a Luddite or zealot against the nuclear industry in general, although I've certainly had unpleasant experiences working in the field." A troubled expression crossed his face.

Adonia broke in, "Even if you had a magic solution to produce all the energy we needed, and we could retire every plant like Granite Bay, we'd still have to deal with the *existing* nuclear waste. You can't just wrap a chain-link fence around all those casks and cooling pools and call them safe."

"But ignoring the necessary transition because it is difficult doesn't help either. We have to start addressing the issue rather than kicking the can down the road. If we had worked seriously on this problem two decades ago, the crisis would no doubt be solved by now—"

"It *was* solved," Doyle said icily. "Yucca Mountain was available decades ago, but people like you prevented the facility from opening."

"And now we have Valiant Locksmith," van Dyckman said. "We know how to safely store the dangerous waste."

"Well, well," Garibaldi said, his voice dripping with sarcasm, "we've seen how well that works."

"It does work!" van Dyckman insisted. Sweat sparkled on his forehead. "If anything, today's debacle shows that our safety and security systems are *too* thorough."

"The waste stored here isn't going anywhere," Shawn said.

"And neither are we," Adonia said.

The intercom clicked, and Harris's voice came back, sounding excited. "Good news! We were able to remotely deactivate the active-denial defenses, since that was one of our newer DOE systems. You won't have to worry about being exposed to millimeter waves anymore."

Senator Pulaski swiveled his chair. "So we can leave this room and get out of here? Head back up the tunnel?"

Harris hesitated. "Not exactly, Senator. Please stay where you are until the facility's completely back online. Just a few hours more, and our emergency teams can get to your location. My sincere apologies for the inconvenience."

"But why do we have to wait here? Six of us crammed in a place built for two." Pulaski looked around the room. "There isn't even room for me to elevate my injured ankle."

"Use this, Senator." Van Dyckman rolled the second chair across the floor, but he pushed too hard and it knocked over a toolbox in the corner, spilling screwdrivers, a wrench, box cutters, and a tin of screws.

Pulaski gruffly refused. "It was a rhetorical question, Stanley!" He got to his feet and hobbled over the spilled tools without bothering to pick them up. Adonia imagined he was the sort who never closed the toilet lid when he was through with the bathroom or added new paper when the printer tray was empty. He leaned close to the intercom speaker. "Harris, are you sure your heat ray has been disengaged?"

"We've deactivated the phased-array antennas, sir. They won't be operational, but—"

"Then at least let us walk back up the tunnel so we can meet your rescue team as soon as this lockdown is over." He limped toward the portal door. Apparently, his grievously injured ankle wasn't as painful as he had implied.

Harris responded sharply, "No, Senator. The shelter in place was designed for personnel to ride out any threat. With our systems still unstable, it really is the safest location—"

Garibaldi said, "I thought you told us *Mrs. Garcia* was in the safest place, locked up in that isolated chamber. Or was that just lip service?"

Anxious to get out of the claustrophobic guard room, Pulaski pushed against the exit door, but it didn't budge.

"Leave it alone, Senator!" Victoria snapped. "The lockdown's still in place, and we'd need to go through the full shutdown protocol before we exit. There are . . . other countermeasures out there." She sounded as if she knew much more about this place than she should.

Pulaski made a rude noise. "And look where that got us! We're stuck down here, and that poor woman is trapped in a chamber full of radioactive waste."

"Waste that you assured us was *safe*," Garibaldi said again.

Victoria spoke with an acid tone. "We're all in this mess because *you* couldn't resist using your phone. You leave this portal and you'll trigger more countermeasures."

Pulaski reddened. "Bullshit. You heard the site manager. He's turned off the microwaves—"

"Ms. Doyle is right, Senator," Adonia said. "Rob switched off the active-denial measures, but *legacy* defenses could still be active, systems that were installed before Valiant Locksmith was put in place."

Victoria continued, "This portal was designed as a last line of defense to prevent a malicious insider from reaching the lower level of the Mountain. That's why two guards are usually stationed here, and why the back and front exits can't be open at the same time. If you do that, you'll trigger more countermeasures—"

"And probably reboot the system," Garibaldi interrupted, "which will set the clock back *another* six hours."

Pulaski jerked a thumb to the rear of the portal. "The back exit isn't open, so we're good to leave." He scrutinized the LED control panel, spotted the door's emergency release. "I want to meet the rescue team at the main door as soon as they get inside."

Adonia intervened. "Senator, we just need to ride this thing out. It's not that long to wait." She had never seen anyone so blatantly ignore a directive and place so many people in jeopardy. "Stay put."

Defiantly, he pushed against the metal crash bar. She grabbed his arm and tried to stop him, but Pulaski used his weight to shove harder, ignoring the chorus of angry shouts. But when he opened the door, no screeching alarms activated, no blast of heat from millimeter waves filled the guard room.

With a huff, Pulaski spread his arms into the surprising silence. "See? Are you going to follow me up to the exit, or am I the only one who'll be rescued?" He stepped gingerly outside the portal and slowly shuffled up the tunnel.

He had taken three steps when, with a loud *whoosh,* a torrent of dull, bloodred liquid gushed down from conduits in the ceiling just outside the portal. Upon contact with the air, the fluid immediately coalesced, fusing into a hard, crystalline froth, like whipped cream turning into cement.

The viscous foam doused the Senator, splattering his head, his shoulders, and his shoes. He lurched backward, tried to stagger into the guard room, but the sticky material glued his foot to the ground. He flailed his stiffening arms, tugged at his jacket. A look of terror filled his face as he tried to fall into the portal chamber. "I'm stuck!"

Adonia smelled the overpowering scent of starch as red foam crawled into the portal, expanding like a flood of crystalline suds. Once, when she had been alone for the first time in a college apartment, she had added too much soap into a dishwasher, and the resulting storm of froth had filled half of the small kitchenette; now, the red foam grew unchecked, gushing from the spray outside in the tunnel and expanding layer upon layer, hardening in seconds.

Shawn shouted, "Pull him in! It's sticky foam. He may suffocate if he's covered!"

The Senator clawed at his face, peeling the hardening material away from his eyes and nose. When Adonia grabbed his arm, her fingers curled around the foam, and her own hand was stuck as she pulled. The foam swelled into the portal, covering everything, like hardening red meringue. The mess filled the tunnel outside and roiled into the guard shack as it expanded through the open door.

Shawn seized Pulaski's shoulders and pulled as hard as he could, yelling for Adonia to do the same, but even together they could not yank him loose from the flash flood of sticky foam. The bubbly sludge crawled forward like a B-movie blob, setting as it was exposed to the air.

Looking wildly around the cramped portal, van Dyckman grabbed for the scattered tools that had spilled from the box. He snatched the box cutter in one hand, a screwdriver in the other, and started hacking away at the hardened foam, slicing off chunks that had set around the Senator's legs. "Try it now!"

"Pull!" Shawn said. Pulaski's feet came free with a loud sucking sound, and all four of them stumbled into the crowded guard shack, where Garibaldi and Victoria caught them.

But with the door now jammed open, the sticky foam oozed into any available space. The red liquid continued to gush from nozzles on the tunnel wall and ceiling, and the sticky foam swelled, bubbled, coalesced, engulfing the chamber.

Behind her, van Dyckman shouted over the noise and commotion. "We're trapped! It's going to suffocate us! We've got to get out!" Crouching, he held out the box cutter as if to ward off the advancing foam.

Garibaldi batted away at the encroaching substance that covered his chest. "Can't breathe. No place to go."

"Move to the back of the room!" Shawn fought through the billowing mountains of hardening foam. He grabbed the open door and tried to pull it shut, but the petrified airy material blocked the hinge pistons and the jamb. He kicked at it, tried to clear a path, but more foam filled the gap, cementing the door open.

Adonia knew that if they didn't get out of the cramped portal, they would be swallowed in deadly foam within seconds.

At the opposite side of the guard chamber, Garibaldi looked through the mesh-embedded window of the second door. "The lower level's clear of foam! We have to go out the other side."

"Don't!" Victoria tried to pull him away. "You'll trigger another system! We have to close the other door first—"

"Not possible," Shawn said, exhausted. "The foam's blocking it."

As the waves of sticky foam kept gushing into the small chamber and the people were crushed backward, Garibaldi threw his full weight against the emergency release of the back door. The rear exit swung open and slammed against the rock wall.

Instantly, another alarm started clanging, and a rotating magenta light flooded the cramped portal. Adonia's ears popped, and a rush of cool air swept into the guard chamber from below.

Garibaldi tumbled out into the lower tunnel, and the others struggled after him to escape.

Van Dyckman, Doyle, and Pulaski fought their way to the exit, their shoes sticking in the expanding foam. Shawn and Adonia were the last to tumble out into the relative safety of the passageway that led into the lower level of Hydra Mountain.

Bright LED lights in the ceiling filled the passage with a sharp, intense glow. Senator Pulaski still pawed at the thick residue of foam that covered him like chewing gum. He peeled his jacket off and cast it aside in disgust, then picked at the hardened globs on his face and in his hair. He took several steps, but the gunk coating his wingtips kept adhering to the concrete tunnel floor.

"Take off your shoes," Adonia said, indicating her own bare feet. Her red dress was also caked with the hardened foam.

The Senator dithered over which was more unpleasant, but opted to take off his shoes, leaning on van Dyckman's shoulder while the other man used the box cutter to slice off chunks of shell-like spume. The laces were cemented together, but van Dyckman cut them, one at a time, and then peeled off the man's shoes.

Pulaski looked displeased when he looked down at his socks, flexing his toes, while van Dyckman retracted the box cutter's sharp blade and then pocketed the tool.

Garibaldi placed his hands on his hips and regarded the portal they had just left, the masses of foam, and the flashing alarm light. He looked like a captain at the prow of a ship. "Well, at least we're safely out of that mess."

"No we're not," Victoria said, her voice shaking. "We've got to move down the tunnel, fast." She pointed at the ceiling. "Look."

A new hissing sound filled the air and Adonia looked up. A plume of yellowish gas jetted out of ceiling nozzles inside the portal.

21

The noxious vapors curled around the top of the tunnel, then started sinking toward the floor—and them.

"Not tear gas again!" Adonia groaned, hurrying them away down the tunnel. "We have to move." They stumbled along, all of them spattered and coated with remnants of the hardening sticky foam.

"It isn't tear gas." Victoria sounded beaten. "That's halothane—an old, potent knockout gas. A big enough whiff, and it'll drop you in your tracks."

"Going to sleep sounds better than getting fried by a wall of microwaves," Pulaski said. "Kinder and gentler."

"If you don't get taken out of the gas quickly enough, you might never wake up," Victoria said.

Victoria continued as they backed away, looking at the gas swirling down from the ceiling, "Halothane gas is one of the final-tier military systems to stop any intruders who might manage to get past the guard portal. I think the designers assumed that only a full-fledged enemy force could possibly get this far in, so these nozzles are spraying enough gas to diffuse down the tunnels and knock out an army before they got to the plutonium pits that were stored in the lower assembly area."

"Then we have to keep ahead of it," Shawn said. "Get moving."

Garibaldi pointed back at the nozzles, frowning and preoccupied. "Halothane is colorless, an invisible old-style anesthetic, been around

159

for years—and it's deadly in large concentrations. But that gas is clearly visible. Are you sure it's halothane, Ms. Doyle?"

"It's mixed with a smoke marker so it can be seen, a psychological edge to scare the hell out of intruders," Victoria said. "Like I said, it was DoD's last line of defense inside the Mountain."

"I . . . I didn't know about this!" van Dyckman said, looking from person to person. "Or about the sticky foam either. I swear." He shook his head. "And this is *my* Mountain!"

"Have your arguments later," Adonia said. "Since we can see the gas coming, let's avoid it."

The vapor wafted down from the nozzles, spreading out as it diffused to the floor. Adonia had no intention of dropping unconscious where she would lie for hours, breathing more and more of the dangerous gas. No rescue team could get to them in time.

Tear gas was a standard deterrent with no lingering effects, good for crowd control; her own site at Granite Bay kept it on hand as a nonlethal defense in case a protest got out of hand. But since Hydra Mountain was designed to store nuclear weapons, its security systems would be much more aggressive against any intruder who managed to penetrate this far inside. She supposed it made sense, on paper.

She caught a whiff of an unusual, almost pleasant smell—which meant they were all inhaling it. "Hurry, before it starts to affect us."

Van Dyckman said, "Keep moving down to where the tunnel widens. We'll be on a high bay above the lower grotto. The farther we go, the more the gas will spread out and diffuse."

"But halothane is heavier than air, and the vapor is rolling downhill, so don't underestimate the concentration," Garibaldi said. "We'll eventually need to get well above it."

Stumbling along, Pulaski glanced at the roiling plumes of gas curling after them. "My God, doesn't this ever stop?" He began coughing as he hobbled forward in his stocking feet.

"Storing nuclear weapons requires many security layers, Senator," Doyle said. "And sometimes they're inconvenient to the good guys."

Van Dyckman persisted, "And look, it's working! This is what Hydra Mountain was originally designed to do. *We aren't supposed to be down here.* No one should be able to break into Valiant Lock-smith and steal the nuclear waste."

"Not even those of us who were sent here to inspect it?" Garibaldi asked.

The cloyingly sweet odor thickened in the air. "We can't afford to have anyone pass out." Adonia breathed shallowly, but she was starting to feel dizzy. "We've got enough troubles without having to carry anyone."

"And once the first person falls, we're all going to follow in quick succession," Shawn said. "Keep moving. We can outrun it."

The tunnel was a wide thoroughfare, built to accommodate transport vehicles hauling twenty-foot-high waste containers, so there were no sharp corners or abrupt inclines. The gradual slope headed ever downhill and deeper into the Mountain.

Garibaldi kept talking as if it helped him to stay calm. "Harris did say the countermeasures would be more severe on this side of the guard portal. Halothane is nasty stuff. Even at less than fatal doses, it can trigger cardiac arrhythmia and cause liver damage. I wouldn't recommend we breathe too much of it."

"We'll keep that in mind," Doyle said with an edge in her voice. "I'd prefer to stay awake, and alive."

They finally outpaced the dissipating gas, and after they had gone well beyond the yellowish mist, they paused to pluck at their foam-encrusted clothes. The Senator, Garibaldi, and van Dyckman had already discarded their suit jackets, and now Adonia and Undersecretary Doyle peeled off their blazers. With an expression of disgust, Pulaski removed his socks, holding on to van Dyckman's shoulder for balance. His limp was more pronounced as he moved again, barefoot on the concrete floor.

They couldn't rest for long, though. Adonia saw the first forerunner wisps of halothane drift like fog, fading as it spread out. "It'll keep rolling downhill. I don't know how potent the gas is now, but we shouldn't just stay here. It'll pool as it reaches a low point, and we want to be above it."

"We shouldn't have left the door open behind us," Doyle said. "The gas keeps coming."

"You're welcome to go back and close it," van Dyckman retorted, and she scowled at him.

"Let's just get to the lower level," Shawn said in a weary voice. "There should be enough room that we won't have to worry about the gas."

Van Dyckman looked inappropriately pleased. "Once we're down in the lower grotto, I can finish showing you the operations. That's why we brought the team here in the first place."

Garibaldi gave him a disbelieving look. "*That's* your priority?"

He shrugged. "We have to wait for the lockdown to end anyway, and this is important."

Adonia sniffed the air, caught a hint of the sickly sweet aroma. "Let's go." She set off in the lead.

Garibaldi offered his arm to support the tall Senator. "You've already had your turn, Colonel Whalen. I'll help him now." Though Pulaski looked embarrassed, he grudgingly accepted the assistance.

Adonia used the older scientist's gesture to boost their morale. "We'll reach the lower level soon, and be safe while we wait for Rob Harris's people to show up."

Victoria Doyle looked uncertain. "How exactly is a team supposed to reach us now? That guard portal was an intentional bottleneck, a single point of entry as a defense against intrusion. The tunnel is now filled with sticky foam. They'll have to clear that away just to get to us. It'll take even more time."

"Harris said he found a way to lift the lockdown and get a team in here," van Dyckman said. "Rescuers are on the way. They'll get to us soon, if we can just stay ahead of the halothane. We need to be ready for them."

"As usual, you weren't *listening,* Stanley," Doyle said. "Harris warned us to shelter in place, *inside the guard portal.* But since the Senator breached the guard portal and set off the countermeasures, now Harris has to reboot the entire system *again* and start it all over from scratch." She scowled at Pulaski. "That should have reset the clock to six hours again. The rescue teams can't even get started yet." She walked briskly ahead.

After they had gone another fifty feet down the tunnel, Adonia couldn't smell the gas, although she still felt a little dizzy and disoriented, either from the effects of the halothane, or maybe just stress. "It'll be fine," she said, still trying to reassure herself as well as the others.

Garibaldi helped the Senator along, and Adonia thanked him. He lifted his bushy gray eyebrows at her. Now his unruly hair was flecked with small clumps of red sticky foam. "Why wouldn't I? We're all in this together."

"Some people don't feel the same way," Adonia said.

Van Dyckman and Doyle led the group, as if each was eager to be the first to reach the main grotto. They walked close together, but not *next* to each other. They didn't talk or otherwise interact. Adonia guessed their affair must have ended bitterly, competitively. She was glad she and Shawn still cared for each other; circumstances had pulled them apart, not their feelings.

Seeing the obvious tension between the two, Garibaldi let out a low chuckle. "That's one of the reasons I left DOE. I got so sick of the infighting. Even in this crisis, when we're fighting for our very survival, those two political appointees can't stop bickering."

"It's all politics," Pulaski retorted, still leaning on the older scientist for support. "Industries, careers, even the future of our nation's energy grid are riding on the success of Valiant Locksmith. You know that, Ms. Rojas. Hydra Mountain is the only feasible, near-term way to ease the existing burden of nuclear waste. Would you rather keep it piled up at a hundred sites around the country, sites that were never intended to hold high-level waste?"

"I don't dispute the problem, Senator, but I would rather have it stored transparently, with more oversight." Adonia felt exasperated with the politics herself. "And as for you, Dr. Garibaldi, I would rather have protest groups like Sanergy work realistically to *solve* what is a significant problem, rather than simply attack any suggested cure. The political environment is so toxic, you would rather denounce a ticking time bomb than work together to defuse it."

Pulaski snorted, and Adonia already knew what he was going to say. "That's why we were forced to establish Valiant Locksmith as a classified SAP here on a military base. What's the alternative? Spend another twenty years and another hundred billion dollars building a replacement for Yucca Mountain? And then *that one* would never be opened because of more red tape and environmental roadblocks!"

Helping Pulaski along, Garibaldi just smiled under the verbal barrage. "I'm not trying to block any solution, Senator. I just want it done right, so the public can be safe. And the best way is to keep it free of politics."

Pulaski made a rude noise. "As if Sanergy is apolitical!"

Adonia sighed. "I try to stay clear of politics in my day-to-day operations at Granite Bay. I prefer to be out in the field, running my own site—which is why *I* left DOE Headquarters."

Ahead, Doyle and van Dyckman reached the bottom of the incline and stopped just before the tunnel opened up to the lower grotto. Victoria stood with her hands on her small hips as she waited for the others to catch up.

Adonia looked back up the long passageway. "We should be far enough away now. The gas would have dropped in concentration."

"Depends on the size of the halothane reservoir," Garibaldi said. "If it was intended to incapacitate an enemy military force inside these tunnels . . ."

"Hopefully the nozzles have a cutoff switch to stop the flow," Adonia said.

"Sensors should shut it off before the gas reached a lethal dose," Garibaldi said. "And hopefully with halothane diffusing through the entire lower level, we may never reach that concentration. But with our luck the defense systems will probably keep pumping gas until the Mountain's entire supply runs out."

Shawn winced. "The military can be redundant to a fault."

They caught up with Doyle and van Dyckman, who stood at the end of the incline, where the tunnel opened into a huge chamber below and ahead. As they approached Adonia called, "It's your facility, Stanley. When was the last time the DoD countermeasures were certified? How much gas are we potentially dealing with?"

Van Dyckman glanced away. "I told you, I didn't know about the sticky foam or this gas. That's Harris's responsibility. Everything should have been inspected when facility oversight was transferred from the military to the DOE."

Adonia wondered what other responsibilities he had overlooked as he basked in his political appointment.

He continued, "But I'm sure all the systems were thoroughly checked before we received the first shipment. I relied on Harris before I authorized the movement of casks, and you know he's a stickler for details." Van Dyckman spoke faster, more insistently, as if to make his point, but Adonia could tell he was already working on diverting blame to the site manager. "We were racing against time—on the President's direct orders."

Sweat glistened on his forehead, and he used his palms to smooth back his dark hair. He looked at Adonia, seeking an ally. "You know the situation. We needed a pressure-release valve for the increasing backlog. Every single shipment we brought into Hydra Mountain reduced the chances of something bad happening on the outside, with the public."

"So, something bad happens in here instead," Garibaldi said. "With us."

Shawn shook his head, unconvinced. "But a waste storage facility shouldn't have any lethal countermeasures at all, no matter how secure it needs to be. Such measures were needed when real nukes were stored here. Why were so many legacy systems left in place after the military decommissioned the site? If the antiquated countermeasures were inspected, then why weren't they deactivated?"

Doyle said slowly, "Probably because they were considered necessary."

"To guard a bunch of dry waste casks? Not likely," Garibaldi said.

"Don't try to understand bureaucracy," Adonia said. "For now, we need to find a functioning intercom so we can tell Rob what happened and explain why we're no longer in the guard portal. We're all flying blind here."

"Everything's just up ahead," van Dyckman said, sounding eager. "You'll see."

They moved to where the tunnel opened up, and they looked out upon Hydra Mountain's vast lower grotto.

22

A cold trickle of sweat ran down Rob Harris's back as he hunched over his desk in the Eagle's Nest. The IR sensors on the screen did not show good news. The team was on the move again after breaching both doors of the guard portal—exactly what he had told them *not* to do. Why was it so hard for them just to stay put? He found it maddening.

Forcing open the upper door of the portal would have released the sticky foam countermeasure, which would be a disaster in itself, but when they opened the opposite door and attempted to pass into the lower levels without authorization, then that would dump the deadly halothane into the tunnels. Those old, extreme measures had all been left in place to protect Victoria Doyle's SAP. Now, the Undersecretary was seeing it all firsthand.

He couldn't understand why they would make the situation worse. Adonia Rojas or Colonel Whalen knew the importance of following strict instructions, Stanley van Dyckman would not have wanted anything else to go wrong, and Undersecretary Doyle certainly understood the dangerous countermeasures deep inside the Mountain. But the Senator and Dr. Garibaldi were both loose cannons.

In the operations center, his techs had just figured out how to deactivate the newly installed nonlethal defenses in the upper level, as required by the DOE. But now the whole countdown had reset to zero and started over again, thanks to the breach in the guard portal. The old, lethal DoD countermeasures were decoupled from the modern DOE systems, and there was no way he could shut them off.

Another six hours before he could do anything!

Harris could only guess what the team was doing deep inside the Mountain. He punched the intercom and called down to his harried-looking ops crew. "I really need to see them. Why aren't my optical sensors working yet?"

Drexler said, "Blame it on the sub-terahertz sources driving the active-denial millimeter waves, sir. They fried the tunnel's new camera circuitry."

Harris couldn't believe it. "Those cameras were just installed. The new electrical components weren't EMP certified?"

It took a moment for his exec to answer. "No reason for that, sir. That requirement was dropped after the Cold War ended."

Harris slumped back into his chair, rubbing his temples. A few months ago, while attending a cocktail party in Albuquerque, he'd spoken to a young Sandia Labs engineer. She explained the work she was doing with high-power microwave weapons, which were similar to Hydra Mountain's active-denial systems. "The smarter you think you are by using sophisticated electronic components, the dumber I can make you by overpowering the circuits. Every increase in complexity offers ten new ways to take you down."

And now, one state-of-the-art security component had tangled with another, perhaps taking more than one down.

Ironically, if they'd kept the old 1950s-vintage circuitry and the legacy cameras, rather than replacing them with higher-resolution and more sensitive optical systems, he might have been able to keep visual tabs on the committee. The original Cold War–era conduits had been certified to survive electromagnetic pulses from atmospheric nuclear detonations. When the DOE converted the Mountain to a waste storage facility, van Dyckman had authorized cheaper electronic solid-state devices rather than using more robust systems, such as enhanced fiber optics that were immune to EMP radiation. Since the purpose of Valiant Locksmith was to store nuclear waste, that shouldn't have been an issue.

And Hydra Mountain possessed far more aggressive countermeasures, old systems that remained in place for the other SAPs inside the facility. Another unintended consequence. Because of the firewalls between the classified SAPs, the interactions of the countermeasures couldn't be fully vetted under all possible circumstances.

Most DOE nuclear sites had been built decades ago, and their operational technology was constantly being upgraded. Under normal circumstances, such upgrades were done in a rigorous, methodical fashion, according to set safety and security procedures. They were monitored by oversight agencies, such as the Nuclear Facilities Safety Board and the Nuclear Regulatory Commission, as well as the nuclear power industry, and in some cases, even nuclear protest watchdogs, like Dr. Garibaldi's Sanergy group. Rob Harris liked it that way, safety net after safety net, a clear set of rules to follow.

But when the President had signed the classified Executive Order to begin moving nuclear waste into Hydra Mountain, van Dyckman rushed the operation, not daring to let anything delay Valiant Locksmith. Once a big government program was operational, the mere inertia of bureaucratic red tape would keep it going, but the tiniest glitch could shut everything down before it got started.

Harris didn't let himself forget that Yucca Mountain had never even opened its doors, killed by politics before it could receive a single spent fuel rod or cask of dry high-level waste. And that boondoggle had cost five times as much as the Apollo program! Van Dyckman had taken emergency measures to make sure the same thing didn't happen to Hydra Mountain . . . and those measures had backfired on the review team.

Drexler adjusted his sweaty shirt collar. "At least the nontraditional sensors still function in the tunnels, sir. We can't see or hear the six team members, but we can track them using infrared and gas sensors that detect their body heat and carbon dioxide emissions." He gave a weary, small smile. "Or, we can always monitor their progress by watching which countermeasures they trigger."

Now that the sticky foam had driven them through the guard portal, he hoped Adonia could find another intercom and report in. But the systems were widely separated and they functioned intermittently. If she and the others were running for their lives from the flood of halothane, their first priority wouldn't be to phone home.

He sagged in his chair, rested his elbows on the desk. He had planned for this to be an important day, resulting in a great administrative upheaval, but he had never expected this. The small plane's hard landing inside the security fence had triggered the high-level security systems, but some members of the inspection team were like bulls in a china shop, and they had caused even worse problems. Someone must have tried to go back up the tunnel, and the motion sensors would have interpreted the movement as an intruder trying to escape.

He suspected Senator Pulaski was responsible. Though the Senator *wanted* this review to go off without a hitch so he could deliver a positive report to the oversight committee, he was his own worst enemy. Pulaski was just a politician who had risen to a position of importance based solely on his seniority in government, not any expertise. He had received his committee position and financial power thanks to his tenure and influence, not through any particular knowledge about the nuclear industry—like a political donor being named the ambassador to France, whether or not he even spoke French. Pulaski had no business making decisions about the complex problem of high-level waste storage, but that's the nature of politics.

Harris paced in his office, gazing out the big windows, feeling isolated. He had to get those people out of there alive.

He had alerted emergency services, and they were standing by just outside the main entrance to the Mountain, ready to rush in as soon as the lockdown recycled. Now, the rescue team would also have to cut their way through the sticky foam barricade just to get down the tunnel.

He glanced at the clock. Time crawled by. Five hours and eight minutes left before the reboot was complete.

He needed to call Secretary Nitta with the news. He knew she wouldn't take it well.

The team members were fighting for their lives in there. The only silver lining was that once the group reached the lower level, they would see the impending problem that had caused him to bring those specific people here in the first place. Then they would understand the real danger at the heart of Hydra Mountain.

And then the shit would *really* hit the fan.

23

The tunnel opened up like a giant window to reveal an enormous high-bay grotto with an arched ceiling stretching out to their right, as if the middle of the Mountain had been hollowed out. Shawn, Garibaldi, and Undersecretary Doyle crowded together at the mouth of the tunnel. As Adonia brought up the rear with the Senator and van Dyckman, she paused, impressed with the enormity of the underground cavern unfolding below them.

All the security and safety measures had herded them here, and they found themselves on a long ledge that extended two hundred yards directly in front of them. Fifty feet on the right, the ledge dropped off to a monstrous rectangular cavern, and she realized that what they had seen as they came down the incline wasn't Hydra Mountain's lower level at all. Rather, it was merely an upper platform that served as a holding area for materials brought down the tunnel, such as the large concrete waste casks. Once placed on the ledge, the cargo could be lifted by a crane and lowered to the floor of the cavern, far below on their right. Years ago the big grotto had been a temporary holding and assembly area for nuclear weapons. It looked big enough to hold a small town.

Running along the right side of the ledge, a painted red line on the concrete floor marked a crosshatched danger zone five feet from the abrupt edge. A chest-high yellow plastic chain draped from metal poles served as a flimsy barricade to prevent anyone from stepping close.

Two open-air hydraulic freight elevators were situated on either end of the ledge; a sign painted on the floor of each elevator read *WARNING 250 TON LIMIT.* From the ledge, two sets of portable metal stairs reached up to the catwalk network, far above the high bay.

On the other side of the plastic chain, the ledge dropped fifty feet down to the floor of the vast cavern. The opposite wall of the grotto was nearly a quarter mile away. Two hundred feet above, the ceiling was supported by giant steel beams at regular intervals.

"The size!" Garibaldi said in a hushed voice. "You could store a dozen aircraft hangars in here."

Adonia drank it in, unable to think of any words. The sheer excavation job, presumably completed during Cold War days, dwarfed anything she'd seen before.

A gargantuan mobile crane was parked in the middle of the cavern—an old red Manitowoc MLC165-1 gantry, capable of lifting over 180 tons. Its 275-foot metal lattice boom was long enough to reach over the ledge where she and her companions stood, lift a load that had been delivered there, and lower it onto the floor of the cavern or deposit it into one of the freight elevators. Right now, the crane's boom had been extended up in its safe position, stretching over several crisscrossed catwalks beneath the ceiling high above.

Oblivious to the other team members, van Dyckman was awed and delighted as they moved closer to the crosshatched warnings painted on the ledge. "No matter how many times I come here, I'm always blown away." He grinned at them all, Adonia in particular. "See what I mean? This can solve the storage problem in one fell swoop. We can fit it all."

Even Shawn seemed at a loss for words. He finally managed, "That crane—how did it get inside here?"

"Piece by piece, down the tunnel. Built like a model ship in a bottle," van Dyckman said. "The old industrial overhead crane from DoD days was only rated to one hundred tons, and we needed more than that to move the dry casks from the ledge down to the lower floor. Structurally, we couldn't retrofit the ceiling for a larger overhead crane, so we installed a high-capacity ventilation system to exhaust the diesel fumes." He pointed to a vent shaft in the rock ceiling overhead.

Staying far from the edge, Adonia looked at the grotto floor as it spread out before her. The broad expanse was clearly still under construction; excavations for large, rectangular structures the size of Olympic swimming pools all being dug in the floor. Mountains of cement mix sacks were piled high in the far corners. She could see stacked construction materials, scaffolding components, piled rebar, copper plumbing pipes, wooden framework braces, and metal sheeting. At least four forklifts were parked against the walls, available to move the materials.

Everything was eerily silent in the gigantic chamber, since Rob Harris had sent away the construction crews on a Sunday. During the normal workweek this place must be a swarm of activity.

"When this was a DoD weapons site, the lower level housed all their equipment and maintenance shops." Van Dyckman pointed to the far corner. "Down there they kept all their high-precision machinery so engineers could simply fabricate whatever parts they needed—except for plutonium, of course, which was done up at Los Alamos's PF-4 facility in Tech Area 55."

He turned to Shawn. "The military left everything in place when they decommissioned Hydra Mountain. Later, DOE had to clean up the mess, which meant covertly clearing everything out to give us space." He grinned. "Our national labs got a windfall of old, unique equipment—it all just showed up on their doorsteps, but we couldn't say where the items came from." He shrugged, looking smug. "Fortunately, budget-tight DOE labs typically don't question getting free stuff."

Adonia struggled to comprehend the scope of Valiant Locksmith. "I had no clue there was so much classified space in the entire country, much less in one location underground."

He nodded. "Between Hydra Mountain's upper and lower levels, you can see why it's a perfect solution for storing one hundred thousand tons of nuclear waste."

"It was quite the political coup," Senator Pulaski said. He sounded as if he had regained some of his confidence. "We can all take a victory lap."

Garibaldi looked more disturbed. "Such an enormous classified construction project could only have been accomplished during the Cold War, when nobody questioned such things. Unlimited budgets, the nuclear arms race, Commies hiding under every bed." He scanned the arched ceiling far above. "This looks bigger even than the interior of Cheyenne Mountain."

Adonia had never been inside the old NORAD command post, but she had seen photographs.

Shawn's expression remained troubled. "But everyone knew NORAD Headquarters was located deep inside Cheyenne Mountain, and it was hardened to survive a direct nuclear strike. Until Hydra Mountain was decommissioned, nobody knew nuclear weapons were being stored here."

"And that fact was never fully declassified or even acknowledged, despite all the rumors," Pulaski said, leaning against the wall to take the weight off his sore foot. "The public doesn't know much about this place at all, which makes it the ideal location for Valiant Locksmith."

Shawn pointed out, "If our adversaries knew that warheads were stored here, the city of Albuquerque would have been a primary target in the event of a nuclear war."

Adonia looked at the wide ledge in front of them. Giant concrete cylinders lined the granite wall, each one marked with the universal radiation symbol. At the end of the line of cement casks, a large seven-foot-diameter steel sphere was anchored in place and connected to piping that led up the inclined tunnel. Was that the halothane reservoir?

The concrete cylinders were much larger than the casks the two flatbed trucks had delivered earlier that morning. These were more than fifteen feet in diameter and nearly thirty feet tall. She couldn't imagine moving something that large through the Mountain tunnels to this ledge. Clearly, the big crane would deliver them down to some holding area on the grotto floor.

She couldn't figure out what kind of high-level nuclear waste would need such massive cylinders. She made out stainless-steel tubing running up their sides and a miniature power supply near the bottom of each cask, complete with backup battery. They looked like small, self-contained plumbing plants. Was this so liquid could circulate inside the casks? But why would dry nuclear waste need to be liquid cooled . . . ?

Then it hit her.

Adonia shifted between disbelief and anger as she shot an astonished glare toward van Dyckman, who stood making grandiose gestures for the benefit of the others crowded next to him. She pushed her way forward. "Those aren't dry-storage containers, Stanley. They're liquid cooled! What are they doing here?"

She had heard of such experimental casks being developed for storing and transporting highly enriched fuel rods removed from a nuclear reactor—the very type of high-level waste that needed to cool in deep pools for up to five years until they could be safely handled in dry storage. But those experimental casks were only meant for limited, temporary storage, as they could be extremely dangerous if the heavy-water coolant ever leaked, stopped circulating, or even heated up.

Every nuclear power reactor produced spent fuel rods much faster than the rods could cool to manageable radiation levels, which meant that power plants like Granite Bay needed to build increasingly more temporary pools just to store the rods in the interim. And with no acceptable place to build more pools, rods were crammed more and more densely in the existing pools, packed closer and closer together— often to dangerous levels, where the radiation could build up to a deadly criticality.

She understood Stanley's desperation, and Hydra Mountain might indeed be a pressure-release valve, but Adonia feared that Valiant Locksmith wasn't qualified to handle still-hot spent fuel rods. Had Harris known about this? How in the world could "Regulation Rob" allow this to happen? Was there some reason why he hadn't simply reported it up the chain?

A new thought occurred to her. Was that why he had wanted this inspection tour, so the broad-based, objective team of experts could see for themselves?

Victoria stood by the aluminum catwalk stairs with her hands on her hips in her familiar stern posture, showing clear astonishment. "What the hell do you think you're doing, Stanley? Ms. Rojas is quite right—if those are liquid-cooling containers, still-hot fuel rods do not belong here under any circumstances."

"We interpreted NRC guidelines, and Senator Pulaski approved it." Van Dyckman sounded defensive. "It is well within our funding mandate."

The Senator looked embarrassed. Adonia knew full well Pulaski would have agreed to whatever Stanley suggested, since he understood little of the underlying science—or implications.

Garibaldi swallowed several times, struggling to breathe. "Have you lost your mind? This is insane. The risks in transporting such highly radioactive casks . . ."

Van Dyckman was annoyed, expecting to receive accolades rather than criticisms. "Nonsense. Safe Secure Transports carry nuclear warheads across the country, and this grotto was designed for storage and assembly of plutonium pits. Cooling fuel rods are far less problematic. Your concerns are baseless, just like Harris's."

Adonia motioned toward the casks behind her. "Don't quote me studies saying these new storage containers are safe. The technology is too immature. The safest option is to keep the spent fuel rods in wet-storage pools near the power plant. You shouldn't transport rods inside those containers, no matter how much coolant they have, or steel and concrete you wrap around them—much less store them here."

Garibaldi gave a firm nod. "She's right. I understand, and even guardedly approve, of the vaults in the upper level—provided poor Mrs. Garcia gets safely out. Those sealed chambers seem to be an adequate system for holding dry waste in isolation." He shook his head. "But Hydra Mountain is no place to store still-hot fuel rods, especially after what we've been through today."

Angry and sickened, Victoria Doyle stood back from the edge and stared across the giant grotto. "Those rods shouldn't be in here at all." She turned a heated glance toward van Dyckman. "*At all,* Stanley. You don't know what you're doing." She insistently pointed across the cavern, where the far granite wall a quarter mile away had a row of embedded vault doors, their tops barely visible; the main lower floor sloped down to the vaults. "Do you even know what's down here? What's in those vaults?"

Van Dyckman lifted his chin. "Those are relics, owned by some other agency. I have plenty of space on the floor for our purposes, and I don't go knocking on old, locked doors."

Adonia turned around and suddenly caught a stronger smell, a sickly sweet odor. No denying it—the halothane was drifting toward them, getting stronger. "Do you smell that? The knockout gas is still coming toward us."

Pulaski suddenly paled. "And we're trapped on this ledge."

"If the gas is still pumping out, it will keep drifting downhill," Shawn said. "But look at all the volume in here. If we get down into the cavern, the gas should diffuse enough to be harmless."

Garibaldi walked to the guard chain at the ledge, peering over the drop-off in search of a way down. He was startled by what he saw. "Oh. I didn't expect that."

When Victoria joined him, her expression turned ashen. "What the hell is this?"

Though van Dyckman stubbornly refused to step beyond the red safety line, Adonia hurried to join them and peered directly down at what had previously been out of view because of the sharp drop-off. Shawn stepped up next to her.

Now the pieces fit together—the thick black plastic panels piled on the tunnel floor, the rebar and concrete mix, and especially the large open excavations being dug in the middle of the grotto. Stanley wasn't worried about keeping the highly radioactive fuel rods in the experimental concrete and steel casks for long.

"You see," van Dyckman said smugly, finally joining them. His face was filled with pride as he looked down. "We have it all taken care of."

Valiant Locksmith wasn't just storing the safer, dry nuclear waste or a few liquid-cooled transportation containers. Not at all.

Van Dyckman's plan was of a much greater scope.

24

Hot with nervous sweat, Harris shifted the classified STE phone against his right shoulder, fighting a cramp as he waited on hold for the Secretary of Energy. Again. His hand was slick around the red handset, but he squeezed harder. His neck ached; his head pounded. Too much tension.

Too many disasters.

With these crises at hand, he would have preferred to use the speakerphone so he could multitask and watch his crew inside the ops center, but speakerphones were strictly prohibited for SAP conversations. It didn't matter that his office, the operations center, and the entire interior of Hydra Mountain were cleared for Valiant Locksmith. DOE SAP regulations and policy covered by U.S. Code Title 50 were not suggestions.

He was horrified by cocky administrators who didn't adhere to procedures, glibly claiming it was better to beg forgiveness than to ask permission. Harris had worked for years at Oakridge in Tennessee, and DOE Headquarters in Washington, earning a solid, reliable reputation. He was not going to throw his career out the window.

He couldn't help but worry about team members cut off from communication, stranded even longer because of yet another systems reboot, with all safety and security systems activated, especially the extreme countermeasures in the lower levels.

And he couldn't help them at all.

The secure line remained quiet for an impossibly long time, and Harris felt a bead of sweat run down his temple. His last report to Secretary Nitta had not been particularly well received, and she had left him waiting, stewing, pacing. Now he had to tell her even more bad news.

Even as the youngest Cabinet official, the DOE Secretary wasn't used to anyone disobeying hard-and-fast regulations, and especially not her specific directives. But someone on the review team had violated the shelter-in-place orders, blundered back up the tunnel, and triggered the sticky foam defense. Now the rest of the team members had breached the other side of the portal, which had dumped enough knockout gas to flood the lower cavern and incapacitate a hostile commando team. The gas reservoir tank was two meters in diameter and filled with cooled liquid halothane ready to be volatilized into a truly significant volume of the anesthetic gas.

Harris chewed four orange-flavored antacid tablets from his desk drawer as he waited. Still silence on the phone. Nothing, no answer, no help.

The line clicked, and a hollow, tinny sound came over the already distorted digitally encrypted link, as if the Secretary had put her own STE phone on speaker. "Rob, I understand we're looking at another five hours." The Secretary's voice sounded deeply frustrated.

"A little longer than that, ma'am, and it's more than enough time for the halothane to fill the lower level to a height of six feet, which should incapacitate all of them even if they get down to the grotto."

An unidentified male voice spoke over the line, not the Secretary of Energy. "Mr. Harris, if the team is overcome and you can't get to them for more than five hours, the gas will almost certainly kill them. Isn't there some brute-force way for a rescue team to break in?"

Although the DOE Secretary may have brought in some sort of adviser, Harris hoped this man had been read into the SAP, per regulations. "I'm afraid not, sir." He cleared his throat. "My operations center has no access to the Mountain's interior during a lockdown. That's the whole purpose of this place. Hydra Mountain is absolutely impregnable, even to a concerted military effort from an adversary."

"But once you *do* have access to the interior, the crisis will be over," Secretary Nitta said. "Correct?"

The stranger's voice broke in again. "Why weren't these malfunctions caught before, and why didn't van Dyckman inform the Secretary there might be problems? Weren't there test runs? A full-up facility dry run before launching Valiant Locksmith? You've been operational for a year."

"Numerous test runs, sir, but we couldn't foresee every conceivable scenario. Even though this facility is equipped with modern digital systems, we're limited by 1950s analog circuitry, legacy DoD systems. And we didn't expect a civilian aircraft being forced down on the side of the Mountain during the inspection." He sighed, gritted his teeth. "Or one of the team members smuggling in a cell phone and making an unauthorized transmission when the systems were already on sensitive lockdown." He heard muted discussion over the secure line. He tried to keep the frustration out of his voice. "We just have to wait this out."

The male voice interrupted, sounding bitter. "So the halothane is still pumping out, and the committee is being forced to the lowest level of the grotto. I'm looking at a diagram now."

Harris pressed ahead, talking faster. "Yes, sir. When nuclear warheads were stored here, the lethal countermeasures were the last line of defense down where the devices were assembled. If any intruder managed to penetrate that deep into our nuclear arsenal, they would need to be stopped at all costs."

"But that was back during the Cold War!" Secretary Nitta said in a harder voice. "In converting Hydra Mountain, van Dyckman should have dismantled the old military security systems and supplemented them with new, nonlethal systems developed to incapacitate rather than kill. And now you've got a U.S. Senator and several high-ranking political appointees trapped in there. Those people are *not* terrorists, and they are *not* expendable!"

Harris struggled to control his breathing. Words caught in his throat like barbed wire. He would be unable to help the trapped team even if he could reveal why the Mountain still required the lethal countermeasures, no matter what this stranger or even the DOE Secretary thought.

"All procedures were followed," he insisted. "Over twelve months ago, when Hydra Mountain opened its doors, each decision was approved by the Congressional Intelligence Oversight Committee, as clearly recorded in the authorization of Valiant Locksmith."

He had done all the paperwork properly, followed every regulation, even though he suspected van Dyckman had circumvented the classified interagency approvals in his rush to impress the President. It was a technicality, but a legal one that could come back to haunt the Assistant Secretary.

Secretary Nitta sounded somewhat cowed when Harris refused to back down. "Due to the urgency of the waste storage problem, I did approve an accelerated process to make the program operational as soon as possible, at the President's insistence—but I insisted that we follow all SAP procedures. Stanley must have pulled some strings, and apparently he cut a few corners as well."

Harris didn't want to cast blame, but the finger-pointing had already begun. Damn the straitjacket of regulations and political blinders that kept one SAP from knowing what the other was doing! "And there were other, uh, security considerations," he said. "As I said before, a cascade of unintended interactions occurred between the legacy and modern systems. We expected to have time to work out the wrinkles, but Senator Pulaski's oversight hearing forced us to move up the timetable."

He heard muffled whispering over the secure comm link. The Secretary seemed to be arguing with the other person in her office. She came back on the line. "We can address this later, Rob. For now, do you know what'll happen next?"

Holding the red phone, Harris stared through the Eagle's Nest window at the operations board on the far wall below. The interior tunnel cameras were still fried, and he had no visual contact with the stranded team. Nevertheless, the heat, oxygen, carbon dioxide, halothane, and other biosensors showed that Adonia and her companions had reached the upper ledge of the high bay above the lower cavern, and that pained him.

Halothane was still flowing down the tunnel, and soon the gas would pool around them and spill over the ledge. They had to get to higher ground before the knockout gas rendered them unconscious. If only he had a way to warn them!

Forcing calm, he spoke to the DOE Secretary. "The team's best bet would be to head up onto the catwalks and climb as high as possible. Again, they'd have a chance to sit tight."

"At least they won't be able to trigger any more countermeasures from up there," said the Secretary. "Simon Garibaldi should come to that conclusion, if no one else does. Can you tell them that?"

"No! They're not near any intercoms, and the loudspeakers are down!" He calmed himself, heaved in a deep breath again. "Once the cavern sensors detect the halothane, the catwalks will retract up into their lockdown position. If the team members can climb up and out of the way before that happens, they will be safe near the grotto ceiling."

The man's voice asked, "And what if they don't think to get onto the catwalks in time?"

Harris longed for another antacid. "Then once they fall unconscious, the system reset time will pass very quickly for them." He hesitated. "Unless the halothane increases to a lethal concentration."

"Why can't they just get out onto the open floor of the lower cavern? Won't the space be large enough to dilute the gas?" Nitta asked.

"For a time," Harris said. "The reservoir was designed to hold enough halothane to cover that lower floor before any adversary could steal the active plutonium pits. The freight elevators are the main means of transporting personnel and equipment down to the cavern, but they'll be locked down as well, retracted to their safe position and out of reach from the upper ledge."

It took a moment for the Secretary to answer. "Considering how persistent the team has been against your countermeasures so far, Rob, and with Garibaldi's presence, I wouldn't underestimate them."

25

Adonia grasped Shawn's arm as they both looked over the ledge. Over the dizzying drop, she saw in the distance exactly what van Dyckman was building at the bottom of the lower cavern: eight massive, in-ground concrete pools in various stages of completion, each forty feet deep and nearly half the size of a football field. At the bottom of each partially constructed pool was a rigid metal frame, a support structure that could hold an array of hundreds upon hundreds of rods upright.

Senator Pulaski frowned as he peered down, following Victoria Doyle's accusing finger, but he didn't seem to understand. "Swimming pools?"

Adonia felt defeated and appalled. "Wet-storage cooling tanks for spent fuel rods." How could Stanley have done this? "He's going to cover the cavern floor with cooling pools."

As spent fuel rods built up at her own nuclear power plant, Adonia had been forced to build similar concrete reservoirs behind the Granite Bay security fences for stopgap storage. She had no place else to put the fuel rods, no sanctioned holding facility where she was *allowed* to send them. But her pools were much smaller than this. The scale of Stanley's project made her own temporary holding tanks at Granite Bay look like wading pools.

"Sixteen of them, when we're all finished." Van Dyckman sounded proud. "We already have two completed and filled, with six more nearly finished, and excavations for an additional eight. Plus," he pointed directly below them, "that large temporary pool just below. We're relieving the backlog of spent fuel rods as quickly as possible, making all those nuclear power plants safer by the day."

Directly below them, Adonia saw another reservoir, an *above-ground* circular pool full of water. It was constructed with inch-thick plastic panels and crowded with submerged fuel rods arranged in an array, held upright at the bottom by a flimsy support structure. This wasn't a secure, concrete-walled, in-ground storage pool like the others being built; rather, it looked like a giant backyard swimming pool, more than a hundred feet in diameter. She couldn't judge the depth of the water from directly above, but the side of the pool was over twenty feet high; basically, a water tank.

Flush with the top of the round pool, a metal mesh platform ten feet wide encircled the outer perimeter, three feet above the water's surface, which would presumably allow inspectors to walk around the top. The platform was supported by a matrix of crisscrossed struts that provided further support to the pool. The surface of the water lay thirty feet below them as they stood on the ledge.

Van Dyckman's eyes were bright. "Those two concrete pools at the far end of the cavern are already packed with rods at the highest allowable density approved by the NRC. I removed them from the most problematic waste sites around the country, and that eased the greatest pressure. We had to do what we could, as fast as we could. I'm sure you'll all agree." He nodded to himself, though no one else chimed in. "But that wasn't enough. As you see from the above-ground pool below us, we're maintaining our momentum and receiving even more spent fuel rods so we can keep nuclear power plants safe around the country." He gave them an embarrassed smile. "The other permanent cooling pools aren't completed yet."

"*Permanent?*" Garibaldi asked, as if he had caught van Dyckman in a lie. "Well, I thought Hydra Mountain was just a temporary measure until we all agreed on a full-scale acceptable solution."

"Or until unicorns fly out my ass," Pulaski muttered. "People like you would prevent *any* solution from ever being constructed."

"Sorry, that was only a figure of speech," van Dyckman said. "Senator Pulaski understood what we meant when he approved the additional funds for construction down here. A good manager improvises. If this day had gone as planned, we would have shown you all aspects of Valiant Locksmith, one step at a time, leading up to this grand finale, so you could put it all into perspective."

Victoria Doyle looked sickened. "Perspective! All these spent fuel rods in here—*in here!*—and some of them in a flimsy plastic pool! You don't have a clue why this is so dangerous."

Undersecretary Doyle always made van Dyckman particularly defensive, and he rounded on her. "I know what I'm doing, Victoria. Is it any less safe than what Ms. Rojas is storing at Granite Bay right now? Some nutcase crashed a *plane* into one of her holding facilities!"

He huffed. "Before we did anything here in the Mountain, I arranged temporary access to specially cleared inspectors so they could certify every aspect of the construction and operation of these pools." He pointed to the half-built structures scattered across the grotto floor. "When the other in-ground pools are completed, we'll fund a full-time NRC inspector resident in Albuquerque to ensure continued safety of operations. Nothing to worry about, everything by the book. Even Rob Harris is comfortable with the arrangement."

Victoria narrowed her eyes, as if she knew something the rest of them didn't. "I doubt he is."

Adonia was put off by Stanley's arrogance. Yes, she supposed it was better that the spent fuel rods were deep inside Hydra Mountain than scattered around nuclear power plants, where they were far more vulnerable, but she also remembered how van Dyckman's erroneous calculations had nearly caused a complete disaster in packing the Granite Bay cooling array. Could she really trust him to do everything properly with a *nation's* worth of high-level nuclear waste? "Stanley, I have grave reservations about this."

"Well, you shouldn't," he said, dismissing her concerns. "We have more than adequate administrative inspection and oversight."

Another Stanley-ism. She felt exasperated with him. "Administrative oversight doesn't ensure safety. You're the Assistant Secretary, and you're the program manager here, but have you ever actually worked at a functioning nuclear site? Spent time in practical day-to-day operations? Ever?"

"Of course. At Brown I interacted with NRC officials. I also ran experiments just down the road on MIT's test reactor. I was responsible for modeling—"

"Universities are *not* equivalent to commercial nuclear or DOE operations. They're great for learning basics and theory, but they cannot simulate large-scale operations, and they certainly don't cover all conceivable situations in real-world operations. You can't play fast and loose with nuclear waste."

Shawn asked a different question. "What will you do when that above-ground pool is full, and the spent fuel rods keep coming?"

"Then we need a new contractor, one who builds pools faster!" he joked. Nobody laughed. "If the in-ground pools aren't yet completed, we'll just have to put up another temporary one. We have enough materials, and we'll catch up sooner or later. Look, you're missing the point. Every shipment of fuel rods we bring into the Mountain makes the nation safer."

"Safer?" Garibaldi groaned. "That is exactly what I warned everyone about. A hasty, easy solution! You are much too confident in design specifications, Stanley."

Feeling increasingly uneasy, Adonia pointed at the massive concrete casks stacked against the ledge's far wall, each one marked with radiation symbols. "How dangerous do you think it is to move the fuel rods from transportation casks into the pools using that crane or the freight elevators? What happens if one of the casks accidentally drops and cracks open?"

"Impossible. Tests at Sandia dropped the casks from twice that height, and they survived."

She turned to the pool directly below. "We're deep underground and isolated. What if the water supply is disrupted? What if the power goes off, and the water can't be circulated or cooled? The water would get superheated, boil away, and if the rods are exposed to the air—"

"Or what if an asteroid slams into New Mexico?" van Dyckman said with a snort.

"Or what if a small plane crashes into Hydra Mountain?" Shawn muttered. "Sometimes unlikely events happen."

"Those scenarios have been assessed, and the risks were deemed acceptable." He scowled around the group that seemed to have turned against him. "Are there any other questions, or should I give you a complete safety briefing?"

Victoria Doyle looked increasingly agitated, struggling with something she refused to say.

Garibaldi stepped closer to the edge, into the red crosshatched area, and pointed to the above-ground pool directly below. "Your in-ground concrete pools may adhere to NRC guidelines, but your temporary pool only has plastic walls—to hold radioactive spent fuel rods! It's a disaster waiting to happen."

"It's fiber-reinforced plastic, Dr. Garibaldi—over an inch thick, greater than industrial standard. And this FRP uses carbon fiber, giving the sides a tensile strength greater than steel. It exceeds the specs for commercial water tanks."

"Except that everyday water tanks don't store nuclear waste." Garibaldi pointed at numerous water outlets, filters, and temperature gauges embedded in the wall near the bottom of the pool, barely visible through the water. "And those fittings make the pool more susceptible to a leak."

Undersecretary Doyle finally blurted out, aghast, "This is ridiculous! If that pool leaks and floods the lower level, a radiation release down here would have . . . unprecedented consequences."

Van Dyckman's tone was withering and defensive. "In a complete worst-case scenario, it would be a mess, yes, but easily contained. We are deep inside a mountain, after all. Who is going to get hurt, even in a disaster?"

Victoria was sweating. Her face had a look of disgust, even fear. "You still don't understand. Even moderated by all this water, those rods have already raised the background radiation level in this cavern well above ambient. With so much nuclear material present, if that damned tank of yours leaks, it would take only a few stray neutrons to cause a potential disaster."

Adonia frowned. What kind of disaster? Was Doyle misinformed?

Her expertise was in nuclear weapons, not power reactors, but surely the Undersecretary could see that the fuel rods in the pool below weren't packed densely enough to go supercritical.

Garibaldi leaned over the edge as he spoke, as if he felt compelled to stare at the temporary holding pool far below. His voice had a different tenor—unlike his previous biting sarcasms, he now sounded deeply frightened. "Stanley, are you storing standard-sized fuel rods in that temporary pool?"

"Of course."

Garibaldi nodded. "So, those rods are four meters long, but that pool below us is clearly not as deep as NRC standards would dictate."

Van Dyckman grew more agitated. "It's twenty feet deep—the maximum depth we could use and still guarantee the FRP integrity, so that the water wouldn't burst out the sides. There's at least six feet of water above the top of the fuel rods, and that's acceptable to moderate the emitted neutrons." He looked around the committee members, flushed, and then insisted again. "That is fully within the NRC's safety guidelines!"

"Six feet of water is plenty," Senator Pulaski repeated, clearly repeating what van Dyckman had told him.

Garibaldi said in a scornful tone, "Yes, I'm sure you completed the rigorous calculations, Senator."

"It's barely within the guidelines," Adonia said. "That temporary pool has almost zero safety margin, fiber-reinforced plastic or not. And any drop in the water level could result in an enormous increase in radioactivity." She glanced at Doyle, who seemed unaccountably worried. "But probably not the disastrous scenario the Undersecretary is so worried about."

Doyle shook her head. "You don't have a clue. None of you."

Stanley grew increasingly agitated. "This is only for three months, max! The next six concrete pools should be completed soon. The contractors are penalized for every day they go over the schedule, and we're still constructing eight more."

Shawn stood next to Adonia. "Again, what if there's a leak? Or a power failure that would stop the cooling water from circulating.

The fuel rods would heat up and evaporate the water, leaving the rods exposed, which would make the situation worse."

Van Dyckman paced along the wide ledge, increasingly upset. "We covered all these scenarios in simulations. What if a magnitude 7 earthquake strikes at the same time a plague of locusts sweeps across New Mexico? And on a national holiday during a full moon?" His sarcasm was clear. "That's the sort of idiocy that kept Yucca Mountain from opening its doors for the past two decades, and you all know it. The problem is far worse if we *don't* accept this solution. That's why the President assigned me as program manager, because he knew I could get the job done. Who else do you think has the right expertise and background?"

"*Any* DOE site manager, and not you," Victoria said sharply. "Now that I see what you're doing here, it's clear you haven't been fully briefed on the unintended consequences. Any of them." She swallowed hard, letting her voice drop further. "Apparently, no one else has either. The Departments of State, Defense, and Energy should all have coordinated on this from the beginning."

Pacing frenetically, van Dyckman looked as if he had swallowed something sour. "You don't understand. Everyone is trying to micromanage my program, but I'm not going to countermand the President." He looked directly at Shawn. "I have to deal with the practicalities and make sure Valiant Locksmith achieves its goals, for the good of the nation. Senator Pulaski understands this, and that's why he increased our black funding line, and allowed me to circumvent the classified interagency review." He looked intently at Adonia, as if expecting an ally. "Don't you see? We are *up . . . and . . . running!*"

"Unless a forklift accidentally punctures those plastic walls," Garibaldi said. "Or a seam leaks, or the pool is accidentally overfilled— which makes the water pressure exceed the FRP's tensile strength, causing the pool to burst."

Adonia said, "No matter how many thumbscrews you felt in Washington, Stanley, sometimes you just have to put down your foot and say *no*."

Victoria turned to face them all. "I told him when he first read us into his program that there were things going on inside the Mountain he doesn't know about, and he brushed me aside."

"Valiant Locksmith *is* Hydra Mountain!" Van Dyckman sounded exasperated.

"Not by half," she said. "Now that I've seen these pools, this review committee is over. I have grounds to shut down your entire program. You have no idea what danger you've put us all in. Not only us, but possibly the entire Southwest." She glared at him. "I just wish I'd been read into your program at the beginning, and I would have pulled the plug a year and a half ago, before this crazy scheme was ever started. Would've saved everyone time. And money."

26

His tense phone call with the DOE Secretary had yielded no solutions, only confusion and criticisms. Harris had looked to his superiors two thousand miles away in Washington for a bureaucratic safety net, but now it didn't feel much more secure than spiderwebs. He was on his own.

Harris felt blind and hamstrung in his Eagle's Nest office above the operations center. His techs still hadn't been able to give him visuals in the lower level, so he couldn't see Adonia and her companions, but sensors implied they had reached the high bay overlooking the wet-storage pools.

Had Undersecretary Doyle put the pieces together yet? She *had* to understand. But even if she did, and explained it to the others on the team, they still had to get out alive.

He pressed his hands down on the conference table so hard that his knuckles turned white. He chewed four more antacids. He fidgeted, longing to be down there on the ops center floor, discussing solutions with his engineers, meticulously reviewing every report as it came in. He wanted to be in on the brainstorming as his techs tried to think of ways to circumvent the lockdown.

But breathing down their necks wasn't going to help anything. His people were self-motivated, bright, extremely creative, and his frantic impatience would only dampen their efforts. He was the site manager, and he had seen some eager techs bend over backward to agree with his suggestions, just because he was the boss. That wasn't what Harris needed. No, he needed their imagination, their skills, and their *solutions,* not butt-kissing.

Stuck in his office, he waited . . . and waited. The original lockdown would have been long over, but the team had forced a reset. Now more than four hours remained for the system to finish rebooting. Worse, the aggressive DoD countermeasures were active, ready to protect Velvet Hammer.

Data from the facility sensors splashed on the oversized monitor outside his office. Halothane levels continued to build up in the inclined tunnel. Thanks to the tracer smoke, the team members would see the hazard approaching, and he hoped they would get out of the way in time.

He placed high confidence in Adonia Rojas, and he had done the right thing putting her in charge. Harris had mentored the bright young woman at Oakridge, and he knew she was a solid worker, a cool-headed thinker. Without a second thought he had given her the responsibility when Drexler called him away to respond to the small-plane incident.

He looked at the numbers on the screen, the rising levels of halothane in the air. Very shortly, the automated sensors in the bay would detect the gas and trigger yet another set of countermeasures. The catwalks and freight elevators would reset and strand the team members high on the ledge, with no place to go.

27

Adonia took a step back from the sheer drop-off, baffled by Victoria's sudden anger. The Undersecretary retreated back up the tunnel, her fists clenched so tight her arms shook.

Alarmed, Adonia called after her, "Wait—it may not be safe to go back up there."

Victoria spoke over her shoulder. "You don't have a clue how dangerous it is *down here*. I'll take my chances."

With a snort, van Dyckman spoke loudly enough that she could hear him. "I expected a little more professional behavior from someone of her rank."

"What does she mean that you don't know about everything inside the Mountain?" Shawn asked him.

"I thought you were the national program manager, Stanley," Garibaldi said. "Aren't you the big cheese here?"

Van Dyckman dismissed the comment. "Victoria's a weapons person, and some people are still fighting the Cold War. She resents the fact that her program is winding down, but that's ancient history."

Adonia looked across the huge underground grotto, her attention drawn to the distant vault doors embedded in the far wall, below the main floor level. Van Dyckman admitted he had no idea what was stored there. Some old program, he had said. . . .

Adonia narrowed her eyes, trying to make out details a quarter mile away. *The vaults!* Did the Undersecretary know about some other program that was being kept secret from van Dyckman? Even the Valiant Locksmith program manager might have been kept in the dark about another SAP that was outside of his clearance. Often hugely important programs were classified from each other, and if the other SAP was also unacknowledged, van Dyckman wouldn't even know another program existed, much less what it was about.

Only Rob Harris, as site manager, would know everything that took place inside the Mountain, but he would have been strait-jacketed by bureaucratic secrecy and tangled restrictions. Adonia knew Regulation Rob would never budge from the rules, refusing to state the obvious because of immutable security prohibitions.

With growing hesitation, Adonia looked at Undersecretary Doyle as she marched up the tunnel, then she glanced at Garibaldi, thinking again how odd those two were as choices to be part of this inspection team. But Harris had personally selected everyone for a specific reason.

Senator Pulaski was the quintessential politician, and van Dyckman had blinders on. Garibaldi was a skeptic, though he had a detailed engineering background and he retained his security clearance. He was also a whistle-blower. Undersecretary Doyle worked for the DOE, but on the nuclear weapons side, so she should have nothing to do with nuclear power operations.

Unless Doyle knew something the others didn't? Was that why she had been invited? Did Rob Harris want the rest of them to see something?

Trying to understand the scattered pieces, Adonia looked at the liquid-cooled transportation casks next to the large metal sphere, and the pipes strung along the walls. Sitting on the lower floor, the thick, plastic-walled pool held rows and rows of submerged spent fuel rods held upright by metal cradles, the tops of the rods covered by only six feet of water. As she pondered, Adonia caught a sudden whiff of the sickly sweet smell, and turned to see the wisps of yellow gas creeping down toward them.

Victoria had paused on her way to the tunnel, looking at the faint curls of tracer smoke at her feet. "It's . . . still coming. How much of that gas is there?"

"Won't it ever stop?" van Dyckman groaned. "Shouldn't it have dissipated by now?"

Adonia did mental calculations, guessing that at a quarter mile long and two hundred feet high, the grotto had a volume of around 160 million cubic feet. The halothane reservoirs couldn't possibly hold that much, but since the knockout gas was heavier than air, it didn't need to fill the entire chamber, only to six feet or so above the sprawling floor, which would incapacitate any intruders. A tank the size of that giant metal sphere on the ledge filled with liquid halothane could hold enough gas to expand into an enormous volume, and these were old military defensive systems. . . .

Eventually, gas from the guard portal jets would flow down the tunnel and spill over the ledge onto the grotto floor fifty feet below like a vaporous waterfall. The flowing halothane would slowly diffuse, but it would still be toxic—and it kept rolling down toward them. If it continued flowing forward, the gas would overwhelm them if they stayed on the ledge.

Victoria began to cough. She took a few uncertain steps, then stopped and bent over. Turning, she covered her face and staggered back toward the group on the ledge, reconsidering her retreat.

Adonia grabbed the Undersecretary by the arm and pulled her away from the flowing gas. They didn't have much room to maneuver with the sheer drop-off.

Shawn searched for a ladder or a walkway down, then considered the freight elevators. Instead, he looked up toward the ceiling. "We need to head up, not down, get above the gas. Quick, everyone—up on the catwalk. Climb as high as you can!"

Senator Pulaski frowned at the precarious metal latticework that extended out above the high bay. "On that rickety thing?"

Garibaldi agreed. "Colonel Whalen's right. Halothane is heavier than air, so we have to climb above it. The gas will pour over the ledge to the lower floor, but we'll be safe up there."

Adonia pulled Victoria toward the aluminum stairs leading up to the catwalk. The Undersecretary still coughed, wiping at her eyes. Van Dyckman hurried to join them, with Garibaldi following. Shawn took the hesitant Senator's arm, urging him to move. "Come on, sir. We can't stay here—up the stairs! We've got to get to those catwalks."

Pulaski shrugged him off. "I heard you. I'm going."

Just when Adonia and Victoria reached the base of the stairs, a new whistling siren wailed throughout the cavern, echoing off the walls. The din was deafening, as though all the military's stockpiled old sirens had gone off at once.

"Now what?" the Senator cried. "I didn't trigger anything!"

A waist-high metal gate at the base of the catwalk stairs swung shut like a guillotine blade. Adonia yanked the Undersecretary away as the gate slammed, cutting them off from the metal steps.

With a sudden mechanical jerk, the catwalk rotated up away from the access stairs with a creaking, clanking sound that was loud even above the alarms.

"Sensors must have detected the halothane," Shawn said, looking at the tendrils of gas rolling toward them. "The release of the gas would signal the other countermeasures and isolate anyone down in the grotto."

"This is insane!" Garibaldi exclaimed.

Simultaneously, the two freight elevators on either side of the ledge whirred into motion and dropped to the lower floor in their safe position, further isolating the team members above the high bay. The opposite catwalk rotated up into the arched ceiling as well and locked in place, just missing the extended metal boom of the massive crane, completely inaccessible.

"We're trapped!" van Dyckman said.

The metal staircase that had connected with the catwalk still extended up, but stopped at a blind end, disconnected. The last step hung over the precipitous drop down to the grotto floor.

Adonia felt as if someone had just kicked the wind out of her. The alarm siren continued to wail.

As the yellow tracer smoke crawled closer, the Senator showed panic, waiting for someone to save him. Van Dyckman moaned in sick dismay. "The catwalks were our only way to get above the gas!"

Victoria Doyle had managed to get her coughing under control, and glared at him. "Another thing you didn't count on, Stanley? How do we get out of here?"

"On the metal stairs, everybody," Adonia said, helping Victoria back to her feet. It was the only option she could see. "Climb while we can."

"But they don't go anywhere!" Garibaldi said. "They just dangle out in open air."

"We might still get high enough to be safe." She swung one leg over the metal half gate and climbed over. Wasting no time, she stepped onto the now-disengaged aluminum ladder, which wobbled, unstable without the connecting catwalk to hold it in place. Once she balanced on the metal stairs, she grabbed the railing and helped Victoria climb over to join her. The others covered their faces with their hands, hoping to block the halothane as they swung themselves over the gate.

Victoria ascended the steps, holding the metal rails to keep her balance as Adonia helped van Dyckman get to the stairs. But as Victoria climbed higher, the unstable staircase creaked from the weight. If she went much higher, the unsupported metal structure would bend.

The remaining steps telescoped up at an angle, wavering free. Adonia realized that was why the gates had swung shut, to prevent anyone from climbing the stairs without the supporting catwalk in place.

While the Undersecretary held on to the swaying staircase, Adonia shouted over the alarm noise, "Wait! It's not stable enough to hold us."

Victoria stopped where she was, and the wobbly stairs stopped swaying, but when she gingerly tried to climb one step higher, the metal frame creaked and swung to the left, then back in a pendulum-like motion. She looked down at the others, her face ashen. "This is as high as I can go. I don't think more than a few of us will be able to get up here. It won't hold our weight."

Adonia knew it would never support all six of them. On the far side of the ledge, the second staircase also extended to nowhere. The disconnected steps might support two people high enough above the encroaching gas, but a third person would certainly overstress the metal.

The air currents in the grotto would stir the gas, waft some of it up, maybe enough to incapacitate them high on the rickety steps. And they would fall to their deaths. . . .

Adonia was already dizzy, and the relentless sirens disoriented her even more. "Dead end." Breathing hard, she caught more of the halothane scent, growing stronger. Her world focused into nothing but survival. She searched for another way to climb higher, but the catwalks were now far out of reach.

Shawn called to her from below. "We have to go down instead—get out on the cavern floor, keep far enough ahead of the gas until it's diluted."

Looking down from her perch on the detached aluminum steps, Adonia saw the piles of construction material, mounds of cement bags, even the crane itself. Once out in the lower cavern, they could reach the far end and climb above the gas.

"One small problem, Colonel Whalen," Garibaldi said. "We have no way to get down there."

Close to the plastic safety chain, Adonia peered over the drop-off to see the stone floor impossibly far below.

The original emergency stairs that led from the ledge to the grotto floor had been disengaged and pushed to the other side of the construction material to make room for the temporary pool. She looked up and saw that the crane boom was out of reach high overhead, extending from the huge Manitowoc cab anchored in the middle of the cavern.

Both freight elevators were now locked and secured down on the floor. "Stanley!" Adonia said. "Where are the controls to the freight elevator?"

Van Dyckman lifted a shaky arm and pointed back toward the tunnel, where the ominous wave of gas continued to boil out. "The override is up in the guard portal."

"No good," Shawn said.

Adonia looked down, saw the surface of the cooling pool only thirty feet below, the entire structure encircled by the metal mesh observation platform. And it was clear what they had to do.

"Good news," she said, turning to face them as the alarms continued to clamor. "We have two choices. Stay here on the ledge and hope we don't die from the halothane." She calmed herself, then said the unthinkable alternative. "Or we jump into the pool of radioactive fuel rods and climb down to the floor."

28

Even with the blaring alarms and the encroaching yellow gas, Adonia knew the others would balk at the jump—and with good reason. But it was the only way out she could see. She hoped she and Shawn wouldn't have to throw them over the ledge. If the halothane incapacitated them on the ledge, they would surely die, lying in the lethal concentration for hours before a rescue team could make their way inside.

Before she could defend her crazy suggestion, Garibaldi raised his voice over their growing alarm. "She's right! This much halothane will kill us if we stay here. We're going to be incapacitated within minutes, so we have to move now."

Shawn added, "Any rescue team is still hours away. Jumping in the pool is less hazardous than staying here. Once we're in the water we can swim to the side and climb down to the floor. We've got to jump."

"Are you insane?" Senator Pulaski stumbled backward in his haste to get away from the edge. "The water and the rods—they're radioactive!"

Adonia raised her voice over the sirens. "Water moderates the radiation, Senator. You'll be all right for a short period of time. If you jump in and swim across quickly, your exposure will be minimal. Scuba divers clean out fuel rod storage pools at Granite Bay all the time. Just stay clear of the fuel rods when you're in the water."

"Sorry to cut off any further debate, but we'd better jump before we get too weak," Shawn said. The yellow mist was thickening around them. "The halothane will hit us fast."

Van Dyckman peered over the drop-off, queasy. "But that's . . . that's like jumping off a three-story building."

Adonia said, "I know it looks far, but it's the height of a high-dive board. *I've* done it. You'll survive if you jump, but the halothane will kill you if you stay here."

"I *can't* jump down there," Pulaski insisted. "And I can't swim across the pool—"

"Yet you will have to, Senator," Garibaldi said.

"Listen up!" Shawn stood by Adonia, using a voice he must have learned when he commanded troops in the Air Force. "Since I'm already feeling the effects of the halothane, I know you can feel them, too." He went to the edge and looked decidedly unsteady. "I won't kid you, that jump isn't going to be easy, but the longer you wait, the more the gas will affect you, and the more you decrease your chances of surviving."

Pulaski stood frozen. "But if we stay here, what's the worst that could happen? We'll fall asleep and lie unconscious until we're rescued."

"You'll never wake up," Victoria said, climbing down from the rickety metal stairs and back over the lowered gate. "So you're better off jumping." She looked grim. "That fall is probably the least dangerous thing Stanley has left for us in this madhouse."

Van Dyckman looked wobbly, unable to make a decision. Shawn approached the yellow chain, and she could tell he was preparing to jump, to lead by example. He waved them over. "Once we're in the pool, we'll boost someone onto the platform, and they can help everyone out. We can climb down that metal side framework to the floor." He stretched his arms, flexed his torso from side to side. "I'll jump first. Piece of cake. Easier than rock climbing."

Adonia interrupted and put a hand on his chest. "No, I'm the better swimmer, Shawn. I'll go first, show everybody how it's done. You stay up here and make sure everybody takes the plunge. No stragglers." She turned to van Dyckman. "Stanley—you jump right after me."

"It's so high! I don't know if I can do it."

"Yes, you can. Just watch what I do." Adonia unfastened the yellow chain links and stepped up to the edge.

Behind her, Garibaldi sucked in loud, deep breaths, as if to gather his courage. When he broke out coughing, the older scientist turned to look at the yellow gas flowing out of the tunnel. "Sorry to sound impatient, but if we don't go soon, we're not going to make it."

Pulaski backed away. "I'll take my chances up here rather than jump into that radioactive cesspool."

Shawn grabbed the Senator's arm. "I will not let you stay here and die. We jump in and cross the pool."

Pulaski struggled to yank away from Shawn's grip. "I can't swim across the pool! I *can't* do this. You can't make me jump. The . . . the radiation!"

Garibaldi joined Shawn and, with apparent glee, grabbed the Senator's other arm. "Look: the rods are all clustered in the middle of the pool, away from the sides. Just aim for the open area near the edge and you'll miss them."

Pulaski dug his feet against the floor, but his heels slipped on the concrete. "The pool is full of them!"

"Hurry, Adonia," Shawn called over the alarms. "Show them, and you can help once they get in the water. I'll make sure the Senator goes." He resolutely grasped Pulaski's arm. "Don't worry, sir. I've taken water survival courses at the Academy. We had to jump with a buddy off the thirty-foot diving board at the Cadet Fieldhouse, so I know how to jump with another person. It'll be as easy as skydiving."

Pulaski did not seem reassured.

Adonia flexed her arms, drew in a deep breath. The fuel rods shimmered in the water thirty feet below. The radioactive cylinders were arranged upright in a matrix in the center of the pool with only ten feet of open water along the sides. The pool was already filled to capacity, and van Dyckman intended to build more temporary pools, just to accommodate all the waste rods he was shipping into Hydra Mountain. Very soon, this slapdash solution would be as bad as the problem he was trying to fix.

But she focused on the problem at hand. Looking down, ready for the plunge, Adonia remembered the exhilarating times when she had used the high dive. "When you jump, be sure to leap forward, but not too much. You'll only have to clear a few feet on the fall to miss the side of the pool. As soon as you're in the air, keep your feet down, your head up. Close your eyes and cover your face with your hands before you hit. And aim for the open space away from the rods. There should be plenty of room." *Provided they could fall straight.*

Victoria Doyle came close, swallowing hard. "I'll be right behind you."

Garibaldi coughed loudly. "That sweet smell's getting stronger."

Van Dyckman stepped to the edge, squirming. "What if we miss the water?"

"Then you'll be a stain on the floor," Victoria said. "Another mess for someone else to clean up."

"What she means is, don't miss," Shawn said.

Adonia put her feet on the edge, telling herself that this really wasn't a big deal. She had made many dives from such a height in her swimming competitions, but she had to do this right—not for herself, but to show the others.

No sense in waiting. She took a deep breath, crouched, and pushed out over the edge.

She leaped in an arc and extended her arms to keep her balance. She waved them in small circles to keep herself upright; holding her head straight and level, she watched for the water by just looking down with her eyes. As she plummeted toward the pool's surface, she pointed her toes and threw her hands up to her face, covering her nose and eyes against the impact.

She tried not to hold her breath when she hit, but the plunge into the pool still jarred her. With the enormous slap of water pressure against her chest, she exhaled a burst of air. It wasn't like diving into a competition pool at all, but rather like jumping into a hot spring. The water was extremely warm from the fuel rods.

She stroked for the surface. Underwater, she could hear a low hum of water-recirculating pumps, exchanging the heated water with cold, filling the pool and maintaining a constant flow pattern.

Adonia opened her eyes and saw bubbles rising around her. She spotted the rounded tops of the fuel rods like nightmarish metal tree trunks to her left, only a few feet from where she'd entered the water. Seeing how close she had come to striking the tops of the rods, she realized there wasn't a lot of safety margin.

With a few short, strong scissor kicks, she burst to the surface. Instinctively, she started treading water. The temperature was alarmingly warm and unexpected, like a hot bath. Even though she convinced herself—intellectually—that the radiation would be tolerable, the heat prompted irrational fears. She was concerned about how the already-panicked Senator would react once he hit the water.

If he jumped at all.

She waved urgently up at the group on the high ledge above. They seemed very far away. Victoria Doyle looked surreal, framed against a backdrop of the crane's metal lattice boom, with Stanley and Garibaldi next to her. "Come on!" she yelled. "Not much time!"

Blessedly, the alarms suddenly stopped, plunging the cavern into relative silence. But that didn't stop the urgency as yellow-tinged halothane started to spill over the ledge; it flowed down the wall, keeping away from the pool—for now.

Crossing her hands over her chest, Victoria crouched and leaped out, as if she had something to prove in front of van Dyckman. Once airborne, she threw out her arms and tried to keep vertical.

Adonia swam backward as hard as she could to get out of the way. "Cover your face!"

Victoria's feet hit the surface, and her petite body disappeared beneath the water with a great splash. Adonia stroked to the churning ripples to help the other woman, and within seconds the Undersecretary's head appeared, her short hair plastered to her face. She sputtered as Adonia reached her. "I'm okay." She blinked water from her eyes. "The water is . . . really warm."

"Can you make it to the edge?" Adonia nudged her toward the plastic wall, and got herself into position again and waited for the next jumper. "Head straight to the side of the pool and keep away from the rods. Six feet of water isn't much clearance above them." Each upright fuel rod was secured in a holding cradle, but unlike the fixtures in Granite Bay's permanent pools, these looked as if they could be dislodged.

Victoria stroked toward the pool's curved plastic wall, and Adonia waved back up at the ledge. "Stanley! You're next—jump!"

Swinging his arms back and forth, van Dyckman leaped out, yelling. As he fell, he started kicking his legs and waving his arms, flailing in the air. He began to tumble, rotating forward. If he hit the water headfirst . . .

"Bend backwards!"

Before van Dyckman could right himself, he struck the surface with his body bent, his knees striking only seconds before his chest and face. He hit the water with a loud smack, and spray erupted in an oval geyser as he disappeared beneath the surface.

Adonia swam toward him, hoping he hadn't broken any bones. She had to get him out of the way so the others could jump. When she reached van Dyckman, he was trying to claw his way back to the surface. She caught him, pulled him along. "Stanley, are you all right?" At least he hadn't been knocked unconscious.

Water ran from his nose as he coughed. His voice croaked when he answered. "As long as I don't have to jump again." He saw Victoria hanging on the edge of the walkway, three feet above the surface of the water. "If she can make it, so can I."

"You're done for today." She nudged him toward the side. "Keep swimming and stay next to the side—away from the rods." He started off without answering, and she shouted up at the ledge. "We're ready!"

Thin curtains of the yellow-marked gas continued to flow, increasing in volume like a waterfall of smoke over the ledge. It drifted down the wall, barely missing the pool and spilling down to the lower level.

Instead of Garibaldi taking the next position, Shawn came up, wrestling the reluctant Senator forward. Garibaldi helped hold him, pushing the big man ahead, but he was struggling. Shawn and Garibaldi seemed to have made their plans together. Shawn turned his back to the edge, grabbed Pulaski's shirt with both hands, and jumped backward over the brink, pulling the Senator with him. As they plummeted together, Shawn wrapped the larger man in a bear hug, preventing him from flailing.

Up on the ledge, Garibaldi reeled, coughing from the halothane. The yellow vapors swirled around his legs, stirred up in the air. Even as the other two men were falling, Garibaldi staggered forward and followed them over the edge without waiting for them to get clear.

Adonia was already swimming toward the impact point to help as Shawn and the Senator smashed into the water. Garibaldi plunged into the pool less than a second later, only a few feet away. An enormous spray of hot water gushed into the air, accompanied by a wave that sloshed over the side of the pool.

Before Adonia could dive underwater to retrieve the Senator, someone behind her started coughing, retching, and splashing. Already half-stunned from hitting the pool, van Dyckman had not yet made it to the plastic wall, and the wave had caught him full in the face. He groped wildly, thrashing for the access walkway that ran along the pool's edge.

With Shawn there to help Pulaski, Adonia swam back for van Dyckman. Clinging with an outstretched arm to the walkway, Victoria did not seem to know what she should do to offer assistance.

The Senator's head had breached the surface, and he thrashed about, gasping for breath, yelling in panic. Shawn reached him and employed all the correct lifeguard procedures, keeping Pulaski's head above water and moving him to the side.

Garibaldi surfaced, spluttering, steadying himself.

Adonia grabbed van Dyckman's shoulder, flipped him around, and placed a hand behind his neck to keep his head above water. Kicking hard, she pulled him to the metal mesh platform where Victoria waited. Van Dyckman blinked at her with bleary eyes, obviously still smarting from his initial clumsy impact.

Reaching the wall, Adonia shook her former boss, making sure he was conscious so he wouldn't slip back under the water. She boosted him partially up until he was able to grab the edge of the metal platform. "Stanley, hold on. We'll get both of you up there in a minute." She left him with Victoria. "Watch him, could you?"

"Right." The Undersecretary made no move to help van Dyckman, but he clung to the platform himself.

Garibaldi started swimming toward them, but Shawn kept having real difficulties with the Senator. Pulaski had become more frantic and violent after the fall, and the unnaturally hot water spooked him further. He twisted back and forth, trying to pull away from Shawn, lashing out at his would-be rescuer. "You're drowning me! Get away!"

Shawn went under in his attempts to dodge the Senator's frantic blows. Adonia stroked over to help, but Pulaski was beyond reason.

"I can't swim—I told you!" He gulped a mouthful of the heated water, which only increased his spiral of panic. "I can't swim!"

Shawn tried to grapple with him, but the big man fought like a madman. He arched his back and flailed away from the side. Pulaski went under, and then clawed his way back up again. As he sank once more, he kicked, found some purchase underneath, and pushed off of something, but the water was too deep. He struggled to rise to the surface again.

Adonia swam underwater as she tried to reach him in time. With her eyes open, she saw that he had kicked one of the upright spent fuel rods, and he was now trying to stand on it. Despite the heated water, she felt a cold knife of dread. She swam faster.

Pulaski squirmed in panicked convulsions and struck out at Shawn, who tried to wrestle him under control. "Help!" When the Senator yelled, he gulped another mouthful of water.

As a championship swimmer, Adonia had more experience in lifeguarding than Shawn did. Drowning victims often sabotaged their own rescues by fighting back, and sometimes the only solution was to slug them hard and knock them out cold.

Shawn was exhausted from wrestling with the man, and the frantic struggles were putting him at risk, too.

Pulaski went under, kicked, and his long legs again pushed against one of the upright fuel rods set in a support cradle. In the standard configuration of a permanent cooling pool, the rods would be immobile, locked in place—but Stanley's temporary cradle wasn't designed to have a two-hundred-and-fifty-pound man kick off against them.

As Shawn grappled with him, somehow Pulaski twisted in the water and kicked him hard in the face with his heel. Shawn jerked back in pain as he was hit in the eye.

Adonia surfaced, racing toward them. She knew this was the most dangerous time of the whole rescue. The deadly AVIR syndrome—aquatic victim instead of rescuer—had killed hundreds of would-be helpers. "Back off, Shawn. I'll handle it."

Treading water and looking blearily through one eye, Shawn reluctantly let her take over. Pulaski kept rolling around in the water, gasping for breath, and Adonia circled behind him where he couldn't see her. She had to let him exhaust himself so he wouldn't pull her down.

She needed life-saving equipment, but this was not a recreational pool. It was a plastic-walled tank for storing spent fuel rods. There would be no buoy, life ring, or other rescue device on the platform that encircled the pool.

Pulaski seemed to stabilize himself, gaining purchase, upright in the water with his head tilted back. She knew his foot was balanced on the fuel rod six feet down, probably pushing on it with his tip-toes or the balls of his feet. Although he was terrified about the radioactivity, his instinctive dread about drowning superseded that. He gaped at the ceiling, the retracted catwalks, and the boom of the giant crane, all of which were far out of reach.

Adonia made her move, lunging in to grab him around the neck and wrap her arm under his chin. She tightened her grip and kept her body far from his as she began stroking with her free arm and kicking for the side of the pool.

With both hands, Pulaski clawed at her forearm. "Stop—I'm . . . drowning!" He writhed in the water and slipped down in her grip. She fought to pull him back up, but he bit her arm.

She cried out as shards of pain sliced along her forearm. She yanked her arm back, releasing him. His teeth had broken her skin, and blood oozed up.

As soon as she let him go, the Senator sank again, kicking down, as if trying to stand on the fuel rods just out of reach underwater. His head went under, and a gush of air bubbles flooded to the surface.

Adonia ignored the pain in her arm as she dove after him. Shawn swam toward her to help, squeezing his swollen eye shut.

She opened her eyes beneath the surface to find the sinking Senator, and to her horror saw that several of the fuel rods were tilted, bumped off-kilter like dominoes about to fall. Two of the rods closest to the side had rotated out of their cradles and slowly toppled underwater against the thick, fiber-reinforced plastic wall.

As he sank, the bottom of Pulaski's pant leg had caught on the top of one of the heavy rods. Struggling, he dislodged that rod as well. The heavy metal-clad cylinder began to fall, pulling him down in a gradual collapse, deeper and deeper. In the rippling pool, he looked like a marionette at the end of a stick.

Adonia swam down, trying to reach him as the heavy rod dragged him toward the bottom. The Senator's struggles weakened as he sank, trapped. A last gush of air bubbles spewed from his mouth. He twitched and jerked convulsively.

Adonia swam harder, knowing that if she could somehow disentangle him, then lift him to the surface, she would still have to pull him out of the pool and perform CPR and mouth-to-mouth resuscitation. She might be able to save him—

A hand grabbed her shoulder and yanked her up. She twisted wildly to see who was trying to stop her. She was still far from the fallen rod, and now the Senator's motionless body was lodged against the side of the pool at an angle, deep under water.

Shawn was dragging her back up. He shook his head and mouthed *No!*, pointing with his free hand to the surface.

She tried jerking away, but Shawn gripped her with both hands and hauled them both upward with powerful kicks. She resisted, still desperate to get to the Senator, to rescue him before it was too late, but the toppled fuel rod had pinned him down to the bottom of the twenty-foot pool.

Pulaski no longer moved, no longer showed any sign of life. She knew it was already too late.

29

Splashing and gasping, Adonia and Shawn broke the surface of the hot water. She pulled in deep breaths of air and felt the sharp sting of pain from where Pulaski had bit her arm, but the sick sadness inside ran deeper. The two of them swam in grim, exhausted silence to the side wall where Stanley, Victoria, and Garibaldi waited, still clinging to the mesh of the metal walkway. Adonia could not shake the image of the Senator pinned underwater, trapped by the fallen fuel rods he himself had dislodged. "He's gone," she said.

Victoria looked stunned and disgusted at what she had seen. "Why didn't he tell us he couldn't swim? How much more could he screw things up?" She did not sound sympathetic.

Holding the wall, van Dyckman stared in disbelief. "And . . . and he dislodged part of the array! Those rods were widely separated."

"Obviously not widely enough." Garibaldi's face was gray. "We can mourn the Senator later, but it would be a very good idea for us to get out of this pool. Now that some of the rods have toppled out of their support structure, possibly with damaged zirconium alloy cladding, I have no idea how close to critical they are."

Victoria struggled to get on the metal grid platform that encircled the pool, but it was too high above the water for her to pull herself out. Moving behind her, Shawn grasped her waist and helped boost her up. The older woman hauled herself onto the top, then turned to help the others. One by one they scrambled up onto the platform, dripping and gasping, relieved to be out of the unnaturally hot water.

The last one still in the pool, Shawn looked grim and hardened, ready to do what was necessary. "I can swim down there and try to push the rods back upright by brute force." He squinted up at Adonia, favoring his injured eye. "Put them back in their support structure."

She reacted with alarm. "No! If you touched the rods with your bare hands, you'd be giving yourself a death sentence. You'd need gloves, protective clothing. And you'd still get a near-lethal dose." Though she was still sickened from being unable to rescue Pulaski, she realized that from his direct exposure to the rods during his struggles, he had probably received a deadly exposure even if he did get out of the water. The Senator would have perished in weeks anyway, a long, slow, painful decline from radiation poisoning. "He's already dead. We're not."

"Unless we stay here," Garibaldi said. Crawling to the edge, he stuck his hand over the side, reaching down for Shawn, who grasped his arm. He pulled him up onto the platform with the others.

From above, wispy tendrils of yellow-marked gas continued pouring over the high ledge, but Victoria looked across to the far end of the cavern, seemingly more concerned about some other danger. "We have to get in touch with Harris. Forget the alarms and the lockdown. He needs to send a nuclear response team in here as soon as possible. We have to remove these rods from the grotto and dismantle this pool."

"Damn right he does," Garibaldi said, dripping as he stood on the metal grid platform above the pool. "But if he *could* get here, then all our problems would have been solved from the beginning."

Van Dyckman looked at Adonia with bloodshot eyes, defeated. "So what now?"

Adonia was surprised that he would even ask such a question. "We find a way to stay safe until the lockdown is over. No more disasters."

Van Dyckman shook his head. "The Senator's dead. Shouldn't we stay here until we're rescued?"

Sitting on the metal grid platform with her knees drawn up to her chest, Adonia pointed up at the ledge above and the turbulent, falling gas. "Can't stay here, Stanley. The gas is still coming, and the system was designed to flood the entire grotto floor. We have to keep moving."

Even here, Adonia could smell the sickly sweet halothane and felt an even heavier dread in her heart. The edge of the pool was several feet from where the smoky waterfall flowed over the ledge, but wisps of the knockout gas tumbled down onto the surface of the water and started to spread out over the pool.

"We'll have to keep above it, or we'll succumb," Shawn said.

"But we're high enough here, and if the water is moderating the fuel rods, we're reasonably protected from the radiation." Van Dyckman wanted just to huddle in place and not move.

"Some of the fallen rods are touching," Garibaldi explained. "No telling how much radiation we've already received. We should get as far away as possible."

Adonia said, "The gas is building up, so we've got to find some way to stay above it while we wait out the lockdown."

Shawn stared at the huge crane in the middle of the cavern. Its boom extended far above the temporary pool and reached nearly to the rock ceiling. "We could get to the crane, lower the trestle, and lift ourselves up to the catwalk."

"Does anyone have experience operating a large crane?" Garibaldi said. "We know rocket science and nuclear physics, but this is heavy machinery."

A pall of silence dropped over the group. Adonia had depended on numerous technical experts to run operations at Granite Bay, from radiation workers to health and safety professionals, and she'd always made an effort to understand the basics of their jobs. But running the large Manitowoc crane? She had taken the blue-collar construction jobs for granted, not thinking about the skills of crane operators who were just as important to the success of her nuclear site. She doubted anyone in the review team had that basic expertise.

She turned hopefully to Shawn, but he shook his head. "I can figure out the controls of any kind of aircraft, but running a big crane is out of my wheelhouse. One mistake, and I could send the boom crashing into a catwalk, and then who knows what debris would tumble into the pools."

"We've had enough disasters for one day," Victoria said.

Garibaldi stood on the narrow platform that ringed the pool. "Let's run through the options, then, shall we? We have to get far from this pool, but we can't stay on the cavern floor for long, because the gas is building up. Even though we can't operate the crane, we *can* climb up the boom, hand over hand, and get ourselves high above the floor, and wait out the lockdown."

Adonia peered up to the cavern ceiling high overhead where the air ducts converged. "Worst case, if the gas doesn't stop rising, we could always climb through those air shafts, where the catwalks intersect. They must vent the crane's diesel fumes outside."

Victoria said slowly, "That would be one way out of Hydra Mountain, but it seems awfully risky."

Van Dyckman pointed well past the crane to the far wall of the grotto. "Even at a walk, we can still move faster than the gas, but the cavern floor is a dead end. What about those vaults? Harris kept saying how safe Mrs. Garcia is in her chamber in the upper level. Why can't we hide out in one of those? They're old relics."

Adonia looked to the row of large metal doors embedded in the distant granite wall. "We could shelter in place, like we should have done in the guard portal."

As a pilot, Shawn had the best eyesight of all of them. "They do look like the sealed storage vaults in the upper level. Dr. van Dyckman's right. Typical vaults are airtight and have their own environmental controls with constantly monitored conditions."

Adonia nodded. "It would be a lot safer than climbing up the crane's boom. But how would we even get inside the vault?"

Van Dyckman had a smug smile on his face. "With my override code. I control the Mountain, remember. I can use it one time. We'll hide out until the danger's passed."

Looking like a bedraggled cat, Victoria gaped at the group in disbelief. "You're all insane! We need to move higher, get above the gas, not lock ourselves in some chamber. You don't even know what's in there."

"Hiding there is a hell of a lot easier than climbing up an airshaft," van Dyckman said. "Even if it means being confined in a chamber with you."

Catching a whiff of the sweet-smelling gas wafting over the pool, Adonia made up her mind. "If Stanley's override code can get us inside there, we'll hole up."

From the narrow platform, Shawn looked down to the concrete floor more than twenty feet below. "There's a set of portable stairs over by that pile of construction material. I'll climb down and push the stairs here so everyone can get down."

But the curling strands of gas were pooling higher on the cavern floor, and Adonia knew they wouldn't have much time to cross the quarter mile to the far wall. "That'll take too long, Shawn. We can shimmy down these metal struts and get moving. Go ahead, lead the way." Though she was still sickened by the Senator's death, she realized the big man would not have been able to make the climb, which would have forced them into another ordeal to save him. "Once we reach the floor, we'll have to run to stay ahead of the halothane."

Shawn walked gingerly along the narrow metal mesh to where one of the metal cross pipes intersected with the base of the platform. Swinging his legs over the side, he found a footing and lowered himself. Besides being in the best physical shape of anyone in the group, Shawn had done enough rock climbing that he could show them the way.

Holding the metal edge, he lowered his body and extended his leg until he found a foothold on a crossbar. Before he dropped out of sight, he looked up at the rest of them. "Everyone, get on your butts so we can do this quickly. Slide over. There are plenty of footholds."

He clambered down the metal scaffolding and quickly reached the floor, where he looked in dismay at the yellow smoke that had begun to swirl around his feet. "Hurry up. The gas is still faint, but it's building. We've got to move."

Once they all climbed down the side of the pool to the floor, the five surviving team members appeared shaken. Sodden, Adonia breathed hard, exhausted from swimming and struggling in the water. But she couldn't rest, not now.

"When will the lockdown be over?" van Dyckman asked. He sounded lost. "How much more time do we have to wait?"

"Whenever the system is finished rebooting," Adonia said, trying to keep the exasperation out of her voice. "Probably several more hours. We have to wait it out."

"At least Pulaski's done causing us problems," Victoria grumbled. Still shaken by the Senator's death, Adonia was shocked by her glib comment.

Shawn was more businesslike as he got them moving. "We'd know for sure if we had some way to contact Rob Harris. Maybe there's another intercom down in the lower level."

"Or even a working hardline phone," Garibaldi said.

"No landlines," Victoria said. "Only intercoms—they were scared telephone lines might mistakenly be connected to the outside, and then they could be tapped. This was built in the fifties, remember?"

Adonia rallied the people to move. The expansive floor of the cavern seemed to go on forever. "Let's make our way to those vaults. Come on, the smell is getting stronger."

Holding her breath against the drifting tendrils of gas, Victoria paused next to a pile of leftover construction material. She rubbed a thick slab of black carbon fiber reinforced plastic between her fingers. When she glanced up, Adonia saw that the Undersecretary seemed more frightened than at any other point since the first lockdown. "Are you all right, ma'am?"

Without a word, the Undersecretary straightened primly and hurried to join the rest of the group. Because of her petite size, Victoria would probably be the first one affected by the gas. "None of us is all right, Ms. Rojas. And it's still a mistake to go to those vaults."

Staying ahead of the creeping gas, they hurried across the open floor toward the holes still under excavation, then past the looming crane. In the crane cab high above the monstrous treads, the door to the operator's console was open, even though the work crew would not be in for their shift until Monday.

Tracer smoke swirled across the floor like a poisonous mist. Even though they made good time, Adonia smelled the sweet scent that followed them. In the far corner, bags of cement, bundles of metal rebar, and piles of steel beams to support the large pools were stacked high. Shovels and brooms rested against the wall near a parked yellow forklift.

Adonia winced as her bare foot stepped on a chunk of concrete debris among the mess strewn around the construction area. She watched her step more carefully, afraid she would step on a nail or cut her foot on broken cement as they reached the uncompleted in-ground pools. She already had enough problems.

Seeing the empty holes dug in the floor and the rebar set in the wooden frames, Garibaldi remarked, "These pools are months away from being finished, Stanley! If you keep receiving shipments, your plastic tank will be at capacity long before the in-ground ones are completed and ready. It's mostly at capacity right now!"

Van Dyckman's expression soured. "Construction delays and red tape. Not my fault. The contractor has been fined for not meeting the schedule. What else do you want me to do?"

Adonia thought his comment was absurd. "What else do we want you to do? Stop bringing in more radioactive rods until you have a safe, permanent place to store them!"

"After we get out of this place, I will personally ensure that *no* water or rods are stored down here," Victoria said. "Ever."

Adonia knew that after all the disasters they had encountered today, especially the death of a powerful senator, Valiant Locksmith would surely be put on hold, if not shut down. Undersecretary Doyle might even have enough clout to ensure that Hydra Mountain never stored any more radioactive waste. There would be classified reviews, programmatic shutdowns, and intensive investigations. It would go on forever. When called on the carpet, van Dyckman would vehemently insist that he was only doing what he was ordered to do. He would argue that the problems could be fixed—but Pulaski's death could never be covered up.

Which meant the real problem would remain unsolved. Because of van Dyckman's cutting corners and missteps, this relatively viable solution for storing nuclear waste would probably be shelved. And there would be no hope in sight.

Van Dyckman had already shipped large amounts of waste into the Mountain. The plastic-walled cooling pool was an unwise idea on basic principles, and if the concrete pools remained unfinished, what would happen to the submerged fuel rods already in their support structure? Pulaski had dislodged and possibly damaged several of them in his frantic struggles. If the above-ground pool sprang a leak, the cavern floor would be flooded with a few million gallons of water, and the standing fuel rods would be exposed to the air and release radiation throughout the facility.

The Fukushima Daiichi reactor cores in Japan had been in a similar situation. When the devastating tsunami damaged the containment and allowed the coolant to drain away, the rods in the reactor core melted, with disastrous consequences. Although the spent fuel rods in Stanley's temporary pool weren't nearly as enriched or as closely packed as the active Fukushima reactor cores had been, that catastrophe had shut down every nuclear facility in Japan. . . .

Victoria spoke through clenched teeth as they hurried to the far vaults. "I will demand that all rods are moved out of here immediately, back to their original site—every one of them, even the rods in the concrete pools. It's not safe to store them down here. The stray radiation . . . the consequences!"

"I'm inclined to agree," Adonia said. "Whenever we can reestablish communication, we'll inform not only Rob Harris of the situation but also the DOE Secretary."

"What?" Victoria stopped. The team formed an uneasy semicircle around her. "You don't think Secretary Nitta knows about this already? She approved the SAP, so she *has* to know about the fuel rods. Right, Stanley?" Victoria glared, but van Dyckman only reddened.

Victoria pulled up. "Wait, you . . . didn't tell her about the fuel rods and the cooling pools down here?" She looked around. "Does anyone else know?"

"I'm not sure about the President," Shawn said.

"You were there at the meeting, Colonel!" van Dyckman snapped. "Of course he knows!"

"Not about these pools!"

Van Dyckman looked around the group, but no one offered support. He took a few quick breaths. "Okay . . . I didn't tell him every detail. Would *you* want to tell him to be patient, take it slow?"

Still wet from the pool, Victoria looked even more shaken. "You're all missing the point! The Department of Energy isn't the only agency using the Mountain. We have to get the rods out, the pools drained. Immediately!"

Adonia urged them to keep moving toward the vaults in the back. "I'll back you up in our report, ma'am. But if these cooling pools have been here for months, no outside facility is going to accept the spent fuel back into their holding areas. If you pull them out of the Mountain, where will they go?"

Van Dyckman strode off ahead, and Victoria bustled after him. "I may not have been inside the Mountain in over two years, Stanley, but I didn't expect such an idiotic change. Long-term, stable programs tend to remain safe, so there was no need for me to babysit every month. But your grandiose program screwed up everything."

Shawn was confused. "Why would you be involved in Hydra Mountain at all, Ms. Doyle?"

"All that matters is that Stanley did this without coordination, by-passing even the interagency SAP process. He prevented others from reviewing *all* possible negative interactions." Her expression soured. "Stanley and Senator Pulaski managed to pull this off, but they didn't go through the proper classified interagency checks and balances, which violates Federal law. Without those reviews, this problem could quickly escalate." She was seething. "Secretary Nitta is an outstanding person, but she was out of the loop, not fully aware of what was happening here or the unintended consequences that could occur. She does not have all the information."

"Once we reestablish contact with the operations center, Rob Harris can patch in a call to the DOE Secretary's office," Adonia said. "But we've got to get out of here first."

"I'm sure he's been in contact already," Shawn said. "Harris would get all the help available."

By the time they moved past the two finished and filled permanent cooling pools, they were well ahead of the creeping halothane. The floor sloped down at an angle toward the widely spaced metal vault doors in the far wall of granite. To Adonia, the positioning suggested they blocked access to large chambers—and something important. Set a level below where they stood, the doors loomed twenty feet high and just as wide, large enough that even the biggest forklifts could drive in and out of the chambers.

"They look like the world's largest bank vaults," Garibaldi said.

"What are they?" Adonia asked.

"Probably designed to store the bigger warheads during the early Cold War days," Shawn said. "They called them 'crowd-pleasers.' The first hydrogen bombs were as big as a bus and needed cryogenic cooling, so they probably tunneled into the granite and built these vaults below ground level to contain any spills."

With increasing agitation, Victoria pointed to another old-style intercom panel set next to the nearest vault door. "Look, down there! We can contact Harris. We're in a secure area, so he should be able to patch me through to the DOE Secretary. This can't wait."

Adonia remembered Regulation Rob's obsessive penchant for following rules to the letter. He would never let anyone call Washington from a nonsecure line, especially not over an intercom. "My priority is to get us to safety," she said. "Senator Pulaski is already dead, and I don't intend to lose anyone else."

"Your priority is to keep this entire facility safe—not to mention the city of Albuquerque." Victoria's face reddened. "Hell, even the southwestern United States!" Hurrying down the slope, she tried to work the intercom panel.

Adonia was surprised by the Undersecretary's vehemence. Van Dyckman spoke conspiratorially but loudly enough for everyone to hear. "Victoria's prone to hyperbole."

Shawn was firm. "If it's such an important crisis, then Harris can call in a nuclear emergency team, once he knows about it. And I can call the President myself."

"We still have to wait until the system reboots, regardless," Adonia said.

"Harris needs to get a nuclear emergency team in place *now*," Victoria said, "ready to move the instant the lockdown is lifted. Every minute counts."

Adonia doubted the site manager would take preemptive action without full approval, no matter how much Undersecretary Doyle harangued him over the intercom.

The rest of the team crowded around as Victoria pressed the button and shouted into the speaker. "Rob Harris! Answer me, dammit!"

"It's not working," Garibaldi said simply. "What a surprise."

"But we need to get out of here!" van Dyckman said. "Can he even hear us?"

Adonia tried to intercede. "We probably have more than three hours left."

Garibaldi gazed back across the great cavern. "We'll never last that long unless we get inside some kind of shelter. The halothane is spilling across the floor, and it'll pool down here. That's how you would incapacitate an armed force of intruders. Worst-case scenario." Even though they had outrun the gas, they found themselves at a dead end. "We may be incapacitated very shortly, unless Stanley can use his magic decoder ring to open these vaults."

"Well, we can't just stand here and die." Van Dyckman's face was flushed as he pushed past the others to a more modern control panel next to the first towering vault door, which had obviously been upgraded since the Cold War era. His fingers danced across the LED screen. "We need to get into the vault."

Victoria grabbed his shoulder, pulling him away. "Stop it, Stanley!" He knocked her back.

Adonia darted forward and held the man's arm, trying to calm them both. "Enough! We've got to work together to get out of here."

Van Dyckman yanked his arm free. "If Mrs. Garcia is safe in her vault, this will solve our problem, an absolutely secure bolt-hole." Not listening to the shouts, he keyed in his code to open the vault door.

31

The controls on the big vault panel looked much newer than the one outside the guard portal where they had previously tried to shelter in place. Adonia thought the pad resembled a reconfigurable airline cockpit console more than the typical controls for a storage vault.

Doggedly, van Dyckman went to work on the panel despite Victoria's increasing agitation. "Okay, this is a standard, upgraded port found in all the new DOE restricted areas," he muttered to himself. "It's software driven, and my access should let me open any vault in the Mountain."

"Then why didn't you free Mrs. Garcia?" Garibaldi demanded.

"Because he's a jerk," Adonia said under her breath.

Van Dyckman reddened as he worked. "Quiet. It's hard enough when my own life is in danger, much less a mere technician's."

Victoria still tried to block him. "Stanley, dammit—Stop!"

Shawn held her back. "We need to keep ourselves safe for at least three more hours, ma'am. With the halothane flowing toward us, that vault may be the only place that can keep us alive."

"It's *not* safe. You don't know what you're doing!"

"We'll all die if we don't get inside." Van Dyckman punched in a code, which failed, and he tried again. "Keep quiet. I'm trying to remember the mnemonic! It's thirty-two characters, after all."

Victoria grew more frantic. "You have to stop—that vault . . . it's Velvet Hammer!"

Garibaldi rolled his eyes. "Velvet Hammer? Valiant Locksmith? Do you all get drunk and just make up strange-sounding names?"

"It's . . . it's a Special Access Program. State Department, not DOE. We're all in danger—"

A chill went down Adonia's back. "*Another* SAP?"

Victoria pulled free of Shawn's grip. "None of you have the proper clearance. Why do you think so many extreme security measures are down here? Certainly not for Stanley's cooling pools! I didn't even know they were here."

"What in the world did you store in there?" Garibaldi asked, looking at the huge vault.

Adonia demanded to know, "Undersecretary Doyle, what exactly is Velvet Hammer?"

"This is *my* Mountain. Your SAP has no business being here." Van Dyckman finished entering the characters and he grinned, surprised at his own accomplishment. "There! Got it." He pressed Enter, and a whirring noise hummed through the heavy door.

Adonia expected the release would trigger another round of screeching alarms, but van Dyckman's master override code was apparently accepted, and with clicking and humming hydraulic mechanisms, the massive door swung open from the wall, groaning under its weight.

The widening gap revealed a dark enclosure lit only by the light from the grotto while old tungsten halogen bulbs struggled to flicker on, blinking, clicking. Adonia could see little more than a row of shadowy granite cubicles inside a large space.

With a vehement lunge, Victoria threw herself in front of the doorway, spreading her arms out to either side to prevent anyone from entering. "Stanley, dammit, shut the vault door—*now*! Thanks to your fuel rods, there's far too much stray radiation down here." Her petite figure looked laughably small in front of the twenty-foot-wide vault opening.

"All the more reason for us to get inside the shelter," Shawn said. Yellow vapors continued to curl along the grotto floor, adding to the hazard.

Additional banks of lights flickered on inside the vault, revealing more of the interior. Van Dyckman turned and stared inside. "What the hell?"

A row of dark granite cubbyholes lined the inner walls of the vault, and a barrier chain hung across each opening. Each alcove held a squat polished object on a sturdy, raised platform that was bolted to the rock floor.

Her face now ashen, Victoria stood before them. Her voice quavered. "Ms. Rojas, we all know Harris put you in charge. I order you to close this door immediately. Our lives are in danger."

Shawn peered into the garish light and the abrupt shadows in each of the cubbyholes. "I recognize those from my B-2 days—we called them Unscheduled Sunrises: thermonuclear bombs!"

Adonia felt a chill. "What are nuclear weapons doing in this facility?"

"Close the vault door!" Victoria shouted. "They're . . . they're *devices,* not warheads. Not technically, and not *legally.* They have everything but the software, and they aren't recognized by treaty as actual weapons—"

Van Dyckman stared at Victoria. "Hydra Mountain was decommissioned! The DoD handed over the keys, and I supervised it. They relinquished all authority. This facility is supposed to be for storing waste only! How dare you store warheads—"

Victoria's voice was like a hard mallet. "Close the damned vault door, Stanley! The radiation is already a high risk, and now it's far worse because that fool Senator knocked down part of the array of fuel rods." She had gone white with both rage and fear. "And if enough water floods down here, the devices could go critical! I swear, Stanley, I will bring charges against you for exposing my SAP. I warned you—"

Garibaldi suddenly understood what she meant. "Yes, she's right. Shut the vault—now! I don't care what you call them, if stray neutrons interact with those nuclear cores . . . that's the real danger. And it's increasing every second that vault door stays open."

"You heard him," Shawn said in his sharp command voice. He pulled van Dyckman back to the control panel. "Close it."

"Do it!" Victoria sounded hysterical. "If one warhead is triggered, they'll all detonate."

"She's right," Adonia said, feeling dizzy. "They're close enough together there might be a sympathetic detonation that might take out Hydra Mountain along with half of New Mexico." She tried to imagine how many millions of people would die. "And the kill zone would cover the entire Southwest."

Still holding van Dyckman, Shawn looked behind them down into the grotto with the curling gas spilling across the floor. "After we close the vault, we'll have to climb the crane instead. That's our best hope now."

Van Dyckman was too rattled to work the control panel. "But it'll be safe if we get inside and seal the door, even with the warheads! We'll be away from the halothane, and we can last for a few hours next to the shielded cores. We'll die if we stay out here." He seemed most concerned with defying Victoria and asserting his power over Hydra Mountain.

"Stanley, you always were an idiot." Victoria rushed to the panel. "Always needing to be in control—"

Van Dyckman shoved Victoria away, thrusting her backward toward the vault. He scrambled past her. "Everyone, quick! I'll close it once we're inside."

Victoria grabbed the door and caught her balance as he pushed into the large, shielded vault. She yelled, "Wait, you didn't bypass the defensive mechanisms. You initiated the sensors by opening up the—"

Magenta warning lights spun into full alert inside and outside the vault. A new siren blasted up and down, and a threatening recorded voice began a countdown that reverberated from speakers inside the vault.

"Unauthorized breach. Exit immediately. Countermeasures in ten . . . nine . . ."

Reacting without thinking, van Dyckman backed farther inside, and Victoria lunged after him. "Stanley, get out of there!"

"Exit immediately." The countdown continued.

Adonia shouted for the two to run from the vault.

Victoria caught van Dyckman by the arm, but he shook her off. "Let go of me, you bitch!"

"Four . . . three . . ."

Outside the vault at the control panel, Adonia ran her fingers over the LED pad, looking for any kind of emergency override. There had to be a fail-safe button to close the vault.

Victoria spun and lunged toward the big vault door as she raced back out, trying to beat the last second on the countdown.

Adonia must have hit some kind of reset, and she was astonished to see the massive barrier begin to grind closed on powerful hydraulics.

Shawn waved toward Victoria, who was running toward them. "Hurry!"

"Breach neutralized." The voice sounded like an executioner.

An incredible burst of air gushed from the vault. A deluge of red sticky foam erupted from the inner ceiling. Unlike the foam that had swelled and oozed into the guard portal in the tunnel up above, this defense spurted down in a wall that expanded swiftly like glutinous, soapy foam. The substance rapidly filled the warhead vault, trapping everything inside like flies in amber.

The burst of escaping air knocked Shawn backward into Adonia. He hit the floor and rolled away from the solidifying foam that gushed out of the Velvet Hammer vault. The fast-hardening substance mushroomed through the gap, boiling up as it expanded, then froze in place.

Adonia had never seen such a swift and vigorous countermeasure. This was a last line intended to stop an intruder and secure the exposed warheads so that no one could remove them, even if the vault door were breached. The previous sticky foam in the guard portal had been meant to impede or confine the bad guys, but this hardening froth was a lethal measure to protect the stored nuclear weapons.

"Victoria! Stanley!" Adonia had to scramble out of the way as the foam swelled and thickened like a petrified tidal wave. "They're trapped in there."

The vault door groaned and screeched as the heavy hydraulics tried to close, but the movement slowed. The large pistons could not force the door shut with the solidified sticky foam. With a loud straining sound, the door ground to a stop, leaving a gap at least four feet wide.

In closing, the door had pushed a weirdly contoured path through the petrified matrix of rigid material.

Adonia could only hear the muffled wail of the warning siren from inside the vault, now muted through a dozen feet of hardened foam. Everything inside would have been swallowed up, buried—including Victoria and Stanley.

"No refuge for us inside the vault anymore," Garibaldi said, sounding oddly disconnected. "We'd better find another alternative."

All around their feet, the smoky halothane continued to swirl and build.

32

Up in the Eagle's Nest, Rob Harris struggled to breathe. He knew exactly what the latest alarm on his status screen meant.

They had found, and opened, the Velvet Hammer vault.

The main screen above the operations floor gave an urgent alert that one of the ultra-secure doors had been opened—the very scenario that had given him nightmares. To make things worse, minutes before, radiation detectors from the lower cavern showed a dramatic increase in the already-high ambient levels, as if something had interfered with the precarious wet-storage pools.

What were they doing down there?

Worse yet, after opening one of the secure Velvet Hammer vaults, someone must have entered and triggered the most dangerous countermeasures, designed to protect the nuclear devices. He felt the blood drain from his face. The avalanche of sticky foam would have engulfed and killed anyone in its way. This couldn't be happening!

He'd never intended for the team to actually gain entry to the vault. Undersecretary Doyle should have seen the fuel rods, the temporary cooling pool, and recognized the danger. Velvet Hammer was her SAP, but she would *never* have opened the vault, knowing full well what the sealed chambers contained.

It had to be van Dyckman. He must have used the override code, which was valid for all systems throughout the facility.

Velvet Hammer was a separate, waived and unacknowledged

Special Access Program, the sole purview of Undersecretary Doyle in her classified work for the State Department. Two years ago when she had last inspected her SAP, the Mountain was still under DoD control, and the near-finished warheads fit perfectly into the operations, a highly classified State Department program that exploited treaty loopholes and allowed the U.S. to hold a clandestine nuclear trump card.

He knew what the State Department had done: the numbers of nuclear warheads in the nation's stockpile were strictly regulated by international agreement. Each year the U.S. routinely pulled five or ten weapons out of inventory for testing before returning them to the military. While those warheads were out of service, the Department of Defense needed to ensure that its arsenal remained at proper levels in the event of a national crisis. An entirely legal way to ensure that a warhead could be moved rapidly into the active inventory was to stockpile nuclear "devices" that weren't really weapons.

The Velvet Hammer devices stored in the lower vault had everything a nuclear weapon needed to function—a plutonium pit, electronics, fuses—except for one critical, technical detail, an easy-to-install final piece, such as the software. Because the devices were incomplete, those "almost but not quite" weapons could not be legally counted as part of the nation's strategic stockpile.

The Department of State used that subtle distinction to hold an ace in the hole. Since the end of the Cold War, the highest government officials insisted on maintaining this card up their sleeve in case of an international catastrophe.

Thanks to the impenetrable secrecy, the State Department wasn't required to inform the Department of Energy of their classified SAPs. Up until now, however, Stanley van Dyckman's own unacknowledged Valiant Locksmith had created a potential doomsday condition that Rob Harris could not reveal to anyone. His hands were tied, and neither the DOE Inspector General nor his counterpart in the Department of State had the authority to know about the other's highly classified program.

When the facility transitioned to the DOE, the Velvet Hammer vault override codes must not have been changed. Yet another unintended consequence contributing to this mindless cascade of disasters. . . .

The only other place where all that knowledge came together was with the President and the Congressional Intelligence Oversight Committee. But a formerly retired site manager had no direct access to the President, and Senator Pulaski—the man responsible for funding Hydra Mountain—had dismissed Harris's concerns, unable to appreciate the technical details of the risk.

Now, Harris dropped into his seat. He had dreaded exactly this scenario. If he had revealed the existence of Undersecretary Doyle's program to anyone involved with Valiant Locksmith, Harris would go to jail for the rest of his life. That was why he had pulled strings to get the right people here, to *see* the hazard with their own eyes. This review had been his only chance to make someone realize the potential disaster of housing these two SAPs together.

Well, they were all fully aware of the danger now.

Now that the stored warheads were exposed to stray neutrons—the levels of which were significantly increased because of all the fuel rods in the pools—the risk of an accidental detonation was no longer vanishingly small. And if the temporary cooling pool ever leaked and the warheads were submerged in water, then the probability of disaster would increase exponentially.

If a single device went critical, sympathetic detonations might trigger them all. Then it would be good-bye, New Mexico. And more.

By sending the review team in there, he may have set his own nightmare scenario in motion.

Sickened as the avalanche of sticky foam hardened and crackled inside the vault, spilling out in a massive amorphous blockade, Shawn pounded on the rigid mass. His blows peeled off a few chunks, but not enough to make a difference. The substance was like a petrified cloud jammed in the vault, blocking the heavy door open. He kicked at the shell-like substance, then threw his shoulder against the vault door, uselessly pushing.

Adonia helped, but there was nothing either of them could do. "They're buried alive in there." Her voice sounded hoarse and angry. "They probably suffocated."

Garibaldi stood by the control panel, ashen. "How do we close the vault door? We need to seal off the warheads from the stray radiation here in the grotto. Every minute the door remains open and the cores are exposed is like a game of Russian roulette."

Adonia knew the older scientist was right. "Hopefully the ambient radiation isn't significantly higher than normal background levels, especially with all those fuel rods. I'm really worried now."

Shawn looked in vain at the huge vault door and shook his head. "An emergency response team can clear the sticky foam with solvent sprays and break it up with sharp tools, and then they can close the vault. Until then we'll have to gamble."

Garibaldi did not look convinced. "The sticky foam doesn't have any moderating effect, and it's way too porous to absorb neutrons.

Our only hope right now is that the background level doesn't increase any more than it has."

Adonia coughed and felt light-headed. She swayed as she stood, sweating in her damp clothes, and she looked down to see the nebulous soup of halothane curling across the lower floor. Some of the wisps had already reached her ankles. Taking shallow breaths, she worked on the control panel, trying the vault's emergency closure routines one more time, without success. The hydraulics only hummed and groaned against the hardened sticky foam. "No use."

Shawn said, "Right now we've got bigger problems than closing the vault door. Unless we get to higher ground, we won't be conscious much longer, and then we can't warn anybody of the danger. We've got to climb as high as we can until the lockdown is lifted."

"Somebody's got to survive," Garibaldi said, sounding more grim than ever before. "Nuclear waste and nuclear weapons don't play well together. Someone needs to get the word out . . . and we've already lost half our team."

Adonia felt a pang of sadness as the three of them hurried back up the incline to the main floor. Even though Senator Pulaski's blundering had caused most of their problems, he hadn't deserved to die, and neither did Undersecretary Doyle, who had just been trying to protect her SAP and prevent this very thing from happening.

Adonia felt a deeper heaviness at the loss of Stanley van Dyckman, whom she had known for years, even though she often found him maddening. He came across as arrogant and opportunistic, and yet he'd created the Valiant Locksmith program to address an urgent problem, even if it was poorly implemented. Now, what should have been her former boss's great triumph had morphed into a total disaster.

No, it was not a good day for Hydra Mountain.

"We should get moving before we collapse," Shawn said, pointing across the cavern. "Climbing the crane is our only good option— unless you have a better suggestion."

"Better is the enemy of 'good enough,'" Garibaldi said. "So if it works, don't try anything better. Let's do it."

Adonia realized she would probably succumb first, since she was physically the smallest. As they jogged back toward the center of the grotto, closer to the halothane that curled over the ledge from the high bay above, some of the gas already swirled up to their knees, stirred up as they moved.

"I hope you don't make me carry you too far if you collapse," Shawn said to her with a quick, reassuring smile. "Come on, we've got some climbing to do."

She tried to put on a burst of speed, running on bare feet but unable to see debris on the floor. She hurt her sole, but kept running, hoping it wasn't a bad cut. She swayed, and the dizziness increased. Shawn caught her arm. "Steady—the gas is already affecting you. When we reach the crane, you're the first one up."

"As long as you're both right behind me," she said, trying to control her heavy breathing. She just hoped she could keep her balance while climbing the open boom. Vertigo at the wrong moment would result in a big splat on the floor below. She shook her head and pushed on toward the giant industrial machine.

They dodged construction material, steel support columns that rose to the ceiling, the trenches, walls, and pouring forms for half-finished concrete pools. The yellow gas stirred as they jogged, causing loops of vapor to rise higher. Coughing and dizzy, Adonia staggered along.

Finally, they reached the huge industrial crane that crouched like some mythical monster: a massive foundation and enormous treads, a high control cab, and the lattice boom that stretched up to the cavern ceiling. Disoriented, barely able to keep her balance, Adonia stared up at the towering structure she would have to climb.

34

When the sirens and warnings started blaring in the Velvet Hammer vault, Stanley van Dyckman was already well inside the chamber. He panicked, reacting instead of thinking.

He lurched deeper into the dimly lit vault, scrambling to get away. Just as he neared the far end, the ominous countdown stopped. He heard an explosion behind him, and gouts of fast-hardening polymer gel dumped all around him, engulfing the open space in less than a second, like a car airbag slamming into his back.

He instantly responded, throwing himself to the side. Back in the guard portal when Senator Pulaski had set off a lesser sticky foam defense, the man had nearly been smothered, and this was a thousand times worse! Van Dyckman dove sideways, sprawling headfirst. By sheer luck, he rolled into the last cubbyhole. He clambered on his knees to a sturdy pedestal that held a round-topped cylinder.

Sirens and alarms hammered the vault, becoming muffled by the explosively expanding foam. Screaming, he scrambled on top of the storage pedestal to get away before the sticky foam enveloped him.

His outstretched hands grabbed at the metal cylinder that was almost as tall as he was. His arms could barely wrap around it. He hauled himself higher, like a man trying to climb above a raging flood as swelling foam expanded to fill the vault. Wrapping his arms around the warm cylinder, he hung on and watched as the mountain of foam froze into place as a hard, pocked meringue. Sealing him in.

He waited, holding his breath. The foam creaked and cracked as it stiffened, plugging the chamber and the vault opening, but it did not advance further. The lights in the chamber glowed weirdly through the translucent obstruction. He was trapped, but he was still alive. He took two quick breaths to reassure himself.

Somewhere near the front of the vault, the bitch Victoria was completely buried under an avalanche of hardened sticky foam, like a concrete straitjacket.

The realization that she was dead sent strange feelings through him. They'd had good times, and good sex, but there weren't all that many instances to remember, and she had always been concerned with her own career, her own needs, instead of his. Just like now. This was all her fault. Her Velvet Hammer SAP had put them all at risk. Nuclear devices should never have been in his Mountain, and because of them Hydra Mountain's worst countermeasures had tried to kill them all.

Sealed in the cocoon of hardened sticky foam, he listened to the oppressive silence. Were the others still alive outside the vault? Adonia, Colonel Whalen, and Dr. Garibaldi had been out of reach of the sticky foam. But, unable to take refuge in the protected vault, as planned, maybe they had already succumbed to the halothane in the open grotto.

The gas! With the door blocked open, the knockout gas could still penetrate here. Van Dyckman sniffed, afraid he'd fall unconscious in here and be suffocated even more slowly, but the volatile, starchy odors of the foam drowned out any trace of the halothane scent. Would he be safe? Maybe the blockage would cut off enough of it.

It would take hours before any rescue could possibly come, and he needed to wait it out someplace. Here in the Velvet Hammer vault, he had light, he had air. It wasn't Club Med, but he even felt comfortable, almost hot compared to what he'd been in the chilly main grotto. . . .

He gasped as he realized why he felt so warm.

He frantically released his grip around the metal cylinder, the thermonuclear weapon.

The warhead was physically warm, and he was trapped right next to it, crowded into the alcove. He looked around the claustrophobic granite vault. A wall of hard red foam covered the rock floor and rose up nearly to the ceiling like a mountain of discolored snow left by an out-of-control plow.

He was buried alive inside the storage vault with dozens of nuclear bombs, and he knew that if they were generating heat, they were also generating radiation. His skin crawled as he imagined the invisible particles shooting all around him, being absorbed into his body. If an old-fashioned Geiger counter hung on the wall, it would have been clicking and crackling like crazy.

He tried to worm his way around the warhead, but the impenetrable foam blocked his way like a petrified cumulus cloud. He was trapped.

Again seeking someone to blame, he cursed Victoria. What had she been thinking to hide all these illicit nuclear devices here? Her program had to be illegal! At least *he* had been trying to solve a crucial problem and help the nation. Thanks to him and his close connection to the President, Hydra Mountain had been reopened and put to good use. This facility was ideal for storing enormous amounts of nuclear waste . . . but active warheads in a secret back room changed the equation entirely! Well, she had died for it.

He had to get out of here.

Moving carefully in the small amount of space available, van Dyckman squeezed down behind the platform and stepped onto the uneven mass of hardened foam piled around the cubbyhole. The substance held under his weight, although it felt uncertain, slippery.

He worked his way around the warhead in its protected alcove and tried to crawl up the wall of hard foam. It was like climbing a gritty, crusty old snowdrift. A piece of the material broke off in his fingers as he tried to get a handhold. The sticky foam had little substance, and if he had a jackhammer, a pickax—even a spoon!—he could chop away at the starchy barricade.

He pounded and clawed at the foam, and little by little he managed to smash away a few chunks. He needed some kind of tool to dig his way out. As he worked with greater desperation, he felt something hard in his pants pocket. Keys? Maybe he could use those—

He found the box cutter he had pocketed from the guard portal, after he'd freed Senator Pulaski from that sticky foam. Sharp and hard; it would work!

He extended the blade and stabbed the hardened foam like a serial killer. Another jagged block broke off, opening a gap, and his hopes soared. Breathing heavily, van Dyckman started chopping away, piece by piece.

Staggering, helping each other as they reeled from the effects of the spreading knockout gas, Adonia and her two companions reached the base of the enormous crane. Large letters, MLC165-1, were painted on the side of the red cab, which rode high on six-foot-tall crawler treads.

"All we have to do is climb above the gas." Adonia felt dizzy as she broke into a fit of coughing. The deadly gas swirled higher and higher on the stone floor at their feet. "No problem."

Shawn trudged around to the opposite side of the crane, looking for a way to climb the high treads to reach the cab. "This way! I can boost you up, Adonia."

When she looked up from below, the towering boom looked much larger than it had seemed from across the cavern. Although the crawler footprint was only twenty-five square feet or so, the crane's swollen main body allowed a clearance of less than five feet from the ground. Even Adonia had to duck as they circled the crane.

Shawn pointed her to the end of the crawler. "You first. I can hoist you onto the tread, but you'll have to get up onto the cab yourself and start climbing the boom to get high enough." He glanced at her bare feet. "Are you up to it?"

Out of breath, woozy from the gas, Adonia nodded. "I can climb. I'll just have to live with sore feet." From here, the crane looked enormous, but she couldn't let it bother her. "As long as I'm alive, I can deal with it."

"We're not going for a speed record," Shawn said. "Take your time."

She saw how high the operator's cab stood above the cavern floor. "Maybe the cab will be high enough. We'll be safe."

"No, get as high as you can," Garibaldi coughed. "We don't know how much halothane is in that reservoir, and air currents will stir the gas higher."

Shawn put his hands around her waist in a firm grip. "Here you go, get to the top!" He boosted her up, and she grabbed with her hands and pulled herself onto the giant tread, scrambling for footing. When she caught her balance, she called down, "You'll look less graceful when you hoist Dr. Garibaldi."

Taller than Shawn, the older scientist responded with a skeptical look. "Frankly, I don't care how graceful he looks. Boost me up, Colonel."

On her hands and knees, Adonia crawled across the giant treads, once again wishing she had worn jeans instead of a stylish business dress. Not her only miscalculation of the day. When she reached up to grab the side of the crane's cab, she pulled herself up, balanced on tiptoes so she could glance inside the compartment. In addition to the controls and a seat for the operator, the cab held several manuals in plastic binders, a metal toolbox, and a long yellow rope curled in a loop. She couldn't carry the heavy toolbox with her as she climbed, but she thought the rope might come in handy for securing themselves to the lattice.

Grasping the cab's flimsy metal door, she stretched her other arm up and tried to pull herself into the compartment, but she slipped, barely caught herself on the edge of the door before falling off the tread. The halothane fumes were making her dizzy, even this high above the floor. "Now who's being graceful?" she muttered.

"Adonia, what are you doing?" Shawn called up. "You have to gain more height. Start climbing the boom!"

"I was trying to fetch a rope in the operator's compartment. We can use it for a safety line." She thought it sounded like a good idea.

"I'll get it when I come up," he called. "You just keep moving, so I don't have to worry about you. We're right behind you." He and Garibaldi were both coughing. He helped the older scientist up onto the big tread, who then reached down to give him a hand up.

Adonia held on to the edge of the cab for balance, then worked her way around the base. She reached the metal lattice of the boom and put her bare foot on the lowest horizontal strut. Each lattice element consisted of an open box, the edges made of thick horizontal and vertical steel rods, or struts. Diagonal rods alternated direction on each face of the box; the lattice of struts continued up the length of the boom.

Fortunately, the struts were thick enough that their rounded surfaces didn't cut her skin, though she knew she'd be hobbling around for a week on bruised feet. That was a problem she could live with. Reaching up, she grabbed the next horizontal strut and pulled herself up. She looked down at the other two as they climbed to the cab.

She slowly scaled the trestle one horizontal strut after another, methodically moving higher each time, as the boom extended up at a steep angle. "Just like an inclined ladder," she muttered to herself. "Not a problem." She made sure her foot was well positioned and her hands had a solid grip on the cold metal before she boosted herself to the next lattice element.

If the lockdown lasted another three hours, plus even more time for the emergency crews to break through to the lower cavern, she wanted more than enough margin of safety above the gas. Falling unconscious and plummeting to the concrete floor far below would probably be fatal.

Strut by strut, not looking down, she kept climbing until she was at least seventy feet above the floor.

As the boom extended across the open cavern, she saw she had made her way to just above the above-ground pool. She looked up to see she had another fifty or sixty feet to reach the lowest catwalk, but knew she didn't need to climb any farther, as she must be well above the gas. Still feeling uncoordinated, she rearranged her arms and legs to pull herself into a sitting position, curling an arm around a metal strut. Oddly, even in this precarious position, she felt more secure than she had in hours.

Twenty feet below, Dr. Garibaldi kept making his way up the trestle, with Shawn behind him, offering encouragement. She smiled when she saw he had coiled the rope from the cab around his shoulder and carried it up.

Before long, Garibaldi had reached the level of Adonia's perch, out of breath but not complaining. "I believe Colonel Whalen is chasing me."

"I'm sure he calls it a motivational exercise," she said. Now that they seemed to be safe, Adonia felt a warm glow. The air up at this level was cleaner, easier to breathe. "He is a good climber."

"And in better shape than I am." Garibaldi twisted around to look at the ceiling of the cavern overhead, studying the catwalks that had retracted up to their lockdown position. "Not exactly what I'd call fresh air, but it's an improvement."

Shawn joined them shortly. "That was easy enough, wasn't it? We're above most of the gas now, but if we keep climbing, we could reach one of those catwalks and make our way home free across the ceiling. Wherever we want to go."

"Sounds like fun," Adonia said. "For someone else."

"Is that necessary?" Garibaldi asked. "We've triggered enough alarms already. Let's just sit tight for a while."

Adonia looked at the nearest catwalk, which the end of the boom overshot. "If we climb all the way up, it's still a ten-foot drop to the walkway." Her feet were already sore, and she winced at the thought of slamming down on the metal grid of the catwalk.

Shawn tapped the looped rope on his shoulder. "We can lower ourselves down. It'll be easier on your feet."

"But why would we need to?" Adonia asked.

As he hung balanced on the boom, Garibaldi extended a finger to follow the path of the catwalk around the ceiling, where it intersected with the supporting columns throughout the ceiling. "Look to the middle of the cavern ceiling. Do you see it?"

Shawn pulled himself level with them and they all hung together on the grid structure. With his sharp eyesight, he spotted what the older scientist indicated. "There's a panel in the ceiling above the main catwalk. And look at the cables going into it. I have a hunch that's a communications conduit shared with an air vent."

"You mean a maintenance shaft?" Adonia said.

Garibaldi pointed at an enclosed safety tube in the far corner of the grotto near the Velvet Hammer vaults, just above a stack of cement bags. "I'd expect that one over there is the maintenance shaft. More accessible. Probably just goes to the upper level inside the Mountain. Too bad we didn't spot it before we made our way all the way over here."

The older scientist turned his attention back to the grotto ceiling. "Hydra Mountain would still need to run communications and control lines from down here up to the next level, maybe even to the outside. In the old days that shaft would be the only way to fix breaks or shorts in the transmission lines. It would need to be big enough to allow access for a worker attempting to make repairs." He waited a beat, then smiled. "If we get up there, we can use that duct to reach the main level. We could bypass the reboot—and get out of here now, instead of hours from now."

Shawn said, "We'd risk triggering other alarms. Better part of valor would be to stay here and wait it out."

"Exactly as Rob Harris told us to do," Adonia said.

Garibaldi gave him a dubious frown. "And when Mr. Harris left us, he said the lockdown wouldn't last more than a few minutes. Are you certain everything will continue to go smoothly?"

Shawn lifted a brow. "Smoothly? We have three people dead already."

Adonia felt more urgency. "With the Velvet Hammer vault jammed open and the warheads exposed to increased radiation, I don't think we can afford to wait three more hours. Harris needs to know what he's dealing with, and he has to get a nuclear emergency response team ready to move immediately. Undersecretary Doyle was right to be panicked."

"I agree . . ." Garibaldi's voice trailed off as he stared down at the concrete floor below, which was partially obscured by the swirling smoke markers of the halothane. He gripped the struts with both hands. "Well, that might not be the worst of it." Anchoring himself with one hand, he leaned farther out. "Look over by the temporary cooling pool."

Adonia peered down to see what he had noticed. Squinting, she saw a wide and expanding puddle near the round pool. A foot above the floor, near the bottom of the metal-supported plastic walls, a thin spray of water spewed from a breach.

"The pool is leaking!" Adonia cried.

Shawn muttered a curse. "Van Dyckman swore those plastic sheets have more tensile strength than steel."

"When our dear Senator knocked over the fuel rods, one of them must have struck a cooling pipe or sensor embedded in the side of the pool wall with enough force to create a punching shear," Garibaldi said.

Adonia held on to the metal struts of the boom. "That's a substantial leak, but at the rate water is spilling out, it'll take days for the water level to drain completely. We'll be out of here long before that."

"If it stays localized," Garibaldi warned. "With the amount of water pressure inside the pool, that small punching shear can easily grow. It could cause a catastrophic failure of the plastic wall, completely collapsing the sides." He paused. "And if that happens, the water will spill out and the entire array of fuel rods will be exposed within seconds. With nothing to moderate the radioactivity, the neutron levels in the grotto will increase exponentially."

Adonia felt her brief respite dissolve. "*Catastrophic failure* are my two least favorite words in the world."

Without emotion, Garibaldi continued his assessment. "In less than a minute the warheads in Victoria's vault will be simultaneously flooded with water and neutrons. As I said before, it'll be like playing Russian roulette, but now with a billion more bullets. Just how confident are you that something else won't go wrong today?"

Adonia suddenly felt ice in her veins. "Victoria said that if even one of the nukes goes critical, they're close enough in proximity that cascading detonations of all the others would wipe out the city and most of the state."

"Oh, surely no more than a third of the state," Garibaldi said with wry sarcasm. "Although the deadly fallout would certainly reach the East Coast. I would prefer to stop that before it happens."

Climbing across the slippery mound of sticky foam, van Dyckman squirmed close to the top of the vault, pulling himself forward. The hard, uneven barrier nearly blocked him off, but he found just enough room to wiggle through, scraping his back against the granite ceiling. He hoped the massive vault door hadn't completely closed, which would have allowed some of the thickening foam to spill outside rather than fill the entire chamber. That might have saved his life.

Struggling for room to maneuver, he used the box cutter, along with adrenaline and desperation, to chip through the substance and pull forward. With each second, he felt increasing urgency to hack his way free.

Like a spelunker squeezing through a tight passage, he crawled and followed the steel pipe that enclosed the wires to the inset lights, so he knew he was heading in the right direction. When he finally reached the inside wall above the chamber entrance, it would be a simple matter to dig and chop his way to the vault door. And out.

His arms ached, his hands were bloody, and each gasping breath felt like razors in his lungs. Somewhere beneath him, Victoria Doyle was dead, engulfed in a mass of hardened foam, like a fossil trapped in limestone.

He remembered hearing her terrified scream cut off as the foam gushed in. Only by sheer luck had he stumbled into the warhead cubbyhole. As he worked his way over the barricade of sticky foam, he knew her entombed body was down there. . . .

He remembered their relationship with only a brief fondness. The affair had seemed inevitable with their shared ambitions, their mutual traveling, the innumerable late-night planning sessions when he was Senator Pulaski's Chief of Staff. But even the sex had evolved into more of a competition than a release. Objectively speaking, he was glad to have her gone, and now he could achieve his potential.

His swift career advancement had been the death knell for romance, since Victoria couldn't stand any scenario where he upstaged her. Even so, he had never imagined she would threaten to shut down his vital program just to keep her illicit warheads hidden here in Hydra Mountain. He had lost a lot of respect for her since they'd broken up, and these last few hours validated the reason why.

Unlike Victoria, at least Stanley van Dyckman was still alive, and he could still escape.

Nearing the jammed vault door, he dreaded that he would have to chop his way down through more hardened foam to reach the interior controls to let himself loose, but if the entrance was blocked open by the petrified foam, he'd only have to cut his way out.

Working his way through the last gap in the hardened material, he felt a rush of excitement as a large block broke off to expose the outside grotto. He frantically chopped and tore away pieces of the foam, then rolled down a steep, bumpy slope. He sprawled out of the vault and onto the grotto floor, dropping to his hands and knees. Reeling, shaking, he sprang to his feet, holding his breath. Like a poisonous fog, the wispy yellow halothane swirled nearly at chest level.

The gas was settling in the lower point of the cavern, driven downward to the Velvet Hammer vaults. Worse, as he moved, he stirred the deadly gas and swirled the sickening fumes up toward his face. Trying not to breathe, van Dyckman coughed and staggered away, knowing he had to get to higher ground.

Though he had escaped from the vault filled with nukes, he still wasn't safe.

The box cutter in his hand was ruined, gummed up by remnants of sticky foam. He threw the tool to the side and heard it clatter along the cement floor, swallowed in the blanket of yellow gas.

Pressing his mouth and nose against the crook of his elbow, he staggered up the incline to the main floor, gaining ground to where the level of gas dropped to just above his knees. But he could still smell it. Frantic, he debated with himself what to do and how to survive. He couldn't go all the way back to the cooling pool, where the halothane continued to spill over the ledge and onto the main floor. He would collapse long before he made it.

He turned toward the back of the cavern and saw the sacks of cement mix piled in the corner. Maybe if he climbed those, he would gain enough height, at least ten feet above the ground, above most of the halothane.

He felt like a wreck, bleeding from his hands, but desperation gave him the energy he needed. He stumbled toward the corner, struggling to take only sips of air, but he couldn't hold his breath much longer. Soon he was forced to gasp in a lungful, which stank of the sickly sweet halothane. He reeled, needing fresh air. He began to cough and almost passed out, but forced himself to stagger forward. Almost there.

He couldn't collapse, or he would die in this soup of deadly gas. Reaching the stack, he slumped against the pile of cement bags. He could find purchase for his feet, climb the sacks like a rock pile, get above the floor. He pulled himself higher, using his knees. One level. Then the next. His hands left bloody prints on the dusty sacks, but his arms and feet felt numb. He wanted to collapse.

His feet ripped holes in the paper bags, spilling gray-white powder. His body was turning to jelly, pulling him back down. He would just slide over the side, fall asleep. . . . *No!* He slapped the hard cement mix bag, and the sharp pain roused him. He kept going. One more level.

He clambered up, finally reaching the top of the pile, where he knelt and caught his balance, wheezing and shuddering. Then he forced himself to stand, gaining another few feet of height. Now he drew in a deep breath.

The air was clearer here, and even though he felt ready to drop unconscious, so sleepy and so dizzy, he made himself stay upright. Heaving, he inhaled some of the stirred cement powder, which set him to coughing again. Even here, though, he could still smell the distinctive halothane.

Panicked, he looked wildly around, sure that he was trapped. Wasn't he high enough above the gas? This mound of concrete mix sacks was like an island in the swirling halothane, and he had no way to go anywhere else. He stretched upward, gaining just a few more inches.

Swaying, he reached up to steady himself against the granite wall— and his hand hit something hard, metal. He squirmed around and saw a line of rungs set into the wall, painted gray so as to be nearly invisible against the rock.

Rungs! He could keep climbing. There was a way up the wall!

Spaced every eighteen inches, the horizontal iron bars ran up the corner and vanished into a metal mesh tube, also painted gray, five feet above his head. Some kind of maintenance tube or shaft, leading upward? If so, then it was the way out. He felt giddy with relief.

Catching a whiff of halothane stirred up from below drove him into motion. Van Dyckman grabbed the rung just above his shoulders and found another one at the level of his right foot. He started to scale the rungs, feeling the layers of grime and crud against his palm. With all the collected grit, he wondered when was the last time any worker had used them. Maybe not since the 1960s.

No matter. He was going to use the ladder now.

He climbed to the next rung, pulling himself higher. Each step lifted him another foot and a half above the halothane . . . but he no longer just wanted to rise above the knockout gas and wait out the lockdown. No, he needed to get as far from those radioactive warheads as possible. This maintenance shaft should take him out of the cavern, lead him to safety, and get him out of here! He might be the only one to survive.

In that case, it would be a lot easier to keep his story straight.

Senator Pulaski and Victoria Doyle were already dead, but what about the others? Just before he climbed into the half-enclosed mesh tunnel, he scanned across the floor outside the vault, but he saw no sign of Adonia Rojas, Colonel Whalen, or Simon Garibaldi. He assumed their unconscious—or dead—bodies lay somewhere beneath the thickening yellow mist.

He kept climbing, vanishing into the maintenance shaft with a renewed sense of vigor and optimism. He was the national program manager, the only man who could salvage Valiant Locksmith for the good of the country.

Desperate times, desperate measures. He had to make damn sure Victoria's illicit weapons stockpile was cleared out. An outrageous hazard! This was *his* Mountain, dammit—his and no one else's!

His throat and lungs burned from the exertion, but as van Dyckman climbed higher, he stopped smelling any hint of halothane. Yes, he was going to make it.

Next, he started planning how he could fix the administrative mess that would explode as soon as Rob Harris got the emergency team inside, which would start another cascade of political disasters. So many tangled moving parts!

How was he going to manage the revelations of all the screwups that had happened today, especially the stockpile of State Department "devices" hidden in a clandestine DOE nuclear waste site? The unacknowledged nukes would have to be moved immediately, under special protection. Maybe behind the scenes there would be enough political will, and embarrassment, to keep Velvet Hammer quiet, have the incomplete warheads whisked away to some other classified location—somewhere *he* didn't have to worry about.

The only drawback would be if Adonia, Colonel Whalen, and Garibaldi had somehow survived. They had observed Victoria's nukes, as well as all the safety and security blunders, driven by the Mountain's competing systems. But Valiant Locksmith had to remain intact, by any means necessary.

Van Dyckman was confident enough in his political skills that he could manage Adonia and Whalen, if they were still alive. They were government employees, and as an Assistant Secretary, he could order them to keep quiet. And if they didn't cooperate, he could torpedo their careers. They had signed the nondisclosure paperwork, and they knew they could go to jail if they revealed unauthorized information.

But if Simon Garibaldi managed to blab to his Sanergy protesters, that would ruin everything. If not for the whining of such gadflies, the scientific community would have solved the nuclear waste problem decades ago. Yucca Mountain would be a successful, secure site to stockpile high-level waste. Nuclear energy would be clean and safe, and the United States' power needs would be met inexpensively. The economy would be booming . . . and Garibaldi's extremists would have to keep themselves busy saving chuckwallas or the pink fairy armadillo.

Realistically, the best scenario would be if the old scientist had succumbed to a halothane overdose. That way, van Dyckman could properly focus the story, keep the narrative under tight control.

Losing Colonel Whalen and Adonia saddened him, personally. Both were good people, though politically naïve. Years ago he had been Adonia's mentor, and even after his so-called miscalculation about the Granite Bay storage arrays, when she could have humiliated him, she had been savvy enough to keep the misunderstanding—all on her part!—to herself.

Even after the suicidal plane crash, when she accused him of nearly causing civilian first responders to be exposed to radiation, she could have used the incident to bootstrap her own career. In any case she hadn't . . . and he'd never quite understood why. Did she have no ambitions of her own? He appreciated the courtesy, nevertheless.

He knew about Adonia's relationship with Colonel Whalen from years earlier. Government employees fed on gossip. No matter how much sensitive data might be kept secret, personal news was fair game. Stanley's own affair with Victoria had generated a lot of whispering, but Adonia's romance with Colonel Whalen hadn't caused much of a stir. No one gave a damn about two people much lower on the ladder. Adonia and that oversized Boy Scout were made for each other.

The loss of Senator Pulaski was a disaster to the industry, though. As an unwitting advocate, he was a cooperative and reliable funding source who knew when to listen to his scientific advisers, like van Dyckman, even if he didn't understand the science himself.

It certainly was a bad day all around, no denying that.

As he climbed higher up the shaft, he felt a warm breeze flowing down from the top of the cavern. He heard a faint whistling sound, like wind moving from a vent in the ceiling, whispering through the outer safety mesh that wrapped around the metal ladder.

Several rungs higher, the rushing air strengthened, and he realized that the maintenance shaft must be connected to an air duct that pulled fresh, outside air down into Hydra Mountain. Maybe it would lead him out! He really needed to get to the operations center, since he had a lot of damage control to do.

Across the cavern, van Dyckman could see other ducts that must be carrying air up *out* of the Mountain, perhaps designed to vent diesel fumes from that gigantic crane. Eventually, the exhaust flow would draw out the halothane gas pooled down on the floor and make the lower level safe again.

He paused just long enough to feel his bloody hands throb on the dirt-encrusted rungs. He had no intention of waiting for the system reboot to finish.

The maintenance shaft extended up into the grotto ceiling above, and as he climbed higher, the wind rushed down from the opening. In the narrowing tunnel above, van Dyckman saw two lines of lights that led up into the solid rock, showing a clear path for him to climb. A way out.

As he ascended into the granite ceiling, he struggled against the increasing airstream. Rung after rung, he climbed straight up. He was well clear of the knockout gas, so his head was clear, but he still worried about falling. Once inside the ceiling, he felt much more claustrophobic than when he could see the expansive cavern.

The rock around him muffled the ambient noise, but he heard a rhythmic throbbing high overhead. The string of dim lights that ran up the shaft showed him a little detail, but the shaft looked the same, and endless. He moved on, rung after rung, deeper and deeper into the grotto's ceiling.

Eventually, van Dyckman glimpsed light coming from the side—another tunnel, perpendicular to the vertical maintenance shaft. He reached a horizontal air vent that crossed into the shaft. Far above, he could definitely see rotating blades—a fan pulling outside air down into the cavern. That made sense, but it would block his way out from that direction if he climbed higher.

A constant, gentler stream of air flowed into the horizontal duct, and he considered what he knew of the ventilation channels inside the Mountain. He must have reached the upper level, where the storage tunnels and the operations center were located.

The choice was obvious. Van Dyckman could follow this horizontal vent until he found a place to get out. Now he was thankful for the health and safety regulations that required retrofitting this place under the new DOE stewardship.

Squirming, he pulled himself into the horizontal shaft, sliding against its cold metal surface. He crawled forward on his stomach, smearing a path through the accumulated dust. At last, he had an escape plan.

Shawn hung on the crane boom as he studied the water spraying from the breach in the pool. "We've got to plug the leak. It's the only way to keep the wall from collapsing and exposing the rods."

Adonia knew what a collapse of the pool would mean: radiation burst. A scattershot of billions of neutrons interacting with the Velvet Hammer nuclear pits . . . criticality, multiple detonations.

"The water level is dropping already, and there wasn't much clearance above the rods in the first place," Garibaldi said. "With all that water pressure at the bottom of the pool, the breach will rip soon, and then we'll have a catastrophic failure. It's simple engineering."

Adonia said, "We've got to patch the wall at all costs, but what can we use to plug the leak? Do we lower ourselves down there and press some metal up against the side? Or maybe use those plastic slabs on the floor? Would that be enough?"

The water sprayed out as if from a high-pressure hose, and the force of the water would blast away anything they tried to apply from the outside. They couldn't stand there and plug the leak with their thumbs, like the Dutch boy did with the hole in the dike—it might undergo a catastrophic failure at any moment.

"You couldn't possibly adhere it well enough," Garibaldi said. "And we'd fall unconscious in seconds in that swamp of halothane gas. How would we get to the materials? We'd never finish the job before we were overcome."

Shawn started working his way back down the crane's boom. "You can't patch it from the outside. The water pressure is too great. The only way to stop the leak is from the inside. The water pressure would hold a patch in place, form a seal."

"Like a bathtub stopper," Adonia said. "But how do we apply a patch from the inside? The leak is twenty feet down, and the rod that caused the breach is in the way."

Shawn stated the obvious, sounding grim. "Somebody has to go down there. A lot of people will die if we don't fix this."

Gray-skinned, Garibaldi looked exhausted and fatalistic. "When we swam across before, we were safe because the rods were set in the center of the pool, the water level was higher, and we stayed near the side, but now the situation has changed. When the rods toppled together there's a good chance their cladding was damaged." Somehow, he still managed to sound professorial. "As I'm sure you've guessed by now, anyone who moves the rods out of the way and patches the breach will surely receive a lethal exposure."

Shawn took a deep breath. "Not a good way to go."

Adonia swallowed hard, and the water continued to spray out. "A thousand violins, but we'll all be dead if that plastic fails."

"No time to lose," Shawn said.

Adonia didn't bother to think, didn't hesitate. "It's got to be me. The breach is twenty feet down, and I'm the best swimmer." She looked at Shawn. "You know it. Don't argue."

He scrambled down the boom's metal framework to get to her. "Not a chance. I'm not letting you."

Garibaldi reached up to block Shawn. "Stick to your climbing, boy. She's right—she's a much better swimmer than you." He looked up at the ceiling and the catwalk that led to the communications shaft up above. "We can't afford to wait three more hours for a rescue team. We've got to let them know now, and they'd better have the right emergency equipment when they finally get in here." His brow furrowed. "Whatever we do, you know the patch on that pool will be only a temporary solution, but it may buy enough time."

Adonia nodded. "Harris doesn't know that Victoria's vault is open and the nuclear cores exposed, and he'll need special equipment to secure and shield those warheads. There's a Nuclear Emergency Support Team on base, stationed at Sandia labs. The NEST team can take care of the nukes, and Rob's emergency crew can close down this pool."

She swallowed again, realizing the consequences of what she had volunteered to do—but it had to be done. What happened in the next few minutes might well affect the lives of millions of people. . . .

Garibaldi stared down at the pool, his eyes darting back and forth. From above, Adonia could see the fuel rods toppled near the breach in the pool wall. Even in the deep, rippled water she could see the Senator's body trapped by the rods, deep underwater, and she felt sickened.

"I'll climb down to the floor, hold my breath against the gas," Shawn said. "I'm sure I can push some of the construction material into the pool. If I collapse after that, you'll still have what you need to make a patch, Adonia."

The cavern floor was a soup of marker smoke from the halothane, now five or six feet deep. Even if he got safely down to the floor, she knew Shawn could never make his way to the construction material, carry it to the top of the pool, and dump it into the water before the halothane rendered him unconscious. "You'd never make it."

His face was flushed. "We have to try!"

"Your effort would be irrelevant, Colonel," Garibaldi said. "I doubt even a strong swimmer like Ms. Rojas could pull it down twenty feet to the breach."

Adonia held on to the crane boom, feeling her desperation increase. "Then what are we going to use as a patch? If we don't do something—"

Garibaldi kept peering into the pool. "One must use whatever resources are available." His smile reflected a moment of black humor. "And it's about time Senator Pulaski finally made himself useful." He pointed down at the corpse trapped under the water near the dislodged rods. "Human skin is waterproof and pliable enough to conform to a leak. Press the Senator's body up against the tear, and it would form enough of a plug to stop the flow of water and temporarily prevent the wall from rupturing."

Adonia pulled back. "You want me to use his *body* as a patch?"

"It's already in the pool and down at the depth we need. It could be maneuvered in place without too much difficulty, and the water pressure will seal his body against the leak, acting as a plug. It would serve the purpose of keeping the water from draining and the side from collapsing, at least for a while. An emergency team can make permanent repairs as soon as they get in here."

"There's nothing else we can use," Shawn said, resigned. "And if we don't do it, the alternative is a big nuclear flash, turning the Southwest into the world's largest glass parking lot."

Adonia remained doubtful. "How would we move the fuel rod that's pinning the Senator to the bottom? They weigh nearly a ton—too heavy to lift, even in water."

Garibaldi patted a horizontal strut on the boom. "Make a pulley by looping Colonel Whalen's rope around this strut and lowering one end to the pool. We tie the rope around the top of the rod, and lever it up, two of us pulling down, as a counterweight. Once the rod is lifted off the Senator, the person in the pool can move the body."

"Brilliant." Shawn tried to jockey around Garibaldi. "I'll tie the rope, then wrestle the body into place at the bottom of the pool to seal the breach. It has to be done."

"Not a chance, Shawn," Adonia said. "I already told you that requires swimming skills, and at that depth it's easier for me. Arguing is only going to delay us until the nukes go off! Now let me do this."

They were partway up the crane's extended boom, directly above the pool, but still nearly twenty feet higher than when they had jumped from the ledge. Adonia's stomach lurched at the thought of missing the side and hitting one of the rods. No margin for error.

Then she had an idea. "The rope," she said to Shawn. "Drop it down into the water, and I can shimmy down before I tie it to the top of the rod."

"I don't like this—"

"You're wasting time arguing."

His face set, Shawn looped the rope around a horizontal strut, secured one end on the lattice, and knotted the rope several times on the boom framework. He dropped the other end, and the yellow line snaked down until it hit the surface fifty feet below them, leaving plenty of slack for Adonia to pull to the bottom.

"I'll keep it tied, so we won't strand you in the pool," he said, avoiding her eyes, looking angry and ashamed. "We can rotate the rod, then pull you up. If we're quick enough, we can limit your exposure."

Shawn didn't say anything more, but she knew he was churning through numerous arguments in his own head, failing to convince himself.

Adonia forced herself to inhale deep breaths, getting ready to work her way down the rope to the pool. She was sure her mind was playing tricks when she smelled faint wisps of sweet gas stirred up from far below. Water continued to spray out from the puncture, but in a wider stream, clearly growing. If the pool suffered a catastrophic failure, she could never stop it.

Adonia also knew in her heart that when she wrapped the rope around the fuel rod to move it, she would receive a massive lethal exposure. Before long, she would be just as dead as Senator Pulaski, although her death would be much slower and more painful.

But she would have averted the catastrophe and saved countless lives. That was what mattered.

She focused her thoughts, concentrating only on what she had to do. Simple, easy steps: slide down the rope, drop into the water, swim to the bottom, wrap the rope around the fallen fuel rod, free the Senator's body, then press his skin against the breach in the wall as a temporary plug.

As she performed the task, Adonia didn't dare think about what the radiation would be doing to her cells, her internal organs. Even if she made it back out, she wouldn't feel the effects immediately. But the damage would be done, and her body would quickly, painfully, fall apart in the next days or weeks.

But if she didn't do this, the water would keep pouring out and the plastic wall would soon fail. And that would be an incredibly bad day for everyone.

Standing beneath her on a horizontal strut, Garibaldi leaned out and took hold of the rope, tugging it to him.

Adonia pulled back. "What are you doing?"

But the older scientist had already looped the rope around himself and was swinging half of his body away from the boom and out over the pool. He stared at the water below as he levered himself out farther. "I am perfectly capable of swimming deep and moving that man's body. You may be the best swimmer, Ms. Rojas, but you're too small. I've got the weight and height to move him." He screwed up his face. "As soon as I free the Senator, you and Colonel Whalen need to escape up that maintenance shaft while there's still time. Tell Harris everything that's happened down here. You know what needs to be done to make the Mountain safe again. Don't let them cover this up!"

Precariously balanced, Adonia reached down to grab him by the arm. "I won't let you do it. Don't be—"

Garibaldi used his momentum and pulled himself back toward the boom, balling his free hand into a fist. He punched Adonia full in the face, taking her completely by surprise. A bright flash of pain exploded from her nose, behind her eyes, and into her head.

She reeled, nearly lost her grip, but hooked her elbow around one of the vertical struts. White and red flashes sparkled in front of her vision. Shawn was shouting. She drew back her hand from her nose and saw it covered with blood.

"Sometimes you have to use more than pacifist methods," Garibaldi said.

She cleared her vision just in time to see him count silently to himself, then let go at the apex of his swing and slide fifty feet straight down into the pool.

38

After his ordeal so far, van Dyckman was surprised to be so flustered by something as trivial as a second sneeze, but the noise echoed inside the cramped metal duct, and it was damned annoying. As he crawled along on his bloody hands and knees, he stirred the dust buildup, and as the air flowed past him, it blew more grit and dust into his face. He sneezed again.

Crawling through the cramped, dusty duct was better than climbing up those endless metal rungs, but the rectangular galvanized steel vent seemed to go on forever. At least he was still alive, unlike Victoria and the rest of the team. He was good at finding silver linings.

He kept his head down, rehearsing what he would do once he found an exit, what he would say when he reached the operations center. Right now his entire universe consisted of a three-foot-wide and two-foot-high metal box that was infinitely long. He kept slithering ahead.

Every twenty feet he passed a grid on the side of the duct that vented air into the tunnel, but he could see only concrete floor and granite walls covered with steel mesh. At last, he came to a larger vent grid, and when he peered through the slats, he found himself above one of the dry-storage side tunnels. Squinting, he could see a huge vault door, just like the one that had trapped them inside the

Mountain when the shit first hit the fan. Through the vent he saw individual chambers—was Mrs. Garcia still trapped in one of them?

He tried to orient himself. With all the administrative paperwork he had completed for Valiant Locksmith, he had seen maps of Hydra Mountain, the tunnels and lockdown vault doors, but he had never paid close attention to the details. During the first part of the inspection tour, he recalled seeing the metal air ducts along the tunnel ceiling. That must be where he was now, which meant he was crawling toward the interior corridor—not far from the operations center.

No one could have predicted that a civilian plane would make an emergency landing inside the fence and trigger a cascade of chaos. Van Dyckman couldn't be blamed for that, but the fool Pulaski had made the situation a thousand times worse by using his damned cell phone. The Senator had been Valiant Locksmith's staunchest ally, but he was also an idiot.

The State Department would probably play the national security trump card with Victoria's covertly stored nukes. They'd argue to the President that Velvet Hammer was much more important than storing nuclear waste. Van Dyckman would find his own head on the chopping block, and Valiant Locksmith would be shut down, once again leaving all the nation's nuclear power plants vulnerable.

Pressed to show real progress as soon as possible, van Dyckman had cut a few corners by shipping highly enriched fuel rods into Hydra Mountain, and he'd done it much faster than he could build the pools to cool them. Senator Pulaski had facilitated that by circumventing the interagency review process, which probably would have stopped the rods from being shipped. And for sure, the pools from being built.

So what if skipping that one small review just happened to be illegal? His program had already reduced the amount of waste inadequately stored across the country by over 15 percent!

Now, without powerful Senator Pulaski flying high cover for him, he knew that *his* ass would be fried—by the President, the DOE Secretary, the Secretary of State, the SECDEF, the Congressional

Intelligence Oversight Committee, the Justice Department, the FBI . . . hell, maybe even the American Humane Society.

His career would be over, just like that.

An influential senator was also dead, drowned in a cooling pool for radioactive waste—the tabloids would love that! And Valiant Locksmith was on the doorstep of another outrageous program of stockpiling undocumented nuclear devices. Oh, and by the way, a DOE Undersecretary was also dead.

Only yesterday, he had been so confident that he would quickly and efficiently wrap up this high-level review. Senator Pulaski should have obtained the go-ahead to continue Valiant Locksmith. And when the program was complete and all the nation's nuclear waste safely stored inside the Mountain, he himself would have been a shoo-in for the next Secretary of Energy.

Now, he faced the real possibility of being indicted and serving time in Federal prison. His spirits sank as he crawled along. What could he do? How quickly would the hammer come down? Would he even have time to fly back to Washington, D.C., so he could start damage control, spin the narrative? There were a lot of bodies to explain away.

He couldn't do anything about it until he got out of here. As soon as he reached the ops center, he would demand that Harris send the Nuclear Emergency Support Team in to close up Victoria's vault and shield the warheads from the increased background radiation in the grotto. Second priority would be to send divers in protective suits to rearrange the toppled fuel rods and restore the array.

Maybe if he played his cards right, he could shift all the blame onto Victoria for her malicious carelessness. If given the chance, he would demand the immediate shutdown of Velvet Hammer. If that failed, Senator Pulaski would also make an excellent scapegoat. The Senator had indeed been the cause of this debacle, and everyone in the industry knew that despite his position, the man knew absolutely nothing about the programs he oversaw.

Van Dyckman crawled past another storage tunnel intersection, where the overhead vent took a right turn. This ventilation duct wouldn't connect with the main interior corridor—too much of a security risk. Even the DOE Health and Safety people wouldn't be permitted to run a vent from the interior Special Access Program area out to the receiving space.

But he had to get out of here somehow.

Squirming forward, using his elbows and knees, he realized that the duct *did* end directly next to the operations center, which was still within the security envelope. Though his bloody hands ached and his elbows and knees were raw, he crawled forward with greater speed. He could see the light at the end of the tunnel—literally!

He pressed his face against a metal screen that overlooked the operations center, far below. People stood together in clumps, pointing at their monitors, speaking animatedly, clearly on an emergency footing.

At this height above the bustling floor, he couldn't hear them, but maybe he could bang on the ventilation screen, dislodge it. The drop was much too far for him to fall, but a screen crashing down among the techs would certainly get their attention. Somebody would see him, rescue him.

And then a second catapult of shit would hit the fan. What other choice did he have?

Farther along the duct, though, he glimpsed a second mesh screen, another opening. He needed to look at his options before he did anything. Breathing hard and fast, he choked on a spray of disturbed dust. He scooted down the duct and peered through the second screen. This vent opened into Harris's private Eagle's Nest overlooking the ops center! The site manager was alone inside the office, deep in concentration as he pondered a screen, moving his finger to trace a detailed map of the tunnel complex.

Van Dyckman was about to hammer on the duct and shout for help, but he caught himself, suddenly having reservations. How was he going to explain this to Harris? What story would he tell?

A lie would be exposed quickly enough, and the site manager would certainly know, so it was best for van Dyckman to tell as much of the truth as possible. But the truth could be viewed through many different filters and alternative facts. He had to figure out what to say, how to perform damage control . . . whom to blame.

With the exception of Rob Harris, they were the only ones who even knew about the potential deadly interaction of the two SAPs. Every other member of the review team was dead or unconscious. If van Dyckman could find a way to secure Victoria's vault and protect the illicit devices, then he could order the warheads moved to an appropriate DoD location, quickly and without a fuss. From what he could tell, the State Department also had the incentive to take care of the problem cleanly, keep this as quiet as possible. Maybe van Dyckman could fix the mess and keep Valiant Locksmith alive.

Because of the highly classified nature of both SAPs, these problems were designed to be kept in the dark, away from public scrutiny. So long as everyone cooperated.

Rob Harris, "Regulation Rob," was the only complicating piece left. The Hydra Mountain site manager knew about both SAPs, but had chosen not to reveal the hazard to anyone who could do something about it. The moron had tied himself up in so much red tape that he refused to tell the right hand what the left hand was doing. *He* had almost caused this terrible disaster!

Harris had hand-picked the members of the inspection team to observe and to ask questions. Several of the people had seemed odd choices, so maybe Harris had set them up on purpose, hoping one of them would blow the whistle on a problem that he didn't have the balls to reveal himself.

The pieces began to fall into place for van Dyckman. Yes, Harris must have assembled this team so he could keep his hands clean and follow the damned rules. The site manager was playing a clumsy game of political checkers in a world of complex chess.

Van Dyckman knew that *he* had to form the narrative. Harris didn't have the political savvy to wiggle out of this. Van Dyckman counted on that. He needed to make the man keep his mouth shut.

He realized how he could blame the disaster on Harris. The site manager's poor, unqualified choices for the review team were at the root of the problem. And then Harris had conveniently separated himself from the others just before the alarms went off.

No, that would not look good for Regulation Rob at all.

Van Dyckman just needed to get through the next few hours. It was his best-case scenario. If Adonia, Whalen, and Garibaldi were indeed dead, along with Victoria and the Senator, then he could easily concoct a cover story that used Harris as a scapegoat, and the man would be prevented from talking for security reasons. Rob Harris would never again see the light of day after being buried deep in a Federal prison.

39

Still holding her smashed nose, Adonia watched Garibaldi shimmy down the rope. He slipped, trying to keep his grip, then finally, half-way down, he let go and dropped like a stone the remaining twenty feet to the pool. The water level had dropped noticeably, leaving less than six feet of water above the tall radioactive rods.

For an agonizing moment as she clung to the boom high above, Adonia thought he was going to hit one of the upright rods as he fell in the pool. Garibaldi struck feetfirst, his toes pointed down, and a geyser of water shot up as he plunged deep. Adonia wiped drip-ping blood from her face as she struggled to see.

A few seconds later, Garibaldi splashed back to the surface and began stroking over to where the toppled rods had fallen against the fiber-reinforced plastic wall. Water still sprayed from the breach, but at least the shock wave from his impact hadn't made the damage worse.

Shawn swung down the boom and climbed next to her. He was angry and worried. "What the hell does he think he's doing?" He reached out to touch her throbbing face, and his fingers came away wet with red. "He hit you!"

"I wasn't going to let him go." Pinching her smashed nose, she looked down as blood dripped onto her fingers and then fell into the open air. "He took me by surprise, made sure I wouldn't be able to stop him." Her voice sounded strange in her ears.

"He's down there now. It is what it is." Shawn watched Garibaldi swim into position. "Now we've got to help him raise the rod." He started pulling down on the rope to give them enough slack to serve as a counterweight. "I can't say I'm not glad that it wasn't you."

She sniffled, coughed blood. "He told us to head up the ventilation shaft. If we can alert Rob Harris, we could really help the nuclear response team take care of this before it gets worse."

"We can't leave Garibaldi here, no matter what he says. He still needs our help." Shawn looped the slack around a horizontal strut to serve as a pulley and handed a portion of the rope to Adonia. "Pull down when he's ready—I'll get below you and help."

Down in the pool, Garibaldi swam to the other end of the rope. Adonia leaned over and called down, "Take the rope and loop it around the fuel rod. Let us know when it's secure and we'll lever it up."

He gave a brisk nod, grabbed the end of the line, and plunged underwater. Adonia's heart felt heavy, knowing what the scientist was doing to himself as he stroked down to the highly radioactive rods. But she also knew what was at stake; they all did.

Focusing on the task at hand, she and Shawn positioned themselves on the sturdy boom, getting ready to use their body weight to pull their end of the line and haul up the end of the rod. She was just below the horizontal strut they would use as a pulley; Shawn was two struts below her.

Garibaldi's wavering form went deeper, pulling the rope with him as he worked his way down to the fallen fuel rod that trapped the body. He seemed to be struggling.

Adonia felt a lump in her throat. She knew how hard it was to dive that deep, even for a championship swimmer like herself, especially holding a rope in one hand.

"He thought it would be easy," she said, looking down at Shawn. "The rods are about twenty feet down, and that would be a challenge under normal circumstances." By now, she knew his lungs must be ready to explode as he ran out of air.

"I should have been the one to do it, Shawn." If Garibaldi failed, she would have to jump down to save him anyway, and then both of them would receive a lethal exposure. She felt sick at the thought.

Bubbles rose from the ripples where Garibaldi had submerged. She and Shawn could still see him working among the fallen rods. He would be looping the end of the rope around the top of the fuel rod, near Pulaski's trapped body. The temperature would be much warmer in the pool now, and Garibaldi would severely burn his hands just by handling the long radioactive cylinder. He wouldn't even see the flood of neutrons pouring through his body.

He seemed to stay down forever.

Finally, Garibaldi stroked upward, moving urgently, and burst to the surface again, gasping and coughing. Treading water, he finally called up at them. "Go ahead . . . pull it up! I'll go back down and free the body." He heaved deep breaths, getting ready to dive again.

Two struts below, Shawn tugged on the rope looped around the horizontal strut above her, taking in the excess slack until it was taut. He looked up at Adonia. "On your count, pull down on the rope as hard as you can. With the two of us throwing our weight into it, we should be able to raise the end of the rod enough for Garibaldi to pull the body free." He hesitated. "How's your nose?"

She wiped her face, but by now the bleeding had slowed. "Still hurts. Let's do this."

Grasping the rope with both hands, Shawn leaned back at an angle on the lattice boom, using the rope for balance. Adonia wrapped a leg around one of the diagonal struts, also bracing herself. She called down to Garibaldi. "Ready!"

The older scientist gulped one more deep breath and dove. He stroked down, heading toward the bottom. Just before he reached the Senator's body, she shouted to Shawn, "Pull!" They both threw their weight onto the rope, helping Garibaldi. As she exerted herself, blood dripped from her nose again, and she felt dizzy.

The rope barely moved.

"Again!"

The rope moved a few inches.

Hand over hand, Adonia and Shawn pulled down, serving as a

counterweight for the heavy fallen rod. She wished she had gloves for a better grip on the line.

They had pulled no more than a foot when Shawn spoke in a strained voice: "Hold it there—that might be enough."

Throwing their weight against the rope, they watched Garibaldi's uncertain form struggle to free the dead man from the fallen rod, finally dragging the figure loose. Pulling his burden, he swam, kicking toward the lower wall of the pool.

The Senator's drowned body would be close to neutral buoyancy, easily maneuverable. Once Garibaldi positioned the corpse to cover the breach in the inside wall, the force of the water pressure would hold the plug firmly in place.

Holding her breath, Adonia watched the gushing water from the breach in the wall slow to a trickle, then stop. "He plugged the leak!" she said.

"There's that at least," Shawn said. "The water level will stay stable for now."

Seconds later, Garibaldi's head broke the surface, his gray-white hair plastered to his skull. He gasped for breath. "Got to get the rope free." Without waiting for a response, he dove back down.

"Give the rope some slack so he can untie the knot," Shawn said.

They slowly loosened the line, letting the fuel rod settle back against the adjacent rod. Garibaldi didn't stay down long, and soon popped back to the surface, gasping and exhausted.

Adonia knew that with the halothane still thick on the floor of the cavern, the scientist could never climb down the side of the pool and make his way back to the crane and climb up again. "We'll have to haul him up with the rope," she said.

Utterly weary, Garibaldi grabbed the rope still dangling from the crane boom high above. After Adonia shouted instructions, he tied the end in a loop around his chest and waved up. His voice was rough and weak. "You don't expect me to spend the rest of the day in this hot tub, do you?"

With her hands sore and her nose still bleeding, she didn't know how they would pull up two hundred pounds of dead weight, but it was obvious he would never be able to scale the rope himself.

"He weighs a lot less than a fuel rod," Shawn said, and again positioned himself below her, determined to try. "Again, if we pull together, we'll haul him up, one foot at a time. Piece of cake." He gave her a wan smile. "Just don't let go of the rope."

"Right. Let's do it." Adonia adjusted herself for stability on the struts. "Ready, ready, *now*." She yanked down as hard as she could.

She felt the rope move, this time much more than when they were pulling up the rod. Shawn had used his legs to push back, raising Garibaldi up a few feet with a lurch, then readied himself for another short gain.

She gritted her teeth and they pulled again—two feet, and then another two feet. He rose out of the water, swaying above the pool. Adonia disengaged her thoughts, trying not to think of how long it would take. They methodically heaved the rope and moved the dangling man closer to the crane, foot by foot. Garibaldi just hung there, and water dripped from his clothes back into the pool like widely spaced raindrops.

"When he gets closer, I'll reach out and bring him in if you can secure the line."

"Copy."

After an eternity, they pulled the older scientist high above the pool, almost to their height, but with the angle of the boom, he slowly twisted on the rope a few yards away. "A little more!" Adonia said. "He's just about here."

Garibaldi reached out to grab the metal lattice, but missed. His jerky movement made him swing and spin as he dangled, and the rope slipped.

"Hold it! *Hold!*" Adonia braced herself hard as the dead weight slammed against the framework.

Shawn grunted as he stabilized Garibaldi high above the water. "Stop moving! Let us pull you in."

"Just trying to help!"

"You've done more than enough to save us all." Adonia still felt the heavy weight of guilt as she tugged on the rope again. Though Garibaldi wouldn't feel any internal effects of the radiation yet, he must know that he had suffered a fatal exposure. Finally, he swung close enough that she could reach out to grab his outstretched hand as Shawn secured the line around the metal lattice.

Garibaldi's skin was wet and clammy, but his grip was firm. He clasped her wrist, and she swung him in. His hands were already an angry red, severely burned. His feet hit the boom, and he pulled himself onto a strut. When he was balanced again, he wrapped his arms around the lattice and shuddered.

Adonia broke the tense, awkward silence. "Saying thanks doesn't come close to acknowledging what you just did. The nation owes you a debt of gratitude, even if they never find out what happened."

Garibaldi glanced at her, embarrassed. "Sorry about hitting you in the nose. I couldn't think of any other way to convince you."

"You didn't convince me anyway." She touched her face, felt the sticky blood there. "I'll get over it."

Shawn was quiet for a moment before he asked, "How long were you in direct contact with the rod? How much—"

Garibaldi looked at his red and blistered hands. "Don't dance around it, Colonel. I received a lethal dose, probably many times over. I could see some of the cladding had been scraped off as well."

"I'm sorry," Adonia said in a soft voice.

Garibaldi lifted his chin. "Don't get maudlin. Now, we need to climb out of here, find some way to communicate with Harris. I don't know how much time is left on the lockdown, or how long the emergency team will take to get in here, or even how long the Senator's body will plug that leak. Remember that even though I sealed the breach temporarily, there are plenty of stray neutrons that could hit one of Victoria's warhead cores and trigger a reaction."

Shawn looked up to study where the air vents converged in the ceiling near the catwalks. An aluminum ladder led from the high catwalk to a hatch in the center vent. "We can climb to that access shaft. Up the boom, drop onto the catwalk, and make our way to the ladder. If you think you're up to it, sir? Otherwise, you can rest here, wait it out."

The older scientist nodded wearily. "I feel adequate enough, for the time being. Let's get moving."

Shawn nodded and started looping the long rope around his shoulder.

Adonia clung to a different sort of hope. "We also need to get you to a hospital. Several of them specialize in radiation exposure, like one of the Mayo Clinics."

"Right now, I wouldn't mind just a comfortable bed, but that's only prolonging the inevitable. I've . . . only got a few weeks to live, at most."

"A person can do a lot of useful things in a few weeks," Adonia said. "If you spoke out, you could focus the nation on solving the problem nobody wants to talk about."

"You want me to convince them to open Yucca Mountain after all? Or keep storing the waste in here?" He let out a quick laugh. "Maybe I can talk them into using an alternative to nuclear power."

Adonia shook her head, surprised that she had been distracted into the debate. "I'd rather have this discussion in a more comfortable place—outside the Mountain."

Garibaldi gave her a curious smile. "Oh, we will have the debate, a very prominent and public one. As I'm dying of radiation poisoning, I'll have a platform like I've never had before." He wiped at his wet hair. "See, there's always a silver lining."

40

In the midst of the emergency, with Hydra Mountain's systems still rebooting, actions that would have seemed preposterous under normal circumstances now seemed possible. Van Dyckman knew it was time to act.

As he observed Rob Harris through the air ventilation screen, the site manager seemed overwhelmed by indecisiveness, waiting for some superior to give him instructions, not to mention political cover. Regulation Rob had no playbook for this situation, and he never took his own initiative, never colored outside the lines. Now that van Dyckman knew about the Velvet Hammer SAP, he understood why Harris had tied himself in dithering knots: the man just didn't have the balls or the imagination to bend the rules and find a solution.

He watched as Harris frowned at the touchscreen, wavering his extended finger over the facility map. His standard emergency checklist probably didn't tell him what to do. Time for van Dyckman to exert his authority and take advantage of Harris's character flaw. He could get the matter taken care of, right now, start working on damage control to offset this lackluster flunky and prevent him from doing further harm.

Valiant Locksmith was an unacknowledged, waived Special Access Program, and with the right finesse van Dyckman could salvage it, blame the right people, make the right excuses. But it had to be done carefully, and it was all predicated on Harris.

Because of his plodding attention to detail, the site manager no doubt had documentation and justification for all his actions, and that might be problematic. But politically, Rob Harris was deaf as a post, so he would make a good scapegoat.

In contrast, as the national program manager, van Dyckman often left the specifics to others while he concentrated on the big picture. And he always knew *exactly* what he had to do.

Huddled in the air duct above the Eagle's Nest, he made his final plans, going over every last detail. He began to convince himself, without a flicker of doubt, that *Rob Harris* was responsible for the whole mess. The site manager had not only caused it, in fact, but was actively trying to cover it up!

Bad enough that Harris would abandon the high-level review team just before the initial lockdown, but a small plane crash, *really*? How contrived! And now five people were dead because of the man's gross incompetence. If Dr. Garibaldi was correct about the potential for catastrophic interaction between the two SAPs, then they were all at risk of a massive nuclear detonation.

Yes, Harris must have known about this danger all along! And he had hidden behind red tape to prevent anyone from knowing about it? He couldn't find a way to communicate his concerns, even via classified channels? If Harris had mentioned it to his superior, van Dyckman would have pulled strings himself and taken care of the issue before it ever became a problem. Too late now, and all because of the man's incompetence and cowardice.

Assistant Secretary Stanley L. van Dyckman was the national program manager for Valiant Locksmith, and Rob Harris was just a tired old retread dragged out of retirement. By hiding behind a veil of red tape, Harris had put the entire *nation* in danger. And he should be held liable for his mistakes.

It was time.

Van Dyckman squirmed inside the rectangular duct until he lay on his back, knees bent, feet against the metal ventilation screen. He kicked as hard as he could. The loud banging sound reverberated, and the metal barrier mesh rattled, bent, but remained stubbornly attached.

From his desk, Harris lurched out of his chair, looked up at the ceiling, and cried out.

With greater force, van Dyckman kicked again and again until two corners broke and the screen bent down. His feet dangled out of the air duct, and he finally managed to slide out and drop to the office floor. The maneuver was clumsy and undignified, and he looked a disheveled mess, but he brushed himself off and regained his composure.

Harris ran from his desk, gaping in disbelief and surprise. "Mr. van Dyckman! How . . . how did you get out? Thank goodness you're all right." He tried to help him, but van Dyckman pushed his assistance aside. Harris asked, "Did anyone else escape? Are the others okay?"

Instead of answering, van Dyckman lashed out with the accusations that were building inside him. "Dammit, Harris—your actions could kill everyone in the Mountain!" As the man recoiled, taken aback by this vehemence, van Dyckman continued, "The others are dead. You let us all go in there without telling us about the deadly countermeasures, without telling us what Victoria Doyle was storing right next to my cooling pools! Do you realize the danger that poses?"

"But, sir . . . I was not allowed—"

Van Dyckman's eyes darted to the phone in the center of the desk, and he strode over, grabbing it like a hawk seizing a rabbit. Harris spluttered, hurrying after him. Van Dyckman grabbed the phone and shouted into it. "This is Assistant Secretary van Dyckman. Get Protective Services to the site manager's office, ASAP."

The voice sounded startled. "Sir, may I ask—"

"You heard me! Security, here—now! And scramble an emergency nuclear response team to the lower levels the moment the reboot is finished and the lockdown is lifted. We are in full crisis." Harris stared at him with wide eyes, panicked and also cowed. As the voice on the phone acknowledged the instructions, van Dyckman also demanded, "And get me the Incident Commander. Understand?"

"Yes, sir, Mr. van Dyckman. Right away." The phone clicked off.

Reeling next to the table in the spacious office, Harris looked as though he'd been hit by a baseball bat. "Sir, what do you mean they're all dead? How did you get past the lockdown? And . . . and why did you just call Protective Services? Is there a new security threat I need to know about?"

"*You're* the security threat, Harris." He thrust a finger in the other man's face. "Do you know what you've done? There's a nuclear disaster waiting to happen because you failed to take proper Class One safety precautions down in the lower vault. You knew about Velvet Hammer and the danger it posed, but you neglected to inform *me* about it."

Harris stepped back. "I . . . I was not legally allowed, sir. Both SAPs are unacknowledged programs—"

But van Dyckman was on a roll. "Your actions, or *inactions,* created a dangerous situation with extreme consequences for the entire nation. Your inattention to both safety and security, not to mention common sense, has put Hydra Mountain at great risk, as well as the future of Valiant Locksmith itself."

Heavy footfalls crashed up the stairs outside, and a sharp knock came at the office door. Van Dyckman snapped, "Enter!"

Two DOE Protective Services officers wearing short-sleeved black uniforms prowled into Harris's office, both wearing sidearms, both looking on edge. The older officer, with buzz-cut hair and a chiseled face, frowned as he looked from van Dyckman to Harris. "Is there a situation here?"

Though he looked a mess from crawling through the filthy ducts, van Dyckman took control. He drew himself up and pointed at Harris. "Arrest this man for violating DOE Order 471.5, Special Access Programs, and hold him in strict isolation. He has committed a SAP security breach and must not be allowed to speak to anyone until he has been debriefed by the proper authorities."

Unable to believe what he heard, Harris could barely find the words. "I followed the regulations to the letter. I am not culpable—"

Van Dyckman raised his voice, adding a firm undertone of command. "Furthermore, his inactions have put this facility and the local population in great danger. If we can't get a handle on this crisis immediately, we may have to begin a full-scale evacuation of Kirtland Air Force Base and the greater Albuquerque area."

Stunned for only a moment, the security guards swept forward to the astonished Harris. When they had seized the site manager by the arms, van Dyckman turned to face him. "Mr. Harris, as Assistant Secretary for Nuclear Energy, and your immediate supervisor in your chain of command, I hereby relieve you of all authority as site manager of Hydra Mountain."

Harris opened his mouth to speak, but he lowered his eyes, unable to respond to the barrage. He shook his head, and his shoulders slumped, as if he realized the inevitable. He mumbled, "You . . . do have the authority to do that, Mr. van Dyckman. Yes . . . I understand."

The Protective Services officers turned Harris around, and even though he cooperated fully, they applied handcuffs and marched him out of the office.

Standing next to the conference table in the Eagle's Nest, looking through the broad windows to the busy operations center floor, van Dyckman felt a flush of satisfaction. At last something had gone right. The person truly responsible for this disaster would pay for it. Van Dyckman had been dealt a lousy hand, but if he played his cards right he just might salvage his career.

He reached for the site-wide intercom. He'd make an announcement of Rob Harris's arrest, ensure that everyone knew *he* was in charge and that he had the dire situation under control. Composing the words in his mind, he spun the volume and channel dials, but discovered to his consternation that the intercom wouldn't work.

As the guards escorted Harris away, one of the ops center techs poked her head through the door. She watched Harris being led off and looked questioningly at the unkempt van Dyckman. Impatient, he barked, "Yes? I am now acting site manager for Hydra Mountain. What is it?"

The woman frowned, but regained her composure as van Dyckman took his place behind Harris's desk. She issued her report. "Sir,

Ms. Jennings, the nuclear response incident commander, is on the red line, as you requested."

"Thank you." He placed the intercom mike down on the table. "And get this intercom fixed. High priority. I need to make a facility-wide announcement. Connect me to all the loudspeakers." Van Dyckman reached for the red phone, and when the young tech hesitated at the door, he motioned with his head. "Did you hear me? Get this intercom working—now!"

"Yes, sir." She backed out and closed the door of the upper office.

Van Dyckman picked up the red STE handset, and a curt female voice responded. "Incident Commander Jennings. May I have the situation, sir?"

"Are you cleared for Valiant Locksmith?"

"I have all the tickets for everything inside, sir, but my team is not cognizant of any of the SAPs."

"Well, then," he said, pulling Harris's chair up to the desk. He felt so filthy, his hair clotted with dried dust, his clothes and skin flecked with remnants of sticky foam. "There will be security implications, Jennings, but first things first—once you get inside, you have to mitigate the danger. You'll need full protective gear." He briefed her on the halothane gas, the toppled spent fuel rods in the pool, the open vault that left nuclear devices exposed to the increased neutron flux, and the sticky foam barriers both in the inclined tunnel and the lower vault.

Without hesitating, the commander recited her prioritized actions for when she had access inside the facility. Wearing gas masks and protective clothing, her team would enter the lower level with the appropriate solvents and tools to remove the extensive blockage of hardened sticky foam at the guard portal. Once past that obstacle, they could get to the lower cavern and similarly clear the foam from the Velvet Hammer vault, after which they would seal the door and secure the clandestine nuclear warheads. Finally, in a more in-volved procedure, divers would rig up robotic lifts to restore the disrupted fuel rod array in the temporary pool, while industrial venti-lation pumps would force any remnants of halothane up into the Mountain's vertical exhaust shaft. Once exposed to the UV radiation in sunlight, the gas would quickly break down into harmless constituents.

The team's last priority was to sweep for survivors.

As van Dyckman hung up the red phone, he settled back in the site manager's chair. Once her team broke into the lower cavern, Commander Jennings would shoot a video feed to the office. That would let him watch the response in real time.

But he wasn't through managing the crisis—this was only the beginning. He still had to prevent the existence of both SAPs from being revealed to the public. It was the only way to salvage Valiant Locksmith. If either unacknowledged program was revealed, the uproar would shut down Hydra Mountain, and he couldn't allow that.

Once the nuclear response team mitigated the highest-priority dangers, special workers could perform a full cleanup, and no one would know any better. Harris would be locked away, held incommunicado, and no one could contradict van Dyckman . . . so long as there were no survivors in the lower cavern.

He couldn't imagine how any of them might still be alive, but he had to close the loop, tie up the loose ends, and make sure nothing else went wrong.

That was what made him such an outstanding leader.

41

Climbing the crane's high boom toward the cavern ceiling, Adonia gripped a horizontal strut as she paused to catch her breath. They were nearly to the end, high enough now that the elevated metal walkway ran ten feet below.

"We can lower ourselves and drop safely to the catwalk," she said.

Garibaldi paused, looking down and breathing hard. "It's a narrow target. If we miss, that's a long way to fall. . . ."

Shawn sounded encouraging. "After what you've done today, Dr. Garibaldi, this will be a piece of cake."

"Yes, piece of cake." He sounded intensely weary. "I prefer cookies."

Though he shouldn't be feeling direct effects yet from the severe radiation exposure, he already looked weak. His red and blistered hands grew more inflamed by the minute, making the rigorous climb an excruciating activity. But the older scientist did not complain. He flexed his fingers and winced. "After all this effort, it would be embarrassing for us all if the pool wall failed and a random neutron set off one of those warheads anyway."

Adonia forced a smile for his sake. "Are you suggesting we're unlucky?"

"We've already used up all our bad luck for one day," Shawn said. He looped the rope around the metal lattice, secured the line, and handed Adonia the doubled end. "Wrap it around your waist, and I can lower you to the catwalk."

Adonia shook her head. "It's not that far, and we don't have time. I'll just shimmy down the line, and then I can hold the rope steady from the catwalk. Dr. Garibaldi may need the help."

The scientist heaved a deep breath and also waved the rope away. "If I fall, I fall. It's only ten feet to the walkway—unless I miss. Then it's a lot farther to the floor. I'll take my chances."

Grasping the rope, Adonia swung out above the catwalk and kept her focus on the corrugated steel walkway just below. She worked her way down the rope, and then let herself drop the last two feet, rattling the metal as she landed barefoot on the grid. She winced, but after climbing the crane's boom for so long, it felt good to stand on a flat surface rather than trying to balance on metal struts. She held the end of the rope steady. "Come on, Dr. Garibaldi."

He painstakingly lowered himself, finally sliding the rest of the way down. His knees buckled as he landed on the catwalk, but Adonia grabbed him, steadied him. He brushed himself off to recover his dignity.

Shawn followed, hand over hand, joining them on the metal grid, before he pulled the doubled rope down and coiled it over his shoulder. "Head for the ladder."

Adonia used the diagonal catwalk as a switchback to move across the cavern, padding gingerly along. She did not look down through the open gridwork to see the empty gulf below them. Garibaldi plodded forward, keeping his head down, and she worried how he would be able to climb the vertical shaft into the ceiling once they got up the ladder. She hoped the actual exit from the cavern wasn't too far above. . . .

If nothing else, Shawn could climb swiftly ahead, get out of the Mountain, and sound the alarm. Adonia doubted he would be willing to leave the two of them behind, but what mattered most was that *someone* managed to get out and alert the response teams to the looming disaster inside the massive grotto.

She reached an intersection with the next catwalk and climbed the connecting stairs, heading up toward the middle of the ceiling. Far below, she could see the half-finished in-ground cooling pools amid construction supplies, everything blanketed with a yellowish mist of knockout gas. She reassured herself that the above-ground pool remained plugged with its macabre patch.

Even though water was no longer draining out, the fallen and damaged fuel rods had substantially increased the ambient radiation levels in the chamber. Maybe their efforts minimized the possibility of setting off the Velvet Hammer warheads, but the risk still remained. It seemed like weeks ago that Mrs. Garcia had given her spontaneous tutorial of how neutrons could be reflected, absorbed, and re-radiated until they struck a critical target.

Adonia stopped at the ladder that hung down from an access hatch in the rock ceiling, the only way to reach the shaft drilled up toward the top of Hydra Mountain. They would have to climb the thirty feet on the open, unsupported metal steps. "I feel like we've all joined the circus. I knew I should have taken those trapeze lessons."

Shawn grasped a rung at shoulder height and rattled the hanging ladder. "I'll climb first and open the hatch. Adonia, help Dr. Garibaldi up the ladder."

"I'm fine," the scientist protested unconvincingly. "Don't let me slow you down. This is too important."

Adonia lifted her eyebrows. "Shawn, you know I don't have the strength to haul him up, rung by rung, if he needs it. Let me open the access hatch while you secure him with the line. I'll take the other end of the rope with me, as security." She leaned over and gave him a quick kiss on the cheek. "You know I'm right."

Shawn pushed her gently forward after handing her one end of the rope. "You usually are."

She tied the rope around her waist. "I'll secure it to something stable once I open the hatch." She grasped the ladder's thin metal sides and gave it a shake, not impressed with its sturdiness. "On top of everything else, I'm going to have Rob Harris write up a safety violation for this ladder once we get out of here."

Garibaldi coughed as he tried to stop laughing.

With the rope trailing at her side, she climbed the ladder, didn't look down, didn't look back. Staring only at her hands, she relaxed into a clockwork motion of reach, step, reach, step, and soon found herself at the granite ceiling. The round access hatch rotated up into the shaft; a lever on the door served as a handle.

Keeping a hand on the ladder, she reached up and grabbed the lever, tried to turn the handle—and the lever didn't move at all. She grunted and tried harder, but still nothing. Her heart pounded. After all this, they were stymied by a stuck *handle*?

Trying not to panic, she inspected the area around the lever, dreading that a padlock might secure the hatch—which made no sense at all, but considering the intersecting red tape of the classified SAPs, she wouldn't have been surprised if some mid-level clerk had added a lock for "extra security."

She struggled again to turn the handle, and in the process, pushed straight up. A spring-loaded mechanism popped, released the latch, and the metal hatch swung up into the shaft, recessed into the rock wall. "Oh," she said, embarrassed as she realized that the handle was only necessary to pull the hatch back down into place.

She climbed two more rungs and poked her head into the vertical shaft bored up through the rock ceiling. Four metal ducts vented into the shaft, directed upward. She could smell the residue of stale, oily fumes; this must be where the diesel exhaust from the crane engine and other heavy machinery was vented.

LED lights ran up opposite walls of the shaft and disappeared high above, showing an endless line of steel rungs that went up to a vanishing point. Safety mesh lined the shaft's inner walls to keep dislodged rocks and debris from tumbling into the cavern. The walls and rungs were covered with layers of grime, dust, and dark grease. Adonia couldn't guess the last time anyone had entered the shaft.

Shawn called from below. "Everything all right?"

She untied the rope around her waist, looped it around the lowest two rungs in the shaft, and securely tied it. She gave it a quick yank and climbed back down far enough to poke her head out. "Ready. The line's secure."

From below, Shawn gave it a tug, then turned to the weary scientist, securing him with the rope. "Up you go, sir. Hold on to that ladder." With a grunt, Garibaldi began the thirty-foot climb on the open ladder toward the rock ceiling, rung over rung. Keeping two rungs behind, Shawn called up. "I'll follow him, Adonia. You keep climbing, and we'll be right behind you. I'll close the access hatch after I'm inside."

Adonia started up the metal rungs, giving the other two enough room to follow her. The lines of LED lights converged high above her head, but since she had no points of reference, she couldn't gauge how high the shaft actually went. Somewhere up there the shaft had to vent to the outside. When she'd first arrived at the guard gate that morning, she remembered how high and rugged Hydra Mountain had seemed.

They might really have some climbing to do.

A loud feedback noise squealed throughout the underground cavern, a clicking sound, then another sharp staccato of feedback boomed from old-fashioned facility loudspeakers mounted on the rocky walls.

Garibaldi hung on to a rung, pausing. "The intercom system must be active now. Harris is trying to contact us."

"About time," Shawn said. "If the intercoms are working again, maybe the reboot is almost over."

But none of them were prepared to hear the voice that came over the loudspeakers.

42

The speakers blared through the enormous cavern, and the voice sounded like a pronouncement from Olympus. "Ms. Rojas? Colonel Whalen? I don't know if you can hear me. Dr. Garibaldi?"

Adonia couldn't believe it. "That's not Harris—it's Stanley!"

"Van Dyckman's alive?" Shawn held himself steady on the ladder. "How did he get out of the vault and the sticky foam?"

Garibaldi asked, "And how did he get out of the cavern?"

The voice continued to boom out. "I hope against hope that you managed to survive. I'm afraid Undersecretary Doyle is dead, but I made it out through a maintenance shaft. I'm back in the operations center now."

Shawn hung on the lower ladder and yelled, "We're here!"

"He can't hear you," Garibaldi said. "Loudspeakers aren't made for two-way communication."

"If you're alive and can hear me, please stay where you are," van Dyckman continued. "You'll be safe. The system reboot will be over in eighty-seven minutes, and then we'll finally have access to the facility's inner storage levels. We'll rescue you, don't worry. Specially cleared recovery and decontamination crews are waiting just outside Hydra's main entrance, as well as NEST teams. We have everything under control out here. There's nothing you need to worry about."

"If Stanley escaped, then he would have told the rescue teams exactly what they'll find down here, the cooling pools and the nuclear devices," Adonia said, feeling great relief. "They'll be prepared when they enter."

"But he doesn't know about the leaking pool with the damaged fuel rods," Garibaldi pointed out. "Or the Senator's body plugging the breach."

Van Dyckman's voice sounded pompous, and much too loud. "I have assumed control of Hydra Mountain and relieved Site Manager Harris of his responsibilities for gross negligence. He is being held, pending arrest. I've already announced this to the rest of the facility—"

Adonia realized he wasn't speaking for their benefit at all. She was rattled. "He's relieved Rob Harris? Arrested him?" She remembered how van Dyckman had held that ill-advised press conference after the extremist attack on Granite Bay and claimed credit for supervising the recovery effort. "Harris wasn't the one playing fast and loose with regulations."

Over the loudspeaker, van Dyckman's voice sounded businesslike and commanding. "I'm doing everything in my power to bring you safely out on the assumption that you're still alive, and then we can determine what to do. Once Mountain operations get back to normal, I'll work with the staffs of Senator Pulaski and Undersecretary Doyle to make appropriate decisions. We will find a way to preserve Valiant Locksmith for the good of the country. Again, I don't know if you can hear me—"

"He sounds more concerned with his nuclear storage plan than with our well-being," Garibaldi said, then added more ominously, "It would be a terrible inconvenience to him if we were still alive."

Van Dyckman's amplified voice grew harder. "You must be very careful not to let word get out, which could cause a widespread panic. All Hydra Mountain internal matters must remain at the highest level of secrecy, until we can determine a proper framework for disseminating any information."

"What's he talking about?" Garibaldi said, appalled.

Van Dyckman rambled, probably assuming that he was speaking to an empty chamber full of dead people. Was this a sort of confessional for him?

"—far greater ramifications than this temporary setback. A black mark on the program now could turn Valiant Locksmith into another expensive political disaster like Yucca Mountain, and we can't let that happen."

Shawn frowned. "He's covering his butt faster than he can rescue us."

"Simon's right. I don't expect he wants to find us alive," Adonia said. "If he's the only one, he can tell the story however he likes."

"—you have my personal assurance that each of you will be cared for in a special medical facility, where you will also be debriefed in a secure environment until all of this can be worked out. So hold on just a little longer. We're coming for you! The emergency teams will soon be on their way with all due speed. When they find you, they'll escort you to safety. Good luck, and Godspeed."

The loudspeakers fell silent, leaving the huge cavern to echo and hum with background noise.

"Like hell they will," Garibaldi said. "You know he'll squirrel me away in some covert, undisclosed location until I die. I doubt the word 'radiation' will ever even be used in any public announcements. If he expects me to go quietly and pretend I suffered a heart attack, he's in for a big surprise."

Adonia began to shake with anger. If a prominent activist like Simon Garibaldi died from radiation exposure, such a casualty would cause a public uproar. If van Dyckman was already sweeping the deaths of Victoria Doyle and Senator Pulaski under the rug, would he whisk Dr. Garibaldi away to a locked-down hospital wing for "special medical attention," keep the scientist away from his Sanergy activists until he succumbed from radiation sickness? Just so Garibaldi couldn't blow the whistle?

The older scientist looked to Shawn and Adonia, red with frustration. "And while I'm in quarantine, you two will be transferred to the Aleutian Islands. You'll have no chance to make a public comment."

"At least we'll be together," Shawn said to Adonia with wry humor. "For the first time in our careers."

"I'd rather be together somewhere other than Shemya, Alaska," she replied, then made up her mind. "Keep climbing. We'll get out on our own." She ascended, rung by rung, toward the converging lights far overhead.

Garibaldi panted as he climbed after her. "We need to get the word out, fast. Give me a phone and a few minutes, and I can mobilize my Sanergy contacts. Then we won't be swept under the rug."

Shawn called up from below. "Van Dyckman got out, and so can we."

Garibaldi flexed his burned hand, then gripped the next rung. "We escape, spread the word, and stop this 'temporary storage' insanity without widespread public discussion and agreement. Or we die trying to get out of here—and believe me, that would not be my preferred outcome. We have to stop kicking the can down the road and figure out a permanent, long-term solution." He was quiet for a moment. "Maybe that means opening Yucca Mountain after all. With the accelerating pace of science and technology, I suppose it might be possible to solve the current environmental concerns—so long as someone actually works on it. I just worry that an easy solution will be a disincentive to develop cleaner, safer energy alternatives."

"Or there's another possibility," Adonia said. "If one of those random neutrons rattling around the lower cavern hits its mark, the Velvet Hammer warheads could detonate any second now."

"Look on the bright side," Shawn called up. "That would solve the problem of what to do about Hydra Mountain."

43

As she climbed higher into the shaft, air currents whistled around Adonia, whooshing up from below like a hurricane squeezed through a straw. Several rungs below her, Shawn encouraged Dr. Garibaldi to keep climbing.

Soon she reached a horizontal vent screen that covered another tunnel recessed into the granite, going sideways instead of up. She called down over the roaring flow of air. "Hold up! I think we've reached an access hatch to the upper-level ventilation ducts."

Shawn called up to her, "Is it open? Can we get inside?"

Air blew in Adonia's face as she tried to peer through the slats of the opening, but she saw only white pleated layers of fabric. "It's covered with a filter."

"No surprise, considering all the dust in here," Garibaldi said.

Adonia pushed, then pounded against the screen, but it didn't budge. Both the hatch and the inside frame were secured with numerous screws sunk deep into the granite. "We're not getting in without a toolkit."

Garibaldi looked past Adonia, straight up the shaft. "Then we keep going. Top of the Mountain, all the way up—and outside."

"Could be five hundred more feet," Adonia said, not looking forward to it herself. "Are you going to be able to make it?"

"Well, I'll have to. Dying here at this point would be a waste of my efforts. I might have only two weeks left, but I intend to make good use of them. So much to do and so little time." He paused. "Ah, that phrase never meant so much before." He heaved a deep breath, then continued in an angrier voice. "If I'm going to die, I don't want my death to help cover up the mess van Dyckman created by cutting corners.

"Why do you think I became an activist in the first place? I used to work for the DOE, really bought into the mission. I followed the procedures, believed that everything was safe at Oakridge. I had major responsibilities, a decent salary, great benefits, challenging work."

A troubled look crossed his face. "Until a routine system failed in one of the Oakridge storage chambers, a power outage and a traditional lockdown. I . . . was inside one of the small vaults, just like Mrs. Garcia. The power went off, and I was trapped alone in the dark. But the worst part was the terror of the unknown, sure there was radiation all around me."

He made a self-deprecating sound. "Oh, I'm a scientist and I know full well what you need to worry about and what you don't—but that's all on paper and computer simulation. It's completely different when you're cold, dark, and all alone. I tried to convince myself I had nothing to worry about. I was sealed inside a pitch-black chamber filled with radioactive casks. At least I had an intercom, and the team on the outside—led by Rob Harris himself, in fact—kept in contact, reassuring me throughout those terrifying hours until the lockdown was over, but they were just detached voices in the dark.

"Over the intercom, Harris walked me through calculations for those two hours, forcing me to go through what I already knew, but had forgotten in my panic. He helped me understand the exposure, convinced me that I wasn't going to die. But during that long, dark limbo, your eyes play tricks on you and you begin to experience false light, hallucinations . . . spurious flashes that you think are radiation bursts. Oh, it's so convincing! All the science in the world doesn't make up for one unexplained bump in the night."

Adonia was fascinated and horrified. This was the first time she'd seen the erudite Garibaldi open up about what had turned him so strongly against the nuclear industry.

"After I was rescued, a young public defender worked like hell to get me medical care, psychological counseling—it was the young attorney's first job out of law school . . . but the DOE rolled over her. They showed her my dosimeter, told her that my exposure was 'acceptable,' although high enough that I had to stay away from radiation sources for quite some time. I was assigned to a desk job at DOE Headquarters, far from any active nuclear site. They even gave me a nice raise, but acted as if everything was fine. Nothing to worry about. They were so glib and dismissive.

"That experience changed my worldview. The fact that they said I would have no lasting consequences from my 'unfortunate ordeal' made me realize we weren't speaking the same language. And I no longer believed we were on the same side."

He was quiet for a moment as he hung there, resting. "I knew I had to leave the DOE. I had to fight for safe alternatives to nuclear power, for a sustainable energy grid that doesn't endanger the environment just to power our hair dryers." He chuckled. "Yes, that sounds like pie in the sky, but I refuse to believe that a goal can't be achieved just because it's ambitious. I had hoped to make more of myself, do something significant with my scientific career. Well, well, maybe this gives me the opportunity, even if it's a shitty one, if you'll pardon my language."

"We'll get you out of here, Simon," Adonia said. Although she knew his dream was not realistic, she really meant it.

Shawn agreed. "That's why we have to stick together. Valiant Locksmith may have been a viable solution for a long-standing problem, but a mismanaged mess like this won't accomplish anything. It wasn't what the President signed up for. I know—I was there when Dr. van Dyckman presented his idea for Hydra Mountain. We'll get out, and then he won't be able to keep us all quiet."

Garibaldi summoned his energy. "Let's get going. We're wasting time."

They climbed higher into the Mountain, far out of range of the loud-speakers, so they would not have been able to hear van Dyckman if he'd made more pronouncements. When the lockdown ended, the NEST teams and emergency responders would break through the sticky foam that blocked the guard portal and arrive in the lower level wearing full respirators and decontamination suits, but she didn't think they expected to find anyone alive.

Adonia knew they had to get out of the Mountain.

As they climbed higher, she heard a muted roar far overhead. The air currents whistled past them, sucked up from below to be exhausted outside. Adonia occasionally caught a cloying whiff, and she knew that halothane was being drawn up the shaft in the turnover of the huge volume of air exchanged from the massive underground cavern. If enough knockout gas swirled up past them, rendering them unconscious, the three of them would slip from the rungs and fall all the way down.

No! They were going to make it.

Shawn brought up the rear. Adonia knew a five-hundred-foot climb would have been an exhilarating exercise for him, but she worried most about Garibaldi. He kept doggedly ascending, holding the rungs with his raw and blistered hands.

"We'll be out of here in another fifteen, twenty minutes at the most," she said. It was entirely a guess, and she didn't know what they would find when they did reach the top of the shaft. Could they even get out? If air vented from the Mountain, there had to be some sort of opening up there for the flow to escape. But she wouldn't be surprised if they encountered an impenetrable barricade of filters for scrubbing the air.

The roar above them increased, as did the wind streaming past them. She could feel the metal rungs vibrating in her hands. Considering the size of the huge mountain complex, all the air needed to recirculate, and such a significant volume had to exit somewhere.

She craned her neck upward to see how far they still had to go, then reeled in shock, letting her grip momentarily slip. Her other arm wrapped around the bar, catching her before she could fall.

A hundred feet above them was a giant, rotating fan, turning furiously to pull the air out. The blades extended across the shaft, blocking where they needed to go.

44

Settling into the Eagle's Nest office, van Dyckman felt a knot in his stomach as he surveyed the operations center below. On the big wall screens, he watched the DOE's Special Response Teams gather just outside Hydra Mountain's massive exterior doors. Incident Commander Jennings had relayed that the Nuclear Emergency Support Team, the Accident Response Group, and personnel from the Radiological Assistance Program were all in place to assist as soon as the lockdown ended. They had already entered through the multiple chain-link and razor-wire fences, guard gate after guard gate, and were now positioned just outside the vehicle entrance.

Due to the uncertain nature of the initial lockdown and the subsequent systems reboot, the SRT weapons were hot-cocked and ready, including a deadly Dillon M134 7.62 mm Minigun. The team members had been hand-selected from DOE's Protective Services for the elite team, and they had trained for years to protect nuclear weapons and material. Additional SRT members had already been placed at strategic locations around the Mountain in full-bore support, but they kept a low profile so that the outside world, including satellite surveillance, would see only minimal activity.

As the reboot timer finally counted down, emergency nuclear cleanup teams from both Los Alamos and Sandia National Laboratories joined the team. Wearing yellow protective clothing complete with self-contained breathing supplies, they carried a range of equipment from radiation detectors to solvent sprayers. The trained scientists would follow the Special Response Team inside, prepared for the worst.

But they couldn't get inside. Not yet.

The DOE Incident Commander worked with her military counterpart in a command post two hundred yards upwind from where the team would enter. Although this emergency was in a DOE facility, Kirtland Air Force Base provided critical infrastructure support; even so, Kirtland personnel remained in the dark about the real nature of the problem inside Hydra Mountain—van Dyckman had made sure of that, now that Rob Harris was sequestered. From now on, all information had to come and go through him.

Van Dyckman maintained contact from the Eagle's Nest and watched via an encrypted link that the Nuclear Incident Command System had set up. But he had put his foot down with Jennings, refusing to let the video feed go directly to DOE Headquarters. Not now. He didn't dare let outside officials monitor his operations in real time. The Incident Commander protested, but he overruled her.

As Valiant Locksmith's national program manager—and now Hydra Mountain's acting site manager—Stanley van Dyckman had absolute control over the flow of information. By the time the neophyte Secretary of Energy learned details about the incident, he would have cleaned up any nasty contradictions that might implicate him.

Except for Incident Commander Jennings herself, the response teams weren't at all cognizant of the SAPs inside the Mountain; the people did not know about the nuclear waste stored there, or the cooling pools in the lower level—and most especially they didn't know about Victoria's covert stockpile of nuclear devices. The teams received only basic information couched in vague terms about a possible spill of high-level nuclear waste inside and that nuclear weapon components might be involved.

No explanations, no details. No need to know.

But every team member understood that the SRT would never have been activated if this weren't a real-world event. They knew this was not a training exercise. Waiting outside in the relentless New

Mexico afternoon heat and blustery desert winds, the SRT and cleanup teams remained on high alert, ready to engage as soon as the lockdown lifted. By now, everyone was getting edgy.

Van Dyckman watched the countdown finally reach zero with a sense of both relief and trepidation. Time to go!

A warning horn blared outside the Mountain. The massive outer steel vault doors began to crawl open, not for a truck delivery this time but to allow access to the Special Response Team. Simultaneously, the large wall monitors in the operations center below blinked as their systems came fully back online, restoring normal routines.

"We are open for business!" van Dyckman shouted aloud, realizing his enthusiasm might seem inappropriate. No one could hear him anyway.

Jennings barked her orders, and the Special Response Team readied their weapons. As soon as the heavy door had opened far enough, the team sprinted through the gap and into Hydra Mountain. The first man slid through the widening door and hustled ahead to set up a security perimeter.

The SRT split into two subteams, the first covering the door to the inner storage area, and the second team jogging down the tunnels to the portal at the incline that led to the lower cavern. As Jennings took point, they would sweep the entire upper and lower levels, making sure they overlooked no potential intruder. But van Dyckman had given them clear instructions: their primary focus was to secure the Velvet Hammer vault, to seal the clogged door and block off the devices from dangerous stray radiation.

Watching the bustling military-style operation on the wall screens, van Dyckman thought their aggressive caution was a bit excessive, but the Incident Commander refused to back down. Jennings had been read into Victoria's SAP and she knew her team might be dealing with unsecured nuclear weapons.

After the SRT detected no immediate threat in the upper tunnels and declared that portion of the Mountain secure, both the Los Alamos and Sandia nuclear accident cleanup teams were escorted into the main corridor. After the last scientist entered the Mountain, the massive vehicle vault door ground slowly shut. Once the outer barrier was closed, the inner storage doors opened, and the Special Response Team entered the even more highly classified interior of the facility.

As if they were invading a small country, the SRT thundered down the incline. Van Dyckman had made sure the countermeasures were deactivated now, and he'd informed the Incident Commander that there was minimal risk of any active threat—in fact, he doubted anyone was still alive down there—but she again opted for extreme caution. To make certain no radiofrequency signals triggered yet another lockdown—like Senator Pulaski's cell phone—the teams left their normal communication equipment outside; instead, they unreeled spools of shielded fiber-optic line.

Reaching the security portal down the inclined tunnel, a waste cleanup tech in full protective suit sprayed solvent on the hardened sticky foam that covered the entry, softening the mass of material. Just behind him, two other cleanup team members used heavy barricade-clearing equipment to punch through the opening. The cleanup operator sprayed more solvent, dissolving the obstruction. The sticky foam faded almost as quickly as it had hardened.

One by one, the team members squeezed through the cramped guard portal and jogged down the slope. One man remained inside the guard chamber, working the controls to disengage the halothane pumps and serve as a back observer.

The Los Alamos and Sandia cleanup team followed the vigilant SRT down, and soon they stood on the high bay ledge overlooking the huge main cavern. The first team members had already rappelled down the fifty-foot drop-off and fanned out on the lowest floor, wearing gas masks against the halothane. One engineer worked the reset controls to activate the freight elevators and return them to the ledge, which let the cleanup crew descend to the floor, where they could install industrial ventilation pumps, though it would take some time to vent all the deadly gas.

The SRT point men raced to the far end of the cavern with orders to clear the hardened sticky foam from the Velvet Hammer vault.

Getting that massive metal door shut again was their highest priority, partly to secure any nuclear "components," but primarily to block off the stray radiation.

With their voices muffled by gas masks, team members shouted for survivors while they spread out to search the giant chamber. Hearing no answer, they combed the floor and the piled construction materials, expecting to find three dead human forms sprawled in the dissipating yellowish mist.

Using the fiber-optic line they'd trailed after them, the Special Response Team reported back up to Jennings in the Incident Command Post. "No survivors so far, ma'am. No dead bodies either."

Listening in from his upper office, van Dyckman leaned forward and interrupted the report. "Have you entered the vault itself? I'm sure you'll recover Undersecretary Doyle when you clear the sticky foam." He frowned down at the screen. "You will also find Senator Pulaski in the temporary cooling pool, where he drowned."

Commander Jennings's voice came over the speaker. "Mr. van Dyckman, please clear the line—"

Harris's harried-looking exec, Drexler, came running in, his face flushed. "Sir, I have some very good news!"

Van Dyckman caught his breath. "I could certainly use some." He tried to imagine what the man might be talking about, but he wasn't sure he would agree it was good news.

"They've released the technician who was trapped in the dry-storage chamber. Mrs. Garcia is flustered, but just fine." Drexler chuckled. "She's asked for tomorrow off, and I told her it was the least we could do. You don't need to worry about her anymore, sir. She's safe."

He tried to hide his acute disappointment. He had forgotten all about the older woman. "Wonderful, Mr. Drexler. I won't give it another thought. She's in good hands." Far better news would be when they discovered the bodies of the others. Then no one could tell a different version of the story. He would be in control of all the details.

For the next half hour, he watched with increasing anxiety as the cleanup crew continued their work and the NEST team verified that

Victoria's nuclear devices were secure, the Velvet Hammer vault closed against the increased radiation in the cavern.

During the mop-up operation, they did indeed find Victoria's body trapped like a bug in amber, overwhelmed and suffocated by the sticky foam. He experienced a queasy chill when they sent him images of her. He hadn't expected to react so emotionally, since he had no leftover feelings for her. Maybe it was just the aftershock of realizing that he could have suffered the same fate if he'd been even a second slower. Yes, that was all it was.

Oddly, when the team searched the temporary holding pool to retrieve the drowned body of Senator Pulaski, they reported back to the Incident Commander that the corpse had been moved, and used as a bizarre sort of patch to plug a puncture hole in the above-ground storage pool.

Hearing this, van Dyckman felt a deep chill. A hole in the plastic pool? Probably from the fallen fuel rods. Was the water draining, which would expose the rods? Then he paused as his thought shot off in a different direction. How had Pulaski's body been moved? Did it just drift up against the leak? But he had been pinned down by the rods. Did that mean one or more of the three missing team members had moved him on purpose? That someone had gone back in the pool, risking a significant radiation exposure?

Maybe someone remained alive. But where were they now? The SRT hadn't found anybody.

The toppled rods posed an immediate danger, and the cleanup team worked to reset the array and patch the weakened pool wall.

The Sandia lead transmitted a message: "Mr. van Dyckman, sir, both labs strongly recommend that you immediately remove all spent fuel rods from this facility and transport them back to their original nuclear sites. With the nuclear components stored in that vault, this location should not be used for wet storage."

He replied in a glacial voice, "I will take that under advisement."

His hands began to shake as the Incident Commander completed the full inspection and sent her report. "Our sweep of the lower level is complete, sir. This chamber is secure. We've started pumping the halothane up the vertical ventilation shaft. Once it vents outside, UV radiation will break down the gas. However, although we discovered the bodies of Senator Pulaski and Undersecretary Doyle, we found no sign of the three remaining people. There's nobody else down here."

45

The giant rotating fan overhead was like a twirling executioner's ax, blocking their way. The whooshing hum grew louder, nearly overwhelming as the blades spun, pulling a river of air that flowed past them to vent somewhere high above. Adonia knew the shaft led to outside and freedom—if they could just get past this obstacle.

On the ladder just below, Garibaldi hung exhausted and dejected. Until now, he had focused on the climb, one rung at a time, almost in a trance. Now he just stared without hope at the revolving blades.

Just beneath him, Shawn clung to the wall, shaking his head in grim frustration. "Can you see any controls, Adonia? Is there some way to shut it down?"

"You know that would be too easy." She doggedly climbed closer to the impregnable barrier. Directly above, the giant fan looked ancient. "Must be part of the 1950s vintage ventilation system."

Garibaldi seemed to be pondering an engineering problem. "How . . . many blades?"

She didn't know what that had to do with anything. "Four, like propeller vanes. They're moving pretty fast, and completely blocking our way."

Sagging on the rung, Garibaldi nodded. "Good. At least . . . it's not a new industrial fan, a centrifugal type. Otherwise we'd never be able to get through."

Shawn called up, his voice sounding urgent. "Do you smell that?"

Adonia drew in a deep breath as she looked down at Shawn's worried face. The faint sweet odor was unmistakable, and she knew what it meant. "If the lockdown finally ended, they're purging the cavern, venting the gas to the outside—and it will flow right past us. All of it."

"Which means we can't go back down," Shawn said. "The halothane would overwhelm us as we descend."

Garibaldi looked up. "The quickest way to slow the gas—and for us to escape, of course—is to stop that fan."

"An excellent suggestion, but how do we do that?" Adonia asked. "I don't even see any power lines to cut."

With a raw, radiation-burned hand, Garibaldi patted one of the LED lights that illuminated the shaft. A small dull-colored conduit ran up the granite wall. "This must cover a power line. It looks plastic instead of metal."

Adonia struck it with her knuckles. "We still don't have any way to cut it."

"You don't need to—there's another way to stop the power. Quickly now, climb closer to the rotating blades. I'll follow you so I can inspect the apparatus." As they hung twenty feet below the spinning blades, the old scientist now seemed stronger, energized. "Good. There's no grill or grating on either side."

"It's not a tourist attraction," Adonia said. "There shouldn't be anyone up here except for maintenance crews, and they would have to get through any safety barriers."

"If the blades weren't moving, there'd be plenty of room for us to squeeze between them," Shawn said.

Garibaldi tightened his grip on the rungs. "Colonel, if you would please untie the rope around my waist? I'd do it myself, but I would rather save my strength—"

Shawn shook his head. "You're too unsteady, sir. And the halothane fumes aren't helping."

Garibaldi continued lecturing, undeterred. "We'll just have to risk it. Untie yours as well, Colonel. Then Ms. Rojas can climb right up and feed the loose line into the rotating blades. That should make a thorough mess of things."

Adonia grinned as she understood. "The rope will jam it up in no time, burn out the rotor."

After Shawn untied the rope from himself and from the older man's waist, Garibaldi handed the end up to Adonia. "This will require some skill, and maybe luck. If you toss it in too quickly, the blades will kick the rope straight up and eject it, without ruining the motor. If you feed in the line too slowly, the blades will whip the rope around and it will flail us like a bullwhip."

"Sure, no pressure." Adonia was quiet for a moment, studying the fan as she pulled up the rope. The cloying smell of rising halothane grew stronger, and she started to feel light-headed. But they were so close to the outside she could taste it, and if they jammed the fan, it would stop drawing the fumes up the shaft. "So I get one chance. I feed the rope into the blades, and release it right away?"

"Release it right after the rope catches. The rotation will pull it in, snag the line, and clog the fan."

Adonia glanced back up at the old machinery, then worked her way up until she hung only a few feet below the spinning blades. She removed one end of the rope from her shoulder, tied a small loop, then let a few feet of rope drop. She twirled the line. "I feel like a rodeo cowboy."

"With the grime smeared over you, you look more like a coal miner," Shawn said.

"I'll take a shower when we're out of here. Right now, you'll have to put up with me." She twirled the rope faster, then jerked it up toward the blades. The small lasso caught in the fan with a loud clang, spun around as the blades rotated, whipping it, tangling it. The rope swiftly snaked up, and Adonia played it out for a few seconds, then let go of the line.

She ducked. The other end of the rope snapped around, just missing her head as it shot into the fan blades like a spaghetti noodle being slurped up by a child. The fan's drive motor made an increasingly loud whine, accompanied by a sharp rhythmic banging that echoed throughout the shaft. Adonia pressed herself flat against the rungs and the granite wall, afraid the entire old fan system might break from its moorings and collapse on top of them.

The wide metal blades slowed, strained, and then ground to a halt. The fan thrummed with leftover vibrations, and the roaring air current quieted to a barely perceptible breeze. The halothane's distinct odor was replaced by the smell of smoke and burning wire.

The LED lights in the walls blinked out, plunging the shaft into darkness, but now Adonia could make out a faint halo of light between the motionless fan blades.

It was light from outside.

"I can see daylight up there!"

They waited, making sure that the motor had really burned out, and then they cheered simultaneously. Garibaldi sounded breathless and weary as he urged Adonia upward. "We can celebrate later, but I'd just as soon get into the open with all due haste. I . . . I am anxious to see the sky again."

Adonia worked her way up into the enclosure that held the fan in place, where she could smell the hot oil and burning grease from the wrecked motor. Around the shaft and blades, the mangled rope looked like a noose. "Climb on up. It's safe—this fan is never turning again. We can squeeze between the blades."

Adonia clambered into the motionless turbine, squirming her way between the flat metal vanes. She cautiously raised her head above the frozen blade. "I feel like I'm sticking my head into a guillotine." Briefly stuck, she grunted and pushed the fan through part of its rotation to widen the gap for the two men to climb through.

A faint curl of greasy white smoke still drifted from the direct-drive motor, but the mechanism made no more straining sounds. She silently told herself she would be fine and squirmed through, finally climbing up to reach the rungs above the ominous blockage. "It's a little tight, but we'll make it to the top."

Bending down, she extended her arm through the motionless blades to help Garibaldi, who wheezed as he wormed his way up to join her. His shoulders barely fit through the gap.

Adonia worked her way around the framework and found a secure position so she could help Garibaldi climb past her. "Go on, lead the way to the top. I'm right behind you."

The scientist started up the rungs without a word. His face wore a perpetual wince from the pain in his hands.

Shawn squeezed through the fan blades until he emerged next to Adonia. Without a word, he reached out to touch her face. Soot, dust, and grime smeared his cheeks, and his uniform was in a frightful state. Adonia knew she must look worse. "You can't report to the President looking like that. I better hose you off when we get outside."

"And I would be honored to do the same for you," he said. "That's what friends are for."

Garibaldi was already two body lengths above them. He kept ponderously climbing as he shouted down to them. "You're right, it's daylight. I can see ahead."

Energized, Adonia climbed after him, feeling a desperate need to get out of the tunnel, to breathe fresh air, and be away from Hydra Mountain. The glimpse of sunshine above gave her a renewed sense of purpose.

The halo overhead grew brighter with every rung. Now that the fan's roar had fallen silent, she could hear Garibaldi breathing hard with the effort, but the sunlight also illuminated more of the vertical shaft. Garibaldi stopped a few feet from the top. He lowered his head and called down. "The exit is blocked off, covered by a structure of some sort."

Despite her discouragement, she realized it made sense. Hydra Mountain wouldn't just vent out of an open chimney.

"It's a cylindrical structure with slits on the sides," Garibaldi reported. "Some kind of baffle to emit the exhaust air horizontally, rather than straight up into the atmosphere."

"More difficult for overhead surveillance to detect any plume that way," Shawn said. "And the layered slits in the baffle would reduce any temperature signature for infrared sensors."

Thinking of the original Cold War–era construction, Adonia understood the measures installed to keep the site covert. "It probably also has filters or air scrubbers to make sure no chemical signatures from the vented air could be detected." She climbed up next to the scientist, assessing the barricade. So close . . .

Garibaldi said, "Most important question is whether we can get through it."

The cylindrical cap was no larger than a crawlspace, big enough for a worker to exit the shaft. The daylight filtering in through the baffle cast deeper shadows in the cramped space. She looked around for a lock or handle. "Workers would need to have an exit. There must be—"

Then she saw a crash bar, identical to the emergency device they had used to break out of the guard portal. "Three cheers for safety systems." Her voice cracked with relief. "We can get out."

Before she could push her way through, Garibaldi touched her arm to stop her. Wires led from a contact sensor embedded in the exit door, connected to the crash bar. "That's an alarm. It probably signals Hydra Mountain's operations center, maybe even DOE Protective Services. They would be monitoring site security."

"Triggering another alarm doesn't bother me," Adonia said. "We've had enough of them today. Let them come rescue us at last."

"Unless it sets off a defensive measure designed to stop a bad guy from exiting the Mountain," Shawn said. "Or someone trying to get in."

"That would be just our luck," she said. "But we've got to get out of here. Dr. Garibaldi—"

"Yes. We do," Garibaldi said. "And after surviving tear gas, sonic bombardments, avalanches of sticky foam, a flood of knockout gas, radioactive fuel rods, and a very inconveniently placed ventilation fan, I'm not about to throw in the towel. Let's just go."

Shawn said, "If it's any consolation, an alarm probably already went off when we shut down the ventilation fan. What have we got to lose?"

With her hand on the crash bar, Adonia looked at them. "I'm ready if you both are."

Garibaldi said, "I would really rather get out of here and have my feet on solid ground. But we also can't let them silence us, whisk us into some secure facility where they can cover up what happened. We know Stanley's alive, and we know he would do anything to cover his butt and spin what happened in there. Two people are already dead. We need to find a way to tell the story before he sanitizes the scene—and us."

Adonia nodded. If van Dyckman had already put a gag on Rob Harris, he would likely do the same thing to them. "We'll have to figure something out once we get into the open air. We're deep inside a military base and behind several layers of security fences. We can't just hold a news conference."

Garibaldi was grim. "I do not intend to go quietly as part of a cover-up. I have a long list of things to do in whatever time I've got left."

Adonia knew that van Dyckman was an expert politician, and he had railroaded Valiant Locksmith through when all public attempts to address the crisis had stalled for decades. But by circumventing the classified interagency review process, what he'd done was clearly illegal; probably just one of many other illegal actions. How far would he go to keep himself out of jail?

Bringing in multiple shipments of still-hot fuel rods and cramming them into a flimsy above-ground pool made things even more dangerous. If they turned themselves in, Adonia was sure he would find a way to detain Garibaldi until the radiation sickness killed him. She and Shawn would be put on ice until the problem was hushed up.

Adonia asked, "Even if we got the chance to expose this, who are we going to tell? And how?"

"Site security will round us up before we go very far," Shawn said.

She heard the sound of Garibaldi's wheezing breath as he struggled to find an answer, and she made up her mind. "Doesn't matter. We're getting out." She placed a hand on the crash bar. "Ready for all hell to break loose?"

"It already has," Garibaldi said, barely louder than a whisper. "What's a little more going to hurt?"

Adonia slammed against the crash bar with a vengeance. With a crack, the exit swung open, and sunlight flooded the cramped crawlspace.

An alarm clanged far below, echoing up the shaft, but she didn't care. She tumbled onto the rocky, scrub-covered ground on the rough summit of Hydra Mountain. Far in the distance, she heard sirens wail, and soon the three of them stood together in the hot desert air, outside at last.

46

Another alarm rang in the Eagle's Nest and alerts lit up the ops center screens—but this was not the alarm van Dyckman was expecting. Not at all. This had nothing to do with the cleanup or the Special Response Team.

It was an exterior *breach* alarm! What the hell?

Light-headed and enraged at the same time, he rose from behind Harris's desk. One of the few access points to Hydra Mountain had been compromised. How could anyone possibly break in with security teams everywhere? He felt a chill, suddenly wondering if that blundering small aircraft really had been part of some wild conspiracy, a distraction to drop in an intruder. Someone was using the chaos of the multiple lockdowns to break into the facility!

Frantically, he swept his eyes across the tall screens in the operations center below. Drexler and his tech teams scrambled to their stations in a sudden flurry, struggling to pinpoint the new alarm.

The young exec pointed at the upper right corner of the screen, which showed a schematic of Hydra Mountain's two underground levels. A small, innocuous red square glowed at the top of a long narrow air duct that ran from the lower cavern through the rock ceiling to the outside. Somebody had compromised an emergency exit at the top of the shaft.

Van Dyckman felt sick, panicked. Did someone else know about

Velvet Hammer and Victoria's hidden warheads? There might be a full assault team trying to work their way in.

But he still couldn't believe it. Four fences surrounded the Mountain. All were heavily alarmed and covered with sensors, ranging from motion detectors to thermal cameras, so sensitive that they were frequently triggered by prairie dogs and jackrabbits. The inner two fences were electrified.

That breach was on the very summit, and no person or team could have slipped so far inside the heavily fortified perimeter without being detected. And the outside of Hydra Mountain was swarming with security and safety personnel. No one could have climbed all the way up there unseen!

According to the schematics he was studying, the only mechanism to open the vent was a crash bar, accessible only from the inside.

Then he actually gasped as he realized someone wasn't attempting to break in. Someone was trying to *get out*!

Van Dyckman found it hard to breathe, and his stomach twisted. The red encrypted phone on Harris's desk started ringing, and the small screen identified the caller as Secretary Nitta, but he let it ring. The bitch was probably in micromanagement mode, and she would only screw things up.

This couldn't be a coincidence. Impossible as it seemed, someone from the inside was still alive. The SRT had not found the bodies of Colonel Whalen, Dr. Garibaldi, or Adonia Rojas. Fifteen minutes earlier, circuit breakers in the ventilation system had been tripped, signaling that an old piece of equipment had burned out, but he'd assumed that the nuclear response team or the cleanup team had overloaded the antique grid. Pumps and some lighting on the lower floor near the temporary storage pools had gone down.

Now he knew otherwise.

The phone fell silent, then instantly started to ring once more. This time it was someone from security, but he ignored it again.

Studying the diagram of the Mountain, looking at the location of the compromised access, he confirmed his suspicions. An old ventilation duct led directly up from the catwalks, and if the three survivors had somehow climbed the crane, gotten above the halothane mists, made their way to the catwalks . . . they could have worked their way out, just as he had. He had called out to them through the loudspeaker, but he'd never believed they were listening. That was all just for show, so he could demonstrate his concern in full view of everyone in the ops center.

But they were really still alive, and now they had gotten out. This was turning out to be his worst nightmare.

He had to develop yet *another* emergency plan to bottle up those three before they compromised Valiant Locksmith. Who knew what they might say? He had already neatly taken care of Rob Harris, and now he had to keep these three from talking. He would order Incident Commander Jennings and her team to round them up before they got any farther. Surely they would want to be rescued, and then he could deal with them.

He forced himself to be calm, slowing his breathing. Van Dyckman would quickly put a lid on this, snuff out any problem. Yes, it could still be done.

The office door burst open, and Drexler ran into the room, frantically pointing at the phone on the desk. "Sir, both the Secretary and the DOE Incident Commander have been trying to reach you. Commander Jennings says it's urgent and she is still on the line."

Jumpy, he punched at the encrypted phone, listened as Jennings spoke in a rush. "Mr. van Dyckman, there's been a breach at the top of the Mountain—"

"I know. I *know*!" He squeezed his eyes tight. "Get your people there as soon as possible. We may have some intruders trying to get away. Intercept them, take them into custody, and don't let them talk to anyone. I'll debrief them myself."

"Already taken care of, sir. Our air surveillance has spotted three individuals outside of an emergency egress hatch near the summit. They appear to be unarmed. But it may be good news, sir—they're quite likely the missing team members. They survived somehow."

He could not let her treat this lightly. "Exercise extreme caution until you're sure, and even then don't let down your guard. It's quite possible that one or more of those people intentionally caused the lockdown inside the facility and may even be attempting sabotage. Take them into custody." His thoughts raced. He had to keep them quiet, at least until he could make Adonia and Colonel Whalen see reason. With their high-level connections to the President, the military, and the Department of Energy, those two might be manageable. They might do what was best for the program, if he could explain the dire consequences facing them if they didn't.

But if Simon Garibaldi got word out to his large network of protesters at Sanergy, that would be a public relations disaster. They might even close Hydra Mountain and send all the high-level waste back to dangerous temporary storage areas across the country. Worse yet, the public outcry might force the closure of *all* nuclear plants—it had happened in Japan after Fukushima. Could it happen here?

Sick to his stomach, van Dyckman knew he couldn't afford to take any chances. "We have to . . . contain this."

The Incident Commander was in her element now, reacting swiftly and professionally. "Don't worry, sir. Even with the rugged terrain, I estimate my team arriving on scene in less than fifteen minutes. Backup air support can be called, if needed."

Van Dyckman found himself nodding. "They must be held and questioned. After everything that's happened today, we can't be too careful."

"Maybe we should call in medical rescue, too," she suggested.

He had to say it. "As a precaution, yes." Another thought struck him, and he quickly smiled with relief. "But operate under the assumption that these people may be contaminated. It's possible they may have radioactive material in their possession." *That's it!* "For safety's sake, treat them as dangerous. Keep them away from as many people as possible."

He would have to start making calls to the DOE, the Department of Defense, the State Department. Everyone had a stake here. They all had a common goal to keep the waived, unacknowledged programs under wraps at any cost. All three departments would support him and take whatever actions were necessary.

"Yes, sir, I understand. My team is prepared to deal with any possibility. Our decontamination procedures are quite effective—"

"*And* they may also have possession of highly classified material, which if revealed, could cause grave and permanent danger to national security." Van Dyckman could feel the pieces fall into place.

Jennings responded, although she didn't sound pleased with his directive. "Yes, sir. I . . . understand completely. We'll take care of it."

Van Dyckman hung up, relieved that he had a little bit of breathing room.

Fortunately, the three escapees were still deep inside the security fences, so they would not be seen in public. They had no way to communicate with the outside, and Jennings would keep them contained, at least for now.

He slumped into the site manager's chair and leaned back, considering his next step.

That was the beauty of operating under an unacknowledged program. As the national program manager, he controlled all access and information. With the loss of Senator Pulaski, Valiant Locksmith no longer had its most important advocate or political high cover. The man's death would bring down far more scrutiny than van Dyckman would have liked, but congressional oversight would be temporarily absent.

With Victoria Doyle also dead, and Harris, Adonia, Whalen, and Garibaldi out of the picture, he would be able to cover his tracks.

He put his hands behind his head and glanced at the clock. Soon, the Incident Commander would apprehend the three, and then van Dyckman could tie up that final loose end.

47

After emerging from the shaft, Adonia, Shawn, and Garibaldi stood on a flat area with scattered boulders, low piñon pines, and clumps of sparse dry grass. The afternoon was warm, and heat shimmers rose from the ground. Adonia drew a deep breath, just tasting the dry, fresh air. It smelled wonderful.

Shielding her eyes from the bright sun, listening to the whistle of the desert wind, Adonia looked back at the camouflaged duct housing that stuck up from the ground. Light brown paint flaked off the metal surface, but the sculptured vents were nearly invisible against the backdrop of boulders and outcroppings. The flat area around the duct was obviously man-made, carved out to provide egress in an emergency.

Garibaldi bent over, coughing from the exertion. Adonia helped to steady him. "Are you all right?"

"Of course not." He squinted up at her. "But you don't look very pristine yourself. Your nose is bleeding again, and I didn't even have to punch you this time."

She touched her nose, felt the sticky blood at the base of her nostrils. "I'll be fine." They were all disheveled and filthy after their ordeal. "I just hope they don't shoot us on sight."

"They won't," Shawn said. "They're professionals." Around the facility, alarms kept ringing. He narrowed his eyes. "But they'll be here soon enough. We have to decide what to do."

"We're out of that death trap, so I'll count my little victories," Adonia said.

Garibaldi sat down on a rock. "We cannot let them silence us. I'm going to die because of what happened today, and I insist that it mean something. Too much went wrong in there, a cascade of unintended consequences. Even if Hydra Mountain *is* an acceptable place to store nuclear waste, the way van Dyckman went about it is totally wrong. The left hand didn't know what the right hand was doing—or the left foot, or the chin. I admit the problems were caused by bureaucratic incompetence rather than the science, but if the government is going to store dangerous waste inside that facility, it cannot be under such conditions." He looked up.

"If the lockdown is ended, the nuclear response team will already be deep inside the Mountain," Shawn said. "By now they may have cleared the way to the lower level—and I hope they've sealed the warhead vault. That's the most important thing."

"And the leaking pool," Adonia said. "We have to warn them, no matter what."

"We can't stop there," Garibaldi insisted. "These complications, the bad decisions, the gaps in knowledge—no one has any clue about the big picture on high-level waste. Groups like Sanergy have to be involved, to make sure the right decision is made."

"Some would say that groups like Sanergy made it politically impossible to do *anything* with all the nuclear waste, which led to our present problem," Adonia said with a hint of bitterness. "Look what happened to Yucca Mountain. That stubbornness is what forced people like van Dyckman and Senator Pulaski to do a political end run like this. We need to *solve* the problem, not stonewall it."

"Maybe there's a middle ground," Garibaldi admitted. "We have to make the public and Congress have serious, open discussions, not clouded by politics; and especially not on emotion. If I'm lucky, I'll have two weeks to make my case—two exhausting weeks that'll take a lot out of me. So I'd better make a difference."

Adonia looked down the rocky incline, where a score of armed protective service officers in tan camouflage battle fatigues swarmed

up the dirt road, converging toward their location. They were followed by six people dressed in yellow radiation gear.

Garibaldi shaded his eyes. "Looks like the welcome wagon is on
its way."

She was quiet for a moment. "If they take us into custody, you'll
never be able to speak your piece. We'll fall into a black hole. You
need to get the word out!"

From the high ridge, seeing the fences and the surrounding desert
of the expansive Air Force base, Adonia could see no point in running.
"Stanley muzzled Rob Harris already, and he'll do the same to us. If
we blow the whistle and call attention to what happened here, Rob
would back us up. The deaths would not have been in vain. Stanley's the one at fault here."

Shawn squared his shoulders and stood with his arms at his sides,
watching the guards approaching. "I count twenty of them, and
they're armed to the teeth. We have ten minutes." He gave an odd
smile. "Not much time to sound off, so we'd better speak our piece
first. It's our only chance to be heard." He hesitated. "But how? We
have to do it the right way. Ending our careers is the least that can
happen if we reveal what's in Stanley's SAP. We'd be looking at jail."

"So what's more important?" Adonia said, having arrived at the
conclusion hours before. "Following rules or saving lives? If only
Rob Harris had made that decision a long time ago, we wouldn't
have this debacle now."

Garibaldi drew himself up. "Colonel Whalen's right." He closed
his eyes, his face twisted in pain. "We'd be breaking the law. Just
because van Dyckman did it, doesn't justify us doing it."

"But you can't just give up! We could go to the press." Adonia
felt exasperated, but then her heart sank. At first she'd naively hoped
that the three of them would be hailed for their efforts, heroic whistle-
blowers, but now she doubted they would have the chance to tell
their side of the story. With the security team closing in, as well as
the motion detectors, weight sensors, and thermal imagers planted
all around them, they had nowhere to run, nowhere to hide.

Garibaldi smiled sadly. "Only as a last resort. Imagine the outcry if
it was made public—there are a few on the Sanergy fringe who might

overact, do something as crazy as that suicidal pilot who attacked your site. And that would defeat everything we're trying to do."

"It doesn't matter," Adonia said. "This is too important. People have to know!"

"Yes, it *does* matter. You and Colonel Whalen can work from the inside to change things, but if your careers are ruined, you'd be on the outside, nothing more than a gadfly, like myself. And the system would plod on, undeterred, and things would never change."

He coughed. "We were so close. We almost had the chance. If we could make just one call out of here, I could contact the Secretary of Energy directly. She knows me and I trust her. Give it one more try before going public. She's a damned smart lawyer, and an ethical one as well; I was her first client out of law school, long before she entered the government. In less than a minute, I could connect the dots for her."

"And you really think the government would follow through?" Adonia said. "Not bury it under a shroud of secrecy? Lost forever, like in that warehouse in *Raiders of the Lost Ark*."

"The Secretary will do the right thing, I know. And in my last days, I can concentrate on the larger debate, demand public discussion about the nuclear waste problem with my dying breath. That's what I'll do, if we get out of here . . . but I can't do that if the press is only screaming about the scandal." He closed his eyes, as if driving back some inner pain. "But I'll still give you something to hold over them, to force the government to really change. All I need is one call with Secretary Nitta. Alas, I see no convenient phone booths."

From their position, Adonia could see the fences down below at the base of Hydra Mountain, as well as the guard shack just outside the main fence. "My cell phone is right down there, locked in a box a thousand feet away. Might as well be a thousand miles."

Shawn responded with a widening smile, and he hugged Adonia hard. "Thanks for reminding me." He rummaged in the pocket of his ABU uniform and pulled a blue waterproof pouch from his baggy pants. He ripped open the seal and took out a phone.

Senator Pulaski's cell phone.

Shawn powered it up and turned to Garibaldi, but held the cell phone back. "What about Undersecretary Doyle's SAP? This phone's encrypted, but Nitta doesn't know about the other SAP in the Mountain. She's not allowed to know."

Garibaldi shrugged. "I don't agree with Velvet Hammer, but it's a policy disagreement, not safety. And if it's been in place since the Cold War, it must have bipartisan support." He coughed. "My problem is how van Dyckman broke the law and common sense." He let out a sigh. "But I won't tell her about the Undersecretary's SAP, if that's what you're asking."

"It will eventually come out," Adonia said. "It has to."

"But in the right place at the right time," Shawn said.

Full signal reception showed on the face of the cell phone's screen. Shawn locked eyes with Adonia as he handed the phone to her. "You know the Secretary's number?"

"Nuclear plant site managers have a direct line." She looked at Garibaldi. "You said I could hold something over the government, ensure they'll follow through. What did you have in mind?"

Garibaldi coughed. "Set the phone to record and encrypt this conversation. Then send the coded file to Sanergy . . . but *you* keep the password. If the government doesn't come up with a realistic solution to this nuclear waste debacle, then this recording will be your ultimate ace in the hole to release the hounds of hell, bring in the press, whatever you think." He hesitated. "I'll tell that to the Secretary . . . and that she's got only two weeks to get things rolling. I won't be around any longer than that."

Adonia drew in a breath. "And . . . she'll believe you? Not take it as a threat?"

Garibaldi nodded. "She was the young lawyer who represented me at Oakridge after my accident there. She was rolled over by DOE once and swore she'd never let it happen again." He smiled. "How do you think I *really* got on this review panel?"

Adonia quickly punched in the settings, then took a moment to enter a long password. She dialed the number. When it began to ring, she handed the phone to Garibaldi. "It's recording now and will send the encrypted file to Sanergy as soon as you hang up."

"Thank you." Closing his eyes, he took the cell and held it tightly to his ear. After a long moment he said, "Madam Secretary, this is

Simon Garibaldi. I may not have much time." He caught a quick breath and his voice grew more somber. "Not much time at all."

As he explained in a measured voice what had happened, Adonia wrapped her arms around Shawn, and he responded by folding her into an embrace. They watched a distant plane take off from the Albuquerque airport, miles to the northwest; below them, approaching guards jogged up the rocky path, closing in as they stood outside the shaft.

"With Garibaldi talking to the Secretary, I don't think we'll be in custody long, if at all. I'll insist on speaking directly to the President, give him the whole story about what really happened," Shawn said. "And the disaster Dr. Garibaldi prevented."

"We'll both add to Garibaldi's testimony and explain the need for transparency. Stanley won't be able to keep us quiet."

"Now that I know Garibaldi's past with the Energy Secretary, van Dyckman is toast," Shawn said. "Garibaldi will get top medical care, but we both need to make sure whatever he has to say isn't swept under the rug."

She was silent for a moment, then whispered something to him under her breath.

Shawn glanced at her, not understanding. "Excuse me?"

"The password—just in case anything happens to me." She turned to him. "You'll recognize the line. 'Now I am become Death, the destroyer of worlds.'"

Shawn nodded and turned back to watch for the guards. "Oppenheimer's quote from the Bhagavad Gita. At Trinity Site, just after the first atomic bomb test." He drew her close. "I'm confident we'll never have to use it."

"I hope you're right—but I won't hesitate."

"Neither will I."

Next to them, Garibaldi kept talking in a rush. He looked up as the security teams closed in. "Are you sure you've got the specifics, Madam Secretary? Everything? From now on, it's up to you." He nodded, and ended the connection.

As they watched the approaching guards, she whispered, "Actually, Dr. Garibaldi, after this, it'll be up to us. *All* of us."

ACKNOWLEDGMENTS

Dr. Marv Alme; Dr. Mark Barnett, M.D.; Dr. Ed Bucheron; Dr. Ron Fursteneau; Dr. Sharif Heger; Dr. Steve Howe; Andrew Hundley; John Kienholz; Dave Schneider; our agent, John Silbersack; and our editor, Bob Gleason.